Chris Bunch was part of the first troop commitment into Vietnam. Both Ranger and airborne-qualified, he served as a patrol commander and a combat correspondent for *Stars and Stripes*. Later, he edited outlaw motorcycle magazines and wrote for everything from the underground press to *Look* magazine, *Rolling Stone* and prime-time television. He is now a full-time novelist.

Find out more about Chris Bunch and other Orbit authors by registering for the free monthly newsletter at www.orbitbooks.co.uk

DRAGONMASTER

BOOK ONE
Storm of Wings

Chris Bunch

www.orbitbooks.co.uk

An *Orbit* Book

First published in Great Britain by Orbit 2002
This edition published 2003
Reprinted 2004

A CIP catalogue record for this book
is available from the British Library.

ISBN 1 84149 192 6

Printed and bound in Great Britain by
Mackays of Chatham plc

Orbit
An imprint of
Time Warner Book Group UK
Brettenham House
Lancaster Place
London WC2E 7EN

Again, for L'il Karen

1

Hal Kailas heard the distant chittering of the dragon as he plodded home. He looked up eagerly, needing to see color beside the gray cobbles, stone houses, mountains, drab mine buildings, high-piled tailings, even the overcast sky.

The crimson and deep-green monster, he guessed a cow, although the beast was really too high for him to see the female's characteristic darker belly stripes, banked back and forth, horned head darting from side to side, looking down.

Somewhere in the crags just above the village, and Hal thought he knew just where from his solitary, but not lonely, hill explorations, the beast had its nest. The nest where dragons had hatched their young for over a century.

He wondered what had sparked its curiosity, what could spark any creature's interest in the village of Caerly. Nothing but gray, including, he thought morosely, all the people who lived there and went down the tin mine for their slender living.

He'd ducked his schooling this day, thinking that if he had to hear the tutor drone on once more about the workers' duty to support the way things are, which meant obediently going down the Tregonys' mine, and kissing their hands in gratitude, he'd go mad.

He dreamed, or rather tried to dream, for it seemed impossible, of the hillmen's legendary past. A past of fierce reivers and warriors, until the king of Deraine's army came through, and slew all those who didn't bend, kiss the sword, and become good little servitors to those nobles the king named as the region's overlords and exploiters.

Two hundred years gone, certainly. But there were still those who muttered about the injustice.

A wind blew cold across his face, and he pulled his wool coat, new only last birthday, closer about him.

Kailas was a bit past thirteen, tall for his age, but he had never been gawky. He had slender arms and legs, belying his strength. His brown hair was tousled, and he had green eyes in a somewhat long face.

The dragon shrilled loudly, and Hal started, for very close to him came an answering cry, higher, not as loud, from seemingly around the corner.

He rounded the corner, and saw four boys torturing a dragon kit. He guessed it to be fresh-hatched, for it was no more than a yard long. It must have fallen from its nest on to something that cushioned its landing.

Now the mother was frantically trying to recover it.

One of the boys was Nanpean Tregony, the local lord's son, and Hal knew the kit wouldn't be allowed to live beyond the hour. Tregony, a year older than Hal, good-looking, always ready with a smile for his elders, kept his cruel streak well hidden.

Hal knew better, having come on him laughing in hysterical glee after he'd soaked a kitten in lantern oil, and struck a spark.

None of the four noticed him. Tregony had a broken broom across the dragon's neck, pinning it to the cobbles, while the other three poked at it with sharp sticks.

Hal knew the other three as well, Tregony's toadies, like Nanpean a year or two older than Kailas, always sucking around him, hoping for favor from the mine owner's son.

The dragon screamed in pain, and an answering scream came from above, drowned by Tregony's jeering laughter. Tregony reached into a pouch inside his waistband, took out a slender, evil-looking spring knife. He touched a button, and its blade sprung out.

"Hold it still," he told one of his cohorts, passing him the broomstick. "And watch this, now," he said, and bent over the struggling kit.

Hal Kailas didn't have much of a temper ... Or so he thought. But when he became truly angry, his voice sank to a whisper, and the world seemed to slow to a crawl, so that he had all the time in the world to do as he wished. That cold rage had made him more than a bit feared by the other village boys.

So it was now, on this gray, windy street.

He saw a length of wood, almost as long as he was tall, lying in a pile of scrap nearby. Hal soon had the wood, half as thick as his wrist, in both hands.

"Stop!" he shouted, and ran toward the four boys. One turned, was hit on the head, very hard, howled in panic, and started running.

Tregony jumped to one side.

"Kailas!" he shouted. "Get your peasant ass away from here, or my father'll roast you!"

Hal barely heard the words. He lifted the wood, and another boy raised his hands to fight back. Hal kicked him in the belly. The boy collapsed, near the dragon, and his face was ravaged by the kit's tiny claws as it flailed. The fourth boy was running after the first.

But Tregony had a bit of courage.

"Come on, then," he said, his face a smiling rictus. "Come on," he said again, waving the knife back and forth in front of him.

Hal had the stick in both hands, like a fighting stave wielded by men in paintings in his father's taproom, moving it up, down, keeping the knife away.

Tregony lunged, and Hal jerked sideways, had the stick

like a spear at one end, and thrust hard. He caught Tregony along the neck, and the jagged end tore flesh. Hal pulled back, lunged once more, into Tregony's breastbone, heard ribs crack. Nanpean howled in agony, had hold of the spear's end, then stumbled back, fell hard against the stone wall beside him. He tried to get up and Hal kicked him, quite deliberately, in the face.

His eyes stared hard at Hal, then glazed, closed. For an instant Kailas thought he'd killed Tregony, then saw the steady rise and fall of the young man's chest.

Instantly he forgot him, knelt over the dragon, who was up on unsteady feet.

It shrieked fear, and, from above, his mother answered.

"Now for you," Hal muttered. "You little pain in the ass."

The dragon kit wriggled, wrapped in Hal's coat, as the boy reached for another handhold. He almost slipped, feet scrabbling on wet stone, then he was safe, inside a jagged crevice that led straight upward.

He looked down at Caerly a thousand feet below him, and was surprised he felt no vertigo, no particular fear beyond what any fool should feel high on this huge crag, only a few yards below a dragon's nest.

"Dammit!" he said, trying to sound like an adult. "Stay still! I'm on your side!"

The kit didn't seem to understand, squirming more frantically.

Across the valley, gray rain was sweeping toward him in the dusk, and he realized, unless he wanted to be trapped here by nightfall, he'd best keep moving.

He scanned the skies for the mother dragon, saw nothing. Hal wondered where the bull was, hoped not diving at the back of his head.

The musky scent of the nest came to him, something he'd heard others describe as nauseating. He found it quite otherwise, not attractive, but certainly not disgusting.

Realizing he was avoiding the last of the climb, he hitched his coat more securely to his waist, saw that the little dragon had ripped the cloth, knew he'd pay for what he was doing when winter winds struck, put his back to the crevice wall, and pushed upward with his feet.

He'd seen egg-gatherers walk their way up sheer cliffs like this, their grass baskets tied to their chests, tried to imitate them.

The rock wall behind him tore at his linen shirt, scratching his skin, but he ignored it, looking only up, only at that huge nest, looking like a pile of abandoned lumber and brush.

The nest had been built in an alcove of the crag, out of the way of wind and most weather. It was huge, thirty feet in diameter. As Hal got closer, he smelt carrion over the dragon-reek, and his stomach churned, wondering what he'd find inside the nest.

A shriek tore at his ears, and he jumped, almost losing his hold, and a wind pulled at him as the mother dragon dove past him, less than ten feet away.

"Go away, dammit!" he shouted. "I've got your baby! Go away or you'll kill us both!"

The baby dragon wiggled, squealed, and the mother heard. Hal had enough of a hold to let the kit's head snake out of the jacket.

The cow roared at him again, climbed, leathery wings, over a hundred feet across, slowly stroking down, lifting the monster high into the air.

The dragon caught the wind, banked, came back, mouth open, fangs menacing. The kit saw its mother, screeched, and again the cow turned away.

Hal scrambled up the last few feet, tumbled into the nest, landed on the decaying, half-eaten carcass of a lamb.

The nest was a litter of bones and debris. Here and there were tattered clothes, stolen from washlines below, bits of shabby rug that the dragons evidently fancied for either padding or decoration.

A deep roar sounded, and Hal saw the bull dragon, above its mate, fifty feet long, its spiked tail, a twenty-foot-long killing whip, lashing, head darting back and forth on the ten-foot-long neck.

"Here," he said, and unwrapped the kit, spilling it into the nest.

He pulled his coat and arm away, not quite fast enough as the kit caught him below the elbow with its fangs, tearing his arm open to the wrist.

The kit shrilled in evident triumph, and the bull dove at the nest.

Hal had one instant of pure awe, seeing the dragon, jaws yawning, foreleg talons extended, wing talons reaching, coming at him, and the thought flashed of how few people could have seen this and lived, realized if he didn't move quickly he might not be one of those survivors, and eeled over the edge of the nest, almost falling, then had a hold on a two-inch length of lumber sticking out of the brush.

The cow flared her wings and landed above him, in the nest, her interest only in her kit.

The bull had climbed, dropped a wing and came back at him, but Hal was tucked in the crevice, slithering down as fast as he could.

The dragon tried again for him, couldn't slow enough to reach into the cranny, screaming rage.

It was below him then, and Hal looked at its wide shoulder blades, at the carapace behind the dragon's long neck and horned head, thought, insanely, that could be a seat, and you could be flying yourself, if you could figure a way to make the dragon do your bidding, and he forced that away, climbing down and down.

The dragon's rage receded as he shinnied down the outcropping, and cold fear finally came, fear of what would greet him when he reached the ground and his parents' tavern.

"I hope that'll not leave the scar I fear," Hal's mother said, as she finished bandaging Hal's arm with the spell-impregnated bandage she'd gotten from the village witch.

"It'll be fine, Mother," Hal said.

"Then that'll be the only thing that shall," she said. She rubbed her eyes wearily. "Twenty years gone for us now."

"Lees," Hal's father, Faadi, said quietly, "that's not going to make our son feel any better about what happened . . . nor is it likely to offer any solutions to our problem."

"I'm sorry for what happened, Da," Hal said.

"Are you really?" his father asked.

Hal started to reply, thought, then shook his head. "No. Nossir, I'm not. That Nanpean ought not to be able to pain others, even a dragon."

"No," Faadi said. "He ought not. Any more than his father ought to be able to use his gold and power given by the king to rule our lives." He shrugged. "But that seems to be the way of the world."

"Some of Lord Tregony's men—" Lees began.

"Thugs," Faadi corrected. "Goons. Bullyboys. Hardly men of good or free will."

"Regardless," Lees said. "They wanted you, Hal."

"Naturally, we told them to go away or we'd call the warder," Faadi said.

"They laughed at that, and said that even if they didn't find you," Lees went on, "there'd be charges pressed, and our tavern would be theirs, and we'd be beggars on the road. We should know full well the warders and the magistrate are on their side, like they side with everyone of riches."

"Tomorrow, before dawn, I'll ride for the city, and hire the best advocate I can," Faadi said. "That'll put a bit of a stave in their wheel."

"But aren't those expensive?" Hal asked.

"We own this building clear," Faadi said. "That should pay at least some of his price. For the rest, he – or she – will have to take payments."

"Which will be a time in coming," Lees said. "Tregony's

men also said that Tregony would order none of his miners –
his miners, indeed, as if they were his slaves – to drink here.
That's the greater part of our business."

"Not everyone in Caerly dances to the Lord's precise flut-
ing," Faadi said.

"Most do."

"But there's others who'll still come here for their pint and
pasty," Faadi said.

"I wish . . ." Hal said forlornly, his voice trailing away.

"What?" Faadi asked.

"Never mind," Hal said, trying to keep from crying. Lees
put an arm around him.

"We'll fight them, Hal," she said firmly. "Fight them and
win."

Hal wanted to believe her, but heard the doubt in her voice.

Later, in his attic room, Hal did cry, feeling like a stupid baby,
knowing that wouldn't do any good at all.

He stared out the window, at the rainy street below,
remembering his mother's words about being "beggars on the
road."

No. That would never happen. Not to his parents.

The clock downstairs in the taproom rang midnight.
There'd been no customers to run out to their homes. The
whole village seemed to be holding its breath, waiting to see
what Lord Tregony would do to the boy who dared hurt his
only son.

Hal thought of what his father had said, about going to the
city with his hat in his hand to hire an advocate who'd stand
firm against Tregony's pocket magistrate.

No, he thought. That would never do. Not for his parents.

He thought about them, about their careful lives, careful
budgeting, here in this tiny mining village in the back of
beyond. And he considered his own life, what he would grow
up to be.

He knew he'd never go down the mines like his fellows.

What, then? Inherit the tavern, and have to listen to the sponges and the old gaffers, mumbling their drunken way toward the grave? Maybe become a tutor to teach the miners' children to barely read and write and bow and scrape before the boys followed their fathers underground, and the girls began to bear baby after baby until they were worn out at thirty?

No.

At least, he thought a bit forlornly, he didn't have to worry about saying goodbye to his friends, since he really didn't think he'd ever had any.

Moving very quietly, he dressed, wearing his best woolen pants, heaviest shoes, a sweater and his rather bedraggled and torn coat. He improvised a pack from another pair of pants, stuffed two shirts into it, along with a toothbrush and a bar of soap.

He started downstairs past his parents' bedroom, heard the sound of their fitful sleep.

In the taproom, he wrote a note that he wished would say everything in his heart, but couldn't.

He took bread, cheese, two pints of the tavern's ale, a small square of smoked ham. He saw a sheathed knife, ancient, a wall hanging, next to an antique sword, took it down, tested its edge.

It would serve, and he found a small sharpening stone in the taproom's utensil drawer, added a knife, fork, spoon to it.

There were a handful of coins in the cash drawer and, feeling for the first time like a thief, he took a few of them.

He looked around the taproom, inviting, warm in the dying firelight, the only world he'd known.

Then he unlocked the front door, pulling his coat on, went down the steps, and off through the rain for a new and better world.

2

Hal looked up at the dragon crouched on the outcropping, put one foot in the step of his stilts and pushed off. He wobbled back and forth, then had his balance.

He glanced back at the dragon. It was, he thought, looking amusedly at Hal's clumsiness, although no one but Kailas would've given the monster that characterization. It was green and white, young, he guessed, perhaps two years old, thirty feet long, and had been hovering around the hopfields for three days now.

The workers had tried to ignore it, in the hopes it meant no harm, although no one knew just what would enrage one of the monsters.

This picking of the hops was too happy a festival for the workers who'd flocked out from the capital of Rozen with their families to allow a damned dragon to ruin things.

It was late summer, hot, dry, the hop flowers beginning to dry, perfect weather for picking. The workers used stilts to walk down the rows of pole-tied vines, as that was faster than using ladders, to reach the cones fifteen feet overhead.

The hops were baled and taken to the big kilns in the

strange-looking circular oasthouses for drying, then pressed and carted away to the breweries.

For centuries, the poor of Rozen had taken this harvest as a holiday, streaming out of their cobbled streets and packed slums. The farm owners provided tents, and vied with each other, claiming to offer better food and stronger beer.

The work wasn't that hard, and there was the night to look forward to, when torches flared, friendships were renewed, and scandals and marriages made in the soft meadow grass.

This was Hal's first festival. He'd been talked into staying on for the hop picking after the peach season ended. The farm owner had vaguely spoke of hiring him full-time, having noted Hal's hard work.

Kailas didn't know if he'd accept, thought not. He'd been offered other steady work in the two years since he'd left the stony mining village, but had never accepted, not sure of the reason.

He'd done just about any job offered that paid quickly, in cash, and didn't try to change him, from road laborer to clerk to wagoneer. The only one that had drawn him, and that for a moment, was being a taleteller, carrying whatever stories and news heard from village to village, performing in a square or tavern for peasants who mostly couldn't read or write. But he realized he had no talent for the dramatics required to wring the last handclap and copper from his audience.

He'd roamed Deraine from north to south, and the road had taught its lessons – never turn down a meal or a warm place to sleep; those who're kindly to passing strangers generally have their own reason for charity; never beg, but offer work and mean it; the first one to make friends with you is most always the last person you want for a companion; it's better to look shabby and clean than rich and filthy, and other messages neither the village tutor nor his father's books had offered.

So he could, possibly, linger on this hopfarm for the winter, although autumn hadn't come yet.

But he could also be far to the south when the first snow came. Perhaps he'd go into one of the coastal cities, as he had a year ago. There, able to read and write, unlike most of his fellow wanderers, he could find work as a clerk or shipper's assistant, out of the tempests.

Last year he'd made the mistake of signing on to a fishing boat, and his bones were still frozen and his fingers prickered from the hooks that ended in his hand.

As Hal thought of the future, his hands worked swiftly, stripping the cones from the stems on the trellis overhead and dropping them into the sack around his neck, then stepping forward, stilt legs striking puffs of dust in the ground ten feet below.

He grinned at himself. When would he learn to let tomorrow take care of itself, and concentrate on the moment?

Such as Dolni, with her waist-length black hair, her smiling red lips, the simple frocks she wore, with nothing beneath. She was sixteen, the daughter of one of the farmer's cooks, with a merry laugh and eyes that promised much.

Late the night before, her arms had fulfilled the promise of her eyes, and it had been close to dawn before she pulled her dress on, pushed Hal away, saying she must be back in her bed before dawn, and perhaps tomorrow night – tonight! – there would be more.

Hal felt like puffing his chest, for hadn't she chosen him over the others she'd gone walking with on other nights of the harvest? Dolni vowed the others had done nothing with her, although they'd begged her for her favors.

Dolni may not have been the first Hal had bedded, but she was far and away the prettiest and the most passionate.

Hal stumbled, taken by his heated lust, almost fell, and brought himself back to work, just as the dragon, on the jutting crag at the far end of the field, snorted, and dove from its perch.

There were yelps of alarm, a scream, from other pickers. But the dragon was merely picking up speed – or, perhaps, harassing the spindly two-legs below, as its great wings caught the afternoon wind, and lifted it high into the air.

Hal stared up at it, banking, gliding.

Now there was where he longed to be, somehow aloft with that fabulous beast, caring nothing for what was below.

Except, perhaps, for Dolni, riding behind him, the sweet tinkle of her laughter ringing through the skies.

Perhaps they would fly north, toward the rumored Black Island, or, more logically, south, beyond Deraine, across the Chicor Straits to the walled city of Paestum, or beyond that small free city, over Sagene and its baronies.

That was too much even for his imagination, and he pulled himself back, and concentrated on his picking, vowing he'd have more full sacks by dusk than any other picker, no matter how experienced, how agile, and shine in Dolni's eyes.

It was hard telling what there was more of: food, or varieties of the various beers the district boasted.

There were barreled oysters, river crayfish, ham, chicken with hot peppers, spiced beef in pasties, kidney pie, cold cuts, breads, pickles, potato cakes, a dozen varieties of barely-steamed vegetables, corn relish, a dozen cheeses, desserts and more.

There was heavily-hopped pale beer, dark porter, heavy stout, lager, wheat beer, even strawberry beer.

All was set on long tables, and everyone was welcome to take as much as he wanted, unlike the meanness of the city.

Some pickers had brought instruments with them, and there were half a dozen guitars playing, a couple of lutes, some woodwinds, three or four small drums, wooden whistles, men and women singers, a chorus that couldn't quite decide whose song to join in.

Children bounced through the throng, intent on their own games. Dogs chased cats, and sometimes were sent howling when they caught them.

Hal Kailas pushed through the crowd, looking for only one thing: Dolni.

He finally saw her, just as she ran, hand in hand with a local farmer's son, notable only for his muscles and blond hair, up a hill and disappeared into a clump of brush.

Her laughter rang behind her.

Hal thought of going after her, but what would he say? He had no rights at all, he realized, just as he also realized those boys who'd gone before him had no rights.

He thought of swearing, knew that wouldn't do any good. If he had any brains, he thought forlornly, he would laugh at his own stupidity for thinking he was more than just one more conquest for the little roundheels. He tried, but the sound was most hollow.

Very well, then, he thought. I shall get drunk. Why that idea came he had no idea. He'd been taken by drink three times, and disliked not only how it made him feel the next morning, but the dizziness, foolishness and sickness it brought that night.

Nevertheless, he found a heavy wooden mug, and went to the barrels of beer. Dark would be the strongest, he guessed, and the most potent, and grimly ladled his mug full.

Maybe he'd hoped for unconsciousness, but after two and a half mugs, it hadn't come. In fact, the brew had made him feel more alert, more alive. He felt strength run through him, had a flashed thought of what vitality Dolni had missed, almost burst into tears.

He looked around for something to do, someone to impress, heard the faint honk of the dragon, saw it settling on to the jutting rock, folding its wings for the night.

An idea came.

If Dolni would not fly with him, he would fly by himself.

Both moons were up, as befitted a harvest, but the higher Hal climbed, even though he could easily make out handholds in the rock, the more he wished it was just a bit darker, for the light showed him entirely too much.

He could see, perhaps two hundred distant feet below, the fires of the festival, heard the sounds of laughter and music, could even pick out a couple of stumbling drunks who couldn't decide whether to fight or to hug each other.

Also, he could see, and now hear, very well, the rumbling snores – he hoped it was snores – of the dragon just around the outcropping and a bit below him.

The effects of the beer had worn off somewhat, and he thought, if he was anything other than a cursed fool, he'd go back the way he came. No one, after all, had seen him begin this stupid climb, or heard him boast of his intent, so he had no foolish pride to sustain.

But he climbed on, another ten feet, thinking that would surely be enough. He slipped across the crag, using an all too convenient crack, and came out in the full flood of the moonlight.

About thirty feet below him was the motionless dragon. He could see its sides heave in sleep, had a sudden wonder what dragons dreamed, or if they dreamed at all.

Meanwhile, without bidding or thought, his hands and legs were finding new holds, and he was moving down toward the monster. Closer, ever closer, and he was within ten feet of its broad back.

Well, he thought, this is as stupid a way to die as ever a man, let alone a boy, ever thought of, and jumped, legs reaching, just for that flat area behind the carapace that guarded the creature's shoulder blades.

He landed fair, and the dragon woke with a screech, wings flailing, trying to reach back with its talons, with its fangs, to tear away the interloper.

But Hal was out of its reach, and the nightmare launched itself out, into empty air.

Hal Kailas was truly flying as the dragon dove for speed, then climbed high, banking, rolling, and he was holding on to the back of the plate, rough scales perfect for handholds, the warmth of the beast beneath him, and he could look up –

seeing down – at the fires below him, people looking up, hearing the dragon scream rage and fear, and faintly he heard shouts as men and women saw him, saw him riding the dragon, flying.

The dragon tucked a wing, and the world was rightside up. Above him were the moons, and all the stars, and below him the world he had little use for.

He tried a kick, a tap really, against the left side of the dragon's neck, and the beast turned as bidden. He kicked with his right foot, and another turn came.

He was not just flying, but he was in command of this wonderful monster, this beast of dreams.

"To the stars," he shouted to the dragon, but the creature tucked its head, and dove, shaking like a horse trying to rid itself of a rider.

The ground was rushing up at him, and Hal could do nothing but hold on, hoping the dragon wasn't about to kill himself just for revenge against this petty creature with the foolhardiness to try to ride him.

The dragon shook himself, the membrane of his wings rattling like great drums, and Hal lost his grip, and fell.

Now the ground, the dark ground, swirled up at him, and the torch fires wound about him as he spun. He kept his eyes open, took, for his last sight before death, that peaceful moon, far above.

Then he landed.

Landed easily in one of the huge wagons filled with bundled hops, and the air was driven out of him, and all was black for an instant.

Then he saw light, fires, heard people running toward him, and he fought his way to his feet, feeling every muscle in his body protest.

A bearded face came over the cart top.

"Whut th' *hells*—"

"Someone said," Hal said, in as careless a voice as he could manage, "dragons couldn't be ridden."

"Boy, you are the *godsdamnedest* fool I ever heard of!" a woman said as she pulled herself up beside the beard.

"Maybe," Hal said. He looked out, saw the pickers running toward him, heard more shouts, thought he saw Dolni, though, now, for some strange reason, it mattered not at all to him.

"Maybe I am," he said thoughtfully. "But I rode the dragon."

3

Autumn had arrived, but only on the calendar. It was hot and dry, the rains promised by the sages and tradition still absent. Dust swirled about Hal's feet as he tramped on, ever south toward the cities along the Chicor Straits.

His purse was full, if of more copper than silver, he had a new cloak rolled on his shoulders, and his pack held bread, cheese, and a flask of beer.

Kailas should have been content, for a wandering worker. But he felt aimless, with nothing north or south to particularly draw him, nor did any of the jobs he considered much interest him.

He heard the clatter of hooves, jumped out of the way as a fast coach drawn by eight thundered past.

Hal coughed his way through the dust cloud it left, the driver of course not bothering to slow for one more shabby wanderer, his unseen master hidden behind drawn curtains.

Such it would always be, Kailas thought, with only a bit of resentment. There would always be those who rode in coaches, like the Tregonys of the village he'd left, and those who walked in the dust or mud.

Like Hal.

He didn't really mind being a poor nomad – at his age, almost everything was an adventure. But he'd seen the older vagrants, tottering along, joints screaming, able to eat only mush, drunkenness their only solace, without kith or kin to care about them until the day they finally died in some road-side ditch.

That was not what he wanted.

But he was damned if he knew what he *did* want.

A shrilling came, and he looked up, saw a large dragon, all shades of green, following the road, about a hundred feet up. He was ready to duck for cover – other travelers had told him dragons haunted this lonely road, ready to swoop, kill and carry off any solitary vagabond.

But then he forgot his caution as he saw, on the dragon's back, a rider.

The dragon soared closer, and Hal could make out more of the man on its back. He was tall, very thin, long-faced, and had a well-trimmed gray beard. He wore brown leather boots, breeches and vest, a tan shirt under the vest, and a slouch hat crammed down on his head.

He held reins in one hand that ran to ringbolts mounted through spikes behind the dragon's mouth, and was sitting comfortably on some sort of pad on its shoulder blades.

He saw Hal, boomed laughter that seemed to ring across the land below.

Hal gaped like a ninny. He'd heard of men who had learned to ride dragons, didn't quite believe the tales even though he'd briefly been on one of the monsters a month gone.

But here was proof – the man appeared in complete control of the beast, touching reins, and the dragon pirouetted through the air.

The man reached in a bag, and scattered a handful of dust.

The dust sparkled in the air, then shimmered, and letters came, floating in the middle of nowhere:

!MAGICK!
!SORCERY!
!ATHELNY OF THE DRAGONS!
SEE THE
WONDROUS DISPLAY OF
ATHELNY'S ART AND SKILL!
RIDE A
DRAGON YOURSELF

NO DANGER BUT ONLY

FOR THE BOLDEST

Hal barely noted that the warning was in quite small letters.

Ride a dragon?

He tore off his cap, waved, shouted, danced in the dusty road.

Again the dragon swooped back, and its rider cupped his hands, and shouted:

"Two villages away, boy! We'll see you there . . . if you've got the silver!"

The dragon banked.

Hal shouted back: "You will! I'll be there!"

But, if Athelny – that must be him – heard, he neither flew nor looked back.

Hal ran after him, then caught himself, slowing to a trot and then a fast walk. Yes. He surely would be there.

He wondered what it cost for a ride.

*

It was one silver coin too much. Hal counted his purse for the fourth time, wasn't able to improve his pelf.

The sign implacably read:

Ride the Dragon
10 Silver Barons

An outrageous sum – but there were people lining up to pay it. Most were young bravos from the village, or merchants' children. Hal noticed half a dozen giggling girls in the line.

He tried to remember where that silver coin he needed so desperately had strayed. A night's lodging and a long, luxuriant bath after leaving the hopfields? That steak with half a bottle of Sagene wine he'd treated himself to? That damned cloak he'd thought a wonderful present to himself, when the weather suggested he wouldn't be needing it for awhile?

It was no use.

Even with his coppers, he was still short . . . and if he managed to find a spare coin in his delvings, what would he do for food on the morrow?

Glumly, he considered Athelny's show.

To someone from a big city, it might have appeared somewhat unimpressive: three wagons, one for sleeping, the other two heavy freight wagons with flat tops and ties to keep the dragons secure. Athelny had three wagoneers, plus two cunning-looking young men, not much older than Hal, obviously city sharpsters. They took tickets, made sure the passengers were securely tied in behind Athelny, jollied the crowd and joked with each other, just a little too loudly, about the rustics around them.

But none of this mattered to Hal, because Athelny had two real dragons, the green one he'd seen on the road, and a slightly younger one, in various dark reds.

The red dragon was sprightlier, constantly trying to take off with the other, the one Athelny was giving rides with. Earlier, the red one had shown his tricks in aerial acrobats, which Hal had seen the last of.

Both monsters were well-tended, scales brushed and oiled so they gleamed, wings shining, talons polished.

Hal had already noted Athelny's riding-pad, a flat saddle tied to two ringbolts drilled through the dragon's neck carapace. Now he saw a second saddle mounted behind the rider's, this one fitted with leather shoulder straps.

If these dragons were his, Hal thought, he wouldn't demean them by giving bumpkins rides for silver.

He would be the bold explorer, finding lands no one from Deraine would know, perhaps even visiting Black Island that the boastful Roche claimed as their own, reputedly the home of the biggest, most dangerous black dragons, a breed unto themselves.

His practical side jeered – and what would he use to feed his dragons, let alone himself?

There were two bullocks, lowing as if knowing their fate, tied behind the wagons, and one of the teamsters had said they would serve as dinner for man and beast.

"Pity they don't breath fire, like tavern talk would have it," one of the teamsters had told him. "That way, we could get 'em cooked in th' bargain."

Perhaps, his dream ran on, he could find a rich lord to sponsor his explorations.

If not, and he must make his way giving jaunts for his wages, he would cater to the rich, and charge accordingly, giving long flights to lords and their ladies. He'd learn about the country around him, and lecture and be thought wise.

And wasn't it you, not long ago, thinking of how much you

despised those rich? I do, Hal thought. It's only their gold I lust for.

Suddenly he grinned.

Nice dreams, he thought, remembering the wanderer's weary joke: If I had some ham, I could have some ham and eggs, if I had some eggs. All I need is some money, some dragons and some wagons, and I'm as good – better, maybe – then Athelny.

Meantime, it's him up there, darting among the clouds, a squealing girl hanging tightly to him, and Hal down here, slumped against a wagon wheel, without the money for even a few seconds aloft.

"Why ain't you in line, since you was so innarested in dragons?"

It was the teamster he'd talked to earlier. Hal thought about it, told her the truth.

The woman nodded.

"Athelny charges fair coin for his pleasures, he does," She thought a moment. "Course, there's always a way for some-one who's not afraid of work to earn a lift."

Hope came.

"Work's no stranger to me," he said.

The woman looked about. "I could be a shit, an' ask if you'd mind killin' those beeves we've got tied up . . . but I ain't.

"Tell you what. By th' way, m'name's Gaeta. I handle the business, day to day, for the show. Our wagons're filthy. I'll have Chapu – he's that fat one over there – drive 'em back to that river we forded.

"You'll find some rags and a bucket from the wagonbox over there."

Hal was on his feet, hurrying toward the wagon she'd pointed out before she finished.

"So you're the lad who's been shining m'wagons for the last half-day, eh?" Athelny asked. He had a bluff, hearty voice, and wanted the listener to think he was one of the upper classes, Hal thought.

Nothing wrong with that, his mind went on, as his fingers linked the two straps, once saddle cinches, that would hold him firm in the seat behind Athelny.

"Have to do you a return, then, and give you a proper ride," Athelny said. "If that's what you want. Or would you rather have the nice lift, the smooth sail, and the gentle landing such as I've been giving the girls of this burg all day?"

"Whatever you want, sir," Hal said.

"Thought you might want a little excitement, which is why I changed saddles for Red. But if you get sick on me," Athelny promised, "you'll think cleaning those wagons was a jolly sport."

"I won't," Hal said, and told his stomach it'd best obey or he'd put nothing in it for the next year, damnit!

"Then hang on."

Athelny slid easily on to the pad in front of Hal, grabbed the reins and slapped them against the dragon's neck. The beast snorted, and its wings uncurled, thrashed, like distant thunder.

"You interested in flying one day?" Athelny asked over his shoulder.

"Yessir." Hal didn't mention his momentary flight over the hopfields.

"Then I'll tell you what's going on. M'dragon, Red, here'd be happier if he had a height to sail down from, instead of having to lift all by himself.

"Another thing that's makin' him a bit unhappy is how hot and muggy 'tis. You'd think, with the air thick like this, a dragon's wings'd have more to push against, and would take off easier.

"But not. Demned if I know why. Now, he'll start trundlin' forward, and then stroke hard, and here we are!

"Airborne!"

Indeed they were, and Hal saw the remnants of the crowd grow smaller, and then he could see the wagons, and then the village.

"We'll climb up for a time," Athelny said, still not having to raise his voice. They weren't moving very fast, so there was little wind rush.

"Now, we're up a couple of hundred. We'll give Red a bit of a relax here, and circle while we're still climbing.

"Not that he believes he needs it for what he knows we'll attempt. You've got to think for a dragon, sometimes, for he's not sure of what he wants. Then, other times . . ." Athelny didn't finish the sentence.

Hal barely noticed, looking down at the road he'd traveled so slowly this morning, hurry as he would, to reach the village. To either side there were trees, farmers' fields, and over there a lake he'd never suspicioned, growing from that small creek he'd forded.

Still farther out, in the blue haze of approaching dusk, were low hills, and unknown valleys.

"How far would we have to go up to see the ocean, sir?" he shouted.

"Don't b'lieve we could from here. Get as high as we could, where men and dragons have trouble breathing, their wings not lifting as they should, I still don't think we'd even see the province cap'tal, let alone any of the Strait Cities."

"Oh," Hal said, a bit disappointed.

"Why? You have people on the coast?"

"Nossir. I was just curious."

"Where are you from?"

Hal didn't feel like giving his biography.

"Not much of anywhere, sir. Some time back, up north."

Athelny turned, looked at him closely.

"You're just on the road, eh?"

He didn't wait for an answer, turned back.

"Now, we've got some height to us. Note how Red responds to the reins. Tap him on the left side of his neck, he turns left. On the right, unless he's in a mood, he goes right.

"Flying, when the weather's calm like this – and when your beast's well-trained and in a proper mood – is easy as walking.

"Other times . . . Well, that's why there's so few dragon-masters."

Dragonmaster. It was a new word.

"How many are there?"

Athelny shrugged.

"Good question. P'raps a dozen here in Deraine, maybe more. I've heard there's some just flyin' for rich lords' pleasure, around their estates or wandering afar, just exploring for the sights."

That was for him, Hal thought.

"Roche has more. Quite a few more. Their queen's interested in anything new. I've heard some say they've got a hundred fliers, though I think that's a bit many for easy belief.

"Sagene . . . maybe ten. Their barons don't seem interested in anything other than their own pleasures and arses. Though I've wondered if there might not be gold to be made across the Straits, showing what a good honest Deraine flier can do.

"Enough of such. Now, hang on, for what we're doing is a climbing turn, taking us back the way we came."

And so Red obeyed, and the village came into sight again.

"Now a diving turn . . ."

The ground grew closer.

"Hang on, for Red's going to loop."

Hal was hanging from his ropes, looking up at down, as he had riding the dragon in the hopfields.

He couldn't hold back, but let out a yelp of pure joy.

"Good boy," Athelny approved. "Mayhap you *are* cut out for a flier. Now we'll do a series of rolls."

The world barreled about Hal, and his stomach made a mild protest, which he ignored.

"Excellent, m'Red," Athelny approved. "You'll get the blood of one steer for that in your meal this night.

"Now, what do you think of this, son?"

Red suddenly dove, again reminding Kailas of his previous adventure. Just below them were the show's wagons, and there were dots getting larger, becoming horses, people, as they closed on the ground.

But it was all quite remote for a few seconds. Then the earth was rushing up at them, fast, faster. Athelny was pulling back hard on the reins, grunting with effort.

The dragon's wings were spread flat, braking the long dive, and rattling loudly.

Then the ground was below them, not fifty feet, as the dragon's dive flattened, and then, once more, Red climbed for the skies.

"Did you have your eyes closed?"

"Nossir."

"Then, did you notice how the world seemed to be coming up at you quicker there at the last?"

"I did, sir." Hal was pleased that his guts were silent now.

"Good. When that happens, means you're within a couple hundred feet, too close, and you'd best be recovering from your dive, or you're about to spread yourself neatly over the landscape.

"Which is not considered proper by any worthwhile flier."

Athelny put Red through a few more turns, these more gentle, then brought the dragon in on the grassy field, braking with its wings, and landing gently on its four legs.

Hal unfastened his straps, and Athelny slid off the beast, gave him a hand to the ground.

"Have you a job around here?"

"Not yet, sir. I was the one you waved at, when you were coming up the road. Tomorrow I guess I'll start looking."

"You still think you might want to learn to fly?"

"I'd do anything, sir."

"Hmm." Athelny was about to say something as Gaeta came up, rethought.

"Did this boy do a good job as it 'pears to me?"

"He did," Gaeta said.

"It'd be nice to have everything always this neat, wouldn't it?" Gaeta shrugged.

"You're welcome to stay and eat with us," Athelny said.

"Thank you, sir. And . . . and if you're looking for some-body, I'll work harder'n anybody, sir."

"We'll see," Athelny said vaguely. "We'll see."

Hal's hopes sank.

But in the morning, when the show moved on, there was a place in one of the wagons for Hal's pack, a bench on the side for him to ride on, and leather harness for him to be rubbing neat's-foot oil into, even if there still was never a mention of what his job actually was, or what his wages might be.

4

"Stand, deliver and such," the bandit drawled casually, although his crossbow was aimed steadily at Hal's belly.

Hal half-raised his hands, dropping his reins across his horse's neck.

Half a dozen other thieves rode out of the brush, weapons ready. At their head was a lean, hard-looking rogue with a carefully waxed goatee.

It was a perfect place for an ambush – about two leagues outside the Sagene walled city of Bedarisi, close enough to safety for a rider to relax his guard a little.

The goateed man peered at Hal.

"Ah. 'Tis the younger who rides for the Deraine dragon-master, eh, the one who came first through last summer?"

"I am he," Hal said.

"And you missed paying your toll when you rode out yesterday for Frechin, did you not?"

"Didn't see anyone to give it to, Cherso."

"We remember each other!" the man with the goatee said with some pleasure. "It's always a good sign when men doing business know each other's names. And the reason no one was out to greet you yesterday was we stopped a brandy merchant yesterday, and he decided to fight, and we had to take all." He smiled sweetly. "It was very good brandy, and so we were sleeping in."

Hal managed a half-smile, took a small pouch from inside his leather vest, tossed it across. Cherso looked at his followers.

"Note, this is a sensible lad, beyond his years, who knows when it's cheaper to pay, not like that merchant, whose bones'll never be seen by his loved ones."

Cherso opened the pouch, looked inside, frowned.

"Nothing in here but silver, lad."

"We've not had the best of seasons," Hal said truthfully. "There's more fliers from Deraine come across doing shows this year."

"Not to mention th' Roche," a pockmarked man said. "A shitpot load of 'em just came in from the east into Bedarisi. Had five great snakes, all tied in cages, biggest I've ever seen."

"Plus so'jers to guard, so we just watched 'em pass," another said.

Hal grimaced. The men of Roche had also discovered flying shows. He'd not seen one yet, but the tales were their perfectly trained fliers, wearing common livery, and performing in formation, shamed most dragon shows, including Athelny of the Dragons, now with only a single beast.

Cherso caught Kailas' expression, tucked the pouch away.

"Now, I'll take your word for having a thin season, boy. For it's good when men can trust each other, and never take more than the other can give, is it not?"

Hal managed a smile.

"Perhaps if I had a better story you'd not be taking any tribute at all?"

"Now, now," Cherso said. "Leave us not press our luck. Each of us has to do what he must, and I think I'm being kindly, most kindly, taking this pittance not only for your safety, but for your master's and crew as well. I assume they'll be passing this way in the next few days?"

"They will," Hal said. "I've been papering Frechin, as you guessed, and Athelny said we'd be leaving in a day or so.

"You know, Cherso, if times get any harder, perhaps you and your men would consider taking your tribute in free rides?"

There was scornful laughter, and Cherso spat on the ground.

"Do we appear mad? Why should anyone want to get off nice solid ground and ride a dragon? We're not fools who willingly court danger."

"But you're bandits."

"That's a trade we know well," Cherso said. "Some of our fathers, brothers, were men of the road as well."

He glanced away, not wanting the obvious rejoinder from Hal asking what rope or headsman's ax they'd encountered to end their careers.

"Speaking of which," he said, ostentatiously changing the subject, "these times we're living in are becoming a bit dangerous, if you haven't noticed."

"I've seen a lot more men with arms about this season," Hal said. "And merchants are travelling in convoys, and few families abroad."

"They sense trouble, as do I," Cherso said. "A man came out, two weeks gone, to talk to us about an amnesty."

"That doesn't seem like trouble to me," Hal said. "Are you going to take it?"

"Nary a chance," the pockmarked man said.

"Not under the conditions he set us," Cherso agreed. "It wasn't a blanket amnesty, such as a baron might offer when his daughter's married or his wizard achieves power over his enemy.

"Seems there's now a Council of Barons, and some say they're considering naming a king from amongst themselves. You heard aught about that?"

Hal shook his head. "I don't pay much attention to politics."

"Nor do we," Cherso said. "But mayhap we'd best start.

This Council has offered an amnesty to men of arms – sorry, I meant men of the road like ourselves, freelances, and such – on condition they join the army they're putting together."

"Armies," the other bandit snorted. "Have to do all the fighting, share your loot with some fatass who sat on a hill lookin' proud in armor, and prob'ly get trampled in some charge anyway. Piddle on armies."

"Worst, they've got a wizard making anyone who takes the amnesty swear a blood oath to him, that if you do something sensible, such as desert after the first pay, you'll be eaten by flaming worms or somethings.

"Not that the barons' alliance will hold together long enough for them to backstab each other until a king wades out of the gore and grabs a crown, but the bastards might hang together long enough to sweep the countryside for us men of daring. As I said, not a good sign."

Hal gnawed at his lip, wondered if any of this would pertain to him, couldn't see how.

"A question for you," the pockmarked thief said. "Does Deraine have highwaymen like Sagene?"

"Not many," Hal answered.

"No men of spirit in your kingdom, eh?"

"No," Hal said, unoffended. "We have laws."

The pockmarked man grinned, tapped the hilt of his sheathed sword. "So do we."

That brought laughter from the other thieves. When it died, Cherso asked, "As I recall, you wintered last year in Paestum. Does your master plan the same?"

"Don't know yet," Hal said. "He was thinking of going into winter quarters early, and voyaging over to the Roche coast for a replacement for the dragon we lost last year.

"But the Roche denied his permit, and he's not taken me into his secrets about what his plans are now."

"Word of advice," Cherso said. "I wouldn't be too eager to spend time in Paestum these days. Far, far too close to Roche, and those bastards and their damned queen keep whining in the broadsheets about having been snookered out of their claim to the city."

"No matter to me," Hal said.

"Nor me," Cherso said, taking the bolt from his crossbow. "Life goes on, and we do the best we can with what we have."

Hal nodded.

"You'd best be getting on to Bedarisi, before dark," Cherso said. "I've heard there's some masterless men who have been lurking just beyond the walls, men without any law to guide them.

"Good luck to you, young dragon man. And we'll see you next spring."

As quietly as they'd come, the bandits were gone, and the road was clear.

Hal thought about what the bandit had told him. Armed men on the roads, a possible amnesty to raise an army, Cherso saying the Roche were growing ambitious. No, it should not pertain to him, at least as long as he kept a wary eye out and his back close to a wall.

It wouldn't hurt if he had a bit more money in the pouch tied to his inner thigh. Athelny wasn't a stingy man, but he had a weakness for the rattle of dice. It was always a race to see whether he'd get his hands on the cash box before Gaeta after a show.

She was the only one left of the troupe Hal had joined that dusty fall day – the others had found better wages with other shows – circuses, traveling bestiaries – or just gotten tired of the wanderer's life.

Hal was still with Athelny because he still wanted, after three years, to become a dragon rider. But so far his master had been stingy training Kailas in his art.

"You don't think I'm mad," he said once, somewhat in his cups, "for if I teach you all I know, wouldn't you just run off, find a dragon of your own and become my competitor?" He laughed in that strange, high-pitched way he had.

Hal had to admit there was truth to that. Athelny, not at all a bad man, had taught him some things. Hal could have found another flier, but he had no guarantee that master would be any more generous with his knowledge.

As for leaving the road, that was absurd, since Hal hadn't seen any trade more enticing, let alone the pure thrill of traveling new roads, seeing new villages and people, even returning to a place not visited for a year, and seeing the changes.

At least once a show, Athelny would give Hal a ride, and recently had let him sit in front, and start learning the basics of flying.

That also never ceased to thrill, from the awkward flapping journey upward, to the easy soaring on wind currents, like a sailing ship of the skies, to darting, carefully, through clouds, always expecting them to taste like the spun candy sold at village fairs, forgetting their dankness, sudden rain and occasional danger.

Even the danger drew him – watching, from aloft, a thunderstorm approach, barely diving down to shelter in time. Or, if there were low clouds, flying just above them, like flying above feathery snowfields. Dragons, too, seemed, as Hal had thought, to enjoy the joy of flight, cool wind across their savage faces, gliding down, silently, to startle a questing eagle, or suddenly appearing above a flock of ducks and hear them raucously dart groundward, away from the claws and fangs.

Athelny had only one dragon now, the green beast called Belle.

The young dragon named Red, Hal's favorite, had managed to break free one afternoon, when the show was camped in the high mountains. There were wild dragons in the heights, and Athelny had said it was mating season.

Dragons, when they came into season, were wildly promiscuous. Then they'd pick a mate from one of the bulls they'd mated with and remain with him through the four-month incubation period, and for a year after the kit was born.

They'd watched, Athelny whispering unconscious obscenities, as Red eagerly flew toward a female. Two males had attacked him. He'd fought hard, lashing with his talons and fangs, but the other two were older, bigger and more savage.

One dove on Red, and had his neck in its claws. He rolled, as Red tore at him, and Hal heard the young dragon's neck snap from hundreds of feet below.

The teamsters had started to object when Athelny ordered them to bury the dragon, but then they saw the terrible look in the flier's eyes and set to.

When Red's corpse was under the mound, and stones were heaped atop it, Athelny had sat, in some strange wake, beside the grave for a day and a night.

Hal, too, had felt aching sadness, such as he'd never felt for another human, and he wondered about himself.

Then the caravan had gone on, and Athelny had never mentioned Red's name again.

What he proposed next, with Roche having refused permission to go to Black Island for a replacement, Hal didn't know. Dragons were most expensive, more so these days. The story was that Roche was buying any trained or half-trained bull or cow, and would even purchase kits.

Athelny had told him he preferred his dragons to be no more than hatchlings when he bought them. "There's only one secret to raising dragons," he said. "You've got to be kind to the little buggers, even when they've ripped your damned arm open. Hate 'em, and they'll sense what you're feeling, and one day ... Well, either they fly off, or else it won't be your arm that's bleeding."

Hal had his own scars now, mostly from Red, but some from the fairly placid Belle. And he had no trouble treating the beasts as Athelny had taught him – he could brook no man's hand being raised against a beast, even one as deadly as a dragon.

It was bad enough, Hal thought, trying to worry about himself, without having to think about kings and queens and armies and such.

The hells with it, he said, deciding to listen to the bandit's advice and not worry about anything behind his horizon.

The Roche dragon fliers were set up just beyond the city gates, and clearly didn't have to worry about any lurking masterless men: Hal counted at least twenty heavily armed men in unfamiliar uniforms around the circled wagons. The Roche had their dragons loose, and were rehearsing.

Hal, never having seen their performance, joined the half-hundred idlers of Bedarisi watching.

He'd never seen anything like it, and certainly Athelny would never be able to put on a show to compare.

The five dragons were dark, greens, blues, browns, with only minor stripes of color. They were big, as big as any Hal had seen, save for a few monsters in the wild, and the Roche flyers had their animals under perfect control.

They flew in close formation, caracoling through various maneuvers – banking, diving, climbing, rolling across each other's back. Then came games – follow-my-leader, mock duels, even a flyer jumping from one dragon to another in midair.

There were two wizards with the show, and they circulated around the crowd, doing various illusions of dragons.

All the while, leather-lunged barkers kept reminding the crowd that this was only a hint of the wonders Roche was bringing to them, that tomorrow, and for three days and nights, this show of *Ky* Yasin's would bring them glories they'd never dreamed of.

Hal heard Yasin referred to as "the *Ky*" by one of the soldiers, gathered that was a title, not a first name.

Kailas was shaken – this was only a rehearsal? Athelny's troupe would be very lucky to attract enough Sagene to cover their expenses here in Bedarisi.

About half the soldiers formed up, as the magicians took a pair of tiny wicker baskets from a case, muttered spells, and the baskets grew until they were about five by ten feet.

Four soldiers, on command, jumped into each basket, and a dragon landed beside each one. Heavy straps connected the baskets with rings fastened through the dragons' outer scales. The beasts, with much shouting from their masters, crashed their wings, beating at the air, and slowly, slowly, climbed into the sky.

Then the dragons turned, and made a mock assault on the crowd. The soldiers fired arrows down into the turf as they passed, very low.

The crowd applauded spatteringly, but was mostly silent. It was very easy, especially considering the way Roche had been behaving of late, to see the obvious military use dragons might provide.

Again, Hal had heard of nothing like this from any flyer of Deraine or Sagene.

The dragons landed, and the soldiers piled out. The barkers changed their tune, and started soliciting for rides, half price because the show hadn't officially opened.

Several people got in line.

Hal was interested to note that the pair of dragons giving rides didn't carry passengers on their backs, but in the wicker baskets, three or four, depending on the size of the passenger, at a time.

Hal thought these dragons older and therefore calmer of temperament than the others.

Their takeoff and flight suggested he was right. These dragons gave very sedate rides up to about 500 feet, toured over Bedarisi, then made a long circle back to a gentle landing. There were no acrobatics or stunts.

Then the rehearsal was over, and the ground staff of the show busied themselves feeding the monsters and cleaning equipment.

It didn't appear as if they minded visitors in their camp, and so Hal left his horse tethered, and wandered about *Ky* Yasin's establishment.

Everything was luxury to Kailas – the flyers had small

wagons to themselves, and servants. The transport wagons –
two to each dragon – were new, and brightly kept. There
were other wagons for the troops, staff, a cookhouse,
equipage, and enough horses and oxen to have fitted out a
regiment of soldiery.

Hal didn't have Gaeta's experience, but had helped her take
care of the books long enough to have some idea of what it
cost to run a show. He couldn't get the numbers for this
troupe to come out right, unless the Roche were charging ten
gold pieces or more for a ride, and he'd seen the priceboard –
rides were even cheaper than with Athelny.

Perhaps Yasin was very rich, and subsidizing the troupe
from his wealth.

Perhaps.

Or, Hal thought, and wondered where he'd developed such
a subterfugous mind, perhaps Yasin and his flyers were
advance scouts for a war being whispered about.

Perhaps.

He was mulling this about as he passed by a medium-sized
wagon, whose door was open. He heard the sound of a man
cursing, then another man laughing.

He knew that high-pitched laugh, and his heart dropped as
he heard someone say, in heavily accented Sagene, "You see,
Ky Athelny, as I promised, your luck was about to change."

Hal went up the steps, trying to concoct a story as he went.

Inside were four men around a table with small, numbered
boards, dice, and piled gold and silver. One, short, very thin,
wore the expensive silks of a Sagene nobleman; another, a
comfortably fat man, wearing gray suede and moleskin
breeches.

The third was a man no more than three years beyond
Kailas' seventeen, with carefully close-trimmed beard and
hair. He wore black leather breeches, with a matching jacket,
unbuttoned to his waist, with a white collarless shirt, a red
scarf around his neck and high boots. He was clearly a flier.
The man, in spite of his youth, bore himself with authority

that was almost arrogance. Hal wondered if he might not be *Ky* Yasin.

The fourth was Athelny. He had the smallest pile of money, mostly silver, of them all, in front of him. It was clear he'd gotten to the cash box, and, remembering how much had been in it when Hal rode out for Frechin with his posters the day before, wasn't winning.

Athelny had been drinking, but what of that? Wine never gave nor took away card sense or luck from him.

He looked up, saw Hal, looked first surprised, then guilty for an instant, then his long face flushed with anger. He tried to cover.

"'Tis a surprise indeed," he said, forcing his would-be upper class drawl, "to see you."

"Uh, yessir," Hal said. "I've just returned from Frechin, and thought you might wish a report."

"Later, lad," Athelny said. "I doubt me if these gentlemen, the noble Bayle Yasin, his manager, or Lord Scaer would be interested in our business."

"But, sir—"

"You may wait outside for me. I shan't be long."

Scaer, the small, thin man, looked at Athelny's pot, snickered, but said nothing.

"I . . . yessir," Hal managed, and went out.

He slumped down against the wagon, not knowing why he was so cast down. So Athelny was gaming? He'd done that before. So he was losing? He almost always did that, too, sometimes wiping them out so they had to steal grain for Belle, who grudgingly would accept fodder other than meat, and beg for their own dinners.

He tried not to listen to the game as it went on, but couldn't. Athelny won a few small rounds, then lost again and again.

Hal sparked awake after an hour, hearing Yasin say quietly:

"*Ky* Athelny, are you sure you wish to chase that wager? 'Twould appear you're bested on the face of things."

"I thank'ee for your wisdom," Athelny said, a bit sharply. "But there're two more draws.

"Lord Scaer, here is the sum total of my stake to say you do not hold the numbers you want me to think."

There was a laugh.

"Give out the counters, then," Scaer said.

Hal heard the clack of the wood, and a breath, sharply intaken.

"Fortune favors the bold, as they say," Scaer said. "To see your last counter will take a deal of gold."

"I'm out of *this* turn," Yasin said.

"As am I," another voice, obviously the Roche troupe's manager, said.

There was silence for a moment.

"I have naught but confidence," Athelny said. "I trust you'll take my note of hand?"

"I'm afraid not," Scaer said. "Meaning no offense, but men who're not of Bedarisi . . . Well . . ."

"All right," Athelny said. "Here. Give me paper and that pen."

Scratching came.

"I trust this deed to my show will allow me to continue in this game?"

"*Ky* Athelny," Yasin said. "Are you sure that's what you wish to do?"

"The Derainian is of age," Scaer said. "Irregular though it is, I accept the bet. The counters, if you will."

Hal was on his feet, mouth dry in panic, fear. Athelny, at least as far as he knew, had never gone this far into madness.

He started up the steps, but there was nothing he could do as wood rattled once more.

"And there you have it," Scaer said.

There was a moan, that could only have come from Athelny.

"So now I own a flying lizard and some wagons," Scaer said, strange triumph in his voice.

"And what will you do with them?" Yasin asked.

"I'm damned if I know. Would you be interested in acquiring that beast?"

"We would not, I'm afraid," Yasin's manager said.

"I know not what I'll do with it either. Perhaps tether it in my park for children to marvel at. Or let it fly on a long rope, and let my guards practice their bowmanship."

"You can't—" Athelny blurted.

"Oh yes, I can," Scaer said. "And I'll arrange for my soldiers to come for the beast, and the rest of your gear, early tomorrow.

"I'm not a hard man, so that will give you time for you and your people to gather their personal belongings. In return, perhaps you'd give my stable master some tips on the care and feeding of dragons. Haw!"

There was a scrape of a chair, and Athelny stumbled out of the wagon, down the steps. He saw Hal, then looked away.

Hal, wanting to hit him, wanting to put a dagger in the guts of that damned Scaer, still not knowing what to do, followed.

They'd reached the patch of cleared ground, not much more than a pair of lots, just inside the walls of the city, where Athelny had set up his show, before the flier could face Hal, who'd walked behind him across the city, leading his horse.

"I'm . . . I'm sorry. It's just when I see the cards, and the silver, I can't seem to hold back, and all my . . . I'm sorry."

Hal thought of things he could say, maybe should say, but pity took him. He shook his head.

"What's done is done."

He called Gaeta, the other two teamsters and their only spieler, told them what had happened.

"What are we going to do?" one of the teamsters said dully.

Hal looked at Athelny, but the flier remained silent.

Something came to Kailas then. If no one took charge, then he must. He dug into his pants, took out his purse. He had saved a dozen gold coins, more in silver. He gave the spieler and the two teamsters a gold coin each.

"Get your things, and go. Cut a horse free if you wish, but you've got to do it before nightfall."

"Where will we go?" a teamster asked plaintively.

Hal shook his head.

"I'm damned if I know. Gaeta and I'll make for Paestum, try to find work to get across the Straits to home, I guess."

"What about him?" The other teamster jerked a shoulder at Athelny, who stood slumped, utterly defeated.

Before Hal could find an answer, ten soldiers doubled up to the lot.

Athelny saw them, shouted something Hal never understood, and ran for the wagon where Belle was tethered.

"Hey! You!" one of them shouted.

"That's his dragon!" Hal shouted back.

"Th' hells 'tis! It now b'longs t' Lord Scaer, an' we're here to make sure there's no trickery."

"There'll be none," Hal said, running toward the soldiers, suddenly sure what Athelny intended.

"That's for damned sure," the soldier said. "You there! Old man! Get away from that monster!"

"He's likely 'bout to sic' 'im on us," another soldier said.

"In a pig's arse he will!" the first said. "Get your bows ready! Fire on my command!"

Athelny had Belle loosed, and her wings were unfurled, clashing in anticipation.

"Stop there, you!" the soldier said. His fingers pulled an arrow from his belt quiver, and he nocked it, lifted the bow.

Hal dove at him, knocked him down, was about to get up, and another soldier had a sword at his throat.

"Stay easy," he ordered, and Hal obeyed.

"Now, Belle," Athelny shouted, pulling himself up on to the beast's neck. Belle's wings thundered again, and she stumbled clear of the ground, was lifting, trying for height.

The soldier had another arrow nocked, aimed, and his bowstring twanged.

Athelny shouted agony, and Hal saw the arrow sticking out of his side.

But he was able to pull himself up behind the carapace as Belle's wings beat stronger.

Other arrows went up, fell short of the dragon, and then it was high in the air, outlined against the sun, setting a true course north, out of sight, flying north toward Paestum, toward Deraine, toward home.

Gaeta and Hal traveled together, taking the road toward Paestum Athelny would have flown above. They stopped at every village, asked every traveler.

Only one man, and he looked unreliable, said he'd seen a green dragon overhead, days earlier. But there was no one mounted aboard it.

No one reported finding a strange body, dead of an arrow wound along the road, either.

Two weeks later, little better than beggars, the two reached Paestum.

There were other dragon fliers there. But none of them had heard anything of Athelny or Belle.

Hal went to the cliffs at the edge of the city, just at sunset, and stared across the Straits.

He hoped, wished really, that somehow Athelny and Belle had made it across them to Deraine and whatever home Athelny had.

He suddenly realized in the two years he'd known the dragonmaster he'd never heard Athelny speak of home or family.

All that he'd had, all that he'd wanted, was the dragons.

Perhaps, he thought sadly, perhaps Belle had taken him on to the land that Athelny might have dreamed of, the land of dragons far bigger, far fiercer than any known, far beyond Black Island and the ken of men.

Then Hal Kailas turned back, toward the city of Paestum.

Now there was another life to begin, a life he had no idea of or dreams for.

5

"You," the man carrying a spear and a half-shield called.
"Over here!"

Hal pretended he wasn't the intended. The man shouted
again, and pointed at Kailas.

Hal put on an innocent face – hard when you're ragged and
hungry – and strolled casually across the oceanfront walk.

"City warder on special duty," the man said importantly.
"Who're you?"

"Hal Kailas."

"Citizen of what country?"

"Deraine."

"You sure you're telling the truth? There's Roche
about in Paestum claiming to be Deraine, which is why we're
checking."

"Deraine," Hal repeated.

"From where?"

"Up country. Caerly, originally."

"Never heard of it."

Hal shrugged, anger starting to grow.

"They've never heard of you, either."

"Don't crack wise," the man growled, "or we'll find my

serjeant and let him sort you out. What's your business in Paestum?"

"I was on the road, and decided it was time to get back home."

"You and what looks like a million others. Damned if I knew there were that many Deraine in Sagene," the man said, loosening a trifle.

Hal didn't answer.

"All right," the warder allowed. "Your accent's too back-woodsy for any Roche to imitate. On your way."

Hal didn't acknowledge, but moved quickly off into the crowd.

The waterfront was crowded, and not with a holiday throng. Men, women, children, some richly dressed, some ragged, some carrying elegant travel cases, others with impro-vised packs of breeches or sheets, eddied up and down the walkway, stopping at the gangways of the tied up ships. Most were looking for one thing – passage they could afford home before the war started.

Hal had been almost three months in Paestum. He and Gaeta had gone their separate ways, figuring their luck would be better alone than in company.

Hal had started looking for work with two dragon fliers he'd found in Paestum. Both were heading back for Deraine, though. The first told Hal he had no interest in hiring some-body who'd pick his brain and end up a competitor.

The other, more kindly, a man named Garadice, said he would, normally, be willing to take on an apprentice, particu-larly one who'd worked for Athelny, which proved Hal had brains, was a hard worker, and had the ability to get along with difficult people. But he was heading for home, "and putting my head under the covers."

Hal asked, and the man explained why. He'd just gotten back from Roche.

"*Damned* scary. Everyone's running around talking about how they're not getting their rightful place in the world, and

Deraine and Sagene are conspiring against 'em, always have, and Queen Norcia's the first to recognize it, and they'll get their own back, and then we'll see what we'll see.

"Don't like it none. Especially when I saw the army warrants combing the villages, enlisting for the army.

"Roche is getting like a damned armed camp. The smithies are churning out swords and spears, the farriers have horses lined up for shoeing, even the damned little old ladies are sewing uniforms for 'their boys.'

"Like I said, a place in the country where nobody comes, a good store of food and wine, and I'll take note of the world again in a year or so.

"Or maybe not."

Hal was driven to casual labor, unloading wagons, clerking for a day, cleaning anything that needed to be cleaned. But there were hundreds, maybe thousands like him, streaming into Paestum, willing to work for a meal, when Hal needed silver for his passage.

And every time he had some money, the price of the passage across the Straits, no more than two days' sail, had gotten dearer and dearer.

Hal had at least found a warm, dry place to sleep in a byre whose owner treated him like he was invisible, not minding him washing up in a trough or even stealing a dipper of milk in the mornings before he went out looking for work.

He was almost hungry and desperate enough to consider the army's recruiters. But not quite. He'd worked too hard to serve any master for longer than a moment, except Athelny. He didn't fancy regimentation, square-bashing or the yessir nossir threebagsfull attitude the army demanded.

Somehow, some way, he'd find a way aboard one of those damned ships with their heartless captains, get across to Deraine and regroup.

As the days passed, he started paying close attention to the rumors, taletellers and broadsheets.

The rumors first said there were raiders abroad, hitting

lonely farms and small villages along the Roche-Sagene border. The rumors were confirmed, and the story was they were actually Roche warriors in mufti.

Queen Norcia denied these rumors, saying it was very like Deraine and Sagene to come up with these lies when they couldn't keep their citizens safe, and perhaps they needed Roche to bring order back.

Rumors said there were Roche infiltrators in Paestum, waiting for the moment to rise and support an attacking army. Frighteningly, these rumors were neither confirmed nor denied by the criers and broadsheets.

Hal gloomily decided it couldn't get much worse.

But it did.

The situation deteriorated by the day.

A company of raiders was wiped out by government cavalry. Strangely enough, the cavalry was a mixed unit of Derainian and Sagene soldiers, strange because it was unknown for the two rival countries, always rivals, to cooperate.

The massacre supposedly happened not many leagues south of Paestum.

Next it was revealed the raiders weren't brigands but Roche military, making provocative raids into Sagene.

The Roche government, rather than disavow the dead bandits, agreed they were Roche dragoons, on an official mission, and had been ambushed well inside the Roche borders.

This was shrilly denied by every official in Sagene, Paestum and Deraine.

Next an official statement from Roche, sent out in Queen Norcia's own hand, said the situation was intolerable, and reparations would be required from both Sagene and Deraine.

The Council of Barons and Deraine's King Asir icily refused.

Queen Norcia increased her demands: reparations, plus a conference, in Roche, which would determine the proper governing of Paestum. At the very least, Deraine must agree to a power-sharing with Roche for the free city.

Failure to meet these "reasonable" demands could have only one response.

Norcia announced her military was being called up, and rumor had it Roche troops were already massing on the border, ready to march against Paestum.

Deraine refused the "offer," King Asir calling it blackmail "no decent man would ever respond to," and force would be met with force, if necessary, although he hoped there was still a chance of peace.

Hal looked up, wondering if that dragon, high above the city, was Roche. Other dragons, all flying in and out to the east, had been overflying Paestum.

No one knew what they were doing, but hearsay had it there were Roche troops hidden not far across the nearby border.

Hal remembered *Ky* Yasin and his flying show, and wondered just where the flier was, and if he might not be wearing a uniform or commanding those dragons overhead.

But it wasn't his concern, since he'd just figured a way that was almost unbeatable to stow away on a fishing boat bound for Deraine.

There were dangers of smothering under a load of fish, being caught and thrown overboard or simply drowning in a fishwell, but what of it? Staying here in Paestum was already dangerous, between the threat of starving, and onrushing war.

His planning was cut short by a stocky warder, flanked by a dozen grinning fellows. All had swords at their waists, carried ready truncheons, and looked as if they were in a transport of delight.

"You, lad. Who's your master?"

"Uh . . . I have none."

"Your work?"

"None, at present."

"You now have both. This is your official announcement that you've been accepted into His Majesty's Army, and your service will be required to defend the walls of Paestum."

"But I'm a civilian, and have no interest in carrying a damned spear," Hal protested.

"That's tough treacle. King Asir has authorized conscription for all Derainians in this present emergency, and you're one of the first to be honored and permitted to become one of the heroes of Paestum.

"Lads, take charge of our new recruit, and escort him to the barracks for outfitting."

6

Hal stared down from the battlement as scouts and dragoons of the oncoming Roche army sacked the outskirts of Paestum.

Overhead, two dragons soared, banking back and forth in the stormy winds coming onshore. Hal supposed they were observing for the Roche commanders, comfortably behind the lines, planning the assault.

Centuries ago, when Deraine had seized by force of arms the seaside city on the border of Sagene and Roche that became Paestum, they'd made it impregnable with high stone walls, sixteen feet thick, covering the peninsula the town occupied from both sea and land assault. Time passed, and Paestum, the most prosperous trading port along the Chicor Straits, had built up to those walls and beyond. After all, it was unlikely there'd be war again, certainly not between the three most powerful countries in the known world.

These suburbs had given fine cover for the Roche army as it entered the city. Cavalry, dragoons and lancers, had been the first to attack the Deraine lines on the outskirts, under the cover of a sorcerous fog. The untrained Deraine, in a moil of confusion, hesitated, and Roche smashed two waves of experienced assault troops into them.

The Deraine fell back, not quite breaking, through the outskirts of Paestum into the ancient fortress.

Hal had been very grateful that he'd been guarding the wall with his newly-issued unsharpened sword, dented shield, and leather armor. That had been – what, he thought dully – three, no four days ago. Or maybe more.

Hal had been assigned to a cavalry formation that lacked only one thing – their horses. He was supposed to be on guard half the day, the rest on other duties including eating and sleeping time. But there'd been continual panics, cries to man the parapets and such, so he didn't remember the last time he'd had two hours of quiet, let alone sleep.

Now Roche was bringing up its main force – Hal had seen, before the storm roared in on them, caterpillar-like columns in their brightly-colored, if campaign-stained, uniforms moving steadily toward the city.

Two soldiers manned a dart thrower in the nearby tower, a pedestal-mounted bow, arms of rigid iron bars. Tension came from hair skeins. The soldiers wound it back to full cock, aimed, and sent a long bolt flashing high at one dragon. The bolt missed by a dozen feet, and the dragon's rider pulled it higher. The next dart fell well below the beast, and the two continued circling.

Roche, fearless and confident, had sent four dragons against the men on the walls after the city was invested. They'd torn several men off the parapets to their deaths, then the dart throwers had been brought up under cover of night.

The bolts, a yard long, iron-headed, tore into the dragon formation when they attacked the next day. Two dragons had been hit hard, and, screaming, snapping at the huge arrows stuck in their bodies, had pinwheeled to the ground. Crossbowmen finished off the one that still floundered in the muck, its rider already sprawled in death beside it. The other dove into a burning building, and both animal and rider had howled down into death.

After that, the dragon fliers were more cautious, flying at greater altitude, doing no more than observing.

Hal looked up at them, wishing he were up there, even in this building storm, a storm that everyone said had been brought by magic, the magic of Roche, so that Deraine wouldn't be able to reinforce Paestum from across the Straits.

Hal didn't know, didn't care about that. But he figured the Roche couldn't try to climb the walls while this wind blew, and squally rain sheeted down.

He scanned his sector again. No movement, save the occasional scuttle of looters. Then he smelt smoke, and saw flames rising from one house, then another.

The Roche had fired the abandoned homes and businesses of the suburbs. Whether deliberately or by accident Hal didn't know. Probably looters had done it, in drunken accident, for nothing happened for an hour or so.

He heard shouts from behind him, looked across, saw a procession coming up the ramp to the next parapet. He was grateful they weren't coming to him – he'd already learned one of a soldier's greatest lessons: that anyone of higher rank showing up can only mean trouble.

The group consisted of four men, wearing the gaudy green and yellow uniform of the King's Protectors of Paestum, the supposedly elite regiment that guarded Paestum's governor, high-ranking officials, nobility and interesting things like the treasury.

Behind them were two young men, heavy-laden with boxes and cases, wearing expensive civilian garb.

Following was the reason for this procession: an impressively-bearded man, wearing dark robes and tall red cap, stalking along with dignity, followed by four more guards.

Hal decided this might be interesting. Interesting things attracted attention, so the first thing he did was plan his retreat – half a dozen steps to the nearest tower and its stairs, then inside against any danger.

That settled, he watched the show, about a hundred feet

away, as the magician's acolytes opened box after box, spread out rugs and set up braziers. Incense went into the braziers, and the magician touched each brazier, lips moving.

In spite of the wind and occasional rain, the incense smoked into life. A crosswind took the smoke under Hal's nose, and he coughed. It was a smell not to his liking, of spices far too strong and unknown.

One of the acolytes and a guard turned and scowled in his direction. Hal put on an innocent air, and walked his rounds until they lost interest.

Evidently, magicians needed silence to work their crafts.

Ribbons were laid out in intricate patterns atop the carpets, and the two acolytes took up stations, each holding a long taper.

Two gestures by the wizard, and the tapers smoked into flame.

The sorcerer picked up a huge book, very ancient and decrepit, opened it, and began chanting.

Hal shivered, for the chanting came very clear to him, in spite of the wind, and grew louder. He didn't know the words as the chant grew louder and louder, the voice deeper in pitch, almost sounding as if no human throat could produce these sounds.

The magician gestured three times toward the Roche lines, and each time thunder slammed against Hal, though he saw no lightning.

The wind backed, then cut, and a flash of sunlight came through the clouds.

The wizard must be casting a counterspell against the storm conjuration.

The dark clouds that had raced overhead broke for certain, a sunny rift growing like a huge arrow over Paestum.

Then the wizard screamed. Hal jolted, saw the man stagger, hurl his grimoire high in the air in a spasm, tear at his robes.

Fire gouted from the tapers, took the two acolytes, curled

like a living thing, and reached a red and black hand for the sorcerer.

He was shrieking, possibly a spell, but the fire-magic was stronger, taking him, and his body roared into flames. He pirouetted, fell, clawing at his body as it burnt.

Hal dove for his cover, out of sight, heard more screams, chanced peering out, saw all of the men on the parapet, soldiers and acolytes, writhe and die in agony.

Then the storm wind began once more.

The next day, at dawn, the Roche attacked.

They struck three times that day, with long ladders covered by archers sheltering in the ruins. Each time they were driven back, the last with cauldrons of boiling pitch.

All was quiet for two days, then Roche soldiers built a heavy wooden passageway to the walls. Flaming pitch was poured down to fire it, but the passage's roof was covered with animal hides, constantly soaked with water.

It crept toward the part of the wall Hal was guarding, butted against it.

Dull thudding began, and word came – Roche was digging a mine under the wall to collapse it.

"Arright, you stumblebums, pay attention," Sancreed Broda grated. The fifty soldiers were instantly silent.

Broda was a puzzlement, and a terror, to them all, officer to recruit. He was old, hard, with a scarred face and ropy-muscled body. He wasn't a member of Hal's cavalry unit, nor was he in uniform. He wore leather breeches so stiff with dirt they could have stood of their own accord, a yellow shirt that might have been white once, some time before the war started, and a leather jerkin even dirtier than his pants. On his feet were some sort of slippers, and a silk scarf was knotted around his long gray hair. He was armed with a hammer, and Hal had seen him use it twice on Roche who'd gotten to the top of "his" wall, grinning madly through yellow, rotting teeth.

No one knew why he was in charge, only that he was, and the gods help anyone who questioned that, although no one had seen him do anything worse than growl at the men under his command.

"This 'ere's a real official docyment from our rulers, gods bless 'em and give 'em royal assaches," Sancreed went on. "It's got all kindsa praise for you lummocks, on account of you're standin' in the most dangerous spot in Paestum, the thin whatever-color-you-yoinks-are line between barb'rism an' civilization, bullshit, bullshit, bullshit . . . I'm givin' you the short version, 'cause we've got to figger out what to do next, ignorin' these eejiots, 'less you feel like dyin'.

"Anyway, everybody's real proud of you, for holdin' firm, even with those friggin' Roche diggin' away under our feet."

He stopped and, without realizing it, everyone listened. All heard the sound from below them of the Roche diggers.

"Now, what you're s'posed to do, an' everybody'll think worlds of you, accordin' to these royal farts back in th' palace," Broda said, his voice withering in scorn, "is go walkin' back and forth atop th' wall 'til the mine's fired, then die real noble in the wreckage, keepin' the Roche back 'til other troops drive 'em back.

"Heroes to a friggin' man," he sneered. "They'd prob'ly name boulevards after your dead young asses if we go an' win this stupid damn war.

"Now, that ain't gonna happen. There'll be four volunteers up on the walls, making sure none of the bassids come up at us. That's you, you, you and you. Get up those ramps.

"The rest of you are gonna pull back, into that old warehouse there. Out of th' weather an' all.

"When they put fire to their mine, you won't be doin' anything like gettin' dead, but comin' out after 'em. Maybe a bit of a su'prise for the bassids.

"'At's fine. You officers can take charge of your troops, an' get 'em under cover now. Half sleep. Get rested, get fed, 'cause I think it'll get shitty in not too long.

"Yeah. One other thing. Four volunteers to listen for when th' diggin' stops. You, you, you and you. Follow me."

Hal was one of the four. He obediently followed Broda into the base of the tower. The old man picked up a bundle of torches, used flint and steel to fire one, went down narrow, spider-webbed steps. There was dank stone all around Hal, and above him.

The sound of digging got louder.

"You wants to keep it quiet when you're down here," Broda said. "Mebbe th' fools think they're doin' all this shit in silence, an' we don't know squat about what's goin' on."

He snorted.

The steps ended in a small cellar. The thudding sounded like it was not quite below them, but very close.

"Right," Broda said. "Here's your posts. Two on, two off. You're listenin' for the diggin' to stop. Like I told you afore, which you likely forgot, when they stop diggin' is when they'll be gettin' ready, pullin' back an' firin' their pit props an' whatever other flam'bles packed in to collapse th' tunnel an' let th' wall cave in atop.

"You're to wait for that silence, an' when it comes, haul ass outa here and find me. Don't hang about, bein' cute and waitin' for th' smell of smoke or like that.

"*Nobody* gets to play a godsdamned hero," he grated, and Hal thought his eyes glowed in the darkness. "If you go and do something dumb like get killed, you'll answer to me. Understand?"

For some reason, none of the four soldiers thought what Broda had said either absurd or stupid.

They waited for another day and a half. Hal swore that if he made it through this, he'd live in a tree or under a bush, and never go under a roof again, let alone this far underground, with the rats and people who wanted to kill him, deadly moles, digging ever closer.

He could have stayed in his village, become a miner, and

died when a shaft collapsed around him if he wanted a fate like this, he thought.

He wasn't meant for this. He was . . . well, he would be, a dragon flier. Let him live through this, let him at least die in the light of day. He thought of praying, couldn't think of any particular god he believed in.

But his fellow listener evidently did, mumbling supplications to many gods, more than Hal thought a priest could honor.

Irritated, driven out of his own funk by the other, he kicked him and told him to shut up.

The other soldier, even younger than Hal, obeyed.

Hal was wondering how long it was until the end of their shift, when they could go up those stairs for a bowl of what everyone had started calling siege stew.

Some said it was made of rats, that all the real meat in Paestum was being hoarded by the rich. Hal didn't believe that, although he'd noticed very few dogs about the last few days.

Quite suddenly, there was silence.

The two soldiers looked at each other, eyes wide against their smoke-darkened faces. His partner started for the stairs.

"Wait," Hal hissed. "Maybe they're only changing diggers."

But the sound of picks and shovels didn't come.

"The hells with you," the other soldier snarled, and was gone.

Hal thought the other right, and went up the stairs behind him, into the spitting rain and dawn light, exulting that he had lived, would live, as long as he made it through the attack that would come.

They found Broda, who grunted, told them to wait, and went down the steps they'd boiled up.

A long time passed, and Broda came back into sight, trying to look as if he wasn't in a hurry.

"'At's right," he said. "They're comin'. You, boy. Go wake up th' other so'jers and tell 'em to get ready."

Two hours later, Hal was smelling smoke as the underground fire built, and then he heard a grinding sound, stones moving against each other.

The drawn-up soldiers moaned, without realizing it.

But Hal saw no sign of movement.

The smell grew stronger and the grinding came now and again.

"Look," someone shouted, and everyone stared up, seeing the wall sway slightly.

"Awright," Broda shouted. "It'll be comin' in a tit. Get y'selfs ready!"

The wall moved more, teetering inward, then with a grinding roar, toppled outward in a boil of dust and ricocheting stones. The wall was down, stones taller than a man bouncing away, sliding.

"Here they come!" someone shouted unnecessarily, and, stumbling over the high-piled rubble, coming toward them, was a wave of Roche infantrymen.

First were spearmen, archers behind.

Deraine bows twanged, and the archers dropped, fell back, but there were grim rows of men with swords behind them.

"Now!" Broda shouted, and Hal was moving forward, when his brain told him to run, that the points of those spears was death. One lunged at him, and he took the strike on his shield, pushed it out of the way as he numbly remembered someone telling him to do, and drove his sword into the Roche's chest.

Then there was another man with a sword, and he parried, ducked, and kicked the man in the kneecap. The man screeched, bent, and Hal booted him out of the way, into another man's spear.

There was a man pushing against him, chest against Hal's shield, and he smelt foul breath, drove his knee up into the man's crotch, killed him as he fell back.

Hal had his back against a high stone, and two men were

coming at him, and then they were both down with arrows in their chests.

Hal didn't know who to thank, saw Broda standing in a circle of bodies, hammer dripping blood.

Chanting came, high-pitched, and something grew out of nothing, a green-skinned demon, dripping slime, crouching, claws scraping the ground.

Someone screamed in terror, and Hal realized he was the one screaming. The demon looked about, pupilless eyes finding a victim, and it leapt toward Sancreed Broda.

The old man moved surprisingly fast, rolled aside, and struck up at the nightmare. It brushed his hammer aside, and claws ripped.

Broda howled in pain, chest torn open, tried for another smash, fell back, dead.

Hal Kailas felt that hard, cold rage build within him.

The demon looked for another target, saw Hal, just as Hal saw, beyond the fiend, a very young man with very long, very blond hair. He had no weapon but a wand, and his lips were moving as the wand moved, pointing at Kailas.

Just before the demon leapt, Hal, having all the time in the world, scooped up a fist-sized rock, and threw it at the magician's head.

The man howled, clawed at the ruins of his face, wand flying away as the demon disappeared.

Hal jumped over a waist-high boulder, and drove his sword into the young wizard's body.

A Roche warrior with a long, two-handed sword was rushing him, and Hal braced. Before the man reached him an eerie wail began, and other apparitions, taller than a man, completely red, body a terrible parody of humanity, with scythe-like claws at the ends of their arms and legs appeared, leaping on to Roche soldiers and tearing at them.

The Roche soldiers paused, confused, terrified, and things that looked like hawks but weren't dove out of nowhere, claws ripping.

The Roche soldiery broke, turned and ran, even as their wizards' counterspell disappeared the red demons and hawks.

But panic had full hold on the Roche, and they didn't stop or look back.

Charging past Hal came wave after wave of Derainian infantry, counterattacking, and he was pulled along with their attack, beyond the shattered walls, and cavalry galloped out of a city gate after the enemy.

Roche magic couldn't recover the advantage, and the attackers were in full flight, through the ruined suburbs back toward their camps, and the siege was broken.

Hal stopped, letting the others run on, killing, pillaging the corpses.

It was not for him.

He turned back, to find Sancreed Broda's body, and get someone to make a pyre. Somehow he knew there'd be no family, no friends to provide the last rites for the terrible old man who'd saved his and many other lives.

Above him, above Paestum's shattered wall, a dragon screamed once, circling in the clean morning sky.

7

The ten horsemen rode at a walk into the glade below a
forested hill. Hal made a swooping motion with his hand,
then at the ground. Obediently, the other nine dismounted.

He pointed to two men, then to his right, two more to his
left. They moved off to provide security for his flanks.

He chose one more, his normal second in command, a pre-
maturely wizened city boy named Jarth Ordinay, and, taking
a long ship's glass from his saddlebag, crept up the hill toward
the hill crest, hoping for no surprises.

There were no ambushers or wizards waiting.

He went on his hands and knees, and crawled into the
heart of a clump of brush, through to the other side, Ordinay,
well-trained, about five feet behind him. He had an arrow and
a strung bow ready.

The hill rolled down, past a nearly dry stream to open
fields that had been well tilled once, but were now choked
with brambles.

The morning was hot, still, and the loudest thing the
buzzing of a swarm of bees nearby.

Half a mile from Hal was the Roche army.

Its tents were struck, rolled into the baggage wagons, and

men were forming up across its front. Behind the infantry, massed cavalry were trotting out toward the flanks.

Hal swept the breaking camp with his glass, found a handful of still-standing tents. There were banners in front of them. Hal read them easily. A year and a half in the cavalry had made him an expert at heraldry.

Duke this, Baron that, Lords the other and his brother, no surprise, seen them before during the campaign, then he started a bit, at one banner he'd never seen before.

It was, he was fairly sure, that of the queen of Roche herself. He couldn't believe she'd decided to take the field, then saw, below the main banner, a longer pennant.

No. Not the queen, but some lord of her household.

That would be, assuming Deraine victory, almost as good.

That also meant that Roche had great hopes for the forthcoming battle.

He slithered back, out of the brush, motioned to Jarth, and they went back to the horses. The flank guards saw his return and, unordered, came back in.

"They're just where the wizard said they'd be," Hal whispered, reporting in the event he didn't make it back to the main Deraine lines. "I'd guess ten, maybe fifteen thousand. Armored infantry, heavy cavalry, maybe a regiment of light cavalry.

"They're getting ready for the march, headed west, again, like we expected.

"They've got flankers out, heavy cavalry, so we'd best skitter back home, for fear of getting pinchered."

The men mounted. Their horses, as well trained as the men, had stayed still, rein-tethered.

Hal led them out of the glade, through the trees, into the open. Fifty yards distant was the ruins of a road.

"At the walk," he said in a low voice, and the horses moved slowly toward the ruined byway.

In unknown territory, using any road, no matter how shattered, could be suicidal. But Hal had taken his patrol nearby less than an hour before, and thought it unlikely there'd been a trap laid in the interim.

He was more worried about being between the two armies – the Deraine army was only half a dozen miles distant.

One reason he'd survived since the siege of Paestum was staying as far away from famous battles as possible. That was why he'd been promoted serjeant, and his troops called him Lucky behind his back.

When he took a patrol out, it was very seldom he didn't bring everyone back, generally without serious wounds.

That was an uncommon boast for these times – after the siege, King Asir had brought a great army across the Chicor Straits, made alliance with Sagene's Council of Barons, and gone after Queen Norcia's army.

They found it, and the two forces smashed each other until they were both tottering, each unable to land the death blow.

They'd broken apart, brought in replacements during their winter quarters, and began skirmishing, each looking for the advantage rather than going toe-to-toe again.

There'd been half a dozen major battles, ten times that in minor brushes that produced no grander results than adding to the casualty lists in the eighteen months since Hal had been dragooned into the army.

One side would move south, the other after it, then the other way around.

Caught in the smash were the Sagene civilians, their villages and farms. A great swathe was cut along the Roche-Sagene border. Here, all was desolation, save the occasionally staunchly garrisoned castle. What trade there was, what merchants there were, stayed close to the army, doing business as they could, when they could.

But the lands weren't empty. There were wanderers, deserters from both sides, and – most to be feared – those who'd turned renegade.

They knew all men's hands were turned against them, so

gave and asked no mercy from any group of soldiers they encountered.

That was one of the jobs of the light cavalry, tracking and destroying the bandits, one reason that Hal Kailas' face showed hard lines, and his smile came but seldom these days.

But it was better, in terms of surviving, than his present task, scouting for the main force as they closed once more for battle.

Everyone knew this encounter was unlikely to be decisive, was not likely to end the war.

Everyone except the high commands on both sides.

Victory would only be won by one army breaking through and laying waste to the other's homeland, yet maintaining its own supply lines.

Sagene and Deraine had more men, more horses. Roche's soldiers were better trained, generally better led. Plus they had more dragons, more magicians.

Just recently, the Roche dragons had changed their tactics. They still scouted overhead, but, just as they'd done in the siege of Paestum, had begun attacking riders and patrols who ventured beyond the safety of the Deraine catapults.

The few Deraine dragons were only used for observation, and what they reported was frequently wrong, and even more frequently disregarded.

Hal sometimes wondered if the end would be all three countries hammered back into barbarism.

All he could hope for, and it was a measure of his strength that he still could hope, was to survive until the war ended. All too many soldiers had given up, dully realized their doom was to be killed, wounded or captured, nothing more.

But an end to this war seemed far in the future.

Hal broke his thoughts, not only because they were veering into gloom, but because anyone who thought of anything other than the minute he was living in was likely to add to the butcher's bill.

He turned in his saddle, looking back at his patrol, scanning the hillsides for movement, then the skies.

As he did, a flight of four dragons, in vee-formation, broke out of the clouds and dove on the patrol.

Hal swore – some Roche magician must have sensed them, and sent out the fliers.

"Dragons!" he shouted. "Spread out, and ride hard for our lines!"

The green-brown dragons swept past above them, then banked back, and dove toward the ground. They flared their wings no more than fifteen feet above the ground, and, almost wingtip to wingtip, beat toward Hal's onrushing patrol, hoping to panic horses and horsemen. But this was not the first, nor the fifth, time Hal had been attacked by dragons.

"Jink!" Kailas shouted, and, obediently, the riders kicked their mounts one way, then another. The dragons tried to turn with them, couldn't, and the ten men rode safely under their attackers. One man – Hal didn't see who – had courage enough to fire an arrow at a dragon.

"Full gallop," and the riders kicked their horses hard, bending low in the saddle, trying to keep from looking back at the closing doom.

It was hard, especially when a scream came. Hal chanced a look, saw a horse pinwheeling through the air, gouting blood from deep talon-wounds in its back, saddle torn away.

Its rider . . . Its rider was tumbling in the dust, getting to his feet, stumbling into a run, knowing no one would turn back for him, following the strictest orders.

Hal wheeled his mount into a curvet, came back at his afoot soldier, saw, out of the corner of his eye, a swooping dragon. He leaned out, arm hooked, and the man had it, was neatly flipped up behind him, and the dragon whipped past, close enough for Hal to have touched its right talon as it missed him.

Again he turned, and his horse was gasping, flanks lathered. Two dragons were coming at him, each not seeing the other, then avoiding collision at the last minute as Hal rode under a torn-apart tree.

A dragon smashed through branches above his head, climbed for height for another attack, and on the other side of the hill were the Deraine lines. Hal's patrol was strung out in front of him, riding for safety.

Two dragons came in for another attack, but the patrol was too close to the lines, and half a dozen catapults sent six-foot darts whipping through the air at them.

All missed, and the Roche dragons were climbing away.

One screamed in rage and disappointment, and Jarth Ordinay blatted an imitation up at him, one of his major talents.

They galloped past the outlying pickets, were in the forward lines, and now they could sit straight, breathe, and even show a cavalryman's panache, laughing at the past danger, easy in the saddle, safe for one more day.

"It has been in my mind for some time," Lord Canista, commander of the Third Deraine Light Cavalry, "that our king might be well served by your being promoted lieutenant and knighted, Serjeant."

Hal gaped. Being made an officer was impressive enough, the Deraine army having three ranks: lieutenant, generally knighted; captain, always knighted; and commander, who'd be a lord, duke or even prince.

Outside Canista's tent, all was a bustle as the army got ready once more for battle.

"First, that pennant you spotted belongs to one Duke Garcao Yasin, who's Lord Commander of Queen Norcia. The two, I was told, are close." Canista coughed suggestively. "Very, very close. So obviously this upcoming battle will be of great import to Roche." He noticed Hal's expression.

"You know of him?"

"Uh . . . nossir." Hal thought back, remembered the Yasin with the flying dragons back in Bedarisi had a first name of Bayle or something like it. "But I may've encountered a relative of his before the war. A dragon flier. Do you know if he's got a brother?"

"Of course not," Canista said, a bit impatiently. "And let us return to more important matters, such as your knighthood. You fight well. But more important . . . Well, did you know your troopers call you Lucky?"

"Uh . . . yessir." Hal was still considering this Baron Yasin. Assuming a relationship, and he had no way of knowing whether Yasin was a common name in Roche, that would certainly indicate the Roche fliers were, indeed, spies. He brought himself back, listened to Canista.

"That's more important . . . for a leader," the lord went on. "Any damned fool with no survival sense can become a great warrior . . . until he's cut down by some lucky sod from the rear.

"Deraine needs lucky officers, Kailas," Canista went on. "The gods know we haven't had many leading us thus far."

Hal looked blankly unopinionated at that.

"Well, I assume you have an opinion?"

"Sir, I'm a commoner."

"Everyone knows that," Canista said. "Where do you think all these damned knights' and barons' and dukes' and whatalls' fathers came from?

"Damned few of us were born to the purple. Time past, time enough for us to get snotty about things, one of our ancestors was good at sticking people with his sword, and lucky enough to do it mostly within the law, or not get caught, plus live through the experience.

"And their descendants are the ones who've ridden out in this war. And are getting themselves killed, like everyone else.

"Deraine will need a whole new generation of nobility, and where the hells do you think it'll come from? From commoners like you.

"It might interest you that my grandsire, ten, no eleven generations gone, was a blacksmith."

"Yessir," Hal said.

"Mmmph," Canista said. "At any rate, that's something

for you to think on, if you want the responsibility. Actually, I'm speaking like a damned fool, for you already have the responsibility. Being knighted would just get you more.

"We've a battle afore us, so think on it. Afterwards, if we all live, you can give me your decision."

"Yessir." Hal clapped his right hand against his breastplate in salute, turned to leave.

"Wait, lad," Canista said. Hal turned back.

"Something I'm required to show you," he said, pulling a rumpled piece of paper from his small field desk, handing it to Hal.

Dragon Men!
Deraine Needs You!
Men . . . and Women
Who Wish to Fly
Mighty Dragons
As the Eyes
Of the Army
Are Bidden
By His Most Holy Majesty
To Volunteer
For the Newly-Forming
Dragon Flights!
Experienced Dragon Handlers
Will Do Deraine
The Greatest Service
By Volunteering
Fly High Above the Fray!
Defy Roche's Evil Monsters!
Extra Pay
Extra Privileges
Bask in the Adulation
Of the Nation!
Join Now!!
Experienced Men and Women Only!!

"I call this damned nonsense," Canista grumbled. "But someone said you'd been around the horrid monsters back before you joined up.

"And doing the king's duty, I decided to show it to you, and give you the chance.

"Even though there's a war, a real war, to be fought down here on the ground, not zooming around peering at the foe and, often as not, making up lies to confuse poor honest lords such as myself!"

Hal barely heard the lord, looking at the sheet of paper, thinking, dreaming.

To be out of the muck, away from the front lines and shouting officers, to be clean. Inadvertently, Hal scratched at a louse bite on his elbow, caught himself.

Gods, how he wanted that . . . to be above the clouds, above this endless cutting and killing, free, alone.

Then he caught himself.

"Thank you, sir," he said, handing the paper back.

"Good man! Not interested at all, I can see, like a proper soldier."

No. It was hardly lack of interest.

It was Hal's mind, suddenly reminding him of the twenty-five cavalrymen he was given charge of, plus another ten supporting troopers.

If he left, who would take care of them?

He thought of other sections, whose warrants had been killed or transferred, and their new commanders, who had caused more than their share of deaths learning the ways of war.

Could Hal give over men, who'd entrusted him with their lives, to some fool, fresh from Deraine's horse academies?

Never.

As long as they lived, Hal Kailas had to be there to lead and, if necessary, die with them.

8

"Water," the soldier gasped, reaching a clawed hand up for Hal's stirrup. "For the mercy of the gods, water!"

Hal saw the gaping wound across the man's stomach, his spilled guts, knew he could do no good, even if orders permitted him to halt.

The Roche soldier's hand fell away.

"Then grant peace," he croaked. "Please, for the sake of your mother's soul."

Hal couldn't bring himself to kill the wounded man, no matter what he wanted. But someone behind him in the column had no qualms. Hal heard the dull thud of a lance going home, the soldier's gasp, and then silence except for the clatter of horses' hooves and the creak of their harness.

This was the battle's fourth day, thus far a sweeping defeat for Roche.

Deraine, given the advance warning by Hal and, no doubt, other scouts, had time to find a strong position along a rocky ridgecrest. Then they'd waited for Roche.

Duke Yasin had taken position on a ridge a mile distant from Deraine's lines, a valley rich with grain between them. Deraine had made no offensive moves, and so Roche attacked first.

Yasin sent his infantry sweeping wide, trying to flank Deraine on the north. But the lines were firmly anchored with heavy cavalry, and Roche was driven back.

They attacked again, and were broken a second time.

Then it was time for the wizards. Roche sent sweeping winds against Deraine, but the spells were broken, and counterspells of dust devils sent back against Roche.

Yasin tried a night attack, with ghostly illuminations. But that barely penetrated the front line, before the Deraine second wave smashed into them.

The third day dawned hot, muggy, promising rain, but none came.

The drums started just before midday, all along the Roche line.

Hal's section had been assigned courier duty, since the light cavalry wasn't needed for scouting, so he was well forward, almost in the front lines, when Duke Yasin's army surged forward behind the drummers across the valley. Hal saw them coming, in wave after wave, and swallowed hard, very glad he wasn't one of the poor bastards in the forward line trying to keep his spearpoint from trembling, trying to gather strength from his equally frightened brothers.

Then sorcery came into play, and this no illusion. Red creatures surged into existence in the Roche line, creatures about the size of a small dog. They were fanged, and clawed, like enormous red ants, but each had the face of a leering man. They tore into the legs of the oncoming soldiers, and when they fell, others fastened their claws into the man's armor, and tore at his face and throat.

The screams rang loud above the drums, and the Deraine front line commanders ordered their troops forward.

The Deraine units obeyed, and the lines came together, and it was a knotted madness. Deraine pulled back, Hal thought beaten back, then realized they'd been ordered to withdraw, regroup, and come in again.

The ant-demons savaged the Roche soldiers but, having

taken mortal form, could be killed, although their fangs still held to their final bite, heads dangling from men's arms, legs, bodies.

As suddenly as they came, they vanished, the Roche sorcerers having found the counterspell.

Deraine attacked again, and once more the lines smashed against each other. Deraine sent their reserves down into the valley, and that broke the Roche. They fell back, up the hill toward their own lines, pursued by Deraine infantry, killing as they went.

The heavy cavalry started forward, to finally break Roche and defeat them in detail. But Roche regained its positions, behind sharp-pointed abatis and piled brush, and the Deraine attack was called off.

The Roche, defeated, should have retreated, back within the safety of their own support lines. But they held on the ridgeline all that day and night.

Perhaps Duke Yasin was afraid to retreat, afraid to reveal his defeat to Queen Norcia. Or perhaps he had another plan in the works. Or perhaps he was simply too stubborn to know when he was beaten.

Regardless, the Third Light Cavalry, augmented with half a regiment of Sagene light, was assembled before dawn, and told to scout the Roche flanks and determine what they were up to.

Hal attended Lord Canista's orders assembly, staying, as deserved a young warrant, well in the back, behind the lords, keeping his doubts to themselves.

One knight, a very slender, very long-haired and mustached man in gleaming armor, did not.

"Sir," he said. "This is no more'n the second time we've ridden together in this strength."

"Third, actually, Sir Kinnear," Lord Canista said. "The other was before you joined us."

"Which means we're not experienced at fighting together. Plus light cavalry," Kinnear went on, "isn't supposed to do more than scout and raid."

"We have our orders," Canista said. "But I believe the reason for us going forth in such strength is the lords of the army wouldn't mind if we ran into some nice fat supply wagons and wreaked a bit of havoc."

"S'posing, sir, that we go a little too far, and supposing their damned heavies charge us?"

"We withdraw in an orderly fashion."

There was a murmur of amusement.

"S'posing, once again, we don't have that luxury," Kinnear persisted.

"According to *my* orders," Canista said, "the Sagene heavy cavalry will be in close support, and if they're outmanned, our own heavies will be committed."

"Sagene?" Kinnear said with a snort.

"I resent that," a Sagene knight, heavy, bearded, scowling said. "Are you accusing my people of cowardice?"

"No," Kinnear drawled, "just a certain . . . tardiness to respond."

"You have been given a chance to withdraw your words," the Sagene knight said. "Now I must demand satisfaction!"

"Now or at any other time," Kinnear said, one hand on his sword.

"Both of you stop!" Canista snapped. "We have an enemy to face, and if either of you persist in your foolishness, I'll have you chained in your tents. After the battle, you're welcome to satisfy your honor by any means you deem necessary.

"But not before! We have a task set before us, gentlemen. Return to your troops and get them ready to ride, for the glory of Deraine and your regiments, and I wish you battleluck!"

Hal was close enough to Sir Kinnear to hear him mutter, "This'll be damned disastrous. Too many troops to move with any sort of subtlety, not enough to stand firm if we're found out. *Damned* disastrous!"

Hal agreed, but there was, of course, nothing that could be done.

*

They went out at dawn, curving out from their lines, intending to skirt the enemy's right flank, and probe, very cautiously, for his intent.

The valley that had been yesterday's battleground was a welter of bodies. Some, thankfully, lay still, quite dead. Others writhed, screaming, or, energy almost gone, managing no more than animal moans.

There were healthy men from both sides afield – men looking for the wounded, dead, from their units, some to-be-blessed chiurgeons, some simply good hearted, trying to tend to the wounded, ease the pain of dying.

And there were others, skulking jackals, looting the dead and, not infrequently, making sure the wounded wouldn't object to being plundered, with a swift dagger.

Hal heard a bowstring twang, saw one such brigand screech, grab at his side, and go down. He turned, saw Jarth Ordinay reaching for another arrow.

"No," he ordered. "We may need them later."

Ordinay hesitated, then nodded, and put the arrow back in his saddle quiver.

Unconsciously Hal's section spread out as they closed on the edges of the ridge Roche supposedly still held, making themselves into less of a target.

Canista's cutting it a little close, Kailas thought. If I held the regiment, I would have taken us straight away from the lines until I was beyond the sight of the fighters, then come back on the Roche from the rear, trying to figure out their intentions from the deployment of their quartermaster wagons and other noncombatants who might not be able to kill you as readily as an infantryman or, worse, a heavy cavalry soldier.

Light cavalrymen wore no more armor than a breastplate and chainmail to mid-thigh and an open helmet. They were generally armed with no more than bow, sword and dagger, although when facing battle, as today, they would carry a light lance, not much more than a spear. They relied on their horses' speed, maneuverability and their own cunning to keep them alive.

Heavy cavalry was their nemesis – men in three-quarters armor to the knee with half-shields, riding great horses that looked suitable for pulling brewery wagons. They were armed with sword, dagger, lance, and frequently a mace or a hammer. They rode in close formation and if the light horsemen were brought to battle by the heavies and couldn't escape, they were almost certainly doomed.

These lumbering monsters were most highly regarded, their units draped with battle honors and their riders among the most noble of any kingdom.

Hal hoped to spend this day without seeing any of them, neither Roche nor on his own side, for that would portend disaster.

All he wanted was to obey orders, get in, get out and get back. Tomorrow, when the armies rumbled back on the move they could resume their patrolling and skirmishing duties.

Before he heard the first warning shout, he felt the earth begin shaking.

Riding out of the forest fringing the Roche lines, coming between the trees in close formation, came the Roche heavy cavalry. Hal was never sure if there were two or three regiments. Not that it mattered. Just one would have given the battle edge to Roche.

Lord Canista shouted to one of his aides to ride back for their promised support, the Sagene heavy cavalry. The young officer saluted, wheeled his horse, and galloped hard for the rear.

He'd gone no more than a quarter of a mile when a crossbowman rose from behind a bush, and shot him off his horse.

Other crossbowmen came up on line, ran toward Hal's unit, closing the jaws of the trap.

Canista shouted for the regiment to turn away from the attackers, and make for a knoll, dismount and fight on foot until their support arrived.

They never made it.

Half a company of Roche were charging Hal's section. He shouted for his men to turn into the attack, comb the lancers, then try for the knoll.

They obeyed, but the heavy cavalrymen held formation, and Hal's section couldn't break through. A knight was coming hard at Hal, and Kailas ducked under his lance, spitted him in the throat, above his gorget, with his sword. Another rider cut at him, missed, and Hal slashed, also going wide.

Then he was behind the first wave, saw another stream of riders thundering toward him.

He pulled at his horse's reins, as the animal screamed and reared. Hal slid off the back as his mount fell back, thrashing, a crossbow bolt in its throat, another between its ribs.

A Roche crossbowman was coming at him, long double-edged dagger held low. Hal parried, ran him through, felt another bolt whip past his face.

A dismounted cavalryman was coming at him, two-handed sword up. Hal went to his knees, drove his sword under the man's breastplate, into his guts.

Then something smashed into the back of his head, and he went flat, world spinning.

He didn't know how long he was out, seconds or minutes, but then he was back on his feet, sword bloody, staggering toward that knoll. Someone was stabbing at him with a spear, and he cut the spearhead away, killed that man.

There were three corpses in front of him, all three members of his section.

A man was standing over them in Roche uniform. Hal killed him, stumbled on.

There was a ditch, and he went down, sprawled face-first, hearing the whine of bolts above him.

A man jumped down, breathing hard, started to stab Hal, saw he wore the same uniform, clambered out and a spear took him in the shoulder. He spun, and another spear went into the back of his neck.

A Roche soldier ran up, not seeing Hal, and Hal's sword took him in the armpit.

There was blood, there was screaming, loud, dying away, and Hal was down in the dust, seeing the Roche heavy cavalry ride past him, back toward their lines, the crossbowmen who'd closed the trap trotting beside them, prodding a few prisoners ahead of them.

Then there was nothing but the sound of men dying.

Hal got back up, waiting to be killed. But there was no one on the field except the dead, dying and desperately wounded.

There was no sign of the promised Sagene heavy cavalry.

Hal considered his injuries. A slash across the back, no more than painful, but bloody enough to have made him look dead, lying in the ditch. An arrow stub stuck out of his upper thigh, and he pushed it through, snapped the arrowhead off. He almost fainted, then pulled the shaft free and tied up the bloody wound with his torn tunic. He was bruised here and there, but felt no broken bones.

He should have gone back to his own lines before the vultures and thieves came.

But he stopped, seeing a man who'd followed his orders, down in death.

A strange fascination came, and he wandered the battlefield, finding one, another, others of his section, all dead.

He saw the body of Lord Canista, half a dozen armored Roche sprawled around him.

A dozen yards away was the body of Sir Kinnear, lying back to back with the Sagene knight who'd challenged him. They, too, had taken their share and more with them.

Time blurred, and it was late afternoon, almost twilight.

He was kneeling beside the body of Jarth Ordinay, who was sprawled on his back, his dagger in the chest of one of the three men who'd died killing him.

Ordinay's face had a quiet, peaceful smile. The lines of premature aging were gone, and he looked the boy he'd been when the army took him.

Hal nodded solemnly, as if Ordinay had told him something, got up, and started back the way he'd come.

Somewhere he found a horse, a bloody slash along its neck, pulled himself into the saddle, and rode slowly back toward safety.

All dead, he mourned. All gone. All dead.

His mind wryly told him, now you can go ride the king's damned dragons if you want, can't you?

The hulk's sails caught the southerly wind, fair for Deraine, a dim line on the horizon. The ship plunged in the swell, yards clattering and sailors scurrying about.

Hal paid little attention to the bustle, eyes on Paestum's harbor they were sailing out of, and the distant border of Roche to his left.

He would be back, though, as a dragon flier.

Back, with a hard vengeance to take.

9

Deraine's capital, Rozen, had he been in another frame of mind, could have angered Hal Kailas. There were no buildings shattered by catapult stones, empty storefronts, shops with only one or two items for sale.

Deraine could almost have been a country at peace.

Almost.

But here was a column of uniformed recruits being chivvied along by a pair of shouting warrants; there another formation of trained soldiers, grim-faced under steel helms and laden with weaponry, and there were far fewer young men to be seen on the streets and in the cafes than in peacetime. Here were a knot of women wearing mourning bands, there other women and children scanning the posted list of those killed or wounded across the Straits.

Small patrols of warders, half civilian, half military, swept the streets.

Kailas paid them no mind, his orders secure in a belt pouch, his mind on other things, specifically the cup of iced custard he was wolfing.

He grinned. The hardened warrior, home at last, was supposed to head for the closest taproom and drink himself senseless on his favorite brew.

Kailas, who'd never thought himself much of a milk drinker, had developed a lust for the rich, cream-heavy Deraine liquid, despising the thin, frequently watered whey of Sagene. He'd had three big glasses, and was topping them off with this custard, flavored with cloves and cinnamon.

Kailas also thought of the other requirement of the home-coming soldier – a lovely girl under his arm, or at least a popsy.

He had no one.

Hal turned his mind away from loneliness, headed for the address he was supposed to report to.

Rozen was a city that had cheerfully "just grown" at the confluence of two rivers. The only coherency it had managed was the result of three fires four hundred years earlier. Then there'd been great architects, working under the king's close supervision, intending to build a city of splendor, the marvel of the world.

There were those great palaces and monuments, but two streets away might be a slum or a silversmith's street or even a knacker's yard.

Hal had been in Rozen twice, before he joined Athelny's circus, and hated it both times, feeling alone and forgotten – which he had been.

Now, an equally faceless figure in battered half-armor, sword-belt tied around his meager roll of belongings, he felt quite at home in the great city.

He felt as if he were watching a camera obscura, arranged for his solitary pleasure. Kailas felt outside this city's life, but it wasn't unpleasant at all.

He'd been offered leave after the destruction of his regiment, and had thought about it, but there was no one for him to go to. He had no desire to return to the tiny village he'd come from, nor any desire to visit his parents, and so he asked for orders to his next duty assignment.

He wondered if soldiering had changed his outlook from

the other times he'd been in the capital. Perhaps he'd seen enough people die young and violently to not mind being an outsider. He decided to give the matter a bit more thought, perhaps over a pint, later, after he'd reported in.

His orders read for him to report to the Main Guildhall, which seemed odd, until he entered the huge building. It had been commandeered by the army, and now was a shouting bustle of recruiting booths.

It was near chaos: a warrant brayed about the virtues of the dragoons, a clerk talked quietly of the safety of the quartermaster corps, an archer chanted about his elite regiment. Other warrants shouted how smart Lord such-and-so's Light Infantry uniforms were, or how Sir whatever would not only outfit a recruit, but send money to his family. Every branch of the service was represented, from chiurgeons to an arrogant-looking pair of magicians to a brawny farrier to a pair of jolly teamsters. There were even a scattering of women, raising nursing, transport, support units.

Most of them had at least one, frequently more, recruits weighing the virtues and dangers of a corps.

Except for one, a stony-faced, leathery-looking serjeant, lean as death, wearing the coronet of a troop warrant over his two stripes.

Behind him, tacked to the wall, was a poster-size version of the leaflet Lord Canista had shown Hal a month ago, announcing the formation of dragon flights.

Civilians prospecting the various booths would look at the warrant, then at the poster, and hasten onward. Evidently dragon flying was thought an advanced form of suicide.

Hal walked up to the man, saluted.

"I'm one of yours, Serjeant." He passed the orders from his corps commander across.

"Fine," the man said, lowering the parchment. "M'name's Ivo Te. I was starting to think I've got plague."

Hal didn't answer. Te looked him over hard.

"You appear to have been rode hard and put away wet, young Serjeant."

"Polishing rags aren't easy to find in Sagene," Hal said.

"Don't I know it," Te said. "Until two months ago, I was top warrant with Eighth Heavy Cavalry."

"I was Third Light. We scouted for you a few times."

"You did," Te said. "I heard about your disaster. But it's nice to have someone else along who knows which end of a sword gets sharpened."

"There are others?"

"There are others," Te said grimly. "And, with one or two exceptions, a bigger lot of shitepokes, crap merchants, layabouts and deeks I've never met before."

Hal grinned. "That good?"

Te sighed. "It's going to be a long war, lad. A long war indeed."

The recruits for dragon school were housed in an inn not far from Guildhall. Hal had little time to assess them before a dozen wagons arrived and, under a steady storm of cursing by Serjeant Te, the forty prospective fliers and their dunnage were loaded aboard and the wagons creaked away for the secret training grounds, somewhere beyond the capital.

The base sat close to a forbiddingly high cliff, on Deraine's west coast. Below, gray surf boomed uninvitingly.

"Be a good place for a morning bath after a good, healthy run," Serjeant Te said briskly, and was glowered at all around.

Before the war, the base had been a religious retreat, gray-stone main buildings and cottages scattered about the huge estate. Hal saw at once why the retreat had been taken over – the religious types must have worshipped a horse god, or else their benefactors were of the galloping set. There were huge barns and corrals, and what must have been a race course at one time, now being leveled by teams of oxen towing rollers back and forth.

"Where are our dragons?" a very young, very redheaded, very confident woman asked.

"Not here yet, and that'll be Serjeant to you," Te growled.

"Then wot the 'ells will we do, waitin'? Play wi' ourselves?" a man who could have been the young brother of Hal's cocky second, Jarth Ordinay, asked, cheekily.

"The Lord Spense will find work for you," Te said. "For all of us."

Hal noted, with a sinking feeling, the serjeant's face didn't look pleased.

Te had good reason.

This was only the second dragon flying class held here at Seabreak – three more schools around Deraine, were also training dragon flights.

Hal asked how the first class had managed, if the school didn't have any dragons, and was told they'd taken their monsters with them to Sagene, just as his class would . . . when the dragons materialized.

The trainees were detailed off to the four-person huts by shouting warrants. One, a Serjeant Patrice, saw Hal's evident status as a combat veteran, but, unlike Te, didn't appear to like it, and chose Kailas for special attention, which meant more close-range shouting than for others.

Hal had learned, trying to sleep in the rain, to put his mind elsewhere, generally soaring with dragons, so it was easy to ignore Patrice.

The huts spread out in four rows, each in a different compass heading, meeting at a common assembly area.

Hal managed to get one as far from the assembly field as possible, knowing which huts would likely be chosen for details by the warrants.

He did manage a minute with Serjeant Te, and requested the diminutive Farren Mariah, and "anybody else you think livable" for hutmates.

The other two were Ev Larnell, a haunted-looking, thin

man a couple of years younger than Kailas; and Rai Garadice, a cheerful, muscled youth the same age as Hal, whose name sounded familiar to Hal.

The thirteen women on the course had their own huts, interspersed with the men's. No one, at least so far, slept anywhere but in the hut assigned him or her. There hadn't been any regulations read out about sex, but everyone automatically sensed it was against the rules. It had to be, since it felt good.

The huts were single open rooms, twenty feet on a side, and there was a wooden bunk and a large open hanging closet for each student. In the center of the room was a stove, which would be welcome as fall became winter, and a wash basin near the door.

Studded amid the huts were privies, with a long door at the rear, and half-barrels to catch the waste. Patrice had told them his favorite detail was telling someone to jockey a wagon down the rows, collecting the barrel's contents. All this was said with Patrice's usual expression, an utterly humorless tight smile the trainees found strangely annoying.

They were allowed half an hour to unpack their gear, then fallen back out. Hal had a few moments to consider a few of the other trainees: the confident, redheaded woman, Saslic Dinapur; a stocky loud man named Vad Feccia; and an arrogant man named Brant Calabar, *Sir* Brant Calabar he was careful to let everyone know. He reminded Hal of his old enemy as a boy, Nanpean Tregony.

Then they were pushed into formation, the experienced soldiers already knowing the drill, the civilians becoming quick studies of the others, for an address by the school's commanding officer.

"This is not my first school command," Lord Pers Spense said. "I've taught at His Majesty's Horse Guards, and was chosen to be Master of the Ring; and half a dozen crack regiments had me as their guest instructor before the war.

"I know little of this dragon flying you men – and women," he added hastily, "are about to attempt, but doubt me that it can be that different from riding any beast, except that you will be high in the skies."

Spense was red-faced, probably balding under the dress helm he wore over a very flashy uniform Hal couldn't identify, but knew it wouldn't last beyond the first archer on the battleground. He was most stocky, hardly appearing to be anyone who was the first to push back from the dinner table.

Spense slapped a riding crop against his highly polished thigh boots.

"Therefore, we shall begin training all of you in what I call the School of the Soldier.

"Serjeant Teh," he went on, mispronouncing the name, "has informed me that some of you have already seen bully fighting against the barbarians, those savages who call themselves the Roche, with barely a hundred years or so since they crawled from the swamp.

"For you, it shall be good to refresh your memory of the most important part of soldiering: drill. For only with the confidence that drill inspires can you go forth into battle, knowing the man on your left will do just what you are doing, and so bring the savages to their knees."

The speech went on, and on. Hal didn't bother listening to more.

He knew why Serjeant Te had winced.

"You *will* run everywhere," Serjeant Patrice bayed, and so the column of trainees ran through the estate grounds, twice around the cookhall, and stopped, some panting hard, in a long line.

Hal, not by accident, found himself behind the redhead, Saslic Dinapur. They introduced themselves, wondered about the food.

"And why'd you join?" she asked.

"I was already in the army," Hal said. "Things . . . changed at my old posting." He didn't elaborate about the massacre. "And I was a oddjob boy for a dragon flier named Athelny, back before the war."

Saslic grinned.

"I met that old rascal once, when he came to the Menagerie, to ask something of my father. Even as a little girl, I thought he was a definite rogue."

"He was that," Hal agreed.

"Do you have any idea what he's doing now? I hope wealthy, perhaps married to some rich dowager, and raising dragons somewhere in the north."

"He's dead," Hal said. "Killed by a bastard . . . Sorry—"

"Don't apologize," Saslic interrupted. "I've heard – used – worse myself. And we are in the army, aren't we?"

"I guess so," Hal said. "But after Lord Spense's uh, enlightening talk, I'm not sure what century's."

Saslic laughed, a very pleasant sound Hal decided he could get used to.

"Anyway, about poor Athelny?"

"Killed by an archer of a Sagene nobleman who'd euchred Athelny out of his dragon," Hal said. "He flew off, north, toward Deraine, I guess, and we never found his body."

Saslic was quiet for a few moments, then said, softly, "A bad way to die . . . but a better funeral than most of us'll see."

"True," Hal agreed.

"Move up, there," a voice behind him grated. "Some of us want our dinner."

Hal turned, looked at the bluff Vad Feccia, thought of saying something, didn't, deciding to fit into this new world as easily as he could, turned back.

Feccia laughed, a grating noise, and Hal realized he'd made a mistake. The man probably thought Kailas was afraid of him. Oh well. Bullies could be sorted out at a later time.

"You said something about the Menagerie?" Hal asked Saslic.

Saslic nodded. "My father is one of the keepers at the King's Own Menagerie, and I helped. I really liked working around the dragons, wanted to learn how to fly them, and when this came up, well, I guess my father'll speak to me sooner or later for running off."

They entered the long building, which was divided into thirds, one the kitchen, the second a dining room for students, the third, closed off with a screen for the cadre. They got tin plates from a pile, had a glop of what looked like stew, some tired vegetables, a pat of butter and bread dumped on the plate as they passed down the line of bored-looking serving women.

"Oh dear," Saslic said.

Hal thought it looked quite a bit better than most of the rations the army fed its troops in Sagene, but he didn't tell Saslic that.

The two looked around the small hall for a seat at one of the benched tables, just as Sir Brant Calabar crashed to his feet.

"This is a damned outrage! Eating with commoners!"

Farren Mariah, evidently the man he objected to, looked up.

"'At's fine, mate. Yer can wait outside, an' I'll save yer the indignity, an' polish off yer plate as a pers'nal favor."

Calabar clashed his plate down.

"Where I come from, a bastard like you'd warrant a whipping!"

A man at the table behind Calabar stood. He was slender, long-faced, with a large, beaked nose.

"Now, sir," he said, in a nasal tone Hal had heard lords in the army use, "best you show some manners here. We're all learners together, and there's surely no call to behave like a pig."

Calabar whirled.

"And who the blazes are you?"

"Sir Loren Damian," the man said. "Former equerry to

His Most Royal Majesty, detached on special duty to this school, also Lord Dulmin of the Northern Reaches, Quinton of Middlewich, and other equally ponderous titles I shan't bore anyone with, but ones I suspect have precedent in the Royal List over yours."

"Oh," Calabar said in a very quiet voice, out-titled to the hilt.

"Now, be a good sort, and sit down, and eat your meal," Sir Loren said.

Calabar started to obey, then crashed out of the hall.

"Tsk," Damian said. "But I suppose he'll come around, when his belly calls, which it appears to do on a rather regular basis."

There was a bit of laughter. Sir Loren picked up his plate, and pointedly walked to the table Calabar'd stormed away from.

"May I join you, sir?"

"Uh . . . surely, I mean, yes m'lord," Mariah managed.

"My title here is Loren," Damian said. "Most likely something resembling scumbucket to our warrants, I'd imagine."

He started eating.

Hal and Saslic found seats. Kailas saw Serjeant Te leaning against the entrance to the cadre's section, a bit of a smile on his face, wondered what it portended for Calabar or Damian, decided that was none of his concern, started eating.

The food was actually fairly awful.

"Forrard . . . harch!" Serjeant Patrice bellowed. "Hep, twoop, threep, fourp . . . hep, twoop, threep, fourp . . . godsdammit, Kailas, get in step!"

Hal almost stumbled over his own feet getting them in the proper military order.

The forty trainees, in a column of fours, marched away from the assembly area, down one of the curving brick paths into an open area.

"Right flank . . . harch!"

Hal turned left, and almost knocked a heavy-set woman, Mynta Gart, spinning.

"Lords of below, Kailas, can't you do anything right?"

The class was in military ranks, and the warrant teaching it had trouble reading the handbook he was holding.

Hal was half-listening, looking at another trainee two rows away. The man kept looking back at him as if he knew him.

As the class was dismissed for a break, Hal recognized him and went up.

"You're Asser, aren't you?"

"I am that . . . and where do I know you from?"

"Hal Kailas. I was Athelny's dogsbody when you were barkering for him. You and . . . Hils, that was his name."

"Right!" Asser smiled delightedly. "I heard Athelny's dead. What're you doing here? Did that old fart ever give you a chance to ride a dragon like you wanted?"

Hal explained, considering Asser as he spoke. Once, a long time ago, he'd thought the young man most dapper, a city slick. But he saw him through different eyes now, no more than another one of those who doesn't sow, but has every hustle in the world for reaping.

"Hils," Asser said sadly. "He's dead, too. I guess he thought he could outrun the warders, and anyway didn't believe one of 'em would cut him down from behind. A pity. He was just about the smoothest bilker I ever knew, and him and me had a great partnership . . . for awhile."

"So what made you join up?" Hal asked.

"It was like you said . . . made's the word. The magistrate didn't believe I had no idea who Hils was, and told me I was either gonna volunteer or be headed for the poogie for five years or so.

"I heard about this dragon thing we're in, figured that'd be a good place to lay low."

"I've seen Roche's dragons," Hal said. "If I weren't a fool, I'd think maybe five years in prison might be a little safer."

"Haw," Asser snorted. "You don't think a smart lad like me'll ever go across the water, now do you?"

Hal didn't reply, excused himself, seeing an angry-looking Saslic motioning to him.

"What's the problem?"

"That frigging Feccia's a lying sod!"

"I'm not surprised," Hal said mildly. "In what category?"

"Probably all of them. But start with his claims to be a dragon rider, back as a civilian, although he's pretty damned vague about the details. But I caught him. Asked him some questions, which he didn't answer quite right. Then I asked him when he thought was the best time to separate a dragon pup from the doe."

"What?"

"And he went and gave me a vague answer, saying it varied, depending on circumstances." Dinapur shook her head. "What a jack! A pup my left nipple!"

"Not to mention a dragon doe," Hal said, starting to laugh. "You know, a man who's so damn dumb he doesn't even know a kit and a cow probably won't get very far around here."

"Who's going to call him? A trainee? I'm not going to peach on someone, and for sure the cadre don't know the difference."

"You're right," Hal said. "I wouldn't nark the idiot off either. I guess we'll just have to wait for his mouth to take care of himself."

"To the rear ... harch! In the name of any god you want, Kailas, can't you learn how to drill? I thought you were some kind of combat hero!"

Hal thought of telling him killing someone, or keeping from being killed yourself, didn't have a lot to do with square-bashing, and no, he'd never had any instruction whatsoever on what foot you were supposed to start marching with. The army across the water was a little too busy to concern itself with left-right, left-right.

But he kept his mouth shut. So far, he'd stayed off the emptying shitter detail.

So far.

The day finally came when they turned in their civilian gear, and Hal his threadbare uniform, which they'd been washing when they could, as they could, and were issued new uniforms.

They were fairly spectacular, which Hal guessed meant higher ranks were particularly interested in dragon flights: black thigh boots, into which tight-fitting white breeches were bloused, a red tunic with white shoulderbelts and gold shoulderboards, and a smart-looking forage cap, also red, which Hal thought would blow away twenty feet off the ground. With the gaudy uniform went very practical, and completely unromantic, undergarments, both in padded winter issue and plain summer wear.

Someone, probably down the line from the uniform's designers, had a bit of practicality, thinking what it would be like, flying in winter, and gauntleted catskin gloves and a heavy thigh-length jacket that must have required an entire sheep to produce were issued.

Another practical item was a set of greenish-brown coveralls, perfect, as Serjeant Patrice said, "for cleaning the shitter."

Hal was starting to think the man had a problem with his bowels.

They were also issued weapons – long spears and swords. Hal couldn't see either having much use aboard a dragon, figured that Sir Spense had called for the issue so the class would look like his idea of proper soldiery.

The only practical weapon was a long, single-edged dagger, which looked as if it had been designed and forged by an experienced bar brawler.

He was a bit surprised Spense hadn't given out spurs.

*

"*Lord*, they let some raggedy-asses into uniform these days," Patrice said, grinning his risus sardonicus. "Now, the reason you're in these ten-deep ranks is we're practicing parade maneuvers, and there aren't enough of you idiots to form a proper parade.

"Forrard . . . harch!"

Hal stepped out correctly, determined for once he wasn't going to make a mistake.

"By the right . . . wheel!"

The way the maneuver should've been done was the right flanker performed a right turn, began marking time, the soldier next to him took one more step, and so forth until the entire ten-man rank had turned right. In the meantime, the second row was doing the same, one step behind.

It didn't work out that way as soldiers slammed into each other, got confused and started marking time when they should've been moving, and everything became absolute chaos.

"Halt, halt, godsdammit, halt," Patrice screamed, and chaos became motionless chaos. He considered the mess.

"I'm starting to think this whole son of a bitching class has got a case of the Kailases."

Hal, who for once had done exactly what he should've, felt injured.

Somewhere in the mess Calabar laughed.

"I heard laughter," Patrice said. "Is there something funny I've missed?"

Silence.

"Who laughed?"

More silence.

"I don't like being lied to," Patrice said. "And nobody confessing is lying, now isn't it?"

Still more silence.

"I asked for an answer."

The class got it, and raggedly boomed, "YES, SERJEANT."

"I have a good ear, I've been told," Patrice said. "Don't you think so, Sir Brant?"

An instant later, he shouted, "Not fast enough, Sir Brant. Front and center!"

Calabar trundled out of the ranks.

"Was that you who laughed?" Patrice cooed.

"Uh . . . uh . . . yessir."

"Don't call me sir! I know who my parents were! You get your young ass to your hut, secure your clothes bucket, and run on down to the ocean and bring me back a bucket of water.

"Move out!"

Patrice watched Calabar run off, then turned back to his victims.

"Now, shall we try it again, children?"

Serjeant Te took Hal aside.

"How're you holding up, Serjeant?"

"I didn't think we had any rank here, Serjeant Te."

"That appears to be one of the good Sir Spense's ideas. You've noticed that no one's been returned to his or her unit yet for failure, either."

"That's right."

Te nodded sagely. "Just a word, or mayhap a suggestion. It could be the good Sir Spense is truly in the dark, and afraid to throw anyone out until he has some idea of what might be required.

"As for Serjeant Patrice—"

"I don't mean to interrupt," Hal said. "But he's water to a duck's back."

Te grinned.

"Good. I didn't figure he'd get under your skin."

"Not a chance, Serjeant. Matter of fact, he's given me an idea on handling a problem of my own."

"I don't suppose," Rai Garadice asked Farren Mariah, "you'd be willing to tell us how you happened into dragon flying, since we've got a whole hour to waste before dear Serjeant Patrice takes us for a nice morning run."

The class was in a stable, looking out at the drizzle beyond. Farren pursed his lips, then shrugged.

"I don't guess there's a'matter. The on'y dragons I've ever been around was oncet, when a show come to Rozen, I got a job cleanin' up the hippodrome a'ter 'em."

"Nice start for a career," Saslic said.

"You name the tisket, I've held it," Farren said. "Crier, runner, butcher's boy, greengrocer's assistant, glazier, changer's messenger, a ferryboat oarsman for a bit, maybe a couple things I don't think I oughta be jawin' about."

"None of this answers Rai's question," Hal said.

"Well . . . I went an' made a bet wi' a friend, don't matter wot, an' lost, an' the wager was the loser hadda take the king's coin."

"Hell of a bet," Saslic said.

"Yeh, well there weren't much goin' on around, so it din't matter," Farren said. "An' then, oncet I was in barracks, there was a certain misunderstanding, an' somebody'd told me about these flights, an' I thought maybe it'd be best to skip outa the line of fire."

"Misunderstanding?"

"Uh . . . the men around me thought I was a witch."

There was a jolt of silence.

"Are you?" Saslic asked gently.

"Course not. I just got a bit of the gift, not like my ma, or my uncle, or his family. And my gran'sire was s'posedly a great wizard, good enough for nobility to consult."

"Oh," Garadice said, forcing himself not to move away. Most people without the gift were quite leery of magicians.

"A wizard," Saslic said in a thoughtful tone. "Maybe we could have you rouse a spell that'd, say, cause Patrice to fall over yon cliff, or make his dick fall off."

"I couldn't do someat like that!" Mariah said, sounding shocked.

"Then what earthly good are you?" Saslic asked.

*

"Broadly speaking," the warrant droned, "if two cavalries of approximately equal mobility maneuver against each other in open country, neither side can afford the loss of time that dismounting to fight on foot entails. Hence, the same fundamental rules apply to all cavalry combats . . ."

Saslic looked at Hal, made a face, mouthed the plaintive words, "When are we gonna learn about dragons?"

Hal shrugged. Maybe some time before they reembarked for the wars.

Somehow Patrice made a mistake on the schedule, and the trainees had a whole two hours after eating before the mandatory late class, this one on Proper Horsemanship.

Not that anyone actually had time for relaxation, busy with boot-blackening, cleaning their weapons – "all this stabbin' and wot really rusts a blade out, eh?" was Farren Mariah's comment – or trying to remember what it was like to be around a dragon.

Since it was an unseasonably warm fall evening, most of them were gathered outside their huts, talking while they polished.

Mynta Gart saw Brant Calabar staggering away from the steps down to the rocky beach with yet another full bucket, said, "Guess our Serjeant Patrice is havin' himself a salt water bath."

"Good for his complexion, I'd bet," Saslic said.

"A better wash'd be to trail him overside for a league or so," Gart said. "And then cut loose the hawser."

"You sound like a sailor," Saslic said.

"That I am," Gart said proudly. "Will be again, once the fighting stops. Once had my own coaster, then got bit by that patriotic fever, and got made a mate on one of the king's patrol boats.

"Which was damn stupid of me, since what navy Roche has looks to be hiding in port until the war's over."

"So why'd you volunteer for dragon flying?" Hal asked.

"Why not? Used to be, when I was up on the north coast, I'd see wild dragons overhead, some heading, no doubt, for Black Island.

"Looked romantic and free to me." She looked around at the trainees.

"*Damn*, but I love this freedom."

"What about you, Kailas?" Feccia asked, when the rueful laughter died. "You have a personal invite from the king to bless us with your company?"

"Where I'm from," Hal said, "that's not a question *civil* men ask."

"Prob'ly wise," Feccia said. "I've heard villains are careful about things like that."

Something snapped inside Hal. He'd made a bit of a joke about solving his problem, and now was suddenly the time. Crossbelts and white polish sailing, he was on his feet and blurred across the ten feet to the bigger man.

His mouth was gaping, and Hal, anger giving him strength, yanked Feccia to his feet. He slapped him hard across the mouth twice, and blood erupted.

Hal let him stumble back, kicked him hard in the stomach, was about to hammer him, double-fisted, across the back of the neck when Ev Larnell pulled him back. Kailas spun, was about to go after Larnell when the red rage faded.

He dropped his hands.

"Sorry."

Hal turned back to Feccia, gagging, bent over, and jerked him erect.

"Now, listen, for I'll only say this once," he said, his voice barely above a whisper even as his fury died. "You'll not talk to me, nor about me to anyone else, unless you're ordered."

Feccia stared up at him, his expression that of a cow staring at the butcher's hammer. Hal backhanded him twice again, grated, "Did you understand?"

The man nodded dumbly, and Hal shoved him away. Feccia

stumbled off, toward the jakes, stopped, vomited, then staggered on.

The anger was now cold, gone in Kailas.

The other trainees were looking at him, quite strangely.

Saslic suddenly grinned.

"Did anyone ever tell you you're lovely when you're angry, soldier?"

The tension broke, and there was a nervous laugh, and the trainees went back to their cleaning.

"You look like you've been in a fight, Feccia," Serjeant Patrice said through his grin. "You know fighting's forbidden here."

"Nossir," Feccia muttered, breathing coming painfully past cracked ribs. His face was puffed, swollen and bruised. "Not fighting, Serjeant. Walked into a doorjamb, Serjeant."

"You sure?"

"Sure, Serjeant."

Patrice stepped back. "Damned surprise, this. Maybe you *might* end up making a soldier."

That night, in their hut, Hal decided to break his own rule, and asked Rai Garadice if his father happened to be a dragon flier.

"He is," Garadice said. "Trained me, even if he thought I was still too young to go on the circuit with him."

"I thought so," Hal said, and said he'd tried to find a job with Garadice just before the war started, and that he'd said he was going to go find a place in the country and let the world go past until it was tired of war.

"That was his intent," Rai said. "Then, after Paestum was besieged, he – what was it Gart said this afternoon? – got bit by patriotic fever, and tried to enlist.

"They told him he was too old, and go home.

"He moped around for awhile, and I thought he'd given up, then he started writing letters to everybody when the war started dragging on. Including, I think, to Saslic's father at the King's Menagerie, saying he knew a lot about dragons, and they could be the key to victory.

"I guess everybody thought he was a little bit mad, since nobody's yet figured out what good dragons are for, other than playing spy in the sky, or so I'm told.

"Anyway, they came to him, made him a lieutenant officer, put him out with twenty others, and now he's a dragon requisition officer, responsible for buying dragons from their owners, or taking young ones from their nests and taming them to be flown.

"I hope he might be with our dragons when they finally arrive."

"Be a damn relief," Farren put in from his corner, "if the king'd give him orders to boot this eejit Spense back into a horse ring, and get some bodies in wot know which end of a dragon poops and which end bites."

"So then we've got three dragon riders in one hut," Ev Larnell put in.

"You've got experience?" Garadice said.

"Course I do," Larnell said. "In my district, we had fairs, and we'd always have dragon riders to top the day."

"And you were one of them?"

"Sure," Larnell said.

"How'd you rig your harness?" Garadice asked.

There was a long silence from Larnell's end of the room, then, "Why, just like everybody, we used ropes as reins, to a heavy metal bit and a chain headstall."

"What about saddles?"

"Just like on a horse," Larnell said, and his voice was thin. "Except with long straps, under the front legs and coming forward from just in front of the back ones."

"Oh," Garadice said flatly.

Hal realized there was more than one phony in the class besides Feccia.

*

The next day, after the forenoon drill, Ev Larnell came to Hal. He licked his lips, and said, tentatively, "I need a favor."

"If I can."

"Last night . . . Well, I guess you and Garadice figured out that I've never really been on a dragon in my life."

Hal made a noncommittal noise.

"You're right," Larnell said, his voice getting desperate. "All I've done is seen 'em fly overhead, and I went to a show once, before I joined up."

"So why'd you lie?"

"Because . . . because I was scared."

"Of what?"

"I joined up when Paestum was surrounded by the Roche, and went to Sagene with the King's Own Borderers.

"We've fought in every battle so far, and generally in the vanguard. Kailas, every man, twice over, in my company's been killed or taken off, grave wounded.

"I'm the only one who's still alive from the first ones, and I know they're going to keep putting us in the thick of things, and then, when we're wiped out, bringing up fresh men, so it's like a whole new unit, and there's no need to give us rest.

"But I remember . . . I'll always remember. Remember what it's like, seeing all your friends, down in death, friends you were joking with an hour earlier. Then you determine you're not going to let anybody close, let anybody be your friend, and maybe that's worse." Larnell's voice was growing higher. "I just couldn't take it any more.

"I'm no shirker . . . I wouldn't run away. But I thought, if I claimed I knew something about dragons, it'd get me out of the lines. Give me a chance to think, to pull myself together.

"Don't tell on me," he pleaded, and his voice was that of a child, terrified of being reported to his parents.

Hal looked into his eyes, saw the wrinkles at the edges, thought Larnell had the gaze of a very old man.

"Look," Hal said after a moment. "I don't nark on people. I've said it before, I'll probably say it again.

"You want to fly dragons, that's good. But don't start things, like you did last night. Keep your mouth shut, and don't go looking to get exposed."

"I won't. I promise I won't. And thanks. Thank you."

He bobbed his head twice, scurried away.

Excellent, Hal thought. Now, you're all of what, twenty, and you're a priest confessor. And what if Larnell finishes training, and then breaks in combat, and puts somebody's ass in a sling?

If that happens, a part of his brain said coldly, you'll have to kill him yourself.

"Can I get you something from the canteen, Hal?" Vad Feccia asked, parading an ingratiating smile.

"No, thanks."

Feccia hesitated, then ran off.

Serjeant Te had witnessed the exchange.

"He's been acting a bit different since he had some kind of accident I heard about," he observed.

"He is that," Hal said shortly.

"Almost like a bully that's been whipped into line ... Or the way a dog licks the arse of a bigger dog that got him on his back, pawing for mercy ... except, of course, there's no fighting at this school."

Hal made no answer. Feccia had been very friendly with Kailas since the "fight," which Hal considered no more than a shoving match.

"Word of advice, young Serjeant," Te said. "A snake that turns once can do it again."

"I'd already figured that."

"Thought you might've."

"This 'un might be in'trestin'," Farren Mariah said. "You see what I'm wigglin' here?"

"Looks like," Hal said carefully, "a kid's toy. You going

back to your childhood, Farren, playing the simpleton, hoping to get away from one of Patrice's little fun details?"

"Heh. Heh." Mariah said deliberately, if uninformatively. "What sort of kid's toy?"

"Uh . . ."

"Like the shitwagon coming down the line, 'bout halfway with its rounds," Rai Garadice said. The four hutmates were crouched in the door to their hut, Farren having cautioned them, without explaining, against being seen.

"Wood, wood, goodwood," Mariah said. By now, the others were used to his occasional rhyming slang. "Just so, just like, and keep thinking that.

"And who's ramblin' up the row toward the shitwagon?"

"Patrice."

"Heh. Heh. Heh," Farren said again, spacing his "hehs" deliberately.

"This center piece's carved by me, out of a bit whittledy from the wagon's arse. It's dipped in real shit – used my own, sackerficin' an sanctifyin', like they said – an' rubbed with some herbs I plucked on the last run beyont the grounds I know the meanin' of. Plus I said some words my gran'sire taught me when I was puttin' it together.

"Th' wheels're toothpicks, an' touched an' charmed by rubbin' against the real ones out there.

"Now, be watchin', that wagon, and I'll be chantin' away."

Garadice drew back, a little nervously. Farren grinned, seeing that.

"Careful m'magic don't slip, an' you go hoppin' out as a toady-frog.

> *Wagon roll*
> *Wagon creak*
> *Full of stuff*
> *I'll not speak*
>
> *Wheel wiggle*

> *Wheel haul*
> *Wheel wobble*
> *Wheel FALL!!"*

At the last words, Farren twisted one of the toothpick wheels off the toy.

But no one noticed.

Outside, a wheel on the real privy carrier groaned, and gave way.

The cart teetered, and Serjeant Patrice had a moment to shout alarm. Then it crashed sideways, spilling a brown wave high into the air, to splash down over the warrant.

He tried to run, but the wagon was turning on its side, and more ordure washed over him.

There were shouts, screams, laughter as the students tumbled out of their huts.

"Paradise," Hal said, solemnly taking Farren by the ears and kissing him.

"Git away!" Mariah spluttered.

"You *are* a wizard," Ev Larnell said.

"It'll be a long night's cleanup he'll be having us doing," Rai said. "But worth every minute."

"Can I ask a question, Serjeant?" Hal asked Te, who'd taken charge of the formation due to Patrice's absence.

"Ask."

"You're assigned to this class, correct?"

"Aye."

"But I haven't seen you doing any teaching, or more than a morning run once a week or so."

"Aye."

"Can I ask why?"

Te smiled, the look of a cat with many, many, secrets, didn't respond.

"I've got a question of my own, Kailas."

"Yes, Serjeant."

"Do you have any ideas how that unfortunate accident could've happened to poor Serjeant Patrice?"

"No, Serjeant."

"Didn't think you would. Nobody else does either." Te smiled, and his skull face looked almost friendly.

"Go after your classmates, young Serjeant. Late class is coming up."

Hal, realizing he wasn't going to get an answer to his question, saluted, and doubled away.

As he ran, a possible answer came – just as a high-ranking officer didn't get where he was without having a bit of a political sense, the same had to be true of a troop serjeant.

Was Te aware of how screwed this school was, and making sure none of the blame would stick to his coat?

Some of the students had gotten in the habit of sitting behind the row of huts, in a quiet glade, between curfew and bed check, when the weather permitted. It gave them a chance to talk about the day, to try to decide if they were ever going to look at a dragon, let alone learn how to ride one.

Since fall was edging toward winter, most brought blankets to sit on and wrap around themselves.

One night, everyone had gone to bed except for Hal and Saslic.

It was clear, a chill in the air, and it seemed very natural for them to lean together, and look up at the almost-full moon.

"Do you suppose," Saslic asked softly, "that over in Roche there are a boy and girl dragon rider, looking up at the same moon . . . I wonder what they're thinking? Romantic things, maybe?"

Hal had been wondering about the Roche as well, except that his thoughts were running more toward some ideas he had for killing Roche dragon fliers, no matter their sex.

"Of course," he said hastily. "Romantic things, and about, umm, dancing in the moonlight, and . . ."

His voice trailed off, and he was looking into her eyes, great moonpools.

It seemed like a good idea to kiss her, and he was moving closer, her lips parting, and a voice whispered in their ear.

"How wonderfully romantic!"

Hal whirled, saw Serjeant Patrice, who'd crept up behind them on his hands and knees.

"We have a great deal of energy, do we, to be wanting to play stinkfinger when we ought to be in bed like good little boys and girls?"

"Uh . . ."

"On your feet, students, and at attention! Move!"

They obeyed.

"I suppose, with all this vim and vigor, you'd appreciate a task to occupy you for the rest of the night, wouldn't you, since you can't be sleepy?"

"Uh . . ." Hal managed.

"Is the shitwagon fixed yet, Serjeant?" Saslic said.

"No, more's the pity. Not that I'd detail you for that, since it makes noise, and I don't want any of your classmates disturbed from their slumber merely because of your . . . pastimes.

"You go change into your fatigue suits, children. And then meet me on the far side of where the horse ring used to be. There's at least one stable that wasn't cleaned thoroughly from the old days."

By false dawn, that stable was as clean as it had been on the day it'd been built, Hal and Saslic working by lantern light and with Patrice's occasional check-in.

"Very good," he approved, just as the drums of reveille began clattering. "Now, back to your huts, and change into class uniform. You've an easy fifteen minutes, and I don't want either of you late, or stinking of horse dung like you do now.

"Fifteen minutes, and I've planned a nice cross-country run for us before breaking our fasts."

Brooms were clattered down and the two pelted for their huts, knowing there was absolutely no way they'd be able to get clean, let alone dressed.

But then came the surprise.

Two huts – Hal's and Saslic's – gleamed with fire- and lamp-light.

"Come on, you eejiots," Farren shouted, and Mynta Gart beckoned from the other hut. "Water's heatin', and yer uniforms're ready."

Busy hands helped Hal out of his stinking fatigue suit, and buckets of soapy water were cascaded about him, as he stood, shivering, outside the hut. Across the way, Saslic was getting similar treatment.

Hal was too tired to even consider lascivious thoughts as his clothes were hurled at him, pulled on.

The only thought that did come, as he and the other students ran toward the shrilling of whistles in the assembly area, was that, with or without dragons, somehow the students had come together, and formed a team, cadre be damned.

The next day the dragons arrived, and everything changed.

10

There were twenty-five dragons, angrily hissing, long necks snaking around, trying to sink their fangs into anyone around. They were chain-lashed to wagons, each drawn by ten oxen.

Hal thought they were just entering their prime.

Saslic agreed, and said they were four, maybe five years old.

"A little young for riding, but easier to train," Rai Garadice added, then yelped in glee, broke formation, in spite of Serjeant Patrice's snarl, and ran into the arms of a medium-height, frothy-bearded man Hal recognized.

"Didjer happen to do a count?" Farren said. "Twenny-five of th' monskers. Assumin' that we, like the eejiots afore, take these mooncalves off to war as our personal mounts, a'ter they've finished trainin' us, that means that somebody's allowin' for either cas'lties or bustouts. So fifteen of us're doom't."

"Most likely both," Ev Larnell said gloomily.

"Yar, well, I don't plan on bein' either," Mariah put in snappily. "Fly the skies, spy the ground, that's my fambly motto."

"Since when?" Larnell asked suspiciously.

"Since right now," Farren said. "What's a good fambly 'less you can shake it, change it, turn it all about?"

There were very immediate changes. Garadice had brought five of his dragon-buying team, all experienced dragon fliers. He announced he had orders to take over command of the school, and everyone would now please help unload the dragons.

"Cadre included," he said.

Sir Pers Spense departed, and no one saw him leave.

Garadice appeared at the dinner formation, told all the students to gather around.

"I'm not one for speeches. I understand from the good Serjeant Te you've been getting marched back and forth a great deal, and it doesn't appear much was done about why you all volunteered.

"That'll change.

"Serjeant Te will take charge of whatever military drill needs doing, which I don't think is much, and the bulk of the time will be spent trying to teach you men and women not only how to fly, but how to stay alive once you reach the front.

"The battle has worsened, and no one is quite sure how dragons will fit in. So it'll be up to you to not only fight bravely, but determine the future of dragon flying.

"There are quite a few . . . well, I shouldn't say old fuds, but that's what they are, who think an army should forget nothing, and learn nothing.

"It'll be your job, and the few that have gone before, and, hopefully, the many that will follow, to make them learn differently.

"Now, go in to eat. I'm afraid tonight's meal is nothing but cold victuals, pickles, tomatoes and bread. I was forced to discharge the cooking staff, since I believe we should eat no worse than dragons, so until we bring in some better qualified people, we'll have to shift for ourselves, and some of you'll be detailed to help prepare and serve.

"Not that any of us will have much time to brood about food. We're all going to be very, very busy."

"Very well," Garadice said, propping a pair of half-moon spectacles on the bridge of his nose, "you might want to pay attention here."

He lifted an enormous folio on to the lectern. It was stuffed with papers, some printed, some scribbled on.

"This is what I think I know about dragons, from twenty years' experience.

"But if any of you know better, or even think you do, please interrupt me.

"Remember, we've only known about dragons for three hundred years or so, when they first appeared on our shores."

"Where did they come from?" Sir Loren Damian asked.

"Almost certainly from the far north, even beyond Black Island."

"Better, why'd they come south?" Farren asked.

"No one knows, precisely. Some have theorized the climate changed, and drove them south.

"Another theory is that they feed naturally on the great herds of oxen that roam the northern wildernesses. Perhaps a plague of oxen, or even overcrowding their natural grounds could have caused this migration."

"More like, somebody was chasin' 'em," Farren said.

"That's not unlikely." Garadice smiled. "Which may be one reason why the far north remains unexplored, besides the problem that Black Island, the logical jumping off place for any such exploration, is claimed by the kingdom of Roche."

The students were paired off, almost two to a dragon, and stable duties began. Somehow Vad Feccia ended as Hal's stable partner. Hal did most of the work, since Feccia seemed terrified of the monsters.

That didn't bother Hal. He cheerfully put Feccia to

pumping the stirrup pump they were given, and sprayed his beast with soapy water, then scrubbed it with stiff-bristled, long-handled brushes.

"His" dragon seemed to like that, at least it only tried to sink its fangs into him at the beginning of the session and at the end.

Saslic determined the dragon's sex was probably female. "All to the good, Hal. Easier to train, easier to keep."

Saslic had a male dragon, which she'd named Nont, after, she said, "one of my imaginary friends when I was a little girl."

Hal didn't name his. He knew that it was going to be a long war, and this dragon might be the first of many, especially if his ideas bore fruition.

After washing, Hal oiled his dragon's scales, checked its talons for splitting, although he wasn't sure what he'd do if one was broken, carted out the amazing amount of waste a dragon could produce, changed the straw it slept on, odorous with the beast's pungent urine.

He then took it, on a very long lead, its wings bound, for a walk around the horse ring. He thought it was a good sign that "his" dragon wasn't very friendly to the other beasts.

The dragon was fed twice a day, generally a sheep or calf in the morning, perhaps some salt fish at night. Hal was grateful there was a butcher attached to Garadice's unit. As a special treat, a handful of rabbits might be tossed into the dragon's cage alive.

"There are four, most likely more, species of dragons. It's also possible that three of these are merely variations.

"The other class, known as the Black Island or black variation, is significantly larger in all dimensions than other dragons, is predominately black in coloration, and is considered untamable, and the deadliest of mankillers.

"As a side note, though," Garadice said, "a number of dragon fliers, back before the war, were able to obtain, tame and successfully ride dragons which had supposedly been gotten from Black Island, so here, again, nothing is certain. Do these other species interbreed with the black dragons?

"I simply do not know."

New cooks had been brought in, Garadice permitted the issue of beer at the end of each week, and one afternoon was given over to free time.

None of this was important to Hal as Rai, who'd quickly been promoted to cadre, gave him a hand up into the rear saddle of a docile dragon cow for his first flight.

"Now, here's the way you steer this brute," he said, "which I suppose you know from your days with Athelny. Slap her with the reins on the left side of her neck, and, with training, she'll turn that way. Hit her on the right – and I don't mean hard, you're not supposed to be cruel – she'll go that way. Drag the reins back, and – with any kind of luck – the beast'll climb. Rap both reins on her neck, and she'll probably dive.

"Kick if you want her to fly faster, pull back on the reins again to slow her down.

"That's the hard way to do things. Some dragons – I remember the one my father gave me – obeyed by voice. Others I've seen can feel the rider bend in the saddle, and will turn with him.

"This lumbering cow is purely stupid, and thinks just getting off the ground is repayment enough for her daily meat.

"Strap yourself in, and let's go flying."

Hal obeyed, and Rai slid into the front saddle.

"Hup," he shouted, and the dragon stirred, got up from her crouch, and staggered forward, out of the pen. Her wings uncurled, beat, beat again, and, very simply, they were flying.

Rai let the dragon climb of her own will, giving no commands.

He looked back, saw Hal's look of pure glee, nodded.

"You *were* a flier, or anyway you've been up, not like some of us."

Hal didn't answer, intent on looking at that most magical of all sights, the ground lower away below him, and the horizon unroll.

"I'll not take her higher," Rai said. "I want you up front here as soon as possible, really learning something, not joyriding with your finger in your nose."

The classroom training was very much by guess and by the gods. Garadice and the other instructors taught map reading, use of a compass, survival skills in case they landed and were trapped in enemy territory.

There was an infantry training camp about half an hour's flight distant, and the trainees helped the class learn what horsemen, marching infantry, a command group looked like from the air.

Hal thought it mildly amusing that the soldiers, when the dragons landed, treated the prospective fliers with a mixture of awe and incredulity that any normal-looking man or woman would trust themselves to the monsters they loved.

He could see the use of most training, but it was evident that no one, instructor or student, was really sure how these dragons, and their fliers, would serve Deraine.

Hal, keeping his own council, was following Garadice's lead, and keeping a notebook that filled up with his own, rather bloody, thoughts on what use dragons might be put.

"Damnation, Kailas," the instructor shouted. "Don't saw at the reins – you're not trying to cut this poor beast's neck in half!"

Hal tried to be lighter with his controls, and the dragon ignored him. He tried leaning to suggest a command, and the dragon ignored him.

He felt sweat on his forehead, under his arms, in spite of the wintry day.

"This isn't producing much," the instructor said. "Bring him down toward the ground, and I'll take the reins.

"I do hope you do better next time," the instructor added, gloomily.

Hal nodded dumbly, terrified that he would be one of the ones found unsatisfactory, and returned to his unit. There were already half a dozen failures, after only two weeks.

Hal Kailas was afraid he'd be the seventh.

Saslic was a natural flier, and her dragon seemed to revel at every moment in the air, the pair quickly progressing to aerial acrobatics, turning, twisting in the stormy skies above the base.

She tried to help Hal on what he was doing wrong, but had to admit, finally, that it was just a matter of "feel," and he should maybe relax, and it would come to him in a flash.

Sir Loren Damian also learned easily, as he seemed to do everything, without effort and with a bit of a smile on his lanky face.

The other knight on the course, Calabar, was stodgy, but competent. One nasty habit he had was carrying a dogwhip with him, and belaboring his dragon at the slightest "failure."

Garadice told him he was heading for trouble, that dragons, like men, loved masters, if masters there had to be, who were easy in the saddle.

Calabar curled a lip and said, "In my experience, a master who gives a serf an ounce of slack is on the way to making a rebel, a bandit, and deserves a whipping as much as his disobedient thrall."

Asser seemed to be learning, then, one day, he was absent from roll call. Two days later, he was brought back, in manacles, by a pair of military warders, who'd caught him on the streets of Rozen.

Everyone expected him to be thrown out, and finally vanish. But he was kept on, although his evenings were spent with a shovel and broom under the tutelage of Serjeant Patrice. No one knew what story he told Garadice, but Farren said, a trace of envy in his voice, "Th' bastid must've a throat that's silver, pure silver."

"It seems fairly certain," Garadice read, "that the dragon's egg, which is about two feet long, is sat upon, in the nest, for about four months before hatching. The Kit is carefully tended by both parents for almost a year, until it is deemed ready to leave the nest. During this time, it's vulnerable only to two things: the weather, and man.

"Dragons seem to return to the same nest, year after year, refurbishing it with considerable skill before the cow deposits the egg."

He closed the book.

"Stop yawning, Mariah, or were you signaling for a break? Outside, all of you, breathe some rain, and wake up."

The class clattered out of the room, and down the hall to the main hall's entranceway, staring out at the rain, almost as gray as the stone and the sea beyond, that sheeted down.

"Damned glad to be inside on a day like this," Saslic said. "Look . . . way out there, to sea. That fisherman's in heavy weather."

Mynta Gart was staring at it.

"Sometimes, I think I wish . . ." Her voice trailed off.

"You were out there, getting bobbed around?" Hal suggested.

"Just so."

"The hells with that," Farren said. "Old Garry – sorry, Rai – goin' on about the dragon's egg, and nary a word about how they ring th' bell for each other, which might've kept me awake.

"D'yer know, I was brushin' that beast of mine, and his wanger came out shootin' out, like a dog's. Big as one of these damn' columns here. I skittered out of the way in a shot for fear he was feelin' lovelorn! Makes a man humble, feelin' inferior, even me, the grandest of lovers, an' ud put me off my feed for a week, were there anyone around here who's feelin' romantic-like about me.

"Which there ain't, an' I'm thinkin' about tryin' a new brand of soap."

Hal sat glumly in the stables, staring at the dragon across from him, which he was thinking of as his less and less. The next beast that would be his, the way things were going, would be another horse, back in the cavalry.

He wasn't supposed to be out of his hut, but the curfew regulations, like most of the others put out by Pers Spense, weren't being enforced, to Serjeant Patrice's annoyance.

"These men and women are adults, or had damned well better be if they're going to be trusted scouting for an entire army," Garadice had said flatly. "So we'll treat them like adults until they give damned good cause to warrant other considerations, in which case it will probably be best to just return them to their parent formations."

The penned dragon across from him had stared at Hal, wondering what he was doing here this deep in the night, but eventually the yellow eyes had closed, and the monster started breathing in a soft bubble.

Hal wasn't really seeing the dragon, but thinking over and over about what he was, what he must, be doing wrong, and why he couldn't seem to get it right.

About half the surviving class were now flying alone, well on their way toward graduation, while Kailas farted about like a stumblebum, having not a clue as to what he should be doing.

He started, hearing the stable door creak open, saw Saslic slip in, close the door behind her.

"What—"

She came over to him. "I couldn't sleep, and went to your hut. Farren said you'd gone out, probably to offer yourself as a sacrifice to the dragon god.

"I figured I'd find you here."

"Farren always makes life easier," Hal said. "Pull up a bucket and help me sulk."

Saslic stayed on her feet.

"You've got to stop worrying, Hal. You get all tensed up, and then you get jerky, and get more tense, like a kitten chasing its tail."

"I know," Kailas said. "But knowing and being able to do something about it seem to be two different things. Hells, I'm such a dunderbrain, I probably deserve being back on a horse, chasing bandits."

Saslic moved behind him, started rubbing his shoulders.

"I can feel the muscles knotted up," she said softly.

"Do you remember," she said after awhile, "the night we got caught, sitting out by Patrice?"

"I do."

"I had the idea you were going to kiss me before that asshole materialized."

"The thought was in my mind."

"Well?"

Hal stood, turned, and was holding her. She was small, light, and felt very good in his arms. He kissed her, and that felt better. She kissed him back, tongue writhing in his mouth, and he couldn't remember having felt that good in a long time.

Then they were lying, close together, in a hay manger. Her tunic was unbuttoned, and he was kissing the small buttons of her nipples, her fingers moving in his hair.

She broke from the kiss, and said, breathing hard, "You could be a gentleman, you know, and take off your breeches and tunic for a bedsheet. Straw isn't the easiest thing on a girl's bottom, you know."

They didn't stop making love until the drums of reveille began tapping.

"Dammit, Hal, quit trying to pull the poor dragon's head off," Rai snapped. "Gently! Feel what you want!"

Hal clenched his teeth, felt, again, his muscles clenching. Then his body remembered Saslic's gentle fingers, and all at once, he had it. He felt one with the dragon he was riding, and the monster responded, banking easily left, tucking a wing, and coming back on its own course.

"Now a right turn," Rai said, his voice suddenly excited.

Again the dragon banked, and this time Hal tapped it into a shallow dive, back toward the base, a gray blur in the grayness.

He didn't feel the cold wind coming off the sea, nor the spatter of rain that caught him as he sent the dragon curveting through the skies.

He did have it, and knew it, and wondered at his own clumsiness of bare minutes ago. It was, he thought, like watching a butterfly stagger out of its chrysalis onto a leaf, and, moments later, soar into the summer air.

He looked back over his shoulder, saw Rai grinning at him.

"See how easy it is?" the young Garadice said.

And it was easy.

"There probably has never been a creature so perfectly adapted for fighting as a dragon," Garadice read, "from its dual horns to the impressive fangs. Dragons, in territorial or mating battles, also use their neck spikes to tear at their opponent.

"The four claws are equally adept at ripping at their enemies with the three talons on each.

"The steering tail is also used to lash at an enemy, easily its most lethal weapon. The wing talons are used not only to impale prey, but to tear away wings, since a beast's wings are more delicate away from the forward, ribbed edge.

"Dragons have remarkable powers of healing and even regeneration, although a dragon that's entirely lost a wing or a limb is doomed.

"It's interesting that the beasts not only fight in earnest, but seem, from what I've observed, to play at fighting, although it appears as if that can become real combat quite easily, which is frequently to the death."

Dragon games, Hal thought, scribbling in his notebook. Men's games.

Like war . . .

Most students weren't slow as Hal had been, nor flashy like Saslic and Damian.

Mynta Gart plugged along, learning steadily, stolidly. Farren learned his new craft readily, always with a ready jest. So did Vad Feccia, in spite of his almost-fear of dragons, to Hal's minor disappointment.

Ev Larnell was quick to learn, even if he was hesitant to try out something new. Hal was glad he hadn't said anything to anyone about Ev's lie about being an experienced flier, although a couple of the cadre wondered aloud why he seemed to be slower than someone with his background should have been.

Other students couldn't seem to learn, were quietly but quickly removed from the school, their gear vanished with them, their mattresses rolled as if no one had ever slept there.

There were other losses . . .

Hal was walking his dragon in the horse ring, and heard a dragon scream. He saw Sir Brant Calabar lashing at his dragon's neck as the creature flapped clear of the ground, savagely yanking back on its reins.

The dragon's wings beat faster, and it climbed for altitude rapidly. But that evidently wasn't quick enough for Calabar, for he kept hitting the creature with his dogwhip. Hal could hear the man's shouting, couldn't make out the words.

The dragon was flying almost straight up, slowing.

Then it tucked a wing, and turned through a semi-circle, back toward the ground.

Calabar lost his hold, flailed, and, screaming, fell, 500 feet or more. He hit near in the middle of one of the exercise rings with a sodden thud, very final, like a bag of grain tossed from a high-bedded wagon.

Hal was the first to reach him. Calabar was motionless, his

eyes glaring straight up. It didn't look as if he had an unbroken bone in his body.

His dragon circled overhead, screaming, and Hal thought his screams were triumphant.

Two more students died and were buried in the next week after Calabar. After their funerals, Garadice behaved as if they'd never been, and pushed the students even harder, spending more and more time in the air.

"Guess there was someat goin' about," Farren joked, and then everyone did as Garadice had, and the three had never lived.

That was the beginning of a ghastly tradition in the dragon flights.

One thing the students had to learn was there were days a dragon simply would not fly. No one seemed to know why, including Garadice, who said that was one problem with his pre-war shows: "You'd have the area filled, and your dragon would be sulking in his wagon, and you'd best leave him alone, or maybe feed him or her choice tidbits until the mood passed."

One student didn't listen to his advice, and kept chivvying her dragon. The brute started hissing, then, before she could jump back, snapped out, taking most of her arm off.

"Now, that's a way to get out of bein' kilt acrost the Straits I've naught considered, an' wi' a nice pension, I'd hope," Farren said, and everyone was a bit more careful around the beasts after that.

Hal, now that he had the flying problem in hand, but still refusing to name his dragon, spent more hours with the beast than most. He had to keep the lead on it, but let the rope and chain slack, and took the monster away from the base, into the trees around it. The dragon seemed to care little for the weather, paying little heed to winds or rain sweeping across its leathery hide.

Saslic caught him having a one-way conversation with the creature one time, and told him he'd gone right over the edge.

Kailas thought, then agreed with her, especially since he fancied the dragon had begun, by claw gestures and hisses, to talk back.

"Now," Serjeant Te said, "Serjeant Kailas has told us how his patrols were stalked by Roche dragons, which is a new tactic.

"We've orders for all of you to start learning the same tactic, which is why you see those dummies on straw horses across that field.

"Each of you is to take your dragon off, and try to bring it close to a dummy. Encourage your dragon – no, I don't have any ideas how – to grab the rider, and tear him from his horse. It's also all right to have him take the horse and rider, too.

"Be careful, and don't run into the ground.

"First man! Kailas! Get out there and give us a good example."

"A question, Serjean'?" Farren said.

"I'm listening."

"I ain't objectin' to killin' Roche . . . I s'pose that's why I'm here, a'ter all. But this grabbin' an' yankin' don't appear economical t' me. One expensive dragon, one expensive rider, riskin' all t' pull some plowboy off a horse, and takin' a chance of some archer yoinkin' you through th' throat. Or puttin' an arrer int' yer dragon, which ain't likely to make *him* happy, either."

Te hesitated, giving Hal enough time to remember the catapults that'd been fired at the Roche dragons who'd attacked his patrol on the way back from that last scout of his.

"Orders're orders," Te said, without conviction. "But I'll pass your word on to Lieutenant Garadice."

Farren looked at Hal, made a face. Kailas nodded slightly, ran for his dragon.

*

Hal and Saslic made love whenever they could get away, which wasn't that often. Their instruction was coming faster and faster, and Kailas fancied he could hear the horror that was war breathing its fetid breath closer and closer.

The winter drove at them, and cut flying time. But Hal still managed to bundle himself in all that wonderfully warm issued gear as often as possible, and prod his beast into the air, and up, through the clouds to where a chill sun gleamed.

His dragon, not happy at first, warmed, and so they would fly, sailing around the huge buttresses of clouds, sometimes through them, and chancing being tossed by the winds hiding in the softness.

Then it was chancy, as he'd lower down into the solid cover, losing altitude foot by foot, hoping there wasn't a hidden outcropping just below.

Once he broke out into the open, only a few feet above the tossing waves, the cliffs of the base dim in the distance.

It was dangerous, but he was teaching himself.

And, as Saslic had said earlier, maybe vanishing in flight wasn't the best way to die, but it made for as good a funeral as anyone could wish.

"That's it," Garadice announced at one morning's formation, a touch of spring in the air. "We've nothing more to teach you.

"You're dragon fliers."

There was a gape of astonishment, then the students began cheering. The noise sounded like a great deal more than the nineteen who'd survived.

Garadice, at his own expense, had small golden dragons cast, and gave one to each student, telling them to pin them on their uniform, to be worn above any other decoration they won.

*

"I wish you all the luck in the world," Serjeant Patrice said. "And I'm proud to have helped make you into soldiers."

Saslic looked scornfully at his outthrust hand, refused to take it.

"No," she said, voice bitter. "Screw the way it works in romances. You're still nothing but a bully and a cheap prick to me."

She stalked away, to laughter. Patrice, face purpling, scurried back into the main hall.

And so the class broke up, each with a wagon carrying his or her distinctly unhappy dragon, creaking toward the Straits ports and Paestum, to report to different units.

Now, Hal thought, the real learning will begin.

11

It was a bit more than six months since Hal had been in Paestum, but the city had changed almost beyond recognition. The ruins from the siege had been mostly razed, and spreading far beyond the walls were caterpillering tents for the replacements and new units streaming across the Straits into Sagene.

When Hal had left, there'd been only *the* army. Now there were four, interspersed with Sagene armies down the Roche border, to meet the building threat of new Roche forces.

But the tactics hadn't changed, still the bloody head-smashing battles as the forces moved back and forth in the wasted, bloody landscape, hoping, each time, without luck, for a breakthrough into the heart of the enemy's country for the capital.

Hal, having a great deal of back pay in his purse, and nowhere to spend it, found a copyist involved with the replacement section who was bribable.

He was negotiating with him to keep Saslic, of course, plus Farren and possibly Ev Larnell, with him, whichever dragon flight he was assigned to, having learned there's no such word as "no" in the military if the pleader has sufficient rank or silver.

There were, at present, two flights assigned to each Deraine army, with Sagene having its own flights, roughly set up the same as Deraine's.

The transport ship had unloaded their dragons, and the new fliers were given a tented area to themselves, while they waited for orders to whichever dragon flight would need them. They were left largely in peace, no warrants rooting through their area for scut-details, since no one seemed to want to get too close to the monsters or the lunatics who rode them.

Contrasting with this were the jokes going around that no one had ever seen a dead dragon rider, and dragon riders were mainly concerned with qualifying for their king's old age pension, whereas an infantryman or cavalryman would certainly never live long enough to worry about it.

Hal was trying to figure out how much he'd have to increase the copyist's bribe to get "his" people assigned to the northernmost First Army area, near Paestum. Even though it was cold, rainy and swampy in spots, it was the area of the border he knew well, and thought that knowledge would improve his, and his friends', chances of surviving.

Then everything shattered.

Roche magicians managed to cloak the assembly of half a dozen armies, south, near the city of Frechin. They'd crossed the border, smashing a Sagene army.

Only the spring rains were holding them back from driving hard toward Sagene's capital of Fovant. But each day, the salient grew longer, a finger reaching into the heart of Sagene.

Deraine's First and Second Armies were stripped of any unit not vitally needed, all offensives against the Roche were put aside, and all replacements arriving in Paestum were detached on temporary duty to units in the Third Army, now engaged with the enemy.

So Hal's entire graduating class of novice fliers, and their beasts, were ordered south, at all possible speed. The Third Army needed them for scouts, spies and couriers.

The roads below were packed with troops, marching, riding, in wagons. Hal was very glad to be high above the roiling mud below. His dragon wanted to find a nice, dry cave and hole up until the weather changed, but he drove it onward, and eventually it gave up squealing protest when he led it out from the canvas aerie the detailed quartermasters set up every night when they camped.

South and south they went, but it never got warmer, and the fliers wore everything they were issued, and still shivered.

Some of them – Feccia among them – got in the habit of buying whatever brandy they could find in their flights. Hal took barely a nip on even especially frozen mornings. He'd already learned brandy as a friend could quickly become brandy as a creaking crutch, and wanted none of that.

Of course the villagers along the roads were either bought or looted out by the time Hal's detachment passed, but the dragons had the option of flying away from the march routes, finding villages who barely knew there was a war, eager to trade, sell or even patriotically give away their produce, eggs, or drink.

It didn't make much of an impression to the ground-bound soldiery, seeing dragons float back to their wagons at dusk, laden with plunder. The elderly infantry warrant who'd been put in charge of the formation seemed to have no objections to what was going on, and Hal shrugged, it not being his concern. It didn't, however, improve his mood to hear the infantry give them new labels: "Defenders of the Veal," "Champions of the Poultry Run," "Guardians of the Keg," "Omelet Defenders," and so forth.

At least he and Saslic were able to be together at least every third night or so, when one or another didn't have guard duty around the dragons.

Other fliers made similar arrangements, or, like Farren,

chased after any women they encountered with the dignity of a hound in heat.

There were persistent rumors of bandits abroad, or cross-border partisans, but Hal never saw any, and these scoundrels were, according to the tales, either a day's march in front of or behind the yarn-spinner.

Before Bedarisi the open roads that had given the soldiers speed changed. Now the roads were packed with refugees, fleeing ahead of the advancing Roche armies.

Hal would always remember a few things from those days.

An old man, pushing an older woman in a barrow, and, from the time they first saw the pair until they vanished around a bend, she never stopped railing at him.

A middle-aged man, wearing nothing but long winter drawers, carrying only an ornate old clock taller than he was.

Three wagons full of young women, who claimed to be from a religious school, and were full of laughter. But if they were religious, they had scandalous rites, although those men – and a few women – who hadn't made bed partners seemed to enjoy their company. Hal and Saslic visited their camp, across from the dragon fliers, for a glass of wine, and Saslic noted, behind the laughter, the fear in the women's eyes, and the way they kept glancing south, toward the oncoming Roche.

A wizard, with two acolytes, their robes stained with travel, trudging along. Farren landed his dragon, got provisions from one of the fliers' wagons, and walked for a third of a league beside them, then came back.

"Dreadful bad it is, in the south," he reported. "Or so the mage says. Roche cavalry ridin' here an' there, lootin', cuttin', murderin', rapin', and the Sagenes don't seem to be able to stop 'em.

"He says we'll have our jobs set for us, an' wished us luck."

Hal asked why the man's magic hadn't kept him from becoming another wanderer, and Mariah, serious for once, had said, "I guess magic don't al'as help the one who's castin' it. Sure fire it didn't make m' grandsire rich, just notable. Guess that the gods, whoreson bastids that they be, don't want wizards comin' up as kings or, worse yet, competin' wi' them.

"That gives us some sort of order, I guess, 'though, thinkin' from present circ'mstances, I wouldn't mind if they let an option out f'r one short amat'ur witch, who's doodlin' around in the wilderness wi' dragons at present, needin' all the help he can get."

One day they were stranded before a washed-out bridge, waiting for the pioneers to rebuild it. There was a small country inn on a promontory over the river, but its proprietor said, mournfully, he'd sold everything he had in the way of provender, and their chickens and ducks had been pirated away by either soldiers or refugees.

Mynta Gart flew away north-west on her dragon, and came back two hours later with a cargo net full of foodstuffs bought in distant villages.

She refused the proprietor's money, told him to build omelets, and the man's two daughters went through dozens of eggs at a time until the fliers thought they might cluck and peck at each other.

Now their forced march from Paestum caught up with them, and Hal could feel fatigue at his back. But he said nothing, and cut Vad Feccia off sharply when he whined about sore muscles, merely pointing to the road they'd pulled away from, at the long lines of infantry, plodding through the mire, a pace at a time, and with nothing but a groundsheet and what they had scrounged from the roadside or begged or stolen from passing wagons for rations.

They reached Bedarisi, the streets crowded with fleeing citizens. It took them two full days to work their way through the jammed streets to open country again.

Feccia suggested low-flying the dragons over the crowd, and hoping some terror would clear the way, but the old warrant forbade it.

Beyond the city, they saw their first Roche dragons,

swooping and diving in the distance, spying the country, and felt the war close on them.

Two of their dragons saw them, and Hal was pleased with their response – angry hissing and snorts, their heads snaking back and forth, mouths open, fangs dripping. He hoped the fliers mirrored their attitude.

Now the roads, such as they were, country tracks worn wide and into sloppy ditches by the army's passings, were empty once more of everything except the military.

They stopped at an enormous post at an intersection of three of these tracks, a log stripped of leaves and branches, and buried vertically. On it were half a hundred wooden boards, each pointing to where a different formation might be found.

Far at the top, Farren saw a small painted dragon.

"Or else't a winged worm," he opined.

They turned the wagons down that track, and went on for several leagues, passing encampments, ration dumps, stables.

The track emptied into a wide meadow, with a pond at one end, and there they found the dragon flight.

Hal kept his face blank, but Farren, Feccia and some others gaped in shock.

Expecting lines of hopefully weatherproof huge stables for the dragons, and neat barracks to the side for the men, they saw, instead, some tattered tents, worse than the ones the former students had brought with them, patched here and there with other colored canvas or even cloth. Some of them had torn grommets, and were held to the ground, flailing in the strong wind, with branches for stakes.

The human quarters were even worse, everything from huge packing crates to tiny infantry tents to sod-roofed shanties supported on logs and "found" lumber.

It looked like a proper base – one that had been struck by a tornado, and then reoccupied by trolls.

There were a handful of people about, most seemingly doing nothing except squelching back and forth on the open meadow in front of the squadron's buildings.

One woman was watering a dragon at the pond.

At both sides of the meadow were catapults, with infantry-men manning them.

A single dragon patrolled the air overhead, flying in endless circles around the meadow.

Hal ignored the moans – as an old soldier, he noted what must be the cooktent, a large, well-pitched tent, with smoke coming from chimneys at the front and back.

Seeing that, he knew that everything had not fallen apart.

"Do you want me to report in, sir?"

"I'd appreciate that," their escort warrant said. "Now we're away from my grounds, and on yours."

Hal caught himself, glanced at Sir Loren Damian, who grinned damply, but made no protest.

There was a guidon pitched in front of a bell tent, and Hal went to it, knocked on the ridgepole.

"Enter."

He pushed the outer flap aside, and walked into a tent crowded with four cots, one piled high with maps and sword-belts.

On another, a man snored loudly, a ragged cloak pulled over him.

Sitting at a field desk sat a man whose body and face were sculpted by exhaustion. Hal was tired, but this man was beyond that.

"Serjeant Hal Kailas," Hal said, clapping a hand to his breast. "With eighteen other dragon fliers and mounts, mobile, as ordered by First Army Headquarters."

The man blinked, rubbed his eyes, picked up a bottle of brandy, and uncorked it. He shook his head, and put the bottle away.

"I am assuming for the moment you're not a magician's imp, sent to taunt me with impossibilities."

"Nossir. I'm . . . we're for real."

"Just maybe there are gods," the man breathed, realized

Hal was still holding the salute. "Sit down . . . or, anyway, find something to lean against.

"I'm Lieutenant Sir Lu Miletus. Someone said I was going to be a captain, but the orders seem to have gone awry.

"You said nineteen dragon fliers?"

"Yessir."

The man stood, extended a hand, and Hal clasped it. Miletus looked as if he'd been studying to become a priest or other ascetic before the war, with his lean, long-faced, somber expression. But Hal saw smile lines on his face.

"Nineteen," Miletus breathed again. "That just might put us back in the war. Any support people?"

"Nossir. We were told you'd have all necessary ground personnel."

"We did," Miletus said. "Until the dragons brought the cavalry on us. At least we didn't lose any of our beasts . . . all ten of them.

"And now, just a little late, we've got those arrow-throwers assigned to keep us safe from intruders."

He shook his head.

"Never mind. We've gotten so good at making do with very little we can probably win this godsdamned war with absolutely nothing."

He pulled on a muddy cloak.

"Let's go see how we can get your people settled, Serjeant. I'll tell you beforehand I'm going to make myself rather loathed, since I'm going to take away five of your dragons from their masters."

Hal kept his face still.

"My fliers – all six of them – have more experience . . . I assume that none of you are more than school-trained?"

"That's correct. Sir."

"Don't look so sour, man. What I'm doing is not only best for the flight, but it might keep some of you alive.

"Also, all of you are grounded until I personally give you permission."

He grinned, noting Hal's deliberately blank look. "And I don't mean to denigrate you by keeping you out of harm's way for the moment.

"You'll see. You'll see your training didn't really give you any help for what's out here.

"Now, let's get your men fed, and start finagling for quarters."

"Four of us are women, sir."

"I'd heard they'd finally gotten around to recognizing the other half," Miletus said. "Not to worry. I don't think any of my men have enough energy to raise a smile, if that was your concern."

The new ones were quartered here and there, some in existing tents, some in the smaller tents they'd brought with them.

The escort warrant and his men rode back the way they came, showing evident relief they wouldn't be required to get any closer to the war zone than they already had.

Miletus didn't, as far as Hal saw, quiz any of the replacements about who was the best flier, who the worst. Instead, he put them up, one by one, over the meadow, ordering them to do certain maneuvers.

Hal quickly found out neither war nor careless habits had driven the flight into slovenry.

They'd been hammered hard when the Roche crossed the lines, losing fliers and dragons to Roche magic, their catapults, which were brought up just behind the front lines, weather, and two to enemy dragons, who'd attacked their beasts until the Deraine dragons went out of control, whipping across the skies and losing their riders, then vanishing into the mists.

Bad enough . . . but then the dragons had guided enemy cavalry through the shattered Deraine positions to the flight's base.

"Everyone," Miletus said tiredly, "became infantry, and

we fought as well as we could." He looked around sadly. "Which wasn't very, I'm afraid, although at least we drove them back.

"The closest thing we had to a hero was Chook, the cook."

Hal waited for an explanation, but none came.

"The Sagene command offered us infantry to guard the base, but I told them to keep the men on the lines, except for those catapult men. There isn't anything here worth another attack." He brightened. "At least not 'til your arrival."

He grinned. "I'm certain you find that reassuring."

Hal found a relatively dry bell tent, with four cots. Three of them were bare, the fourth occupied by a wiry man with amazing mustaches, who introduced himself as Aimard Quesney, and told him to take any bed he wanted.

"Won't I be disturbing anybody?"

"If you are, and anyone says anything, move out sprightly," Aimard said. "For they're all quite dead, and I'm getting tired of waiting for their ghosts."

"Small, but cozy," Saslic said, waving a hand around her hut. "Note the greenery on the roof, which'll go well with my face when I think about what I got myself into wanting to play soldier."

The hut was small, ten feet on a side. But shelves had been built along the walls by a skilled carpenter, and there were cleverly-hinged windows on either wall.

"Built for two," Saslic said. "But I hid the other cot before anyone could claim it."

"Why?" Hal asked.

"Did your mother have any sons with intelligence?"

"I don't guess so. Explain."

"I thought a certain northern fool might want to come visiting from time to time, and since I'm not into either threesies or witnesses, I thought we might like privacy."

"Oh."

"Speaking of which, why don't you slide the door shut? I noticed you coming back from the pond, looking cleaner than you have since we left Paestum, and thought you might be interested in messing about."

In the dimness, Hal saw her slide out of her coveralls, and lay back on the bed.

"Close, but perhaps we can manage," she murmured.

Later, as they lay together, Hal had a question.

"I know men aren't supposed to ask and all. But what's going to happen to us?"

Saslic kissed him on the nose.

"Why, we're going to get killed. Preferably nobly, in battle."

"Oh." Hal thought. "No. I'm going to live through this."

"Of course you are," Saslic drawled. "That's what everybody who filled up all these empty cots knew."

"No," Hal said stubbornly, trying to sound as if he were positive about things. "I'm going to survive."

"Well, good for you," Saslic said. "I'm not. Which is why I haven't bored either one of us talking about love, or after the war, or anything else beyond this moment. So remember me fondly when I'm gone, and name your first child after me.

"And as for immediate moments . . ."

She moved close, hooked a leg over his thighs, and pulled him on top of her.

"Remember, anything you don't see might kill you," Miletus said over his shoulder. "C'mon, Fabulous. Get your arse in the sky."

He tapped reins, and the dragon's wings flapped slowly, and it took a few steps forward. Then it was clear of the mucky ground, and climbed into the skies.

Hal, sitting behind Miletus, tried to keep the map he'd studied ready, and glanced at the compass clipped to his fur-lined jacket, then put it away, mindful of Miletus' orders to keep his eyes on the sky, not anywhere else.

He shivered at the chill spring wind blowing in his face, and decided, before next winter, if he lived that long, he'd have to have someone make him furry thigh boots like Miletus wore, and some sort of tie-down fur-lined cap.

They flew south-south-west, toward the salient.

"I'll skirt the edges of the battleground," Miletus shouted. "No point in giving their damned catapults a shot at a virgin, now is there?"

The lines were clearly demarked – two long scraggly rows of huts, with most of the vegetation in front cleared, the woods around cleared for firewood and building materials. Between them was open, rutted land torn by marchers and horsemen.

They flew down the lines, turned, went back the way they came, turned back to base.

Miletus slid out of the saddle, tossed the reins to one of his handlers, said, "Well? What did you see?"

"Not much of anything," Hal said honestly. "Smoke from fires, a couple of horsemen back of the lines."

"That's all?"

"Yessir."

Miletus shook his head.

"And you're a combat veteran. Kailas, if you expect to be alive in a month, you'd better learn to sharpen your eyes.

"First, you missed a flight of three dragons, ours, but they could well have been Roche, moving east, just west of that little bend in the lines that's marked as the Hook.

"Second, there was a Roche dragon circling a position about a mile north of them.

"Then there was that stationary cloud over that ruined village."

Kailas looked perplexed.

"There was a wind blowing, maybe seven, eight miles an hour. Clouds don't hang about when there's wind, correct?"

"Nossir."

"That'd suggest, if we were a proper scouting patrol, to

take a look. Probably the cloud is magically cast, and there's most likely something underneath it the Roche would rather we not see.

"I'll send a couple of beasts up as soon as I finish with you.

"Then there was a column of cavalry, a company, perhaps more, riding toward the southern end of the salient, which would suggest someone's up to no good.

"Lastly, and you couldn't have known this, we passed over a scruffy little forest that was a nice open piece of land yesterday or the day before."

"Magic?"

"Probably not," Miletus said. "More likely camouflage nets. By the size of the area, I'd guess an encampment of a company, perhaps more, on the move.

"On patrol, it'd be your job to get lower and closer, and find out what sort of unit."

Hal had nothing to say.

"Your most important weapons are your eyeballs," Miletus said. "Keep looking, keep moving your head about. And don't forget to keep looking over your shoulder.

"The Roche love to creep up on you from the rear.

"When you can find one, buy a nice lady's scarf, the softest silk or lamb's wool you can find. That'll keep your neck from getting chafed.

"Pity there's no way to clamp a mirror somewhere on a beast's neck plate.

"Now you see what we face, and what you've got to learn.

"I'll sign you off for patrol – but only with an experienced flier, until he tells me you actually stand a chance of staying alive around here."

Chook was a large, jovial, nearly bald man, who claimed that his family owned the biggest – and, of course, the best – restaurant in Rozen, with a clientele of knights, dukes, even, once or twice, the king himself, "though he came in disguise, of course," plus a goodly contingent of the royal court's magicians.

No one knew if he was lying, but no one cared. Chook was not only a superb cook, but could almost always make something close to edible out of the iron rations they mostly lived on these days.

He prided himself on his "beef in the grand tradition of Chook," which consisted of the smashed dried beef they were issued, the iron-hard crackers, powdered milk, and assorted liquids and spices from the huge wooden cabinet that was always kept locked.

It was this cabinet that'd made him into a hero. When the Roche cavalry attacked, he'd stayed in his mess tent, until four cavalrymen dismounted and, sabers ready, came looking for some food or drink to loot.

Chook told them to get out.

They laughed, started toward him.

The first two were bowled over by one of the long wooden benches he threw at them. The third slashed at the cook, who ducked around the stroke and hurled him against the glowing stove.

The fourth turned to run, and Chook threw, with unerring aim, the cleaver he used to behead any looted chickens. It buried itself, with a dull chunk, in the back of the man's head.

Miletus heard the sounds of sobbing, ran into the tent, saw the fourth corpse, the third man's head stuck into the open oven door, charring nicely, and the other two with ghastly saber wounds in their chests from their own blades.

Chook sat at a bench, crying bitterly.

If few were stupid enough to criticize his cooking before, for fear he'd throw a pet and lose his brilliance, no one at all dared after the slaughter.

"So what should I be most scared of?" Hal asked Aimard Quesney.

He raised an eyebrow almost as groomed as his mustaches.

"Odd for anyone to be owning to fear," he replied. "I thought we were all fearless knights of the air, and so on and so forth and I was the only one who . . ." And he broke into song:.

> *"There's a dragon leaving the border*
> *Limping its way toward its home*
> *With a shit-scared flier a-clinging*
> *With a grip that'd bruise to the bone."*

He hiccuped, pushed the flagon of fairly decent wine at Hal, who shook his head.

"I'm on my first patrol tomorrow."

"Have a drink anyway," Aimard said. "Gods know I will." He swilled, ignoring his glass. "It's easier to die with a hangover. Besides, it gives you an excuse for drinking the next day."

The flight had a separate club/mess for the fliers, administered to by the legendary Chook. It was no more than a raggedy tent, with planed logs for benches, and a long bar their rather pathetic supply of alcohol sat behind. The canvas walls were pinned with cutouts from the broadsheets of Deraine and Sagene: sketches of beautiful ladies, pertinent letters, stories of society and such.

The best thing was that the mess was open around the clock, with either Chook or one of his assistants standing by.

"To be most afraid of," Quesney mused. "First, your own dragon, who'll be the most likely to kill you, chewing your leg off, or just dumping you off to see if you can walk on air like it can.

"Second, the weather closing in, and you getting lost in it, or blown into a mountain or forest.

"Third . . . leave third for a minute.

"Fourth, the Roche on the ground, with their catapults, crossbows and archers. If you're hit, try to steer your dragon as far away from the troops as you can, for they'll treat you most harshly should you fall into their hands.

"At least, try for some soldiers you haven't been spying on, and hope for their tender mercies.

"Fifth, our own soldiery, who'll be as quick to launch a bolt at you as the Roche. Perhaps, since we're losing, a bit more quickly.

"Sixth, our own command, who haven't the foggiest what a dragon's supposed to do, and so will punt us into the most unlikely places and situations.

"Now, to go back to third." Quesney paused.

"That, of course, is the enemy dragons."

"What will they do?" Hal asked.

"What they'll try to do is scare you away, back away from the lines and your scouting.

"If there's one in the vicinity, they might try to attack with one of their teams. That's if their dragons decide they want to attack you, which is very seldom.

"They'll try to tear you off your dragon, or tear at your dragon's wings and body, though that's rare enough. Generally they make great pains of themselves, and occasionally get lucky, and one of them'll be close enough to get in with that snaky head and have a bite of you."

"Has anybody thought of taking a magician up, and having him cast a spell against the Roche dragons?" Hal asked, thinking of some of the ideas in his notebook.

Quesney looked puzzled, shook his head.

"Doubt if you could find a wizard stupid enough to strap himself on the back of a dragon. And it'd take long enough to build a spell so that everyone concerned would be miles away by the time it swirls into life."

"What about an archer?"

"Never heard of such an idea. Can't imagine a bowman astute enough to be able to cling on, and aim while some nasty monster's hissing and snapping at him," Quesney said. "Why? Are you planning on starting a one-man war in the sky?"

Hal smiled, poured a glass of water.

"I don't like that idea," Quesney said. "Just flying's enough of a hazard.

"Start bringing in that kind of thing, and we'd be no better than those poor bastards down in the mud, now would we?"

Hal's stomach was roiling gently, but he had enough remove to think of laughing at himself. As a cavalryman, he'd led patrols into Roche territory a dozen, a hundred, who knew how many times?

But here he was, as his dragon climbed away from the flight's base, with Aimard Quesney to his left and, beyond him, Farren Mariah, on his first dragon patrol.

He determined he'd follow Miletus' suggestion, and kept his head moving, swiveling like his dragon's, who also seemed eager to spy something out.

The day was starting to warm, but there were huge thunderheads towering over the land. Quesney had said they were to fly east along the salient, toward where the lines had been before the Roche attack, until the weather broke, which it would, and then strike back for base.

Hal kept his reins loose, scanning the ground below. Nothing, for a long time, then movement. A column of infantry, heading away from the lines.

Hal jotted a note on the supposedly waterproof pad he had strapped to his knee.

Something moved at the corner of his eye, and he saw two dragons, not far distant, flying toward him.

They closed, and he saw, with relief, they were Deraine, passing no more than a hundred yards away, with a wave.

Hal's dragon, though, cared little about man's definitions, and hissed a loud challenge, which the evidently older and certainly wiser dragons ignored.

Smoke down below . . . He couldn't tell what it came from. But the plume was large enough to warrant a note.

The clouds were closing on them, and he kept glancing at Quesney, who seemed oblivious.

Far in the distance was a flight of three dragons. Quesney

slid a glass out of his boot-top, focused, then lifted a small trumpet, and blatted two notes.

One, Aimard had said, meant return to base. Two was enemy in sight, other toots had other meanings.

So there were the Roche, perhaps half a mile distant, no, more, Hal thought, allowing for the rain-rich air's magnification.

Quesney waved an arm, pointed down, and Hal pulled his reins right, tapped them on the dragon's neck, and the beast's head lowered, and the three dove away from the enemy, who showed no sign of having seen them.

They landed at their base, handlers running out to meet them, just as the rain began.

In the next three days, Hal made five more patrols, finally being trusted with a solo mission. The other novices were cleared for patrol, and enough dragons were assigned so the flight was at full strength, at least in the air, and everyone had a monster of her or his own.

On the ground, the formation was still woefully undermanned: at full strength, a flight should have about eighty men. The fliers were at the top of the pyramid, below them two stablehands for each monster, teamsters, cooks, clerks, blacksmiths, orderlies, leathersmiths, veterinarians, and so forth. Hal wondered why there weren't any magicians assigned, and Miletus laughed hollowly. "I'm sure, eventually, we'll get them. As soon as every infantry and cavalry regiment have them, plus all headquarters, supply people and any other unit who's been around for 150 years or so."

Then the storm closed in on them.

So far, no one had died, and Hal had come the closest to Roche monsters.

No one thought this would continue.

Hal was going through his notebook, staring gloomily out at the driving rain.

Saslic curled on the back of his cot. Quesney snored gently on his own cot, mustaches waving.

"Hey," Saslic said. "Aren't you bored?"

"No," Kailas said. "Thinking."

"I am. You want to go have a beer?"

"Not especially."

"You want to go for a walk in the rain?"

"Why?"

"Fresh air's good for you. What're you thinking about, anyway?"

"Oh . . . crossbows . . . magicians . . . if there's any better way of passing on information than those stupid little trumpets. Things like that."

"Hmmph," Saslic said. "You're bound and determined to grow up to be a dragonmaster, aren't you?"

Hal grinned. "I haven't heard that word used since . . . since before the war. I don't know if it applies."

"Maybe it should," Saslic said. "Maybe if this godsdamned war drags on much longer, it'll come back."

"Meaning what?"

"Considering the way you seem to be thinking, somebody who's figured out a way to kill Roche dragons."

"Dragons," Hal said. "Maybe. Or maybe their fliers. A dragon without a mount isn't all that dangerous."

"Why are men so bloody-minded?" Saslic asked thin air. Receiving no answer, she got to her feet.

"All right. Last offer. You want to go help me make up my bed?"

Hal lifted an eyebrow. Saslic giggled.

They pulled on their cloaks, and went out, into the storm.

Aimard Quesney opened one eye, grinned, then went back to snoring.

The weather broke for an hour, and Hal volunteered for a patrol. Miletus shook his head, muttered something about people too damned eager for a medal, and nobody else on the front would be in the air, but approved. Hal's dragon plodded through puddles, wings thrashing, then came clear of the ground.

By rights, Hal thought, a dragon base ought to be on a bluff somewhere, so the poor monsters didn't have to work that hard to get airborne. But in this sector there was little but rolling flatland for leagues around.

Hal circled the field, picking up height through scattered clouds, then turned his dragon toward the salient.

He was within a league of the lines when he snapped to full alert.

To his left, a flight of three Roche dragons. To his right, two more flights.

Something was very much afoot.

He could see no sign of any other Deraine beasts.

Ahead, he saw another three dragons climbing.

Hal thought quickly. Of course he couldn't proceed. But . . .

He had an idea, turned his dragon back the way he'd come, as if fleeing the watchful Roche, flew for the shelter of a cloud. Hidden, he dove for the ground, then banked back toward the salient. He flew no more than fifteen feet above the ground, his dragon's wings beating hard.

He climbed above trees, over abattis, tents, noted a Deraine flag near one pavilion, then was over broken ground.

Hal gigged his dragon for speed, and the beast's wings thrashed, like a ship's sails in a gale, and he was over the Roche positions, moving too fast for anything other than dimly heard shouts, and one arrow that missed by leagues.

A road junction was in front of him, and Hal's jaw dropped. The roads were packed with Roche troops, marching in close formation.

On another, parallel, rode columns of cavalry.

Below him, quartermaster wagons were being moved closer to the lines, unloaded for fresh supply dumps.

Their army was on the march.

He chanced overflying the junction, further into the salient, and every road, it seemed, had soldiers on the move.

The Roche must've used the break in fighting and the storm to rebuild their forces, and now were mounting an offense intended to end the deadlock, smash into open country, once and for all.

But no Deraine, evidently, had heard, seen or reported anything. No courier had come to the base with any reports of this . . .

Hal heard a screech, looked up and behind, saw a Roche flight, three huge monsters, diving on him. Their talons were reaching out for him, claws working in and out.

He jerked his dragon into a diving bank, turned back for his own lines, barely above spare treetops, his dragon flying as fast as its wings could beat.

Behind him, one dragon was closing fast, the other two hanging back, Hal's young beast having energy on the Roche brutes.

If there was some way of fighting back, Kailas thought, I'd let the bastard close, and try to take care of him.

But there was none, and the Roche flier was getting closer. His dragon was far bigger than Hal's, and he had a slight height advantage. Clearly his intent would be to savage Kailas as he overflew him, or else panic Hal's dragon into diving into the ground.

The two flashed over the lines, and Hal thought for an instant he was safe.

But the Roche must've known Hal had seen the troop movement, and must not be allowed to report.

The rain set in, drenching sheets, and Kailas hoped he could lose his pursuers in the gray dimness. But the Roche remained on his tail.

Long before they reached the base, Hal knew, at least that leading dragon would be on him.

There must be something . . .

Ahead, the ground rose to a stony hillside. Hal forced his dragon even lower, until the beast's talons were tearing across the scrub brush.

He looked back again, and the Roche flier was almost on him, having eyes only for his prey.

Hal forgot about him, saw two trees to his right, aimed his dragon at the gap between them, his monster screeching in unhappiness.

They shot through the gap, the dragon half-closing his wings, branches tearing, the dragon dipping, almost crashing, and Hal heard, behind him, an enormous crash.

The Roche flier hadn't been watching ahead, and his dragon had smashed into the trees, and pinwheeled, throwing its flier high into the air, arms flailing, trying to stay aloft, with no success.

The other two . . . The other two were far back, and Hal forgot about them, and went hard for his base.

The great hall of the half-ruined castle was silent, so quiet Hal could hear the patter of rain outside. Through a still-unshattered window, he could see couriers gallop in and out, wagons arrive, leave, marching men disappear out the gate.

It was the very model of an army headquarters.

There were seven men in the hall: Hal, Sir Lu Miletus, and three staff officers. Another wore a dark robe, breeches, and carried a magician's wand.

Standing behind a huge desk, easily dominating it, and the men around him, was the Third Army Commander, Duke Jaculus Gwithian. He was tall, perfectly white-haired, with a warrior's build. He wore dark brown, with a chain mail gorget. This far from the lines, it couldn't be for protection, more likely to remind everyone Duke Gwithian was a fighting leader. Complementing this was a low-slung leather belt, with a sheathed dagger with a jeweled handle.

His voice was a low, imposing rumble, full of certitude.

As far as Hal could tell, thus far on their first meeting, Duke Gwithian appeared to have less brains than a rabbit ensorcelled by a snake.

Frowning, he held a copy of Hal's report.

"I realize, Sir Lu," he said, "you place great trust in your . . . soldiers, which is a dictate of all commanders. However . . ."

Miletus waited, his face stone.

"What Duke Gwithian means, no doubt," one of the staff officers said, "is your man Kailas isn't the most experienced flier under your orders, isn't that correct?"

"I think any man who's flown that low, and seen what he saw doesn't need to have any more experience than a boarhound's pup to know what he's looking at," Miletus said, trying to keep his voice calm.

"Still," another staff officer added, "you must agree these circumstances are a bit . . . unusual. I mean, none of our wizards, none of our scouts, have reported such a move, and this young man sees . . . sees whatever he thinks he sees."

Hal, perhaps a year older than the staff officer, held his temper with difficulty.

"That is one worrisome point," Duke Gwithian agreed. "Certainly, I have the most powerful wizards, ones I cannot believe the Roche can flummox. Correct, Warleggan?"

The mage nodded frostily. He was slim to the point of emaciation, and his clean-shaven face appeared never to have smiled.

"I am hardly the one to agree with you, Duke Gwithian, not being given to vainglory. However, I do think that myself, and my more than competent aides, would certainly have detected signs, traces, of any spell the Roche thaumaturges could be working, and certainly a great spell such as this one would leave vast traces."

There was an uncomfortable silence, broken by Miletus.

"Sir Oubang," he said to the officer who hadn't spoken, "you specialize in analyzing the information from our scouts."

"I do."

"Has *nothing* been reported by our light cavalry?"

"Well, this is the one thing that troubles me slightly," the small, stout man said. "Actually, over the last two days, our scouting has been most minimal, due to a combination of circumstances.

"We've been shifting our light cavalry to the tip of the salient, expecting an eventual attack by the Roche. Other units have been relocated to the base of the salient, getting ready for . . . well, for an action of ours that should solve our current problems that I'm not at liberty to discuss the details of.

"So, contrary to what Sir Cotehele said, we really haven't had what I'd call a truly effective scouting screen out beyond the lines for over a week."

"Be that as it may," Cotehele said, a bit of anger in his voice, "I find it utterly impossible that no one, no one except this . . ." He didn't finish, but his look made it obvious what he thought of dragon fliers in particular, and Hal Kailas in particular. "This man, saw.

"There is, after all, such a thing as logic, is there not?"

"In war?" Miletus' voice dripped incredulity.

"Now, now, gentlemen," Duke Gwithian said soothingly. "Let's not let ourselves get worked up.

"This young man risked his life to make a report. I commend him for it. And we shall take this information under advisement, and assign the correct value to it.

"Sir Lu . . . and you, Serjeant Kallas, was it? I thank you for doing what you conceived as your duty.

"Be sure to avail yourselves of a good meal before you leave my headquarters.

"A meal . . ." And he looked at the two fliers' weather-worn garb. "And, if you feel there is time before returning to your – what is it, squadron? No, flight, that's it – making proper ablutions and drawing less shabby uniforms.

"Thank you."

Without waiting for the salute, Duke Gwithian walked out through a side door.

Hal was seething as he followed Miletus out of the hall.

"He didn't believe us, did he, sir?"

"Of course not," Miletus said. "He wouldn't've believed just you if you'd come back with a Roche prince's head on your dragon's headspike."

"So what are we going to do?"

"Eat his godsdamned meal – fast – and get our arses back to the flight," Miletus said grimly. "And get ready for the Roche attack."

12

Miletus gave his orders to the flight most cagily. He told them to be ready to move with an hour's notice, not saying which direction they might be moving. Of course most of the fliers, having heard Hal's report of the Roche on the move, assumed the worst.

Miletus made sure all the troops had their weaponry sharpened and ready for use, inspecting them in sections.

Nothing happened in the tag end of that day, and the weather stayed bad the next.

"Hard telling," Miletus said at nightfall, "whether the rain's been encouraged by Roche sorcerers or not. It keeps their movement cloaked, but it can't make their progress any easier.

"We'll go to half alert for the night. You fliers, you're exempt. It's not unlikely you'll be needed soon enough."

Hal woke well before dawn, hearing a sound like thunder, but somehow different, more like a series of great drumrolls. It came from the south, from the salient.

Faintly, he heard the sound of a wind roaring.

Few of the flight members needed awakening.

Chook and his assistants readied a hasty breakfast of

bacon, fried bread and tea, and Miletus ordered the men and women to the cooktent in shifts.

But nothing happened for a time, no one disturbed their isolated camp. The sun came up, blearily, through haze. No couriers with orders rode down the single road that led away from the front.

Miletus had the fliers standing by their dragons, ready for anything.

It was mid-morning when a pair of riders bulled through the brush past the pond and through the meadow. Their horses were slathered, panting, and the men were wild-eyed, and had thrown away their arms.

"They're attacking . . . they've broken through . . . magic . . . their damn wizards had an infernal spell . . . no warning . . . they're just behind us . . . ride for your lives!"

Miletus tried to stop them, but they galloped around him, and were gone.

He hesitated, then ordered the unit into motion. "There's but one road away from here, and we'll not be bottled up."

He looked at Hal.

"If I'm wrong, I hope you'll be a character witness at my court martial."

Before Kailas could answer, Miletus ordered all dragons into the air, scouting ahead of the flight's wagons and horses. He had his own beast chained to its wagon, and stayed on the ground with the soldiery.

Slowly, terribly slowly, the flight started moving. They were held back not only by the nearly ruined road, but by the herd of sheep being driven in the middle of the flight, the dragons' rations.

Hal saw a rider galloping hard toward the flight. The rider pulled up in front of Miletus, hands waving for a few moments. Then he wheeled his horse, and splashed back the way he'd come.

Miletus's trumpet blatted, and the fliers circled, landed in an open patch.

"The Roche have broken through our lines," Miletus said. "They're supposedly coming north, toward us. That rider ordered us to scout south, to try and evaluate the damage."

He looked to his non-flying adjutant.

"Eitner, take charge of the formation. Keep them moving as far as the main north-south road, then wait for us to return. If you're threatened, retreat north, and we'll find you somewhere."

"Sir."

"All dragons in the air! Scout separately, don't take any more risks than you must. Reassemble at that crossroads," Miletus ordered, then ran for the wagon with his dragon. His handlers were already unchaining the creature.

In ragged formation, spreading out as they flew, the dragons flapped south, climbing as they went.

First they came on the retreat – mounted men, riding hard for the north and safety. The roads were no better than cart-tracks, and were jammed with fleeing men. After the riders came wagons, then men on foot.

It was ugly. Soldiers weren't supposed to run like civilians. But the Third Army, and its attached units, were in full retreat.

Hal wondered what horror could have panicked an entire army, then saw it.

A thin greenish cloud was spreading slowly north, holding close to the ground, no more than fifty feet in the air.

Again he heard the rolling thunder, and the whistle of wind, even though none blew.

Something told Hal not to get close to the cloud.

He pulled his reins and the dragon climbed.

Hal looked down again, and saw, in the wake of the cloud, bodies of horses, men, oxen, lying motionless.

Behind the ghastly cloud came the Roche army. Flights of dragons, more than Hal could imagine, floated in front of the waves of cavalry, infantry behind them.

He'd seen enough, and turned his dragon back, over the

panic, to the road junction Miletus had designated as the assembly point.

Other dragons from his flight were making the same track.

Hal spotted the flight, drawn up near the crossroads, which was a roiling chaos of units, groups of soldiers, single men, all fighting to get on that road north, north to Frechin, Bedarisi, safety.

He landed, and found Eitner. With him were two couriers. He made his report as the other fliers streamed in, all with bad news.

Eitner also had some unpleasantries to pass along, learned from passing officers and one near-hysterical magician.

The Roche wizards had cast more than the great spell that'd masked their soldiers' movement to the lines. They had another spell, the one accompanied by the wind-whine and thunder. Eitner'd talked to men who'd paused in their flight long enough to tell him what it was like: suddenly the air had gone bad, not hard to breath, but as if all the goodness that gave life had gone out of it, even as it hazed into the ghastly green.

The green haze killed anyone and anything that lingered for more than a few minutes.

The fliers looked at each other, hoping she or he didn't look as frightened as the other.

"Be wonders if the spell'd work just on m'lice," Farren joked feebly, and no one bothered to respond.

"All right," Miletus ordered. "You, courier. Take the word back to your headquarters. You, stay with us. No. Get your ass out to the road, and grab anyone who's got a good mount and isn't completely crazy, and tell them they're drafted to carry messages for me.

"You fliers, get back in the air. Keep scouting the Roche progress."

"What about that cloud?"

"Just hope to hells our magicians come up with a counter-spell, and keep away from it.

"I'll stay with the flight down here," he said. "I don't have any orders, but we'll do no one any good fighting as a rear guard. We'll try to bash our way into this column, and move north.

"I'll have men paint arrows on the wagon tops so you'll be able to find us. Stay up no more than an hour at a time. Scout away from the roads for abandoned animals, for your dragons, and make sure they're watered.

"Rest them before you take off again, and reassemble before dark."

He stopped, realizing he was caught up by the panic a bit himself if he was telling the fliers what every stablehand knew.

"Get gone," he said.

They flew back and forth all that long day, giving the reports of disaster, of broken, wiped out, decimated units, and the seemingly unstoppable Roche offensive to Miletus, who scrounged riders here and there, gave them dispatches for army headquarters. They rode off, and no one ever knew if they obeyed orders, or just continued their flight.

The Deraine and Sagene forces lost their blind panic, but continued retreating, and the Roche army kept after them.

The sodden roads, further torn by the retreating soldiers, slowed them some.

There were rumors to fuel the flight – this attack was personally led by Duke Garcao Yasin, that Queen Norcia was with her retinue with his headquarters.

That may have frightened some, but Kailas remembered Yasin's failure once before. He wondered if Yasin's brother was on the battlefield with some dragons, vaguely wanted to find him. But without any weapons, other than the instinctual ones of his beast, any encounter was more likely to result in Hal's destruction than anything else.

Eventually the day ended, and Hal found the flight, hasty-camped near the road, still filled with soldiers tramping steadily toward Frechin.

*

The next day, they retreated through Frechin. By now, the city was almost deserted, most of its inhabitants having fled before the rumored horrors of the Roche cavalry and their dragons.

On the other side of the city, Hal, flying very high, high enough to feel a bit dizzy in the thin air, looked back and down, saw Roche dragons swarming in the air as their army continued its advance.

"I think," Aimard Quesney said, tugging at his mustache, "our Rochey friends have stepped upon their fundament."

"Right," Mariah said. "They're comin' on, we're haulin' ass. Surefire screw-up there."

Half of the fliers were crouched around a dying fire, too worked up, too tired, for sleep.

"Shut up, Farren," Saslic said. "Make me feel better, Aimard."

"Well, this probably won't make *you* – or any of the rest of us – feel better."

"I do love your abstract wisdom," Sir Loren said wryly.

"Any wisdom these days is better'n none," Mynta Gart said.

"Would you people shut up and let him explain," Hal said. "I, for one, could use anything cheery, whether it's about me or the King of Deraine."

"Thank you, Serjeant Kailas. The Roche have come a cropper, as I was saying," Quesney said. "Now, this offensive of theirs is intended to win the war, correct?"

"An' here I went an' thought it were just a spring fancy," Farren said.

"The best way to do serious damage would be to make for Fovant. Once Sagene's capital falls, what're the odds their Council of Barons wouldn't sue for peace, together or separately?"

"No kidding," Saslic said. "That's what we were told is why they invaded Sagene in the first place, which brought all us down here."

"Oh," Hal said. "Of course. I got it."

"There's one other great mind among us besides myself," Quesney said smugly. "You may finish my thought, Serjeant."

"If they began the battle, opening the salient," Hal said slowly, "then they *were* going for Fovant. But then, with this new attack, their warlord – Yasin, or whoever it is – has lost sight of what he started out to do, and is chasing us around the country, instead of heading east like he should."

"Precisely," Quesney said. "Perhaps he's lost his head with all the destruction . . . Or, more likely, his queen changed orders on him.

"In either event," he said, stretching and yawning, "we'll most likely get obliterated. But Roche just lost the chance to win the war."

He disappeared toward his bedroll.

"What a *cheerful* man he is," Mynta Gart said sarcastically. "He'll make my dreams this night ever so lovely."

"I'll make them worse," Sir Loren said. "The Roche have learned something we haven't. When this war started, it was wham, a battle, then people regrouped, reformed, looked around, and then wham, another battle.

"Now they're keeping up the offensive, never really letting up.

"We'd better learn to do the same, pretty damned quickly."

Now the Roche unleashed yet another weapon.

Small groups of Roche infantry suddenly materialized here and there in the rear. There were mutters of magic, then Hal saw two dragons, flying close together, with something hanging between them.

He remembered the Roche flying show, before the war, in Bedarisi, and their stunting with soldiers, riding in baskets strung between two dragons, then giving rides.

An idea came, and he flew back to the flight, in the middle of the ponderous retreat.

He landed, found Miletus, told him.

"*Damn,* but I wish I had more rank," Miletus said. "I'd grab some smithy unit, and set them to fabricating . . . But I don't, so I can't. But I'll send men back to that village we just passed through. That temple had iron gates on it, that should work. Our smiths can shape the metal this night, and we'll give your idea a try on the morrow."

By sunrise, all fifteen dragons were equipped. The wrought-iron gates had been cut into pieces, and each section bent into a hook. Three hooks were brazed together into a grapnel. Ropes were requisitioned from a retreating quartermaster unit, and harnesses improvised. Slings hung from each dragon's neck and hindquarters, the hook at their bottom, hanging about twenty feet below each beast.

The dragons didn't object too much to this latest weirdness from their masters, snorting and hissing no more angrily than usual in the dawn grayness.

Miletus gave the flight its orders, told them he'd give the word for takeoff when he sighted some of the Roche dragon-transports, and took off.

Vad Feccia came to Hal, said his dragon wasn't behaving properly, and perhaps he ought to stand down.

Hal told him to get back to his mount.

Asser looked at him with a wry face, quickly looked away.

They ate buttered bread and cheese, cut from a great wheel Chook had liberated, waited. An hour after sunrise, Miletus flew overhead, trumpet blasting.

They mounted their beasts, kicked them into a stumbling run, and were in the air, following Sir Lu back toward Frechin, hooks cradled behind them.

They'd only flown a few minutes when they sighted pairs of dragons, twenty of them, soldier-carrying baskets between them.

Hal forgot the others, tossed his grapnel overside and steered his dragon toward one pair. His monster honked protest for an instant, then screeched a challenge as his courage grew.

Hal closed fast on the pair. One beast was looking up at Hal, head whipping, the other was looking down, ready to flee. Their riders were shouting, kicking their mounts, and Hal steered his dragon just over their heads, going in the opposite direction.

His dragon jerked as the grapnel caught on one of the basket's support lines and tore it away.

The paired dragons banked away from each other, terrified, and the basket spilled soldiery, falling, flailing, to the ground 500 feet below.

Hal came back, tore at another dragon pair. These two held together, diving for the ground, and he let them go, climbing back for another target.

He ripped at a third, and this time his rope broke and he lost his grapnel as the Roche basket broke away from its dragons, and plummeted down.

Saslic's dragon, Nont, flashed past him, and he heard her yelling, face fierce in anger. Behind her came Sir Loren, his grapnel half awry, but still after the Roche beasts.

Hal forced his dragon up, reaching for height above the shattered Roche formation. He saw, in the distance, on-rushing dragons in threes, which could only be Roche.

He turned to meet them, hoping, without a grapnel, to give the others a chance to wreak further damage.

Then they were on him, shouting, dragons hissing, each trying to terrify the other, and the air was a swirling mass of monsters.

There was a dragon turning, just above him, its head darting. He leaned away, and it missed, tried to grab his mount's neck in its fangs, talons ripping at the air, reaching for Hal.

Hal had his dagger out, and thrust hard. It went home in the beast's eye, and it screamed deafeningly, rolled, dumping its rider, who fell, endlessly.

Then he was in empty sky, looked back, saw the Roche dragon-carriers and the other Roche monsters in the distance, no signs of his own flight.

Hal dove for the ground, found the main road, and followed it back to his flight.

There was jubilation – they'd finally found a way to strike back at the beasts.

"Now, let's find a way to kill the damned riders and leave the beasts alone," Saslic said. "They don't deserve what we're dealing out to them, any more than the poor damned horses deserve that green horror."

"I'm thinking about it," Hal said. "And I've got some ideas, if this war would slow down for a little and give me a chance to work them out."

There was one man separate from the others – Vad Feccia. He claimed his dragon was sick, unflyable. Hal noted that, put it aside for later.

There was one man missing – Asser. No one had seen him after they'd taken off that morning, and he was never seen again by the army. Hal didn't know if he'd been killed in the fight, or, more likely, if he'd flown north toward Paestum, toward safety as far as he could, then melted into the crowd and made it across the Straits to Deraine. He guessed he wasn't much as a hard man, for he sort of wished Asser luck.

Twice more that day Miletus sent them against the soldier-carriers. Once they tore a formation apart, the survivors flying back at full speed. The second time the dragon-carriers were escorted by thirty Roche dragons, and Hal's flight couldn't attack.

They were fighting back – but the retreat went on, to Bedarisi.

Bedarisi was an even bigger nightmare than Frechin, units on top of other units, soldiers looking for their fellows, others trying to avoid rejoining a fighting formation, bewildered civilians, officers without commands bawling orders, and always the walking wounded, staggering, looking for a chiurgeon or a wizard to treat them, forcing themselves to keep moving, afraid of what the Roche would do if they captured them.

Everyone was terrified the Roche would bring that greenish fog down once more, but it didn't materialize. Perhaps the Deraine sorcerers *had* found a counterspell.

It was bad enough that the Roche dragons were flying close to the city, and the suburbs were being harried by Roche light cavalry.

Hal remembered a ring road from before the war, led the unit around the city and found a place to set the flight up. Chook and his helpers went looking for a ration point or foodstuffs to buy or steal, and Miletus rode into the city center, looking for Third Army headquarters.

He came back in a few hours, looking very grim.

He'd not found Duke Gwithian's headquarters, but had encountered a lord who was somewhat in authority.

That nobleman had brayed that the army wouldn't need spies or fliers, but only men with swords, and for the flight to leave its dragons and work its way to the front lines forming before the city, and become infantrymen.

Ev Larnell was gray-faced, obviously sure he would never cheat the death he'd avoided.

"Damme," Farren said softly, "wot a waste of all that trainin'. Not to mention some pretty good folks as well."

13

"The Roche are expected to attack before dark," Miletus said. "Every man who can fight is to be on the lines."

He was about to continue when Rai Garadice gasped, and pointed. Everyone turned.

Smoke coiled above Bedarisi, and Hal thought for an instant the Roche killing fog was about to strike. But the smoke firmed, and became the huge figure of a man, armored, sword in hand, but helmetless.

Kailas recognized him. It was Duke Jaculus Gwithian, the Third Army Commander, the man who'd refused to admit the Roche were on the attack, standing more than 300 feet tall, noble, warlike, awe-striking.

He lifted his sword, pointed it south, and spoke, his voice a rumble that shook the ground, or so Hal thought.

"Soldiers of the king! I call on you in this most desperate hour. The enemy has driven us back, but from this hour, this minute, we shall retreat no more.

"I order you as soldiers, and also you of Sagene who fight alongside us. This shall be our finest hour.

"Here we will make our final stand. Not one man, not one woman shall fall back, shall flee.

"We call upon our courage, our gods, our heritage as free men and women to fight to the last man.

"This battle, shall Deraine and Sagene live on for an aeon, will be looked back by those who come after us with awe, and give inspiration for a thousand generations.

"Here we stood, moving back not one yard, not one inch, fighting for our king and, uh, our barons.

"Here we shall stand, like a rock against the tide, firm, to the last man.

"Here, in Bedarisi, a new legend is being born, a legend of—"

Suddenly the figure writhed, and changed, and became a rooster wearing armor, who crowed loudly.

Then the image changed once more, and was a Roche warrior, who looked down at Bedarisi, and began laughing, a grating, ominous laugh.

And then there was nothing.

"Dunno," Farren said skeptically, "what *that* was supposed t' do for my morale."

"That isn't important," Sir Loren said. "We've just got our marching orders . . . or, rather, our dying orders.

"We fight – and die – where we stand."

A few minutes later, they dimly heard the chortle of trumpets, and knew battle was closed.

"I suppose," Saslic said, rather weakly, "we'd best be going forward as Roche fodder."

"Or else runnin'," Farren said, pointing down at the road, where soldiers continued to trail past, "like those, who've gone an' decided they'll go for home and make those other gen'rations the image was talkin' about, to tell them about us."

"There's something we could try that might be a little better than a suicide stand with a sword," Hal said, surprising himself, for his ideas weren't quite formed.

"Anything's better than dying in the muck," Ev Larnell said.

"Agreed," Miletus said. "What do we need?"

"Fifteen brave men . . . or fifteen fools."

"Goin' beyont us fools?" Farren said.

"Sir, if you'll go with me out to the road," Hal said. "We'll go fishing."

"What am I for?" Miletus said, half smiling.

"To give me a little authority."

"After you . . . Serjeant."

It only took half an hour to find the prospective heroes.

There were thirty of them, crossbowmen, shambling along, beaten, with no officers at their head. But Hal, who'd let a group of archers and another of catapult men pass, since they were unarmed, noted that these thirty still had their bows in hand, and bolts in their quivers.

Men who're broken don't bother, generally, worrying about their arms.

"You men," Miletus called at Hal's nudge. "Form up over here."

A few lifted their heads, studied Miletus, looked back at the road.

"I said, over here!" Miletus shouted, and there was a hard snap to his voice.

The thirty came to a scuffling halt. The man at the head of the group was huge, mightily muscled with a gut to match.

"Who're you to order us . . . sir?"

"We need you," Hal said. "To fight. With us."

"Haw." The man spat. "We're done fightin'. Mebbe Paestum's worth fighting for, more likely Deraine, on our own ground.

"Not here, against dragons like you appear to be flying, and the Roche's damned magic, and Sagenies who won't stand up for themselves."

Hal ignored him, but unobtrusively took something from his belt pouch and held it in his fist.

"I need fifteen of you," he continued, "who aren't afraid to fly on – and fight from – the back of a dragon."

Utter silence, except for the shuffle of other soldiers moving steadily past. Then somebody catcalled, and somebody else laughed harshly. But Hal had seen a couple of men shed their fatigue, straighten, and look slightly interested. Very slightly interested.

"Fifteen men," Hal said again. "Who wouldn't mind taking down some Roche fliers."

The big man sneered.

"You want us to go up on them beasts, what, riding behind, and do what? I ain't had shit to do with dragons, but I'll wager they take more than one shitty little bolt to kill."

"I didn't say anything about dragons," Hal said. "We're going after their fliers."

A man, lean, with an intelligent look on his face stepped forward.

"Somebody just came up with this idea," he said. "Nobody ever thought about it before? You'd think *someone* would've tried it, and got himself killed. Or, more likely, some other people killed. Which might make you think this idea isn't all that great from the outset."

"This is the army, remember?" Hal said. "They barely admit to having dragons, let alone how to use them. And since when is any army quick with new ideas?"

That got a few smiles.

"Aw, sod off," the big man said. "I'm not about to get kilt followin' your foolishness, nor am I gonna let any of my friends get et up by monsters.

"Let's go, people. We're moving on."

"Stand where you are," Miletus said. "That's an order. You're still in the army!"

"Naw. Naw, I ain't. Call it uni . . . uni . . . whatever resignation."

"I gave you an order, man."

"And I told you to sod off," the big man said. "If you're hard of hearing, try this."

He started to pull the long sword at his side from its sheath. Hal stepped forward, and snapped a punch into the man's stomach.

The man's sour breath gushed out, and he stumbled forward and threw up. He fought for air, couldn't find it, and fell on his knees, then, moaning, on his face in the dust.

"Toss him on that bank," Hal ordered, picking up the sword, and putting his hand back into his pouch for an instant. "You, and you. I'll not trust a man like him at my back, on a dragon or in a brawl."

He indicated two men, who'd been fingering their crossbows.

"Now, fifteen of you," he went on. "Volunteers. We'll do it the army way. You men there . . . and you four . . . and you two. You just volunteered. The rest of you little boys can keep right on running."

He turned his back, and started back toward the flight. After a dozen yards, he looked back. A bit to his astonishment the fifteen, plus another three, were straggling at his heels.

Hal looked at Miletus beside him, and grinned.

"Not bad, Serjeant," Miletus said. "You're not a bad leader . . . or fighter, either. One punch! That was one enormous bruiser."

"It doesn't hurt," Hal said, "to have a bit of an equalizer." He reached in his pouch again, showed Miletus the paper-wrapped roll of coins that'd been hidden in his fist.

"You ever flown before?" Hal asked the intelligent-looking man.

"No, Serjeant," the man said, looking around curiously from his perch behind the dragon's shoulders on a hastily-improvised saddle. Other crossbowmen were being helped to mount as well. "Thought about going for a ride a couple of times, before the war, when a show'd come to our district. But either I didn't have the coin, or the courage, or enough drink, or, once, the head of the school I was teaching at heard I was thinking about it, and forbade it.

"Said that wouldn't be a good example for my students."

He looked at his ragged uniform, sword-belt, and crossbow across his knees.

"As if this is."

"The name's Kailas. Or Hal. Forget the serjeant. You?"

"Hachir."

"That's a good upcountry name."

Hachir grinned.

"Here's what we're intending," Hal said, although he'd already lectured the drafted crossbowmen, as he hoped each flier was doing to his assigned soldier. "First, you *can't* fall."

The man fingered the ropes that held him securely in place, nodded.

"Keep hold of your bolts, though. Without them, you might as well be riding for joy. Now, have you the strength to recock your bow after each shot?"

"I do," Hachir said. "Assuming I can get a foot in the stirrup, and I'm not being thrown about."

"Good." Hal made a mental note for something to try at another time.

"What we're going to do is simple," Hal said, sounding very confident. He'd learned that with his serjeant's stripes, remembering the number of times his patrol had been utterly lost, yet he'd reassured his fellow riders that they were in exactly the place they were supposed to be.

"I'm going to find some Roche dragons. I'll get as close as I can, and you take a shot. Try and hit the rider in the body. About the only place that'd be vulnerable on a dragon with your crossbow would be under the wing, right where it joins the body, or between the bellyplates, and that'd take, I think, a very sure aim."

"I'm not a bad shot," Hachir said, without boasting. "But I'll aim as you say."

He looked about him once more.

"The woman I'm affianced to will never believe this, and most likely whip me like a dog for making even more of a fool of myself than I did joining up."

Hal laughed, climbed up into his seat, and picked up the dragon's reins.

"Let's go see if we can change the way the war's going, just a little."

Miletus motioned Hal to take the formation lead as they circled over their wagons below. "Since you seem to have all the ideas today," he shouted when their two dragons came close.

Hal waved acknowledgement, shouted back to Hachir, "We'll try to get on top of the Roche before we attack them. Maybe that'll give us surprise."

The crossbowman grunted. Hal glanced back, afraid the man was getting sick, saw he was staring about him, wide-eyed, entranced, reminding Kailas of his first flight with Athelny.

He hoped that was a sign everything would be all right.

Just south of Bedarisi was a throng of dragons, too many to be from Deraine or Sagene. They paid little attention to the tiny formation of dragons a few miles distant, especially as the Deraine monsters appeared to have no interest except possibly flying into the sun.

The Roche dragons were intent on the battle being waged below, lines of infantry crashing together down blocked streets and through ruined buildings, and, to the east, the twisting mêlée of a cavalry fight.

Hal and his flight were a thousand feet above the Roche.

Hal signaled, pulled reins, and his dragon began a long, slanting dive toward the enemy. Behind him streamed the others. This time, even Vad Feccia hadn't backed out.

"Get ready," Hal said, and felt Hachir stir about behind him.

He bent over his dragon.

"That one, that one," he said in a croon, stroking the

monster's neck, pulling the reins with his other hand until the dragon was looking at a beast circling at the edge of the Roche formation.

The creature seemed to understand what Hal intended, wings clattering as it turned, flying faster, closing on the Roche.

The rider saw Hal's onrushing dragon, and his eyes widened.

"Shoot!" Hal called, and the crossbow thwacked. The bolt went just wide of the rider, ricocheting off the dragon's carapace.

"Shit!" Hachir shouted.

"Forget it! Try again!" Hal shouted, pulling the reins, finding another target, closing, wondering if his idea was that great.

"Now!" he shouted, wishing he had the crossbow in his own hands.

Once more, the bow fired, and this time the bolt buried itself in the rider's back. Hal heard him scream, saw him contort, fling himself backward, off the dragon.

"Again," Hal shouted, feeling a fierce grin across his face, and there was a dragon above them, its rider peering down. The crossbow fired, and the man clawed at his throat, collapsed across his mount's neck.

Hal saw a shadow, and reflexively snapped his reins, and his dragon dove, just as an enormous brute whipped past, talons clawing at Hal's dragon's wing.

"Godsdammit!" Hachir shouted, but Hal paid no mind, yanking his dragon into a tight, climbing turn.

"At his guts!"

Hachir pulled the trigger, and his bolt thunked home in the Roche dragon's side. The monster screamed, impossibly loudly, whipped on its back, talons clawing at the wound. Hal saw the rider hanging by his reins below the dragon's head, then the man lost his hold, and fell.

Hal forgot him, and looked for another dragon rider to kill.

He saw Ev Larnell's dragon, pursued by two Roche beasts. He slapped his dragon's reins, trying to go to the rescue, but his dragon was closing slowly, too slowly.

A Roche dragon had a bit of height on Larnell, tucked its wings, and dove. Hal thought it would ram Larnell, but it passed just above him.

A talon reached out, almost casually, took Larnell's head in its grasp, and tore it off.

Larnell's corpse sprayed blood like a fountain, and his dragon squealed in fear, dove away. The crossbowman behind him sat petrified, making no move to reach for the reins, and then the dragon was gone, far below.

There was nothing around Kailas but his fellows.

The Roche dragons were fleeing south, in a ragged mess.

Hal took his flight down, across the battleground, saw, on a knoll, the colors of Deraine and a handful of dismounted knights fighting desperately around the rallying point. Roche soldiers swarmed about the knoll.

There was nothing Hal could do except go back to the flight, get more bolts, and look for more dragons.

He couldn't tell what was happening on the ground below, who might be winning.

Hal looked for that knoll when he was airborne once more, couldn't be sure he found the right one, since there was nothing but high-piled bodies.

At dusk, he landed, dazed with fatigue, mourning Larnell, wondering if he'd still be alive if Hal had exposed him on that long ago day.

But the fliers had learned their lesson about how to mourn their dead.

Chook had found a flagon of brandy, and they, and their crossbowmen, toasted Larnell's memory.

And then they forgot him.

Hal and Hachir had killed five dragons or their riders that day.

The flight had taken out sixteen Roche beasts. Saslic had

taken out three, as had Sir Loren. Rai Garadice had accounted for two.

By their last flight, no Roche dragons were in the air.

But that mattered little, at least at the moment. He asked of the battle, the real battle, down on the ground.

Deraine had held the Roche, driven them back slightly.

Duke Jaculus Gwithian, and his staff, were among the knights who stood their ground to the last man, neither asking nor giving quarter.

He may have been a dumb bastard, Hal thought. But he was surely a brave dumb bastard.

Aimard Quesney was sitting near the dragon lines, away from the others that night. Hal brought him a plate of food. He took it, set it down untasted.

"And so you've got what you wanted," Quesney said. His voice was flat, not pleased, not angry. "You've got your war and your killing.

"Be proud, Kailas. Be very proud. We've bloodied the land and the water, and now you're the first to take it to the skies."

Without waiting for a response, he walked away, into the darkness.

They were in the air at dawn the next day. Again, Miletus, even though he commanded the flight, let Hal control the fighting.

It didn't matter to Kailas – the situation was so desperate nothing mattered except killing Roche.

Again, the battle on the ground was mounted, and again Deraine held.

On the next morning, before the two sides could stumble together and hew away in exhaustion, they heard trumpets from the south and east.

This time the flight's mission was its original – to scout the land.

To the east, they found, proud in its finery, freshness and armor, a massed Sagene army. They barely had time to report the miracle before the Sagene smashed into the unprotected Roche flank.

They were the army that'd been assembled to defend Sagene's capital of Fovant, and the Roche attack on the Deraine soldiers had given them time to march east, and strike where they weren't expected.

The Roche fell back, across the wasteland their soldiers and green mist had created. But they didn't break, as the Deraine soldiers had, but fought stubbornly from hilltop to ravine to draw, killing one Deraine here, half a dozen Sagene there.

But they were pushed all the way back through that bloody summer, back across the border, and several miles into Roche territory.

Deraine and Sagene disengaged, numbly prepared fighting positions, and then collapsed in total exhaustion.

No one knew how many men died in the brutal series of battles. Some said half a million, others said a million, others even more.

"Serjeant Kailas," Miletus said. Hal was helping his hands groom his dragon. Hachir, still with the flight as were the other thirteen crossbowmen, was also helping.

"Sir?"

"I've got orders for you."

Hal waited.

"Since the crisis appears over, you, and six others – Dinapur, Feccia, Garadice, Gart, Mariah, Sir Loren, are reassigned."

"Where?"

"Back where you were supposed to have gone in the first place. The First Army," Miletus said. "Around Paestum."

That was what Hal had wanted, but he was just too tired to celebrate.

"I'll be sorry to leave you, sir," he said, telling the truth.

"Don't be," Miletus said. "Those bastards across the line're too tired to do anything for awhile. Things will be nice and quiet in these parts, and we can recover and maybe think about getting drunk and laid.

"Up north, where you're going, things are just starting to get interesting.

"I've sent dispatches to whatever Lord High Plunk will take over the Third Army about what you did . . . about your ideas.

"And I'm giving you a sealed dispatch, for your new Commander at the First Army, with the same details. Maybe he'll give you a medal, or make you a knight, or even give you a free drunk in Paestum.

"As for leaving us . . . we'll run into each other again, down the road.

"If we live.

"It's looking to be a *very* long war."

14

Again, Paestum had changed, becoming more and more a smooth-running machine to process troops toward the front and, as a byprocess, to relieve them of as much money as possible.

Hal was the ranking warrant of the seven fliers, still with the rank he'd had with the light cavalry. He'd wondered a time or two why no dragon flier ever seemed to get promoted. But he'd learned that if the army had a reason for doing what it did, it seldom chose to share its wisdom with the lower ranks.

Hal's orders read for the seven to report to the Eleventh Dragon Flight. He asked a provost, got instructions to its camp, two leagues west of the city.

All of them were heavy-pursed – there hadn't been much to buy during the retreat and battles. But none seemed in the mood for revel, still tired from the fighting, and Hal didn't think his new commander would be entranced if a warrant decided to stop the war so his charges could get seduced and drunk.

He was very right.

The Eleventh Flight had commandeered a sprawling farm, almost a manor. Most of the buildings were cheery red brick, and the grounds were neat if overgrown, although the land had been fought through during the siege of Paestum, and there were still shattered remnants of outbuildings here and there.

It looked very peaceful in the summer sun.

Hal smiled when he heard the screech of a dragon from behind the manor house, answered by one of their dragons on the wagons.

But his smile vanished, seeing a formation of soldiers marching back and forth to the chant of an iron-lunged warrant.

"Drill," Farren said as he might have mentioned slow torture. "Drill, here?"

"Maybe," Saslic said, from her seat behind the wagon's driver, "maybe those are guards for the flight."

"Maybe," Farren said. "Or, more likely, we've fallen into the clutches of a martynet, who thinks the war's to be won by square-bashint."

Captain Sir Fot Dewlish dabbed delicately at his nose with a handkerchief that, Hal decided, was probably starched and ironed.

Sir Fot was a very dapper officer. His uniform had clearly been tailored, and equally clearly had never seen a muddy battlefield, any more than Sir Fot had.

He sat, very calm, very much at ease, at a desk that wasn't sullied with paper. Dewlish was about to say something when a clock gonged.

Both men turned to look at it. The clock was a bronze monstrosity of a dragon, holding a world in one claw, a clock in the other. It had been carefully painted in exact colors.

"That's our mascot," Dewlish explained. "The lower ranks quite revere him, and call him Bion."

Hal made a vaguely understanding noise. He rather wished

there was a dragon on Dewlish's chest, indicating he was also a flier, instead of on the mantel.

"To continue," Dewlish said. "I cannot say, to be truthful, I'm much impressed by your, or your fellows', appearance. I've always heard that some of the dragon flights permit their fliers to go around looking scruffy, and now believe it."

"There weren't a lot of tailors where we were, sir."

"Do not be impertinent!" Dewlish snapped. "Now, or ever."

"Sorry, sir."

"I'll make arrangements for you to go into Paestum, in turn, and visit my tailor. He's quite good, and fairly economical. I assume that your lot has some money?"

"Yes, sir."

"Good. Now, first let me acquaint you with the way I run this flight. I believe a good soldier keeps himself, or herself, quite smart." He frowned, as if not liking the idea of women being assigned to his flight, but said nothing.

"There is no room for slackers, Serjeant Kailas. Not here, at any rate.

"I believe that was the reason my late predecessor in charge of this flight suffered such terrible casualties."

Hal didn't reply.

"Fortunately, I understand you have had the benefit of being schooled, at least in your first days in dragon school – dreadful name, that – by an old friend of mine, a fellow heavy cavalryman, Sir Pers Spense."

"Uh . . . yessir. We were, sir."

"A pity how he ran afoul of these new thinkers in the army. Now he's over here, responsible for dealing with the recruits that arrive, before they're assigned to their new units.

"He tells me their discipline is shocking, most shocking, and he, and a loyal coterie, are doing their utmost to make them into proper soldiers of the king.

"Poor fellow. He wants, more than anything, to be reassigned to a proper station, perhaps in charge of one of the schools of heavy cavalry.

"But, like all of us, he soldiers on, without complaining."

Dewlish smiled at Hal, and Kailas guessed he was supposed to have some sort of response. He smiled back, more a twitch than anything else, in return.

"Now, Serjeant, I'll acquaint you with my manner of soldiering. I'll be wanting to address the new men, and, er, women, before evening meal. But you can give them the gist of my feelings, and, since it's still morning, help them to begin shaking things out, as I believe you fliers call it, informally.

"I believe, as I said, in running things firmly. All fliers will be neatly dressed at all times, including when flying. I especially despise those disreputable sheepskins you wear."

Hal was grateful it was still summer, hoped that Dewlish would trip over his spurs or a dragon before winter came.

"We assemble before dawn, for calisthenics, and a run, for I believe a sound body breeds sound fighters. Then three flights, of two dragons each, go out on morning patrol, to scout the assigned tasks from army headquarters that we receive during the night.

"Then the fliers return for noon meal and, after, drill, which shall be mounted, once I manage to obtain horses. Then the afternoon flight goes up, on its assigned tasks. Sometimes there will be an evening flight as well, returning just at dusk.

"Are there any questions?"

"Sir, won't the Roche figure out that we're passing over their lines at a certain time, and arrange their affairs to allow for that?"

Dewlish snorted.

"I do not believe those barbarians are capable of that kind of analysis. In any event, those are my orders, and, consequently, that is the way this flight will be run.

"I'm aware," he said, reaching into a desk drawer and taking out a rather thick envelope, "that your former commander allowed a great deal of independence.

"I received an interesting letter from him, suggesting that

certain extraordinarily irregular changes you tried recently might be implemented in my command.

"First, the existing King's Regulations give us quite enough to do as it is.

"But second, and more important, just as I do not tell any officer how to run his command, so I brook no interference from others!"

He ostentatiously tossed Miletus' letter into a red leather wastebasket.

"As for certain other recommendations he made about you . . . well, I think a soldier must prove himself in person before any awards or such can be considered.

"That, I think, is all, Serjeant. My orderly officer will show you your quarters, which of course are rigidly segregated as to the sexes, which is only natural, and the stables for your beasts. The rank and file you brought with you will be integrated into the flight, which should speed up their learning my way of doing things, and your wagons will become part of my establishment.

"Oh yes. One other thing. I believe in a proper reward at the proper time for a man who has distinguished himself. And, on the other hand, I punish offenders uniformly, and with a very severe hand.

"That is all, Serjeant."

Hal stood, saluted smartly, and marched out, wondering what Farren Mariah would say when he found out about the new wind blowing changes.

Mariah offered four absolutely horrifying and anatomically impossible obscenities.

"Worst, the bastid ain't flyin', so that means he's prob'ly immortal," he mourned.

"We could always arrange an accident," Saslic said.

"Careful," Sir Loren warned. "This Dewlish doesn't impress me as someone who can take a joke like that."

"Who was joking?" Saslic said.

"One other thing," Hal said. "Dewlish isn't one for holding hands in the moonlight."

"So what?" Saslic said. "I wasn't considering holding his paw."

"For him . . . or for anybody else."

Saslic used two sentences, and Farren's eyes widened in admiration.

"That eunuch," she added. "I suppose we can't drink, either."

"I already checked," Rai Garadice gloomed. "Fliers are permitted two drinks daily, which are served before dinner in the main mess."

"I was wrong," Saslic decided. "He's not a eunuch, he's a godsdamned Roche secret agent, determined to ruin our morale."

Following a daily briefing, the fliers went out, morning and afternoon, over Paestum, to the Roche positions on the coast, south for a time, then home.

The First Army's orders were always the same: "Scout the Roche lines east of Paestum, and to their rear for any signs of troop build-up."

Of course, since clocks could be set by the time the dragons overflew the lines, there was seldom anything to be seen, other than cavalry skirmishing, or an occasional infantry patrol in contact with the enemy.

Once Hal saw movement, extensive movement, in a forest just inland, and asked permission of Dewlish to take another patrol back over the area at once, to catch whoever was moving about down there by surprise.

Permission, of course, was refused – Dewlish said if it was anything of significance, it would be reported by the afternoon flight.

Nothing was seen.

"What the hell are we going to do about him?" Hal snarled.

"You keep telling me I can't arrange an accident," Saslic complained.

"Even if I did, who would you go to?"

"Probably take care of matters myself," Saslic said. "Buy some poison next time I'm in Paestum. Lord knows if Dewlish ever fell over dead, there'd be no end of suspects.

"The fliers all want him skinned alive, and the rest of the flight think that's too easy a fate."

"Rest easy, children," Sir Loren said. "Concentrate on practicing your flying and getting ready for the next time our peerless leaders decide it's time to go out and get killed.

"Besides, nothing lasts forever. Not even Sir Fot Dewlish."

"You c'n afford to be, what do they call it, c'mplacent," Mariah said. "You're ahead of him in the Royal List, so he gives you little agony."

"True," Sir Loren said, grinning. "And you lesser beings can work out your own fate."

"Can I push him in the pond?" Farren asked Hal.

"With my blessing," Hal said.

"Now, now. Us high-ranking knights deserve a little respect," Sir Loren said.

"And that's what you're getting," Hal said. "Very damned little respect."

Frustrated, Hal took to doing just as Sir Loren suggested – flying his dragon either morning or afternoon around the base area if he wasn't scheduled for a patrol, and doing acrobatics in the sky.

Thinking about the crossbowmen they'd used over Bedarisi, Hal started teaching his dragon to respond to shouts and pressure from his thighs. That would leave his hands free for other actions, which he was still devising. One thing he'd vaguely noted back then, through the haze of exhaustion, was that his dragon flew more slowly, couldn't climb as fast, with Hachir behind him.

His dragon, still nameless, seemed to like curveting about,

either high above the farm, or else flying very low, very fast along the country roads, hopefully terrifying any travelers and, sometimes, sending a wagon careening into a ditch.

The first time it happened, Hal expected the farmer who'd emerged dripping from the green water to complain to Dewlish, but nothing happened.

One of the stablemen said the locals were all terrified of the dragon fliers, swearing they'd made pacts with demons for their powers, and wanting nothing to do with any of them.

"Which's a great laugh f'r us, 'cept when we figger ain't none of us getting' laid by th' local lassies. Though," he said and looked sly, "I've hopes for th' future, puttin' the word about one of th' gifts th' demons give us is double-length dicks."

On the way back from a patrol, Hal landed near an infantry base, and traded some of the wine he'd bought in Paestum for a crossbow and a selection of bolts.

He set up targets at various ranges, and began mastering the weapon. He rated himself a fair shot with a conventional bow, learned when he was with the cavalry, and had little trouble adjusting to the more modern weapon.

But firing at motionless bales of straw on the ground did little to teach him how to hit a moving target in the air. He found a Roche banner, and a length of rope, and convinced Saslic to tow the line behind her dragon, Nont, and let him shoot at the banner.

The first time out, he almost shot Nont in the tail. Saslic had words with him when they landed, made him vow that if he was going to miss, miss to the rear, not forward.

"One more like that – especially if it happens to tweak me – and it'll be a long, long time before this playground'll be open for you," she said.

Two problems were immediately obvious – he wasn't good enough to always hit the banner on the first shot, and reloading the crossbow, while rocking in the saddle, was a good way to suddenly start practicing air-walking; and his bolts were unretrievable.

The crossbowmen he'd traded for the first weapon became his very, very good, if a bit alcoholic, friends, since he had to stop almost every day for new bolts.

Since his stops meant the other dragon in his patrol had to fly about for a time, he was afraid Dewlish would find out his extracurricular pastime, and forbid it, like he arbitrarily had forbidden the fliers associating with their stablehands when not on duty, keeping alcohol in their quarters, and ever appearing out of uniform.

He thought of acquiring more crossbows, but the thought of going flying with a stack of weaponry clattering about behind him, possibly hung on hooks drilled in the dragon's plating made him laugh, wryly.

"How strong're you?" Farren asked without preamble.

"Strong enough, I suppose," Hal said.

"Look 'ere," Farren said, taking a roll of paper from under his arm. "I remember, back as a lad, seein' a toy like this, use't to shoot at the poor larks flyin' about. I took the toy away from the little savage what wielded it, and warmed his butt with the thing.

"It looked sorta like this."

The sketch was of a crossbow. But conventional crossbows had nothing but a length of wood from the butt to the foot stirrup, with perhaps a guard around the trigger. This had a curved grip just behind the trigger, and a second grip in front of it.

"Now, you can't see too good f'rm my sketch, but the fore handle kinda slides, don't remember how, but it's got fingers, up here, t' grab the string and cock the bow.

"Now, this, over here, on the side's a box, wi' I guess some kinda spring inside, for it held bolts. You sorta clamped it on the bow, and worked this fore handle back, cockin' the piece, an' a bolt drops down, and the wretch pointed it an' shot.

"On'y problem is it'd be kinda light for killin' people 'stead of larks.

"Anything innit?"

Hal studied the sketch.

"Maybe. I don't know. I think I need to talk to somebody who knows more about weaponry than I do."

That day, the flight took its first casualty since Hal and the others had joined it.

The afternoon patrol was swarmed by ten Roche dragons, just before it was supposed to turn north. One of the Roche monsters had an archer sitting behind. No one knew if the lost flier – one of Dewlish's – had been hit by an arrow, or ripped from his mount by a dragon.

The dragon came home, bare-saddled, blood drenched down its sides.

Hal waited for Dewlish to react, to change the patrol order, possibly even to investigate Hal's idea of crossbowmen, but, other than a mawkish funeral speech, the commander did nothing.

The sign over the small backstreet house featured an ornately carved dagger, with lettering under it:

Joh Kious
Fine steel
By Appointment
To the Royal Household

Hal entered, and was dazzled. He had never dreamed of, let alone seen, so many different tools of destruction.

There were swords, daggers, maces, morningstars, javelins, short and long spears, arrows of various wickednesses.

Between them were bits of armor, a few ceremonial, most grimly practical. From the rear came the cheerful sound of hammers beating against steel.

The man behind the counter was slender, in his fifties, placid-looking, with an easy smile.

"Uh . . . Sir Kious?"

"There's no sir to it, my friend. Merchants tend not to get much from their supposed betters, except their gold."

Kious had a bit of a sharp tongue, though his accent was soft and country.

"How may I be of service? I've just recently opened this branch across the water to help in our efforts against the Roche."

Hal produced Farren's sketch, explained it, asked if Kious could build one, suitable for combat use. Kious thought a moment, noted the dragon emblem on Kailas' chest.

"Might I ask you to do something, sir?" Kious asked. "Try to pull my arm down straight when I hold it up like this."

Hal obeyed. Kious might have been slender, but was surprisingly strong. Hal put some of his war muscle into it, and succeeded.

"Well," Kious said. "I've built some crossbows, though not for years, and certainly not of this type. I assume you want an adequate poundage, which is why I tested your strength.

"Are you planning on using this in the air?"

"I am." Hal explained his intent.

"That somewhat increases the problem," Kious said and went on in a scholarly fashion. "You would want, oh, about 150 pounds draw weight to be sure of dropping your man. But sitting down, cocking a 150-pound bow, especially more than once, with this rather ingenious arrow-box . . . that could be a strain.

"But if we decrease the poundage of the prod – that's the

bow itself – and increase the draw length – possibly use compound stringing – that will give us the arrow speed we want.

"Hmm. Hmm. Hmm. An interesting project. I'll require a deposit of . . . oh, twenty-five gold coins, sir. The total cost will be . . . oh, seventy-five gold, and that will include a goodly supply of arrows. I notice your wince, sir, and must tell you, I would charge at least double, more likely triple, were you a civilian wanting this for sport.

"And I assume you want it to be ready yesterday, as do the other warriors who've come to me."

Hal grinned.

"Of course I do," he said. "If I'd wanted it tomorrow, I would've come to you tomorrow."

Kious smiled, a bit painfully.

"At least a month, sir. And that will be setting aside some ceremonial daggers I'm quite entranced by, and am already late on.

"But gore takes precedence.

"So if you'll step into the back, sir, we can take appropriate measurements for the bow length and such."

Dewlish summoned him to his office a day later. Hal barely noticed the other man present, other than he was older, slim, white haired with a bristling white mustache, since the CO was purse-lipped, red-faced.

Hal wondered what he'd done wrong this time.

"This man is here to see you," Dewlish said. "I expect you to handle yourself in a soldierly manner.

"That is all."

Hal blinked as Dewlish stormed out the back door of the office.

The other man got up, held out an open palm. Hal, completely bewildered, touched it.

"I'm Thom Lowess," he said. "I'd suppose your commander doesn't like taletellers."

"I, uh . . . I don't know, sir." A taleteller? For him? Hal had no idea what this was all about, but a thought came that Dewlish might like taletellers very well – if they were interested in glorifying him.

"Perhaps we could find a more, um, congenial place to talk?" Lowess said, picking up a slender leather case.

Hal checked the dragon clock.

"The fliers' mess is open. We could go there."

"Good. It's always good to lubricate someone before you tell them what you want."

Lowess tasted the glass of wine set in front of him, nodded approval as Hal sipped beer.

"Very good. This is a thirsty business I'm in," he said, opening his case and taking out a notepad and pen. "I'm sure you're aware of my trade, and hope you don't, like too many soldiers, spit at its mention."

"Not at all, sir," Hal said. "Matter of fact, at one time I thought of becoming a teller. But I really don't have the gift."

"Things have changed since the war," Lowess said. "Some of us still work the villages, telling our stories. But others have been commissioned by the Royal Historian, to visit the armies, and bring back stories for the others to spread abroad in their wanderings. It's our bit for the war . . . and, of course, for recruiting.

"By the way, it's Thom, not sir."

Hal nodded, waited for an explanation.

"I've made it my specialty to interview heroes," Lowess went on.

"I beg your pardon?"

"Please don't be modest, Serjeant . . . Hal, if I may?"

"You may, but I'm still lost."

"Actually," Lowess said, "I'm the one who's lost. I've heard of your exploits in the south, yet I see no medals on your chest. Are you very modest?"

"Medals, sir?"

"I would think," Lowess said dryly, "that a man who's

destroyed ten Roche dragons should have some sort of awards, should he not?"

"I've been given nothing," Hal said. "Nor asked for anything, to be honest. And I've only taken out five dragons – no, six, counting that poor transport brute.

"And I didn't destroy them, actually, but just flew close on the five, so a crossbowman, a soldier named Hachir, could take care of them . . . or their riders."

"Very interesting . . . and still very modest," Lowess said. "I'd like the full story, if you don't mind."

"It'll sound like bragging."

"No, it won't," Lowess said firmly. "If it makes you feel any easier, I have the courtesy rank of captain, which is why your Sir Fot wasn't able to run me off, and can give you an order to tell all, if that would make it easier.

"Or I could merely buy you another beer.

"By the way, there's little use in evading me. I understand there are others in this flight who were with you on that detached duty with the Third Army, and I'll be talking to them before I take my leave."

Hal took a deep breath.

"I don't have any choice, do I?"

"You don't," Lowess said. "Now, you might begin with your first encounter with a dragon."

"It was when I was a kid," Kailas said slowly. "Back in this little mountain village I grew up in . . ."

Lowess stayed for two days, to Dewlish's mounting fury.

Then he left, and matters returned to normal, if the exaggerated awe his six friends paid him at every opportunity, calling him Horrible Hal the Hydra Hobbler, counted as normal.

At least they didn't do it in front of witnesses.

Two weeks later, the entire flight was assembled before evening meal.

Sir Fot Dewlish paced in front of the formation.

"This is an awards ceremony," he said, every word being pulled from his mouth by chains. "Serjeant Hal Kailas ... post!"

Hal pivoted out of ranks, doubled to the end of the line, and then to the front of the formation, saluted Dewlish. Dewlish undid the ties on a scroll, began reading:

"'I, King Asir of Deraine, do in my wisdom grant this Royal Badge of Honor to my faithful servant, Serjeant Hal Kailas, and direct others to render him proper respect.

"'I grant this distinction because of Serjeant Kailas' bravery in combat on several instances, first destroying attempts by the Roche to infiltrate raiders with dragons, then, during battle, using ingenuity to devise a method of destroying the dragon scouts and their riders.

"'Serjeant Kailas is not only a brave man, a worthy soldier of the king, but clever to boot, and it is recommended that any officer who is privileged to have Serjeant Kailas in his command give full attention and implementation to the serjeant's ideas and opinions, knowing that Serjeant Kailas is worthy of my particular notice and favor.

"'Signed, this day, King Asir.'"

Dewlish's lips pursed, unpursed several times before he opened a small box and pinned a medal on Hal's chest.

"Congratulations, Serjeant," Dewlish said, in a voice suggesting he'd rather be reading the citation at graveside.

"Thank you, sir." Hal said.

"That is all. You may return to ranks."

Hal saluted, obeyed, ran back to his place, hoping Hachir the crossbowman had also been recognized. Saslic leaned over a bit, and speaking without moving her lips – a talent all of them had learned under Dewlish's tutelage – said, "And now you're for it, you know."

Hal nodded.

Three days later, he was called to Dewlish's office.

"Serjeant Kailas, I've a request for four fliers, volunteers, for special duty. I've detached you, Mariah, Dinapur and Sir Loren. You'll report to the First Army's headquarters in Paestum at once, with your gear, dragons and handlers, plus volunteers necessary to maintain an independent action, for further details about this special duty."

The way Dewlish's voice savored "special duty" made Hal think the mission would certainly be one that might be better described by the word "suicidal."

15

But there was no briefing at the First Army headquarters. Instead, there was a tall, solidly-muscled man with a barely healed sword-slash across his face, who considered them through yellowish eyes that reminded Hal of a tiger he'd seen in a menagerie once.

He was Sir Bab Cantabri, commanding officer of this special detail, and he took them to a secluded tower room in Paestum Castle.

"I assume the four of you are volunteers, as specified?"

"We're alla that, sir," Farren Mariah piped. "In the smashin' old army style of the first ranks rarin' to march out and die."

Even though it looked as if it hurt to give up a smile, Cantabri managed a rather wintry looking one.

"And the four from the other flight look to be that unit's cheese dongs," Cantabri said. "Figures. Nothing changes about the army, whether it's on land or air.

"At least you look smart enough. We can only hope for the rest. You, Serjeant Kailas. You're ranking warrant?"

"I am, sir."

"Do you happen to have the necessary sea-going experience that was requested?"

"Nossir," Hal said. "The only flier in our flight who does wasn't volunteered."

"And the gods wept," Cantabri murmured. "Do you suppose you can manage to land your dragon aboard a ship? We'll arrange to get your gear and crew out by lighter."

"I don't know, sir," Hal answered honestly. "I've never tried it."

"There's a first time for almost everything. All four of you, over to this window. Here, use this glass. See, far out there on the horizon, five ships?"

They could.

"Two are fast corvettes, three are transports. One transport is towing a barge. You'll land on it, then your dragons will be hoisted aboard and you can lead them to their cages. Aboard ship, you'll draw tropical kit."

"Can we ask what the special duties we've uh, volunteered for now?" Saslic asked.

"When you're aboard, and we've set sail, you'll be told all you need to know. I'll tell you just one thing, in case you fall off your dragon and drown, so you can die in a patriotic fashion, this will be as important a mission as you're likely to be given.

"I'll tell you the rest when we're aboard the *Galgorm Adventurer*." He snorted. "What an absurd name for a spitkit of a horse-hauler."

Hal expected the worst, and, for once in his military career, was disappointed.

The four dragons were unchained from their wagons, and took off, as ordered, away from Paestum, then turned to sea, and flew to the waiting ships.

The sea was a bit rough, tossing whitecaps, and Hal wondered if he came off his mount, if he could stay afloat until rescued.

As senior warrant, the man who should always go last, he waved Sir Loren in to land first.

"I'll let someone else take the honors," Loren shouted.

Hal pointed to Farren, who needed no further encouragement. He sent his dragon spiraling down, then pulled up on its reins. The monster flared its wings, and settled on to the barge with a screech of triumph.

The triumphant call changed to one of dismay and fear as sailors went down ladders to the barge, and a crane swung out. Wide leather bands went under the dragon's belly, and it was muzzled.

Then it was swayed neatly aboard, and Farren, keeping away from its lashing tail, led it to a large cage.

Saslic went next, but her dragon balked, and she had to make another pass before landing on the barge.

Sir Loren landed, was loaded without incident, and then Hal sent his creature diving down, pulling up at the last minute, and the monster's talons scraped on the wooden deck and he was safe.

It tried to bite a sailor, and Hal slapped it with his open hand on the neck in reproof.

Then, it, too, was hoisted aboard the ship.

Hal had a moment to consider the *Galgorm Adventurer*. Not being a sailor like Mynta Gart, Hal had little to judge the former merchantman by. It certainly wasn't the handsomest vessel he'd ever seen, having almost no curves to its construct above the waterline. It was almost 500 feet long, three-masted, square-rigged with a jib, and had one cargo deck, built with ramps to load horses, plus the main deck. These two decks had their stalls enlarged to accommodate small dragons, wooden bars extending to the overhead. Half of the lower deck had been closed off, for troop bunking. The upper and poop decks were large, fitted with cabins, no doubt for the horses' owners or trainers. These were now for the expedition's officers and the fliers.

Wide sliding gangplanks, jutting forward, had been added

to either side of the hull, which didn't improve the ship's lines any.

Sailors escorted the four to their cabins, and they had a chance to meet the other fliers. Hal reserved judgement on them, since a gifted flier, contrary to what Cantabri and Dewlish thought, might not have the shiniest harness of all.

Already aboard were some 200 soldiers. Hal saw by the easy way they handled their weapons, the way their eyes constantly moved, and their air of superiority to everyone, especially the ship's crew, that they were experienced warriors.

Whatever this special duty was, it didn't appear to be one involving either maypole dancing or fishing.

"Tropical kit," Farren said with a smile. "It'd be nice to be flyin' somewheres warm. It's drawin' on toward winter."

But no one knew anything, everyone was waiting for Sir Bab Cantabri to show up.

Eventually his lighter, flanked by others with supplies and the dragon handlers, arrived, and goods and men were transferred aboard ship.

Hal was very glad to see Garadice, Rai's father, and twenty of his dragon specialists with Cantabri. The man asked of his son, seemed both unhappy and relieved that Rai hadn't been volunteered for this mission.

Within the hour, orders were given and the five ships set sail, due west from Paestum, into empty seas.

When all sight of land was gone, Cantabri summoned the infantry officers to the great cabin. An hour later, they were dismissed, and the fliers were called.

There was an elaborate plaster model of an island in the center of a table. Hal couldn't tell the scale, but the island was clearly large, covered with high mountains, interspersed with alpine valleys. There were two noticeable harbors, deep fjords knifing into the land, and a third inlet. The two harbors had tiny wooden houses near their mouth, and there were three other groups of houses further inland.

"This," Sir Bab said, "is Black Island. Our target."

Farren wailed. "I shoulda guessed he was lyin' t' us, an' a long farewell to the tropics. It'll be naught but ice, black dragons, cold, an' bum-freezin'.'"

Cantabri nodded.

"I did lie about the tropical gear. Just as I ordered a false course to be set west, to deceive any Roche spies in Paestum. We'll turn north within the day, and tomorrow issue cold weather gear to all.

"Being fliers, I suppose I don't need to tell you what Black Island's noted for. Dragons. We've heard from reliable sources that Roche is not only taking every dragon it can from the nests to train for their fliers, but their magicians have devised a way to make the dragons breed twins."

He went to a door, rapped. Three men entered. One was in his thirties, the others ten years younger. All wore dark garb, and had close-cropped hair and were clean-shaven. Were it not for the wands they carried, Hal would never have thought them to be magicians, but, perhaps, Cantabri's battle-hardened aides.

"This is Limingo, who's one of the King's Royal Magicians, and his assistants.

"They'll advise us of any Roche magic, hopefully cast counterspells and also keep us from being spotted on our journey north.

"We're at least three weeks or so away from Black Island, likely longer since we'll be hugging Deraine's west coast as we sail. During that time, I want you all to familiarize yourselves with this model, so that you can not only provide scouting as we approach Black Island, but can prevent any Roche fliers from seeing us and guiding their warships to attack us.

"I intend to seize this port, Balfe, here. Once we take the port, we'll attack this settlement here." He touched one of the fjords, then an upland cluster of houses.

"That's where one of our spies reported the Roche have

their dragon breeder, from the time they're taken from their nests to be fattened and become familiar with man for a few months. Then they're taken to Roche to begin training.

"After we seize the island, those dragon babies – I understand you call them kits – will be taken to Deraine, trained and used to reinforce our own dragon flights.

"With any luck, we'll be able to sail in, take them by surprise, and be back out to sea within the day."

Hal and his friends looked at each other.

"With just three warships," Saslic murmured.

"Which impels the question," Sir Loren said. "If this raid's so important, why wasn't half the fleet sent north?"

"Because it's *most* doubtful we could devise a spell to keep a plan of that size a secret," the magician, Limingo said. "Given warning, we think the Roche would cold-bloodedly slaughter those kits we're after rather than let us take them."

Hal thought the Roche weren't that barbaric, but said nothing.

"Supposing," Saslic said, "we do encounter Roche dragons in the air. How are we supposed to deal with them?"

Cantabri hesitated.

"I heard rumors that a flier, down south, devised a way of dealing with them, but I wasn't able to find out his name or any details." He frowned as Farren began chortling. "What's so funny about what I just said?"

Farren looked at Hal, who shrugged a go-ahead.

"Th' flier you're after's standin' right there," Mariah gurgled. "A brave volunteer if I ever saw one."

"You, Kailas?"

"Yessir." Hal briefly explained his use of crossbowmen in the battle down south.

"Hells," Cantabri growled. "And I specifically brought no crossbowmen since we'll be moving fast, and on the offensive. I've never liked crossbowmen when I'm not on the defensive and they don't have a chance to prepare fighting positions.

"Could you do the same – I'll need you to give me details –

for some of my archers? I guarantee you'd have no lack of volunteers."

"With longbows, sir?" Hal asked. "That's a problem."

Saslic nodded. "We'd be darting about, and they'd be wiggling their bows trying to get a firm aim ... I don't think that'd work, sir."

"I know it wouldn't," Sir Loren said. "I've seen cavalry try to shoot a-horseback, and the results are miserable."

Cantabri stood, frowning in thought.

"Kailas, stay after. We need to discuss this matter."

"Yessir."

"I don't know," Cantabri mused, "whether having you aboard is a bit of luck or not. You had success in killing dragon fliers or dragons, which I heartily approve of.

"I maintain this war will only be won when the Roche get tired of being killed, and either defang or depose Queen Norcia. All else is wishful thinking.

"So you and I agree on purpose. The question is, can you come up with any scheme to match our present circumstance, without crossbowmen? Which is why I wondered about my real luck in having you aboard."

Hal thought of mentioning his crossbow a-building, still weeks from readiness, but determined to say nothing, since he had no idea whether his scheme would work. But perhaps his idea could be modified slightly, at least for this operation.

"Possibly, sir," Hal said. "Is there any way we can get our hands on some crossbows? There's eight of us fliers ... maybe forty bows, and a thousand bolts?"

Cantabri considered.

"I can detach one of the corvettes, perhaps with one of Limingo's aides, to one of the west coast fishing ports. Maybe he can contact one of our armories and have the necessary tools waiting here ... in Deraine's north."

"Not good enough, sir," Hal said. "We'll need time to practice."

"I do not like changing a plan," Cantabri said. "But there's no way around it, I suppose, if we wish to have weapons to face the Roche fliers. We'll have to send the corvette, then lay off that port until the crossbows appear.

"That is, if the matter can be arranged at all."

"Frigging dragons don't get seasick," Saslic moaned.

"Guess not," Hal agreed. The wind had freshened, and the waves crashed over the bows of the *Adventurer*.

"But I do, godsdammit," Saslic said, and bent over the railing once more.

Farren, who was distinctly greenish, looked away from her.

"This is the doom," he muttered. "To be sick, sicker, an' then freeze, an be et by black dragons.

"I don't like this even a bit. I've got plans for after the war, I do."

Saslic turned.

"Don't fall in love with them," she said, her voice harsh. "There won't *be* any after the war for a dragon flier."

The corvette was sent off to a medium-sized trading port, and the other ships sailed to and fro, well out of sight of land, away from the chart-marked trading routes and fishing grounds, waiting.

"Now, the question will be," Sir Bab mused to Hal, "how many crossbows will we get?"

"We asked for forty, correct, sir?"

"Kailas, you might have been in the army for a time, and fancy yourself an old soldier. But there are things still for you to learn."

"Not sure I want to learn them, sir."

"Don't think, Serjeant, you'll be able to keep that nice civilian core you had before the war started, and when peace breaks out, you'll be able to drop right back to doing whatever it was you were before being called to the colors."

"I wasn't called, sir, but taken. But you were teaching me about crossbows."

"No. I was teaching you about the army and numbers. If you want, say, forty of anything, ask for 120. They'll look at your requisition, and find reasons why of course you can't get what you thought you needed.

"So, if we're lucky, we get eighty.

"If we're lucky."

Three days later, the corvette returned with sixty crossbows, of which at least half were in sad shape. Fortunately Limingo's aide had looked at them, realized their condition, and bought skeins for bowstrings and wood to repair the prods. There were enough peacetime carpenters among the crew and soldiery to be put to repair work.

With the other crossbows, Hal, and a grizzled infantry serjeant set to, training the fliers how to shoot.

Sir Loren and Saslic became experts. Hal wasn't surprised – Loren was instantly good at anything he undertook, and Hal had learned years ago that women were, generally, better than men with arms, once they decided not to listen to the railings from males.

Farren was an acceptable marksman, which he said, with a shrug, didn't bother him, since "I don't much like the idea of killin' dragons, 'less they're tryin' to fang me, so I'll just have to fly closer an' shoot straighter at their riders." He nudged Hal. "Or get the Master Murderer here to get them for me."

Of the four fliers from the other flight, one was a decent shot, although he was hardly an eager warrior. Another was zealous enough, but was lucky to be able to hit the ship's side, let alone the target pinned to it. The other two were sullen, not caring about much of anything. Hal decided Sir Bab had been right – they'd been stuck with the other unit's cheese dongs.

They continued practicing while the ships sailed steadily north. Sir Bab didn't want any dragons flown, so the handlers and fliers were hard put to keep their mounts happy in their cages, eager as always to get away from the earth and into their natural element.

"It'll come, soon enough," Hal told his monster, while the beast grunted contentedly, munching on a piglet Kailas had tossed into its cage.

"There'll be one way to tell if we're lucky," Sir Bab told Hal. The two had gotten in the habit of exercising on the ship's low poop after evening meal then, when Hal had been worn out by Cantabri's grind, to lean on the stern rail, cooling off in the chill, near-arctic wind, and talk of most anything.

Cantabri was reluctant to talk of before the war, but Hal had learned he was married, had two children and had been a King's Advocate, specializing in land claims.

"A good way to get rich," he told Hal. "Or just make enemies if you're stupid enough, as I was, to stand against the rich when they try to grab some peasant's holdings."

Then, one night, he'd brought up luck.

"What's the way, sir?" Hal asked. "When we're sitting in some bar in Rozen with all our fingers and toes and kits swarming around us like we're their fathers?"

"That's one," Cantabri said. "Another one is if we don't encounter a Roche flier named Yasin. A nobleman, with a brother who's supposedly mounting Queen Norcia. He's—"

"I know him, sir," Hal said. "Ran into him before the war, when he had a flying show."

"I hope he was luckier for you than me," Cantabri said. He touched the livid scar on his face. "His damned dragons pointed me out to some heavy cavalrymen when I was wandering around behind their lines one time, just to see what I could see.

"Another time I was afoot, raiding a supply column, and his beasts caught me out and tore into my men. They weren't as tough as I'd thought, and broke.

"Dragons have no trouble taking men from behind, you know."

"I know," Hal said.

"The first time I noted the black bannerlet he had tied to his dragon's neck spikes. All of his fliers use that as a common emblem, I've been told, though only his has golden fringing. The second time, the same, and there was one more time when he, or at least some of his men, saw me on a diversion. Didn't lose anybody, I'm glad to say, but we had to abort and skit back to our own lines before we got trapped.

"So I'm no fan of this *Ky* Yasin.

"I heard he'd moved north, to Paestum, and hope to hell the bastard – or whatever magicians he's got working for him – hasn't scented us out.

"I was told by one of the First Army's intelligence sorts he – and his dragons – have become some sort of a fire brigade, sent wherever there's trouble along the front.

"He also told me this Yasin was the one trying to train black dragons – I was told they're supposedly untrainable, implacable enemies of man – and having some success, which would explain why the Roche are capturing the monsters up on Black Island.

"Kailas, there are some people who scare me, and he's one of them."

There was a long silence, then: "If I were superstitious, I'd fear the man carries my doom."

Again, stillness, then Cantabri laughed harshly, without humor.

"Talking like this is why soldiers should never be given time to themselves. They're liable to try to teach themselves how to think, and all they manage is brooding.

"Night, Kailas."

And he went to a companionway to his cabin.

Hal lingered on for a few minutes, thinking. How many million men under arms? And this damned Yasin kept cropping up.

At least, Kailas thought, he hadn't encountered Yasin in the air. So far.

And if he were truly learning to ride black dragons, from all that Hal had heard, he certainly didn't want to.

16

They'd been almost three weeks at sea, a few days to the fishing port, and a week waiting for the crossbows, then on north, when Hal went to Sir Bab, and told him the dragons had to be flown. If they were mewed up all the way to Black Island, they'd be lucky to be able to do more than flounder about in the air.

"You have your soldiers exercising," he pointed out. "Dragons are no different."

Cantabri didn't argue, just told Hal not to fly further north than the ships, for fear of being seen. And if they were sighted by any other dragon riders, they could assume they were Roche.

But Hal wasn't quite ready to put his monster into the air. For openers, he had no idea on how to navigate over water, and the constantly changing weather could easily confuse a flier, and lose him in the sea-mist.

He went to the *Adventurer*'s navigator, and asked for help.

The officer showed him astrolabe and chronometer, charts, and the rest of the apparatus he used to find their position. Hal had a bit of trouble envisioning himself standing on the back of his dragon, twiddling dials, a chart braced under one foot, and the chronometer hanging on a chain around his neck.

No.

Saslic said she was willing to take a chance, which made Hal think even harder.

He had an idea, then, and went to Limingo the magician.

"I need a spell that will let me find this ship, no matter what the weather," he said. "A spell that you could lay on all of us."

The magician thought, clucking his tongue against the roof of his mouth.

"An attraction," he said. "For what? Canvas? Ropes? Other dragons? No. Those, especially as we close on Black Island, might lead you into the heart of the enemy."

"What about an aversion spell?" Hal asked.

"To what?"

"Salt beef might do," Hal said, thinking with a shudder of the barrels of meat that'd been boiled, then kept in salty water. Farren had spoken for them all when he said, "This'd be enow to turn me vegetarian. No wonder the poor friggin' sailors spend so much time buggerin' each other. On'y pleasure life gives 'em at sea."

Limingo laughed, said that would certainly be an easy spell to build, and one that would surely take. He wanted an hour to prepare it, asked Hal to have all eight fliers in his cabin then.

The magician's spacious cabin had its furniture pushed back against the bulkheads. Eight small braziers were set in twin arrows, both pointing to a hunk of salt beef. Around it, semi-circles in various colored chalks were drawn, and in each a symbol or letter of a tongue known to none of the fliers.

Farren whispered that if "any of them letters require speakint, I'll never have a tongue snaky enough, despite what m'lady friends've said."

Saslic jabbed him in the ribs, told him to shut up.

Limingo, flanked by his acolytes, explained what Hal had wanted, and what they'd come up with.

"Then I bethought myself a bit," he went on. "An absolute aversion to salt beef, natural though it would be, might spell starvation while we're still aboard. So rather than impregnate you all with this counterspell, we'll give each of you an amulet.

"You can see them on the floor, next to that slab of what's laughingly called beef, which I've linked to the meat aboard this ship. I'll enchant them, and when you wish to know where this ship is, stroke your amulet, think of beef, and you'll immediately know which way to turn your dragon.

"Now, each of you come forward, and take an amulet."

"Strokin' m'amulet, eh?" Farren whispered. "I thought you got toss't out of the army for strokin' it too much."

This time, Hal was the one to kick him.

The amulets were tiny ovals of a variegated brown, each with a silver ring around it and mounting for chain or thong. Hal wondered how Limingo had been able to make these charms in such short order, decided he must have a pack somewhere, ready for various ensorcellments.

"My assistants are now putting various, efficacious herbs on the fire – adders tongue, hellebore, purslane, spurge. We ourselves are chewing bits of clove against the spell, since we don't wish to have it take root among us."

Evil-smelling smoke boiled that might have been pleasant if only one herb at a time was being burnt.

"Take your talisman in your right hand," Limingo went on. "Touch it to your heart, then hold it out toward me."

The fliers obeyed. Limingo began chanting:

> "Beef of old
> Covered with mold
> We shun thee yet
> Your odor set

> *We turn away*
> *Our stomachs at bay*
> *Protect us all*
> *From your horrid pall.*"

He then chanted, in a monotone, words in an unknown language, nodded at his assistants, who capped the braziers, just as Hal was about to break into uncontrollable coughing.

Another assistant opened a vast port on to the seething ocean at the ship's stern, and the chill wind quickly cleared the smoke out.

"I never thought," Sir Loren said, "having a strong stomach is a perquisite for wizardry."

Limingo heard him, grinned.

"It is an *absolute* necessity. I recall the first five years of my apprenticeship as being mostly nausea. I suppose that kept my master's expenses for his larder down, though.

"Now, all of you, try your amulets out."

Hal touched his, thought of salt beef, and instantly did not want to go in three directions. He asked Limingo about it, who had him indicate those directions.

"Very good," he said. "One aversion, of course, is to that bit of beef on the deck there. The other would be to the hold where the provisions are kept. And the third would be to the galley, which suggests what we're having for the evening meal.

"All of you? Did you feel the same?"

All did, but two had only a single response.

"Good enough," Limingo said. "Each of you has his – or her, pardon milady – personal compass.

"So you can go flying now . . . and be content you'll be back aboard before the cooks finish boiling our meal into submission."

They started for the dragon deck.

Saslic noticed Farren Mariah had a long face.

"'Smatter, small one? You don't want to eat some fog?"

"'Tisn't that," Mariah said. "Just realizin' what small beer

I'd be as a wizard. Not only havin' to pack-sack all that gear, and learn all kind of tongues, none of which anyone without a split tongue could ever speak aloud, but havin' such pretty, pretty assistants.

"Not my cut of beef at all. Pardonin' the expression."

Hal and the others took their dragons high, circling in the sheer joy of flying after so long, swooping, making mock attacks on each other.

As the sun sank and it grew colder, the ship's warmth called, and, one by one, they circled back to the *Adventurer* and its salt beef.

"That incantation Limingo was saying," Saslic said to Farren as they groomed their dragons. "It was damned poor poetry."

"'Twas," Mariah agreed.

"Since you're supposed to have some talents as a witch, Farren," she asked, "does it matter how good your poems are? Do demons – or whoever helps magic work out – like good poetry, or crappy stuff, like soldiers go for?"

"Don't seem t' matter," Farren said. "M' gran'sire said it just focused the mind an' will on the spell."

"So a magician could be going doobly, doobly, doobly, and it'd have the same effect?"

"Nope," Farren said. "Best if you've got to slave some, writin' the chant, and then, sayin' it, keeps you payin' attention."

"And if you don't pay attention," Hal asked from his cage, "the spell won't work, right?"

"Mayhap," Farren said. "Or a demon eats you."

"There goes one of my choices for an after-war career," Hal said firmly.

Hal ordered all dragons to have their carapace scales pierced and smallish hooks installed that he'd had the ship's artificer make, patterned after the pelican hooks used in the rigging.

The dragons seemed to have no feelings in their scales, save where they were attached to the beast's skin, and so did no more than growl when the handlers were at work with their bow-drills.

He assembled the dragon riders, gave instructions, and issued two crossbows and four bolts to each rider. The bolts were colored for each rider.

A small raft was tossed overboard from the *Adventurer*, with a block of wood covered with bright cloths in its center and a long towrope connecting it to the ship.

Each dragon rider flew off, then assembled, in a line, behind Hal.

In turn, each dragon swooped on the raft and its rider fired at the block, climbed away while the rider rehung his first crossbow and prepared the second. Four passes per dragon, which took almost three hours as riders aimed, lost their aim, pulled away to try again, and then dragons were landed, and the raft dragged aboard.

The results were fairly wretched – Hal had three hits, as did Saslic. Sir Loren had two, Farren one, and one of the other flight's fliers managed a strike.

Not good, Hal thought, pondered long, but couldn't think of any better way to train the fliers. He talked to Limingo, and asked if magic could help.

"Certainly," the magician said briskly. "If you could bring me a bit of a Roche dragon flier's tunic, preferably with a little of his blood on it, I could cast a similarity spell, and that would do the trick."

Hal grinned wryly, found Sir Bab, told him not to be expecting much if the Roche and Deraine fliers came in contact.

"I always expect nothing, or almost," Cantabri said. "That way, I'm almost never surprised.

"Look at it like this, Serjeant. If you buzz a bolt close to one of their fliers, something he can't be used to, that should scare him off.

"At least for awhile. And maybe, when he gathers his courage and tries again, the flier he goes against will have better aim."

Hal saluted, called the fliers together, told them they'd be flying twice a day against the evil raft until they got better.

They did. Slightly. But only slightly.

They spent almost as much time studying that model of Black Island as they did in the air. The soldiers' warrants and officers did the same.

Hal was impressed, seeing how many of the common warriors spent time in the room, lips moving silently as they walked around the model, then pointing to various places with their eyes closed, whispering the place names to their mates.

And there was always the thunder of soldiers running back and forth on the decks, exercising, practicing swordplay with wooden swords against each other.

When they reached Black Island, they'd be as ready as soldiers could be.

"The problem with war," Sir Loren mused as the four fliers sat on the deck one morning too foggy to fly, "is it's no fun any more."

"Di'n't know it ever was," Farren said. "Killin' people ain't my snappy-poppy idea of pure joy."

"That's the bad side of it," Sir Loren admitted. "But when it's a clear morning, and you can hear the horses neighing across a camp that's bright with banners and knights' tents, or when you're riding out on a spring day on a country patrol, or even when you see a castle besieged in its splendor . . . You've got to admit there's a certain glory."

"No," Saslic said flatly. "I don't."

"Never mind, Sir Loren," Hal said. "You're in the minority here. But what made war no fun . . . in your eyes?"

"The damned quartermasters and victuallers," Sir Loren said.

The other three blinked.

"An' a course, you've an explanation," Farren said.

"It used to be," Sir Loren said, "that soldiers would assemble, at the will of the king or whatever nobleman had their fealty or could offer gold or loot, in either spring or fall, after the harvest or after the roads thawed, most generally in the fall, after the harvest was in.

"We'd campaign for three months, then, when the army couldn't find any more peasants' farms to loot, and if there hadn't been a knockdown battle that settled the issue, everybody went home."

"Except the poor looted peasant, who didn't have a home to go to," Saslic said.

"He could enlist for the next campaign, hoping for loot to compensate," Sir Loren went on. "But now, we've got efficiency, with victuallers riding here and there, dealing with contract merchants for so many hogsheads of hogs' heads or corn or whatever, and all that goes to depots for issuance to the army.

"And so we can stay in the field forever, not like my father and father before him, who'd have a chance to return home, let his wounds heal, and rest for a time."

"And possibly procreate more killers for the next king to call on," Saslic said.

"Well . . ." Sir Loren let his voice trail off.

"Sorry, Sir Loren," Hal said. "No sale here. Although I'm sure Sir Bab'd agree with you."

"Not him," Sir Loren said. "He's of the new school of warrior. Fight until the enemy's down in the ditch, then stab him a few times to make sure, paying no attention to anything like a white flag."

"A bleedin' *monster*," Farren said, mock horror in his voice. "Bet he doesn't curry to ransomin' brave knights, either. Stick a bit of iron in their armpit, where the armor don't cover, an' march on, knowin' they're no more a threat. Right?"

"Aargh," Sir Loren said. "There's no chivalry in the lot of you."

"And thank the gods for that," Saslic said.

It grew colder, and a flier reported he could see the northern-most headland of Deraine, sinking into the ocean. The seas grew larger, sweeping across the vastnesses of open ocean, and Saslic was seasick again, moaning that she thought she'd gotten her sea legs, but somebody lied to her, and if she ever found them she'd either kill them or throw up on them.

But she staggered to Nont, and was airborne with the others. Hal thought the epitome of courage was seeing her tight, pinched face, ignoring nausea, fighting her way into the air.

One day, all fliers were in the air, and a sudden storm swept down from the north, bringing rain and fog with it, the seas rising.

The dragon fliers used their amulets to drive hard for the *Adventurer*, and the handlers rushed each from the landing barge on to the ship, another dragon already approaching, spray reaching up and soaking its belly.

Eight dragon fliers had taken off.

Seven came back.

The missing flier was Saslic Dinapur.

Hal tried to take off, to look for her, but Sir Bab forbade it.

Limingo was afraid to cast any spells this close to Black Island, for fear of being discovered by Roche wizards.

Kailas wanted to rage at him, rage at Cantabri, but fought himself under control.

All that long night, as the storm boomed, and the ships rolled, taking green water over the rails, Hal stood on the poop, out of the way of the watch and helmsmen, feeling no cold, no wind, none of the waves' drenching, eyes burning as he tried to peer into blackness.

His mind kept running the thought – I never told her I love

her, over and over, never willing to change the word to loved.

Cantabri came on deck at dawn, saw Hal, and ordered him below for hot soup and a change of clothes.

Kailas obeyed, his loss overwhelming him, his mind numb.

Less than a turning of a glass later, the lookout reported a dragon, flying toward them.

Hal was on deck, lips murmuring prayers from his childhood, knowing uselessness, knowing that this was nothing but a Roche scout who'd sighted them.

But it wasn't.

It was Nont, and Saslic Dinapur, weaving in the saddle, almost falling, as she brought her dragon down on the barge. A wave almost took it, but there were handlers on the decking, heedless of the storm, fastening bellybands under Nont and bringing it aboard.

Saslic tried to stagger up the gangplank to the *Adventurer*, stumbled, almost went overboard, and Hal had her in his arms, carrying her to her cabin.

She was near-frozen, body unfeeling. Limingo and the ship's chiurgeon were there, stripping her clothes away, and putting her in a tub of heated salt water, constantly refreshed.

She stirred, came back to consciousness, saw Hal, and a smile quirked her lips.

"That," she managed, "was the longest damned night of my life."

Then she went out again. Limingo had herbal rubs, hot plasters and drinks, and she was put to bed with high-piled blankets, and slept for a full day and night.

She woke ravenously hungry, and all the delicacies the mess cooks could provide were hers.

Hal sat beside her while she ate. She burped delicately.

"I think I feel like getting screwed," she said. "Just to convince myself I'm not frozen in some wave."

Kailas was only too happy to comply, and moaned, in the height of passion, his love.

After they were finished, she looked at him strangely.

"You mean that?"

"Yes," Kailas said firmly.

"Me, too," Saslic said. She sounded a little embarrassed, and hid her face against his shoulder.

"Would you like to tell me how you came to live?" Hal said, a bit relieved to change the subject.

"It was all Nont," Saslic said. "Did you know dragons can swim?"

"No," Hal said, then caught himself. "Yes. We take them down to the river for washing. But that's just splashing about."

"They swim like godsdamned ducks," Saslic said. "That's what kept me alive. When the winds got too strong to stay in the air, Nont ignored what I was trying to get him to do, and dove for the water.

"I thought we were dead, but he spread his wings just yards above the waves, and flared us in with a great damned splash.

"Then he folded his wings over his back, over me, and we bobbed around. It was almost warm, like I was in a weird tent.

"It was dark and, well, smelly, and the water kept drizzling in. Then it got colder, and Nont put his head in the tent with me. He was breathing on me, and it was like being on a battlefield three days after the fighting, maybe worse. But it was warmer, and I could just concentrate on not throwing up.

"I wonder if dragons can cross oceans like that, just hunched up, letting the currents carry them? Maybe they don't come from the north, like everybody thinks.

"Anyway, I think I spent a lifetime under his wings, but it got gray out, and the waves didn't look as high. I didn't know what to do, but Nont did. He waited until we were on top of a wave, and then I could feel his feet paddling hard, and his wings spread, and we went up the next wave, before it could break over us.

"The wind caught us, and lifted him in the air, and we

skipped across the water and he flew like he's never flown before, and then started listening to the reins and what I was shouting.

"I used the amulet, and it worked perfectly, and brought me back home."

She was silent for a moment, then smiled, in childlike happiness.

"I do love you, too.

"And I want to sleep again now."

Hal sought out Garadice, told him what Saslic had discovered about dragons.

"I'll be whipped," the trainer said. "This certainly shows that nobody knows anything about the beasts. I can picture this great flotilla, swimming, or being borne by the storms, from some far-distant land to the northern lands. I'd heard tales of dragons settling on water, but I thought just to drink, or rest for a moment.

"Nobody knows anything about dragons," he repeated. "Or, come to think about it, anything else, as far as I can tell, the older I get."

The next morning there were alarums. A lookout on one of the flanking corvettes reported something in the air at a distance.

Hal and Sir Loren hurried their dragons from their cages, went aloft, climbing in tight spirals.

But they saw nothing.

They circled the tiny convoy for an hour, came back in for a landing, chilled to the bone.

No one other than that single lookout had seen anything, and Sir Bab decided it was likely an illusion, for the dragon was reported flying almost due east, rather than north to Black Island or south to Deraine or the mainland.

There was nothing east for leagues, so the lookout had to have been mistaken, or perhaps had sighted a wild dragon.

But no one relaxed after that.

The following day, Hal was on high patrol, and saw something to the west of the convoy. He took his dragon lower, ready to flee, expecting to see ships, and there could be none but Roche in these waters.

But the tiny dots – Hal counted more than forty of them – stayed very small, and he chanced going still lower.

Then he made them out, and a chill went up his spine.

The dots were dragons, wings folded over their backs, heads tucked inside the tent, being carried along by the current and waves.

Dragons migrating . . . toward where? Black Island? The unknown wastelands to the north of the island?

Was this a regular process? Or were the dragons fleeing something?

Hal flew low over the dragons. One, near the lead, lifted its head, looked up at Hal, saw no evident menace, and put his head back under cover.

Hal had no answers, nor did Garadice, who added a further question that perhaps some ultima Thule to the west was the dragons' real homeland, and the northern wastelands a current-ordained temporary destination.

Hal puzzled over it, put the matter aside as one more intrigue about dragons, and returned his mind to the war.

Two mornings later, just at dawn, a high-flying dragon rider reported, just lifting from the northern horizon, gray land bulking out of the gray seas and mist.

Black Island.

17

Black Island, from about five thousand feet, looked exactly like that plaster model in one of the *Adventurer*'s cabins, barring the cloud-scatter below Hal and his three fliers.

Clouds, and the moving dots that were two of the transports, landing soldiers on the horns that enclosed Balfe's harbor.

There seemed to be no other sign of life below them, and then Hal felt a surge of sickness, knew the Roche magicians were casting what spells they could bring up in time.

He scanned the town, saw nothing worth reporting, looked to sea, which was gray, speckled with white.

He motioned to Saslic to stay high on patrol, and pointed to his other three fliers to dive.

They shot down, dragon wings furled, across the northernmost point of land, saw soldiers, in formation, trotting along a dirt road toward the settlement. Still lower, they saw two bodies sprawled outside a shack, couldn't tell if they were Roche or Deraine.

Hal led his flight in a sweep around the island, saw no sign of alarm. They flew past a huge seamount, and saw half a dozen full-grown black dragons crouching, watching. Hal shivered at their size – fifty or sixty feet – far larger than the beasts they rode.

He kept his hand near the two crossbows hooked to his dragon's carapace until the wild dragons were out of sight.

They flew over Balfe, saw no dragons with riders trying to get in the air, but smelt the strong reek of the beasts from long roofed pens below.

Running toward the settlement, from the other point, came other Deraine soldiers, as the *Adventurer* and the other two transports hove toward the settlement's single pier.

The escorting corvettes stayed clear of the bay, watchful for Roche ships.

A handful of Roche soldiers ran out of a guardhouse, and either died or surrendered to Cantabri's soldiery.

The second flight of dragons came off the *Adventurer*, landed near the barracks to wait their turn in the sky.

Hal saw Garadice and his specialists disembark from the *Adventurer*. The other transports unloaded bulky stretchers and small carts. Soldiers were detailed by Sir Bab's warrants to assist Garadice.

Then the craziness began, as dragons were taken out from their pens, and chivvied, coaxed or carried to the transports. Hal, swooping overhead, trying not to fall off in his laughter, counted more than fifty dragons of various ages, saw them snapping, trying to claw, and tail-lashing, heard shouts of pain, and squeals of rage from below. The soldiers trying to help Garadice may have been deadly warriors, but as dragon handlers they were bumblers.

Farren flew close.

"Glad to be out of that!" he called.

"Aye," Hal shouted, pointed up. "Relieve Saslic. It's cold up there."

"Bastard," Farren called amiably, and took his dragon upstairs.

The dragons went up the gangplanks on to the transports reluctantly, but they went.

Saslic's dragon flapped down alongside Hal.

"Nothing here?"

"Nothing," Hal shouted back. "No dragons anywhere but on the ground."

"Can't believe ... Roche sloppy ..." Saslic said, words torn by a gust of wind. But Hal understood.

He swept back and forth over Balfe, then it was his turn to freeze.

Hal kicked his dragon in the ribs, pulled on the reins. The beast's wings beat harder, and he went to altitude and relieved Farren.

He saw nothing, and Sir Loren replaced him.

The biggest of the Roche dragons from the hatchery – they were about twenty feet long, Hal guessed almost yearlings – were being loaded as his flight landed, and the second flight took off on patrol.

Handlers had already offloaded barrels of beef, and hacked their tops open, one for each dragon. The monsters gulped hungrily, eyes darting back and forth, daring any of the two-legs to bother them.

Soldiers were passing out buns stuffed with smoked fish, onions and pickles. The fliers got their noon meal, cups of tea, and watched the madness.

Hal noted Garadice, standing near one of the dragon pens, and went over. The dragon trainer had a worried expression on his face.

"What are you eating your fingers about, sir?" Hal asked.

"I have no idea what secret – if any, other than endless patience – the Roche trainers are using to train these black dragons."

"Whyn't you ask one?"

"The soldiers say all of the trainers fled into the hills while we were landing. Maybe they're telling the truth, or maybe the trainers had time to disguise themselves as common guards.

"I was hoping we'd take prisoners of either the trainers or magicians, and find out the Roche secrets. But no such luck, and we don't have the time to beat the bushes for them," he said, and as he spoke, a trumpet blared.

"Back aboard," Sir Bab was shouting, the command echoed by his warrants.

One of Limingo's assistants scurried by.

"What's the problem?" Hal called.

He shook his head.

"Not sure, not sure at all. But we've detected some sort of magic out there, just a wisp."

"From where?"

"From the east," and the man was gone.

Hal's back prickled. That unknown dragon that maybe didn't exist had flown away to the east, too.

He looked up at the second flight, saw with a grimace they were very low, no more than two thousand feet overhead.

Bastards didn't want to get up there in the wind, where it's freezing. I'll have them sorted out, he thought, starting for his dragon.

Then he saw dots to the east. Five, flying close together.

He shouted a warning, and his three fliers saw the oncoming dragons, had perhaps a moment to hope they were a wild covey, then realized wild dragons never flew that closely together, and were in their saddles.

Hal jumped on to his mount, jerked the reins, and the dragon growled in protest, but turned away from the last of the salt beef, and sprang into the air.

The flight climbed, circling over Balfe as the last soldiers tumbled aboard, pulling up the transport gangplanks. Anchors had been dropped when the ships pulled up to the pier, and now the ships kedged back from shore, laboriously came about, and put on all sail. Hal saw signal flags going back and forth from corvettes to transports, had no time to watch others as five Roche dragons dove toward the second flight, about a mile away from Hal.

The on-rushing Roche dragons flew hard, wings driving, straight into the four.

The air was a swarm of dragons, beasts slashing at each other with their talons, fanged heads snaking.

A Deraine flier was struck by a tail-slash, sent spinning down toward the sea below. Another was fumbling at his crossbow when his dragon banked sharply, away from an attacker.

Hal could hear him scream as he lost his footgrip, above the screech and scream of the dragons and fell. Hal's flight was level with the free-for-all, and Saslic looked at him, for orders. He pointed up. Better to have altitude before they closed, he knew.

He glanced at the mêlée, saw it break apart, one dragon with a Roche pennant on its carapace spinning, wing torn away. Another Roche monster was far below, diving, wings folded, into the ground. The two surviving Deraine dragons howled, attacked the three survivors. The Deraine fliers may not have been the best, but they were certainly brave.

The Roche fliers wheeled their mounts and fled, just as a Deraine flier from the second flight slumped down over the neck of his mount, and slowly slipped out of the saddle, falling limply toward rocks.

Then the Deraine fliers, five of them, were alone in the sky over Black Island.

Hal was amazed how much time had passed, looking down, seeing the five Deraine ships well clear of land, at full sail toward the south-east.

He was about to signal his flight to make for the ships, then saw, against the gray haze on the horizon, the specks of ships. He counted twenty, and his eyes were tearing from the cold and wind, unable to make out more.

Hal's fliers were waiting for orders.

He knew what must be done, knew he was probably sending his fliers to their deaths. Hal waved his hand in a circle – keep patrolling. They must stop any oncoming dragons, to keep the Deraine convoy from being followed and destroyed.

The fliers obeyed, waiting.

Hal knew Limingo and his acolytes would be casting every possible spell to turn away Roche magic.

He thought about his warm bunk, about hot soup, about anything other than the cold creeping up his arms and legs.

Time passed.

The dragons honked unhappiness at the boredom.

The Deraine ships were over the horizon, and the Roche fleet, now counted at thirty-five ships, was closing on Black Island, when Hal saw another flight of dragons – once more, five – flying toward him.

He pointed, and his three, followed by the last survivor of the second flight, flapped toward the Roche.

His dragon whined protest, wing muscles tiring, but obeyed Hal's orders.

He had slight altitude on the Roche, motioned for his dragon flight to climb even higher.

The Roche dragons came up toward him, and Hal saw, with a chill, two of them were huge.

Huge and black.

Roche *had* learned how to train the feared black dragons.

He pushed fear away, picked up one of his crossbows, already cocked, bolt in its trough, steered toward the lead Roche.

They rushed together, and the fear vanished, for icy calm.

At the last instant, the Roche flier broke, afraid of collision, kicking his mount down, trying to dive under Hal. Hal aimed, pulled the trigger and it was an easy shot. The bolt took the Roche in the chest, knocked him back, bolt pinning him to his mount's back.

The dragon bucked, was gone, and Hal forgot him, pulling his dragon's reins as a black monster, almost twice the size of his mount, slashed with its dripping fangs at his dragon's throat.

Then they were past, and Hal pulled his dragon up into a climbing turn, saw a black dragon trying to turn inside him, wings shaking as he slowed into a stall, the sound like dull thunder.

He had his crossbow cocked, a bolt ready, and the black was almost on him, mouth gaping. He put his bolt fair between the beast's jaws, and it howled, bucked, and its flier almost fell, caught himself on the carapace, legs dangling, kicking for a foothold as his dragon rolled on its back, and dove toward the ground.

Again, the brawl was joined. Sir Loren's dragon tore at a Roche's wing, and Saslic took it from the front, talons ripping at its neck.

The last survivor of the second flight was flying in tight circles with a Roche dragon. The Roche broke the circle, was on the Deraine beast, ripping at its chest. Ichor spurted, and the Deraine beast convulsed, fell.

Hal had his second crossbow up, shot the Roche rider in the back, dove under the dragon, fumbling the crossbow string over the cocking fingers, stuffing a quarrel in, and there was a black Roche above him. He sent a bolt toward its gut, missed, hit neck armor, and the bolt skittered away.

The dragon was turning toward him, and Saslic dove on it, shot the dragon in the body as Farren put his bolt into its rider.

A dragon slammed into Hal's mount, almost knocking him free, the Roche monster's fangs ripping at Hal's mount behind the wing. Hal was trying to cock his crossbow as his dragon rolled, lost it, almost grabbed for it, and yanked the other bow from its nook.

Ichor sprayed across Hal's face, almost blinding him, then he saw the Roche dragon turning back to finish him.

But it was very slow, and he had all the time he needed to cock his crossbow, tuck a bolt into the notch, lift it, and fire. The bolt took the Roche rider in his guts, and he grabbed himself with both hands, fell back from his saddle, bounced once on his dragon's tail, and was gone.

His riderless mount dove away, and the sky was clear of Roche, just as Hal felt his dragon shudder and saw the terrible wound in his mount's side.

Then he was diving down toward the sea below, pulling helplessly at his reins, his dragon trying to recover, trying to fly.

He almost made it, lifting himself on one wing and torn remnants of the other, bravely trying for land. But he ran out of sky, and Hal and dragon smashed into the ocean, Hal tossed away, to go deep, water green, turning black, while his thick fingers unfastened his sword-belt, let it fall away.

He kicked at his boots, slid out of his thick coat, and the water was lightening. He broke the surface, gasping.

Not a dozen yards away, his dragon thrashed at the water in death agonies, shrilled, then sank.

Hal Kailas was alone on the tossing gray ocean, the wind catching the tops of waves, turning them white.

Hal waited until a wave lifted him to its crest, rubbed salt-burning eyes clear, looked for land, thought he saw the peaks of Black Island.

A long ways away, but there was nothing else, and so he started the swim, arm over arm. A shadow came over him, and he flinched down before he realized, and looked up.

Saslic's dragon, Nont, banked above him, then, whining in protest, spread its wings as Saslic forced it to the water, splashing down on the back of a wave.

"Need a ride, sailor?" she shouted.

Hal, half drowned, didn't have strength enough for a reply, stroked toward Nont, caught hold of a wing, pulled himself along it and on to the monster's back.

"I guess we should think about going home, hmm?" Saslic called as she goaded Nont into a flapping run through the water, up the back of another wave, and then ponderously in the air, climbing, up to where Sir Loren and Farren flew.

"Before the rest of the party shows up."

18

The five ships docked in one of Deraine's western ports, and the stolen dragons were transferred to barges, and sent upriver to a secret training ground of Garadice's.

Hal and the other dragon fliers had expected to be put on a transport, with their three surviving dragons, and sent back to Paestum, the Eleventh Dragon Flight and the charming attentions of Sir Fot Dewlish.

Instead, the dragon fliers, Sir Bab Cantabri, half a dozen of his soldiers and Limingo were given special orders and transportation to Rozen, Deraine's capital.

"An' what do yer think that pertains to?" Mariah wondered. "We got away wi' it, so there'll not be a court martial."

"Medals, lad," a gray-bearded serjeant said. "We're heroes."

"Mmmh," Farren said, thought for a moment. "That's nice, an' such. But I'll wager it means the army acrost the seas has taken it up the wahiny of late, and the king's lookin' for someat to distract the masses."

"Prob'ly," the soldier agreed. "But haven't you learned to take yer medals where they fall?"

Hal suspected the serjeant was right, since the transportation north wasn't the usual oxcarts soldiers got used to, but carriages more suitable for officers or minor lordlings.

It was cold traveling in the beginnings of winter, but there were crowds down the main street of each village, cheering the soldiers, sometimes even by name, generally Sir Bab, and every night the twelve were put up at decent inns, not crouching over fires in their stables.

Again, Hal noted there were few men about, and the farmers' winter tasks were being done more and more by women.

Saslic and Hal slept in each other's arms each night, waking to make hungry love, evidence they'd lived through the icy seas.

Others took full advantage of the adulation they were getting, and Hal wondered how many village maidens would have children nine months gone.

Saslic commented acidly that she truly admired the patriotism of her fellows, "trying to personally compensate for any war losses. Heroes all."

The two surprises were Sir Bab, who smiled politely at the invitations to linger beyond dinner from the country noblemen's wives and daughters, but no more.

"He's married," Sir Loren announced.

"An' what of that?" Farren asked. "As if anyone'd peach on him."

"No," Sir Loren said. "He's *really* married. Which means all those saddened virgins, mourning widows and lonely wives are forced to make do with the second best." He smiled, stroked the pencil-line moustache he was cultivating.

The other surprise was two-fold: first that Limingo favored young men rather than women, and the second part was how many small villages had boys eager for his embraces.

Saslic was a little taken aback, thinking that such practices were mostly restricted to cities, but Hal just grinned. Between the road and the army, very little of what people did in bed surprised him any longer.

A day beyond Rozen, the soldiers stumbled into the rather casual formation Sir Bab required for a headcount before the carriages moved off.

"Thank some gods," Farren moaned, peering through red-rimmed eyes at Hal, "pick your lot t' pray to, that we'll be in the city tomorrow. I thought when we lit off, I'd as soon spend the rest of m'life ridin' along, eatin' only the best, and beddin' the lustiest. But I'm worn frazzled. An' walkin' bowlegged."

"Better to ride your dragon," Saslic suggested.

"Y'know," Farren said, changing the subject, "there's not been a maid I've met who objects t' the gamy smell of me. One said dragons make her randier."

"I don't even want to think about her dreams," Saslic said, with a shudder. "And if you'd bath more, like we've been doing, you wouldn't still stink of the beasts."

"Lass," Farren mourned, "you're not thinkin'. If th' ladies love it, who'm I to arguefy?"

If the villages and towns were gleeful, Rozen was hysterical.

"Isn't there anybody at work?" Sir Bab marveled as the carriages made their slow way toward the city's center. He smiled at a woman who tossed him a rose from an apartment window overhanging the street, ducked as someone threw half a winter melon through the carriage window.

"*Damn*, but I wish they'd stop thinking we're unbreakable," he muttered.

All of them had learned to wear pleased smiles, and wave slowly, to keep from wearing their arms out.

Again, there were far more women than men to be seen, and those men were generally boys, elders or in uniform.

The warrants were betting on which of the City Guard's barracks they'd be put up in, but nobody won the bet, as the carriages were guided into the great Tower complex, where the government of Deraine and King Asir's main castle were.

"An' aren't we shittin' in tall clover?" Farren marveled as they were given separate rooms built into the walls of the Tower itself. "M'mum'll never believe me. I'll have t' steal somethin' of real moment t' prove I was ever here."

*

The throne room was a dazzle of tapestries, gold, silk and noblemen and women. But Hal barely noticed. He and the other soldiers, save perhaps Sir Bab and Sir Loren, had only eyes for their king.

King Asir was a bit shorter than Hal's six feet, stocky, with very tired eyes. He wore scarlet velvet breeches and vest, over a white silk shirt, and a mere gold ringlet for his crown.

The soldiers had been issued new uniforms that were tailored to fit in a few hours, told to stand by, and the gods help anyone who had brandy on his or her breath when they were summoned.

They were marched into that throne room, surrounded by Deraine's nobility, and all knelt, bowed their heads, as instructed, when trumpets blared and the king entered.

He was flanked by an elderly lord with a beard and martial stance that challenged belief, and a pair of equerries carrying velvet boxes.

Asir went down the line, and Hal was most impressed at *his* training, for he knew the names of each man and woman, although a bit of Kailas snickered about what would happen should, say, he and Saslic change places.

He spoke briefly to each of them, a bit longer to Sir Bab, paused at Hal, looked him carefully up and down for a time. Hal tried to hide his apprehension.

"Serjeant Kailas," the king said. "This is the second medal I've given you in three months, the first in person."

"Yes, Your Highness."

Asir took a case from the equerry, opened it, and looped a medallion on a chain around Hal's neck.

"I'm delighted to honor your bravery, not just over Black Island, but in other places as well. You've served since the beginning," Asir went on. "Quite bravely, without proper recognition, both because of circumstance and evident jealousy.

"Fortunately for your building reputation, you're one of the favorites of the taletellers."

Hal, very nervous now, nodded, gulped.

"Yessir . . . I mean, Your Highness."

Asir smiled.

"Don't get goosey," he said. "Remember, I sit down to crap just like you do."

Hal had no idea whatsoever what the response to that should be.

The king nodded, went on down the line.

Farren, next to him, nudged him, subvocalized: "Whajer get for your medal?"

Hal ignored him.

The king returned to his throne, remained standing.

"I am mindful to make two further awards. Sir Bab Cantabri, come forward."

Cantabri obeyed.

"I now name you Lord Cantabri of Black Island, and declare this title shall be passed down to your heir and his heir, to keep the memory of your bravery fresh in men's minds until the ending of time. It is also in my mind to reward you with more earthly goods, estates, rights, which we shall discuss at a later time.

"Kneel, sir."

Cantabri obeyed, and King Asir took a small, ceremonial sword from the lord, tapped Cantabri on his shoulders and head.

"Rise, Lord Cantabri."

The king embraced him, and Sir Bab saluted, and returned to the ranks. Hal was surprised to see tears running down the hard man's face.

"There shall be one other honor this day," the king went on. "It was in my mind earlier today, but I wanted to meet the man first.

"This is an unusual honor, given not merely because this man is most brave, but is a pioneer member of our dragon fliers, what I have heard some call, before this lamentable war, dragonmasters.

"If any deserves this title more, I know it not.

"Through him, I am also recognizing all those who've struggled under the sometimes imbecilic traditions of the past, of a peacetime service that, at times, seems not to know times have changed, and that we are in the most bitter war of our existence.

"These men, and women, have fought, sometimes without success, to make the army, and I include myself as Supreme Commander, realize that just because something has been done in a certain manner for decades or centuries, that doesn't mean there isn't a better way.

"Frequently it is necessary, and I charge all of us to recognize this, to think hard on the way we fight, and consider other ways of doing things, instead of holding close the dead hand of the past.

"Serjeant Hal Kailas, come forward."

Hal gaped for half a lifetime, then Saslic, beside him, kicked him in the ankle.

"Move, you git!"

Hal obeyed, almost doubling up, as the army required, to the king, realized how unseemly that would be, almost stumbled, crimsoned, hearing a snicker from the rows of nobility.

But he kept his feet, and saluted the king.

"Kneel, sir."

Hal obeyed, and felt three taps on his shoulders and head, taps he felt with the crushing weight of the burden they brought.

"Rise, Sir Hal Kailas," the king said.

Hal did, saluted the broadly grinning king, and was never sure how he got back to his place in the file.

"Not just a friggin' medal," Farren Mariah marveled, "which means I'll not have t' plunder somethin' to show me mum, but a whole week's leave.

"Mayhap I'll not come back. And what'll you think of that, *Sir* Hal?"

"I'll hunt you down in that warren you live in," Hal said. "And drag you, kicking and screaming, back to the war."

"Now, that's not the way a proper knight knights," Farren complained. "Speakin' of which, how're you plannin' t' spend *your* next glorious week?"

Hal came back to a bit of reality, realizing he didn't have anywhere to go, had no family other than Caerly, and that held nothing at all for him.

"Be damned if I know," Hal said. "Thank the gods we got paid, and I can afford an inn."

"Paf to that," Sir Loren said. "You can always come home with me. I haven't a sister for you to lust after, so you'll not have to worry, Saslic. But even though the old manse is gloomy and stony, there's more than enough room for you."

"Or if you don't want to be fartin' around some frigid castle in th' bushes wi' strange beasties an' stranger bushcrawlers," Farren said, "there's an attic room one of m' uncles been wastin' away in too long."

Hal looked at Saslic.

"I'm to be back with my family," she said. "I don't know if you fancy being around dragons, or around suspicious fathers, even if they are Royal Keepers, but there's room."

"Sir Hal's living requirements are already provided for," a voice said, and the three turned, saw the taleteller Thom Lowess. "I'll be claiming my own reward on the man, though he's welcome to visit any of you.

"My townhouse is but ten minutes ride from the Menagerie, Serjeant Dinapur," Lowess said. "And I'm hardly suspicious around nightfall."

"Uh . . ." Hal managed.

"Sir Hal, you're not being consulted. You're being told," Lowess said firmly, taking him by the elbow. "Now, come with me."

The four hastily scribbled addresses and instructions to their respective places, and went their way.

"Now, young man, come pay the price," Lowess said.

"For what?"

"For your knighthood."

"Huh?"

"I would like a little respect, sir," Lowess said. "Who else has been slaving away, night and day, making sure your name is on everyone's lips, that the court itself buzzes with your bravery?"

"Oh. You mean . . ." Hal remembered what the king had said.

"I mean, I've been promoting you as if I were on your payroll."

"Why?" Hal was suddenly suspicious. Lowess spread his hands, smiled blandly.

"Why? How else does a taleteller advance himself, once he's become the voice of the nation, save by pushing causes and people who deserve it?"

Hal looked at him carefully.

"I'm not sure I understand."

"You're not supposed to," Lowess said cheerfully. "Chalk it up to a strange man's strange hobby. Now, come. We'll be late for dinner.

"There are certain ladies of the court who've made it very clear I'll no longer enjoy their favors unless they have an opportunity to meet you."

Thom Lowess' manor house was intended to show Lowess' vast travels in unknown lands, his notable friends, savage and civilized, in those lands, and the dignities that had been shown him.

It did that very well. Walls hung with paintings, weaponry, exotic objects. It was also very clear there was no wife or lady living there. The house oozed masculinity, all leather and dark wood, a bit too much so for Hal's tastes.

Lowess' table was also a marvel, with dishes Hal had never tasted, or heard of only from lords' braggadocio. There were cooks serving splendid items, servitors making sure no plate remained bare or glass empty for more than a few seconds.

And there was Lady Khiri Carstares, just seventeen, but with a glint in her eye suggesting experience beyond her years. She was slender, small breasted, almost as tall as Hal, and wore her dark hair curled and hanging down one side of her neck.

Hal couldn't decide whether her eyes were violet, green or some unknown shade of blue.

Lady Khiri was bright, quick with a laugh, or to be able to bring one. She appeared to follow news of the war closely, and was very aware of Hal's exploits.

Hal, before her eyes drew him in, had the sudden feeling of being a fat bustard, pursued by a relentless hawk. But he put that aside, thinking that he'd been too long in the company of mostly men, and was missing Saslic fiercely.

After the meal, there was dancing in a great ballroom, with a small orchestra. Hal tried to beg off, but Khiri insisted she was the finest teacher, and "surely a dragonmaster like you, Sir Hal, can learn anything as simple as the dance within a moment."

Kailas didn't know about that, but he managed not to step on her feet nor trip.

Hal felt guilty, remembering the men in the mud across the water, then laughed at himself. They surely wouldn't begrudge him, and if they were here in his place wouldn't think of a poor dragon flier's loneliness for even an instant.

There was punch, mild in taste, but strongly alcoholic, and magicians, really sleight of-hand artists, wandering through the crowd showing their tricks.

There was a break, and Hal found himself on a balcony, with a hidden fireplace, where they could look out over the city of Rozen.

"So whereabouts in this maze do you live?" he asked Khiri.

"For the moment, here, with Thom."

"Oh. He's your lover, then, or . . ." Hal let the sentence trail off.

"No, silly. He's just a friend of the family. But my family's holdings are largely on the west coast, or in the north. So, I have my own bedroom . . . a small suite, actually, like four or five other friends of Thom do. All we're required to do, he's said, is keep what he calls the loneliness wolves away, which in fact is no more than laughing at his jokes – which are very, very funny – and pretending not to have heard a story when sometimes you have." She shrugged. "That's a very cheap rent."

Khiri smiled up at Hal, came closer.

"Besides, it gave me an opportunity to meet a real hero, not one of these posers with their brass and polished leather."

The moment hung close, and Hal felt a sudden impulse to kiss her.

Fortunately, the orchestra started again, and he pulled back, took her hand.

"Come on. We're not through dancing, are we?"

Khiri looked disappointed, then smiled brightly.

"You're right. What's now is now . . . and what's later is . . ." She didn't finish.

Hal, feeling very confused, hoped there was a lock on his bedroom door. Or, perhaps, on hers.

But locks weren't needed.

That night he slept as he couldn't remember doing, since . . . since being on solid land in Paestum, with the rain beating down and no flight scheduled for the next dawn.

He woke, yawning, late the next morning, wondered if he could borrow a horse from Lowess and ride over to see Saslic.

As he was dressing, a courier came with a sealed message:

YOUR LEAVE IS CANCELLED. RETURN TO FLIGHT IMMEDIATELY WITH OTHERS. YOU ARE HEREBY ORDERED TO TAKE

COMMAND OF ELEVENTH FLIGHT AND RETURN UNIT TO
FIGHTING STANDARD. FULL SUPPORT AND REINFORCEMENTS
ARE AVAILABLE.

The order was signed by the lord commanding the First
Army.

Somehow, somewhere, disaster had struck.

19

"It is most unfortunate," Lord Egibi rumbled, his snow-white mustaches ruffling in a most martial manner, "the Roche chose to test their new secret weapon, deploying infantrymen in baskets slung below their damned dragons, on your Eleventh Dragon Flight. Sir Fot Dewlish and his men fought hard, but they were sadly outnumbered.

"*Most* unfortunate," he repeated.

Hal tried to hold back his anger, wondering what stove his reports of the Roche tactic months earlier had served as kindling for. Lord Egibi noticed Hal's expression.

"Is something the matter, Sir Hal?"

"Nossir."

The Lord Commander of the First Army had a good reputation among the troops as a man who'd given his life to soldiering in the service of the king, first against bandits in the north of Deraine, then on loan to the barons of Sagene to advise their own campaigns against highwaymen, then, just before the war with Roche, on the east coasts, quelling an outbreak of piracy.

He was a very big man, with very big appetites that he never bothered to deny, and boasted that he had no enemies, other than the Roche, living, who were worth acknowledgement.

The Lord Commander of the First Army got up from his padded chair, moved his bulk to a large-scale map, tapped a point.

"First the Eleventh is hit," he went on. "With the success of their attack, I can only assume the Roche will be striking at other flights.

"Sir Hal, I need a tactic to combat this! That's why I ordered you recalled from your sorely earned leave. I desperately need my dragons to prepare for the summer offensive, and if the Roche continue decimating – hells, destroying – my flights, I'll be blind!"

Hal's anger vanished. Finally someone in high command was admitting the dragons were more than just parade toys, only two years and more since the war had started.

"I've read the citation at your knighting, and agree with the king. We must have new ideas, new thinkers, or this war will just keep grinding us down and down until one side or the other collapses from sheer exhaustion. Which will hardly be a famous victory."

"Yes, milord," Hal said, trying to sound like a man of intelligence and action. "Give me a few days with my squadron, getting a full picture of what happened, and I'll do my best to come up with something."

"Go ahead," Egibi said. "But do more than your best, lad. Deraine needs help, desperately."

Hal saluted, started to leave, turned back.

"I'll need one thing, sir. A magician. A very good one. If possible, I'd like the services of a man named Limingo, who's still in Deraine."

"This matter has the highest priority. I'll have a courier off on a picket boat within the hour, requesting this Limingo be assigned to First Army and to you. And anything else you need will be provided."

"There just might be some other things, sir," Hal said.

"Just ask," Egibi said. "And we'll try to provide. I correct myself. We *shall* provide. Oh, by the way. A serjeant is a poor rank to command a dragon flight. Effective immediately, you're promoted captain on a brevet basis.

"Do well, and I'll confirm the appointment as permanent."

The crossbow thudded, and a bolt whipped down the long room into a target. Hal worked the grip under the bow back, then slid it forward, and another bolt dropped down into the trough from a tray clipped above the bow's stock.

Hal fired, and the second bolt buried itself beside the first.

"Good," he approved.

"Perhaps, as I warned you, sir," Joh Kious said, "a little light on the pull, due to the cocking lever design. But it will kill you your man. And five more with the other bolts.

"Or, precisely aimed," Kious added, eyeing the dragon on Hal's breast, "even a dragon. I applaud your design of this weapon."

"Not mine," Hal said. "One of my men, remembering a sparrow shooter of his youth."

"Very well," Kious said. "Your spare bolt carriers and bolts are already wrapped. Will there be any other way I might be of service?"

"Yes," Hal said. "I'll need crossbows built for my three fliers upstairs, plus thirty more crossbows made to a general pattern, plus ninety bolt carriers. And a thousand bolts. For a beginning."

"Young man," Joh Kious said, sounding slightly shocked, "do I look like a factory?"

"No, but you are about to look very rich," Hal said. "I want you to set up a plant building these crossbows. Hire as many as you need, price the weapons reasonably, which doesn't mean what I'm paying for this one, and start work. Payment will be immediately made by First Army's quartermaster on acceptance by me, in gold."

"Of course you want these crossbows yesterday," Kious said.

"Certainly," Hal said. "As I said when I ordered the first

one, if I'd wanted them tomorrow, I would have ordered them tomorrow."

Kious smiled.

"I've read about you in the broadsheets, Sir Hal. You certainly aren't a man unsure of himself."

Hal didn't reply.

"Very well," Kious said. "I should have known when I came across from Deraine something like this would happen and I'd be drawn into the maws of the military system once more.

"At least I'm providing for my old age," Kious said. "Which, remembering what it's like to deal with the army's quartermaster corps, looms close."

Hal and the three other fliers had expected the Eleventh's base to be thoroughly worked over. But the reality was worse – the farm estate was a shambles.

The main house appeared to have been set afire, and then some sort of explosion had scattered bricks across the grounds. Most of the other buildings had been fired as well, and the survivors of the flight occupied hastily pitched tents, scattered here and there.

Hal, riding behind Saslic on Nont, saw no sign of the flight's dragons as they lowered to land.

Around the flight's base was a garrison of infantry, also quartered in tents.

Very secure, Hal thought. Especially now that the barn's been burnt and the horse butchered for its meat.

Mynta Gart limped out to greet them, saw the captain's tabs Saslic had managed to find in Paestum, saluted.

Hal returned the salute, a bit embarrassed for some unknown reason, looked around as a scattering of handlers, some still bandaged, came out to take charge of the dragons.

"I think," he said, "I want you to tell me what happened, exactly as it happened, before we do anything else."

"Yessir." Gart's use of the title came easily, and Hal knew she must have seen others promoted over her head as a sailor, and thought little of the matter. "I think it best to repair to my tent.

"It's not a particularly lovely tale."

It wasn't.

The Roche, estimated two or three flights, all with basket-mounted infantrymen, had struck just as the sun was coming up.

"The first target was the nine dragons still on the ground, the bastards. That was where I picked up an arrow in my thigh, doing nothing in the way of good, trying to save my beast. I never was much of an infantryman.

"They killed the dragons, and went after anyone wearing flying insignia, then started killing anyone who fought against them.

"I came to just as they were looting and firing the buildings. That was where our fearless leader got killed."

Gart seemed reluctant to go on. Hal nodded at her, and she continued.

"Dewlish was in his office . . . I guess he was hiding. They came in, and saw his rump sticking out from under his desk. Someone put a spear in it, and drove him into the open.

"They beat him to death with that godsdamned dragon statue of his. Broke Bion in about a dozen pieces, and shattered Sir Fot's skull.

"They finally ran out of things to break, got back in their baskets and flew off. I don't think they took more than a dozen casualties, all told. Bastards!"

There were only two good notes.

The attacking dragons had been normal, multi-colored beasts, so evidently the number of black dragons thus far trained was minimal.

And the second was that none of Hal's fellow students in dragon school had been killed. Rai Garadice had been off on a dawn flight, not returning until the carnage was complete.

"Our own Feccia seems to have seen the Roche approach, and vanished. He claims he was going to alert the closest fighting unit, tripped in the woods and knocked himself unconscious, not coming to until the fight was over."

Gart smiled cynically. Hal made a note that, sooner or later, the coward would have to be dealt with. But there were more important matters to deal with.

Hal thought for a moment.

"What's our strength?"

"Five dragons . . . your three, and Garadice's and his partner. Nine fliers. Twenty-three survivors. Not much in the way of equipment. Morale is nonexistent."

"New gear is on its way, as are replacement dragons and fliers," Hal said briskly. "Now, I want you to take over as my adjutant, since Dewlish's crony got killed, simplifying matters.

"And I want the unit assembled in front of the main house in half a glass."

"Adjutant?" Gart said. "But I'm a flier."

"And so you'll remain. On this flight, there'll be only two sorts of people – fliers and those helping them."

Gart managed a smile.

"That'll be a surprise for some people."

"The first of many, I hope," Kailas said.

"Do you know what you're going to say?" Saslic asked.

"I think so," Hal said. "But for the love of the gods, don't you – or Farren – smirk at me, or I know I'll start laughing."

"What's it to be, then?" Saslic asked. "The old tyrant who bites nails in half routine?"

"Pretty much. Now get your ass out to formation, woman."

"Yessir, master sir."

The formation was as ragged as the tents the men and women fell out from. The fliers were at one end of the rank, curiously waiting.

Gart called them to attention, turned the formation over to Kailas.

"If you haven't heard by now, I'm the new flight commander," Hal said. "And I propose that we set about winning this war, instead of farting about the fringes as we've been doing."

There were mutters, some of agreement, others sounding surly.

"Here are the changes we'll start with," he continued.

"First, I want this damned camp straightened up. The tents will be rowed as they're supposed to be, and the grounds'll be cleaned. I don't want a flight that looks like a palace guard, but there's no particular reason you have to frowst about like vagabonds."

"Hard to wash, get clean, when all your gear's been burnt," someone in the ranks called, reluctantly added a "sir."

"Supplies, including rations, will be here by nightfall," Hal said. "For the moment, we'll keep that infantry contingent, in case our Roche friends decide to come back.

"Now, the second thing is from now on this flight is only going to concern itself with one thing – fighting the war. Anybody who thinks anything else is more important is welcome to apply for a transfer.

"I'll be in that tent over there after this assembly. Anyone who wants out will have all the help I can give.

"The same goes for anyone who doesn't want to soldier. The way out is wide open."

"The frigging Roche hit us once, now you're acting as if it's our fault," an unshaven man growled.

"No. It's nobody's fault," Hal said. "As long as it doesn't happen again."

"The hells with it," the man said. "I'll take you up on your transfer."

"Fine," Hal said. "The infantry always needs some more swordsmen."

The man looked alarmed, and there was a ripple of amusement.

"That ain't right," he grumped. "Almost die here, and then you'll put me where I'll get kilt for sure."

"Not my doing, friend," Hal said. "From your own mouth."

"But—"

"But nothing," Hal said. "You're gone as of tonight. And anyone else who's looking for the easy life can go with you.

"We got knocked down, but we're getting back up. And we're going to strike back. I promise you, the Roche who tried to destroy us will be destroyed in their turn.

"They'll be very damned sorry they ever heard of Eleventh Flight.

"We weren't much of a unit before, but all that's going to change, and change now.

"From now on, when anyone thinks of dragon fliers, they'll think of the Eleventh.

"That's all. All surviving section leaders report to me as soon as I dismiss you."

Hal had the beginnings of an idea, and ordered the clean-up crews to carefully set aside any Roche weapons or gear, and marked the spot where the few Roche casualties had been buried.

The wounded had been taken away when the Roche departed, so there weren't any prisoners to interrogate for what he needed, although he questioned the surviving members of the flight again and again.

At least, he noted with relief, none of them reported black dragons being used. But little else came – not the name of the attacking Roche units or anything else of value.

That, he hoped, Limingo the wizard would provide.

Egibi's promise was good. By late afternoon, wagons began rolling into the compound, filled with everything from food-stuffs to new uniforms to the necessary tools to squealing pigs for the still-to-materialize dragons.

Hal had been thinking of other things he needed, specifically one other man. Once more, a rider went off to First

Army headquarters and again the request was granted, and another picket boat set out for Deraine.

"Yer might 'swell go for anywot and everywot," Farren said. "Soon enow the gleam'll be off the rose, and we'll be lookin' for the hind tit to suck like the rest of the army."

"I'll bet," Saslic said, "you haven't thought about us."

"Uh . . . what should I be thinking?" Hal wondered.

"Men!"

"I've had other things on my mind," Hal said, only half apologetically.

Saslic growled incoherently, found calm.

"Look, you. You're now the muckety of this flight, which means you've got to be a moral upright."

"Oh," Hal said in a small voice.

Saslic nodded. "Moral uprights don't go around screwing their underlings. At least, not directly, and not if they want to have their soldiery fawning and yawping at their feet."

Hal sat down heavily on his bunk.

"Hells," he said.

"Just so," Saslic said. "Here I have to go and fall in love with this bastard determined he's gonna be a Lord of Battles, a Dragonmaster above all, which means he better not show any human failings."

"I don't like this," Hal said. "I do love you and don't want things to change."

Saslic softened.

"I know. I don't either. But I don't see any way that can happen."

"What do you want to do?"

"I *have* thought about things," Saslic said. "If I were a tough warrior, which I'm not, I'd transfer to another flight. But I'm not that strong."

"Thank some kind of god for that," Hal said.

"But I can't see any way that we can keep fooling around. At least, not on the flight. Can you?"

"I suppose not," Hal said miserably.

"Maybe we can sneak around, like we're married to other people, when we're in Paestum or away from the Eleventh. But no more."

"Shit."

"Shit indeed," Saslic agreed.

"I guess I shouldn't be whining," Hal said. "Considering what it'd be if I'd never met you, or if I was back in the lines. But . . ."

Saslic shrugged, her face as downcast as Hal's.

"War's a crappy business, all the way around, isn't it?"

Hal very quickly became too busy to worry about his private life or, indeed, to have any.

Support replacements came in, and were fitted into their slots.

Morale stayed low, for there wasn't anything to do until the dragons and the new fliers arrived.

Then ten dragons arrived, chained in great wagons. They were only half-trained, and the handlers had to work very carefully to avoid being bitten or clawed.

Farren Mariah found one handler, a new man, lashing a dragon with a chain. The man went to the infantry that same day, after Hal had assembled the flight and, as scathingly as he knew how, said the handler was no better than a Roche, trying his damnedest to lose the war.

The new fliers arrived, even less trained than the dragons, and Garadice and Sir Loren were put in charge of their training.

Hal had his own worry – training his own dragon not only to obey his commands, but all of the nuances he'd laboriously taught the dragon he'd lost off Black Island.

Remembering Saslic's advice, he grudgingly gave the dragon a name, remembering the tales he'd heard as a child of his mountain people, when they were reivers instead of being miners. The name he picked was Storm, after the fierce hound a legendary warrior owned.

*

Limingo arrived, with a mountain of gear, his two acolytes, a little put out at having to give up the flesh pots of Deraine.

But he forgot his complaints when Hal told him what he needed.

"Hmm," he said. "An interesting idea, and one I'd never thought of before."

Hal showed him the piled Roche equipment, and he seemed unimpressed.

But when Hal took him to the graves of the Roche dead, he brightened.

"Now this," he said, "is matter we can work with."

His smile wasn't pleasant, and Hal's stomach roiled a little.

"I assume you'll want to be present at the ceremony, once I figure it out?"

Hal didn't but knew he must.

Next to arrive was Serjeant Ivo Te, the leathery warrant from flight school.

Hal's orders were simple – Te was to beat the flight into shape. Nothing mattered except flying. He'd report to Gart, to Hal in extraordinary circumstances.

"Any preferences on how I train 'em?" Te asked.

"None," Hal said. "As long as it's quick, and not too bloody."

"I never draw blood," the serjeant said. "Welts and bruises are generally more'n enough.

"The incorrigible'll go off to be Roche fodder."

Hal dreamed, and knew he was dreaming. He was not a man, but a dragon, soaring high, free, with nothing below but tossing waves and ahead a land of mountains, rocks, crags.

Here there were animals for food, animals to hunt.

There were no men in this world, and the dragon rejoiced.

He floated from current to current, diving sometimes through clouds, the harsh wind and rain a balm to him.

Somewhere in those crags was a cave, empty now, but in

time, in season, a place for a mate and kits, a place to live from year to year, while the seasons rolled past, ever familiar, ever unknown.

A reveille bugle sounded, and Hal's eyes came open.

He sat up on his cot, looked out through the flaps of his tent at the flight's other tents, at a dragon grumbling as he was saddled, ready for the first patrol.

Hal remembered his dream, realized he was happy, feeling a great, quiet, sense of joy.

Kious' crossbows came in, and Hal had them issued. He ordered his fliers to begin practicing, first on the ground, then in the air, putting Serjeant Te in charge of the firing range as well. He made sure their confidence wasn't shattered by starting them on large targets, the size of cows, then working his way to man-size targets.

Thirty archers, real volunteers, from the infantry unit still guarding them were detailed off, and instructed in being dragon passengers.

Limingo sent one of his acolytes to Hal, saying he was ready for the ceremony, and would Hal please honor him by attending?

The acolyte said that he would be transcribing the results, assuming there were results, so Hal needn't worry about having to rely on memory.

The ceremony was scheduled at noon, rather than midnight, as Hal had expected, but Limingo had requested that all dragon flight personnel remain in their tents, for fear, the acolyte said, "of disrupting the ceremony." Then he added, a bit disquietingly, "or being disrupted."

The disciple, at the appointed hour, took Hal to the gravesites of the Roche raiders. The air was soft, late autumn, and a thin sun shone through the multi-colored leaves of the trees.

Buried in the gravemounds were spears, swords, arrows, all with their blunt ends pointed at a huge, round, bronze mirror or gong, hung about ten feet above the ground from a tripod.

Directly under it, an arrow had been mounted crosswise on a stake, set loosely in the ground so it could turn easily, like a wind indicator.

Limingo greeted Hal, noted his obvious nervousness.

"You don't have to worry . . . I'm not going to try to raise the dead. That isn't possible. At least I don't think it's possible . . . certainly not without some very potent, very dark magic.

"We're merely looking for some memories. Now, if you'll stand over there . . ."

Braziers were lit, and Hal wrinkled his nose. Maybe this spell wasn't dark magic, but some of its ingredients were certainly foul-smelling enough to qualify.

Limingo stood at one leg of the pyramid, motioned his disciples to the other two, then began chanting:

> *"Once you lived*
> *Saw, fought, lived*
> *Bring back that time*
> *When your eyes still saw*
> *Still saw."*

He reached up with a wand, barely touched the mirror, and it began humming, like a great, strangely tuned gong. Again, he took up his chant:

> *"But then you bled*
> *Then you died*
> *You could not*
> *Return.*
> *But were left*
> *Here on soil not your own*
> *Forever wanting to go back*
> *To the place you should*

> *Not have left*
> *The place with your friends*
> *Your officers*
> *A place of warmth*
> *A place of life*
> *Show us now*
> *The direction of your dead longing."*

The drone of the gong became louder, and the mirror came alive, showing huts, soldiers in Roche uniform, dragons, the dizzying view from one of the infantry baskets, dragons carrying soldiery, then, below, the farm the Eleventh Flight was quartered on. The scenes passed faster, faster, and there were men with swords, spears, soundlessly screaming Deraine soldiers, then the ground rushing up, and the gong's sound rose to a near-scream, then went black.

"Now, watch the arrow," Limingo ordered.

It swung back and forth, then steadied in a single direction.

"Mark!" Limingo ordered, then reached up and touched the gong, dulling it to silence.

"We should have enough power in the mirror to make this spell again," he told Hal. "Perhaps two or three leagues south of here.

"Draw those two lines until they come together, and—"

Hal's smile was wolfish.

"And we'll know just where the Roche came from."

Hal flew out before dawn, by himself. His dragon, Storm, was irritable, and the darkness let him remember a time when he was free, and he snapped experimentally at Hal, got a kick in his armored head for his pains, settled down.

Hal climbed high, then sent his dragon over the barren wasteland that was the front line, static now that winter was close.

His map was on his knees, a tiny dot that marked the intersection of the two magical lines his target, nothing more. In

case he was brought down by the Roche, they would have no
clue as to his mission.

There was heavy cloud for a time, and he flew by compass
heading. Then it broke, and Hal checked his bearings, saw he
was on track, and began scanning the ground far below.

He saw what he was looking for almost immediately.

It was well camouflaged, with huge nets over the two open
areas the Roche dragons would fly from, and the roofs of the
barracks and the fliers' huts were painted to look like farm-
land.

But not well enough.

"I must say, Sir Hal," Lord Egibi said, leaning back in his
oversized chair, "you've taken long enough to return to me."

"Sorry, my lord. But I needed certain things, and then my
magician took some time to prepare his spell."

"*Certain* things," Lord Egibi said with a snort. "You requisition materiel like you're . . . like you're a lord, dammit."

His attempt at looking angry failed, and a smile could be
seen under his mustache. Then it vanished.

"I hope, for all this expenditure of time, supplies and the
king's money, you have something for me."

"I do, sir," Hal said. "I now know where the three Roche
flights that wiped out the Eleventh flew from."

Lord Egibi looked puzzled.

"And with that, you propose what?"

"I am going to obliterate those flights," Hal said quietly.
"Every flier, every dragon, every soldier who attacked us will
die.

"The Roche struck us with terror. Now I propose to give
that back to them. To the last man."

20

The Eleventh Dragon Flight came over the wooded hillcrest just as the sky lightened. Ahead of them was the Roche dragon field.

Hal hadn't dared scout the base more than once, for fear the Roche would realize they were the target. But he assumed almost all armies were the same, and their leaders despised anyone wanting to sleep past a time when he could see his hand in front of his face.

Roche soldiers were, indeed, straggling out of their huts and barracks toward morning formation, and there were three dragons being saddled, prepared for flight.

The Eleventh was in a shallow vee, Hal in front.

Each dragon carried a flier and one archer, except for Vad Feccia's monster. Behind Feccia rode Serjeant Te, who not only had a bow like the others, but a ready dagger.

Hal had told Feccia that Te would be his passenger, and added, "He'll be most helpful to you, and make sure you don't stumble over any more tree roots."

Feccia had protested volubly about being misunderstood, and that he was as proud to be taking part in this revenge attack as anyone, smiling, but his eyes held pure hate for Hal Kailas.

Hal might have worried about being backshot, but not with Te around, and especially not since he'd learned, in his cavalry days, to turn his back on no one.

The dragons overflew the Roche formation, crossbow bolts raining down, and even a few of the archers managing aimed shots. They dove on the three dragons, who were barely awake. One reared, and Saslic's Nont ripped his throat open. The second took three bolts in his chest, thrashed, and died.

The last's wings flared, and he stumbled forward, trying to get aloft, as Sir Loren's dragon tore the rider away, and Garadice's beast's tail smashed its neck.

They banked back, and Hal motioned for a landing. They touched down, and, as ordered, the archers tumbled off, and, carefully picking targets, began their killing.

Hal motioned his dragons up, and they took off again, flying low across the field, shooting at anything that moved.

The Roche base was a howl of confusion and disarray, much, Hal thought, like the Eleventh must have been when the Roche came a-raiding.

He steered Storm over one of the camouflage nets, very low, and the beast seemed to know what he wanted, reaching out and grabbing the net, then, flapping hard, it went for the sky.

The net was far heavier than Hal had figured, and Storm was about to fall out of the sky when, to his considerable surprise, Feccia's dragon was on the net, just beyond Storm's wing-reach, lifting, and then Garadice's dragon was alongside, and the net was coming up and away.

It was like overturning a rock to see scorpions scatter. Under the net were the dragon pens, the monsters screaming in surprise at the sunlight, fliers running for their beasts, handlers trying to get them ready to take to the air.

Hal grabbed the bugle hanging from one of Storm's head-spikes, tootled unmusically, but his flight heard, and responded.

The dragons swept down across the dragon pens, their riders firing at the beasts, banked back, and made another attack.

Hal motioned ahead, seeing his infantrymen beset by

Roche. One was down, then the Roche saw the on-rushing dragons, broke and ran.

Hal brought the dragons down, and the archers scrambled aboard, one pulling the wounded man with him.

Then the dragons were stumbling forward, gracelessly leaving the ground, becoming instantly elegant as they climbed for the heights, back toward the Deraine lines.

But that was not enough. That evening, at dusk, Hal brought his dragons back, with a fresh group of archers.

There were two Roche dragons in the air, and they went down under a hail of crossbow bolts.

The dragons dove, landed their archers, and again, swept back and forth across the base, this time tearing away the second net.

Hal had brought a new weapon with him – thin glass wine bottles filled with lamp oil, and given a conjuration to burn.

The bottles were scattered by the fliers, flaring into life as they struck and smashed.

Flames grew, jumped to the camouflage, spread to huts and barracks.

Other dragons were shot down as they stumbled, screaming, out of their burning pens, their masters shot down in cold blood, no mercy being given.

Then the raiders were gone.

Hal was not through with the Roche.

Again, he came back at dawn, and this time there was little to burn, few to kill. But the dragon fliers methodically combed the fields, shooting down any Roche they saw.

They made one more pass, each flier dropping a pennon of the Eleventh Flight so the Roche would know who had attacked them.

Two days later, word came from spies who'd crossed over the lines.

The Roche squadron had been all but obliterated, with no more than two or three fliers still able to fly, and all dragons killed.

The unit was broken up, its few survivors sent to other Roche dragon flights. This made Hal grin, for these broken men would surely tell the tale, and Roche morale would further dip.

Another report came – responsibility for the Roche dragons opposing the First Army had been taken over by *Ky* Bayle Yasin, and his newly established Black Dragon Squadron.

Some looked fearful, but Hal nodded in satisfaction.

Now he would get a chance, he hoped, to fight the man he illogically felt a grudge against, going all the way back to the death of Athelny of the Dragons.

21

The broadsheet fairly screamed:

The Dragonmaster Strikes!

Hal winced.

"The dragonmaster, eh?" Lord Bab Cantabri said, mock admiration heavy in his voice.

"The broadsheets have a vivid imagination," Hal said.

"Still, that might look good, tastefully embossed on some stationery," Cantabri said. "Here's another good one," and he read the screamer aloud:

Hero of Deraine Modest,
Worshipped by His Men

"Oorg," Hal managed, picking up another sheet from the impressive pile Cantabri had brought to the flight:

"His long, blond hair streaming, Sir Hal shouted his dragon fliers in to the attack with his battlecry, 'The Gods for Deraine and King Asir' . . ."

"Bastards can't even get my hair color right," Hal grumbled, rubbing his close-cropped brown hair.

"Heroes *always* should have long, blond hair," Lord Cantabri said. "Makes 'em much more followable."

"Here's another:

"An exclusive account of the dashing raid against the Roche, as told directly by Sir Hal Kailas to Deraine's favorite taleteller, Thom Lowess—"

"That great liar I haven't seen since getting my leave cut short back in Rozen," Hal interrupted.

"Now, now, Sir Hal," Cantabri said in a soothing voice, his wicked smile undercutting any attempt at comfort. "Never let the truth stand in the way of a good story."

Hal grunted, listened as, outside the window, Farren Mariah read from another broadsheet with suitable emendations:

"Teeth gritted against the bleedin' autumn gales, grindin' his tongue to powder, our own Sir Hal lashed his dragon with his crop, forcing the enormous beast to whirl in his tracks, and smash into two attacking Roche monskers.

"Whirl, whirl, like a friggin' top.

"An' then the dragon took one Roche horror by its neck, usin' two talons of one claw, and dandled it up and down, then hurlin' it away, whilst our own Sir Hal grabbed the second horror by the tail, swung him about his head, and then—"

Hal closed the window with a bang, as a patrol of six soldiers marched past.

"I suppose," Cantabri said, "those square-bashers are just in case *Ky* Yasin decides to come back on you."

"They are."

"Best you should think about changing bases entirely," Cantabri suggested. "But keep the base support at your new post. The Roche have spies as well who might winkle you out."

"I'm already scouting for something," Hal said. "Preferably closer to the lines, so we'll be able to get a little flying in when winter comes."

"Ah, but I have a better suggestion," Cantabri said, smiling blandly. "One guaranteed to keep you out of the winter weather, nice and active, and fighting for your country as proper heroes should.

"And not just you, but the whole flight, should you choose to volunteer them."

"I should've known you came here with more than delivering papers on your mind."

"If you have a map about – in a nice, secure place – I'll show you where the further opportunities to cover yourself with glory are."

"Or get dead."

"That," Cantabri sighed as he followed Hal into an inner room, "seems to go with the territory, does it not?"

He went to one of the maps in the briefing room, a fairly small-scale map of the entire front.

"Now, as we all know," he said, deliberately taking on a false tutorial manner, "the war is currently at something resembling a stalemate.

"What has been proposed by the king and his advisors, is a bold masterstroke, to quietly pull selected units from all four armies, move them to Paestum, together with new units currently training in Deraine, and Sagene allies.

"We'll go by sea, around Sagene's western border, then east, until we're beyond Sagene and the lines, and then make a bold assault on the Roche heartland.

"I'll not tell you just where yet, but it's along a river, that we can follow up to reach Roche's capital of Carcaor."

"How many men?"

"At least a hundred thousand."

"Which you'll be able to keep from talking about their coming glorious adventure?"

"If they don't know, they can't talk. We'll probably arrange some camouflage scheme, like issuing them arctic gear, reversing the promises we made for the Black Island expedition, or arranging for a map of Roche's northern seafront to be captured."

"What happens when we round Sagene's south-western cape? I assume the Roche have some sort of navy."

"Deraine's ships will be screening for the convoy."

"Mmmh. How many dragon flights?"

"Four have been selected."

"Not many for a hundred thousand men."

Cantabri lost, for a moment, his confidence.

"I know ... but dragon fliers are scarce, and new formations won't be ready until spring, at the earliest."

"And you're in command of this operation?"

"No," Cantabri said, realized the note of his voice, and tried to put confidence back into it. "A close friend of the king's, a Lord Eyan Hamil, will command."

"I don't know the name."

"As I said, he and the king are very close. The story I've been given is that he's been in command of the approaches to Northern Deraine, and has begged the king for a more active command. He's an older man, quite charming."

"But he's never led an army in the field."

"No."

The two men stared at each other for a moment.

"Well," Hal said, "I'll put it to my fliers."

"You command most democratically."

"When it's convenient," Hal said. "Has there been any more of a plan developed beyond get ashore in this spot you won't name for me, and start marching upriver?"

"Not really," Cantabri said. "What deployments we'll make after the landing will depend on the Roche reactions."

Hal rubbed his chin.

"Is this the way you would have run this expedition?"

Cantabri stared at him.

"I don't think I'll answer that."

"You don't have to, sir."

Hal got up.

"I'll call the troops together, and have an answer to you – I assume you're at the First Army headquarters – by nightfall."

"You won't find me there," Cantabri said. "But I have a deputy there. As for myself, I have three other armies to canvass for brave men and heroes, so I've leagues still to ride this day."

"You really think we can pull this off?" Hal asked, watching Cantabri closely.

"Yes," Cantabri said, then, with growing confidence, "Yes, I do, and end this damned war for once and all."

22

The sea beyond Paestum was aswarm with ships, from transports converted from merchant ships to hopefully ocean-worthy ferries and deep-water fishing boats without their nets to, Hal was glad to see, the *Galgorm Adventurer*. He was even more pleased to find that someone – he suspected Lord Cantabri – had arranged for it to be the Eleventh's transport.

This operation had been in the planning for some time – the *Adventurer*'s upper troopdeck had been hastily converted, with a raised and arched topdeck, to provide more dragon shelters.

As they were loading the beasts, trying to avoid being maimed by a dragon tail or drowned by being kicked off the quay by one of the fairly unhappy monsters, the rumor ran around that this was the beginnings of a great operation, to attack behind the northern Roche lines, and smash through to the capital.

"Which means codswallop," Farren said. "All we need now is to be gifted with winter gear, and I'll know for surely-certain we're goin' south.

"Friggin' military always thinks it can think, when by now it oughta know better. I could cast a little witchy pissyanty spell and find out where we're going, so you know damn-dast well the Roche wizards are already laying in wait."

Hal thought of telling him to button it, that his guess was far too close, but that would've only made the tale run faster.

"*Damned* fine thing," Saslic said dryly, looking out over the fleet, "that we're able to move in such secrecy. Thankin' the gods there aren't any Roche spies over there on the waterfront, spitting in the water and taking notes."

"Anybody else want to contribute?" Hal said.

"I think not," Sir Loren drawled. "I'm sure we're just off to the homeland for our holidays."

The ships, loosely gathered into lines, sailed north until they were out of sight of land, then swung west down the Chicor Straits, as had the *Adventurer* in its masking maneuvers before turning toward Black Island.

Hal didn't think it would do much good to conceal the operation from the Roche.

Mynta Gart spent a lot of time on deck, when she wasn't tending her new dragon, and Hal asked her if a seaman like her didn't like being below decks.

"Doesn't matter much to me," she said. "And I didn't notice I was above decks as much as you say. Perhaps I'm worried about the weather."

Hal lifted an eyebrow.

"This is damned late in the year to be sailing toward the open ocean," she said. "Winter storms're coming, and that bodes no good for the spit kits we've got around us.

"I can only hope we've got weather luck. Or some damned powerful wizards casting spells in the flagship."

Perhaps so, for no gales tore down on the fleet before it turned north again, and found a sheltered anchorage behind a long, narrow island, the Deraine port of Brouwer, where another great array lay waiting.

Some of these ships were brand new, others converted to merchantmen, and they were packed with troops, mostly new formations raised in Deraine.

Now, Hal thought, we should put out to sea as quickly as possible, before the tales have time to spread.

But they sat at anchor, waiting.

Hal's soldiers began grumbling, and so he put Serjeant Te to work on them, running them around and around the decks, up and down ropes, keeping them fit, with little time to get bored.

He flew off two three-dragon patrols each morning and night, and that kept his fliers from getting bored.

And they waited.

A royal messenger was rowed out to the *Adventurer*, with a request, from Lord Cantabri, to meet the expedition's commander, Lord Hamil, at a dinner to be held by Thom Lowess.

It seemed the taleteller had his fingers in everywhere.

It was a small, intimate gathering, at least by Lowess's standards. He'd rented a beach-front pavilion, and brought several of "his girls," including Lady Khiri Carstares.

A dozen men sipped wine in the antechamber. Hal was the lowest ranking of them all, and Lowess the only one not in uniform.

"Sir Hal," he smiled at Kailas. "At last I'll get a chance to see you in action."

"You mean you're going with us?"

"Lord Hamil has specially invited me, which pleases me no end." However, Lowess didn't look that thrilled. Hal wondered, and thought poorly of himself for the cattiness, whether Lowess preferred concocting his tales of derring-do a bit farther from the clash of battle.

Lady Khiri spotted him, and made for him as if he were magnetized. He tried to make polite conversation, but was all too aware of Saslic, back on the *Adventurer*, not to mention that the gown Khiri wore was scooped low enough in front so that he could've seen the color of her toenail polish without undue effort.

"And so you'll be one of the lucky ones," she said. "Not with us, freezing our poor little heinies off, here in the northland."

"How did you know?" was the best Hal could manage, hardly a way of dissimulating.

"Why, simply *everyone* knows," she said, in considerable astonishment. "It's been the talk of the court for weeks now."

"Wonderful," Hal muttered.

"If I didn't know better, and hadn't been aboard some of the terribly crowded ships you men will be sailing on," she went on, "I'd wish that you and I might be sharing a cabin, watching for the first flying fish, and feeling the wind grow warm around us."

Hal felt a bit warm at that moment, was relieved to see Lord Cantabri beckon him over. He excused himself, joined Cantabri and the other man he was with, medium height, white-haired, distinguished and looking most regal.

"Sir Hal, I'd like to introduce you to Lord Hamil," Cantabri said.

Hal guessed, at an event like this, it would be better to bow than salute. He evidently guessed correctly, for Hamil made a curt bow in return.

"So you're the young man on whom Lord Cantabri said we might well be depending?"

Hal fought for the proper words.

"I'd think, from what I've seen, we're more likely to be depending on him."

"A good, gentlemanly answer, sir," Lord Hamil approved, then turned to Cantabri.

"When this war first began, and the idea of men – and women – flying dragons, I was bothered by the idea, first that a measure of chivalry might be slashed from the nobility of war, and secondly, that these fliers might be less than gentlemanly warriors.

"But from what I've read of this young man, and the men and women he commands, I find that my suspicions were false.

"Indeed, to soar high over the muck and blood of the battleground might be creating a new nobility, a nobility of the air, and one which, were I beginning my military career, I might well envy and wish to join."

Neither Hal nor Cantabri found an answer to that one, although Hal tried feebly.

"I can only hope, Lord Hamil, to be worthy of your hopes."

"I'm sure you shall, lad," and Hamil smiled, and turned to another, passing lord.

"I say, Lord Devett, a word with you?"

Hal was about to say something to Cantabri, when Lowess approached them.

"Ah, the two sharpest arrows in my quiver. Are you enjoying yourselves, gentlemen?"

Hal took the moment.

"I'd be a deal happier, sir, were our expedition not on everyone's lips."

Lowess frowned.

"I know. I like it little myself. But the word has been going about for weeks. There's even been mention of a betting pool as to just what our destination is, and what I've heard mentioned is uncomfortably close to our plans.

"I suggested to Lord – to certain parties – that some replanning might be in order. He chose to disagree with me, so there appears little I can do.

"I wish there was more, since I will be sharing your fate this time."

Cantabri drained his wine glass.

"Might I ask you something, *sir*?" he said.

Hal noticed the slight emphasis on the sir.

"Anything within reason."

"You just said the two brightest arrows in your quiver. I'm not sure I understand."

"What I meant was quite simple. Just as I seem to have made certain people, and perhaps the nation of Deraine, aware of Sir Hal's propensity for valor, so I plan on doing the same for you as we progress to . . . to our eventual goal."

"I would rather not be so favored," Lord Cantabri said dryly.

"But Deraine needs heroes, sir. Don't pursue false modesty, sir," Lowess said, a bit sharply. "Heroism unnoticed, and unrewarded, does the nation little good.

"I'm afraid the burden is one you'll be forced to bear."

Cantabri sought for something to say, forced a smile and nodded.

Lowess fielded a glass from a passing servitor, and left them.

"It's nice to be in the company of a budding hero," Hal said.

"Damn, damn, damn," Cantabri growled.

"Now, what was it you were saying, Lord Cantabri," Hal mocked gently, "about not letting the truth stand in the way of a good story, just a few days ago?"

"Damme for dooming myself with my own mouth," Cantabri grumbled. "Now we'll both be laughing stocks, I fear."

Hal grinned, and a gong sounded. A door opened, and the guests began filtering toward the dining room.

The dinner began with a toast by Lowess:

"To our victory, and to the noblest of Deraine's warriors, gathered here tonight."

That, of course, was drunk to only by the women carefully positioned between each guest.

The next toast was by Lord Hamil:

"Confusion to our enemies."

That everyone drank to, Hal particularly, although he barely tasted the wine, since he'd been doing no drinking lately, and didn't think part of being a noble hero was throwing up on his host's linen.

The room was a marvel of old paintings and silk hangings. Four musicians, behind a screen, played softly, and a magician and two assistants worked interesting illusions that appeared, vanished, against a muslin curtain against one wall.

The illusions were of patriotic themes, great warriors, interspersed with sentimental scenes of life in Deraine. Hal wryly noticed that all these scenes were of the rich and their estates. That made sense, he thought. No one in the room, with the exception of Hal, came from a poor family.

He was seated next to Lady Khiri Carstares, who, he thought, grew prettier each time he saw her.

"I want to apologize," she said.

"For what?"

"I saw you were upset that I know about . . . about certain matters."

"I am," Hal admitted.

"Do I look like a Roche spy?"

"I never saw one wearing a sign yet."

She smiled.

"Maybe not you," Hal went on. "But what about that waiter who just served us this fish pancake?"

"That, you barbaric soldier, is caviar . . . fish eggs. With sour cream."

"Oh." Hal chewed. "I guess I like it. But us barbaric soldiers like anything that isn't trying to eat us."

"Stop trying to be clever," she said. "Leave that for Thom Lowess."

They chatted on, about almost anything and everything except the war, and Hal found Khiri a delightful conversationalist.

Of course you do, a part of his mind said coldly. She's agreeing with almost everything you say.

The next course was perfectly cooked steak in a green peppercorn sauce, followed by herb-baked potato thins, puréed

spiced vegetables, a watercress and endive salad with a
lemony mustard dressing, and dessert was a meringue tort.
Each course was accompanied by a different wine, which, as
before, Hal barely tasted.

"You're quite the abstainer, sir," she said.

"Sometimes," Hal agreed. "When I don't want a thick head
the next day."

"You needn't worry about that," she said, leaning close,
and glancing around to make sure no one was listening.
"You won't be sailing until the winter storm the wizards
have forecast has passed, and that won't be for at least four
days."

Hal was brought back to reality. Again, Khiri noticed.

"I'm sorry," she almost wailed. "Should I be a total ninny,
and not talk about *anything*?"

Hal thought of explaining, decided if she didn't understand
by now, she never would.

But Khiri realized her mistake, and began asking him about
the habits of his dragons. Hal, eager for the change, talked on,
then caught himself, realizing he was probably beginning to
sound like Dinner Bore, Category Thirteen, the Dragon
Expert.

He was about to apologize, when he realized Khiri had
taken off her evening slipper, and, hidden by the long table-
cloth, was rubbing her soft foot up and down his inner calf,
above his dress half-boot.

He found himself gently sweating, looked at Khiri, saw her
smiling, delighted with the effect she was working.

He made some inane comment about one of the illusions, a
soldier and his lover walking arm in arm through a swirling
garden.

"You are married?" Khiri asked.

"No," Hal said.

"But you have a lover."

"Uh . . . well, yes." Hal was ashamed of his hesitation.
"How did you know?"

"The best men always have lovers," Khiri said mournfully. "Tell me about her."

To his surprise, Hal found himself yammering on about Saslic, and Khiri seemed most interested.

Then Hal's glass was empty, and Thom Lowess was standing again.

"I thank you all for attending my gathering," he said. "Boats are at the landing below, and I suggest it's time for those who're aboard ship to leave, since the weather appears likely to change within the hour.

"The promised storm is, indeed, upon us."

Khiri walked him down to the dock, shivered as a chill wind caught her.

"You'll forgive me, Sir Hal, for not staying, but this gale is freezing my poor little marrow."

Before he could respond, she leaned close, and kissed him, her tongue darting for an instant between his lips. He reached for her, reflexively, but she pulled away with a bell-like laugh, and ran up the steps into Lowess's mansion.

Hal tasted that kiss for a long time on the ride through the choppy waters back to the *Adventurer*.

The storm broke as predicted that night, and the ships put out double anchors but still heaved restlessly as the rain and wind beat at them.

Hal spent most of his time, as did the fliers and handlers, making sure the dragons were as happy as they could be, feeding them tidbits of offal the ship's cooks were only too glad to get rid of.

He tried to spend his time thinking about how his fire bottles might be improved, either magically or with better material, but Khiri's face kept intruding.

Saslic asked him why he was so pensive, and he was rude to her, and apologized hastily.

She looked at him strangely, but said nothing.

*

Four days later, the storm ended, and the sky was a wintry blue, the seas calm as a lake.

Signal flags went slatting up and down masts, and anchors were weighed, and slowly, laboriously, the great fleet made its way out into the open sea.

Hal was standing next to Sir Loren, Vad Feccia and Mynta Gart, awestruck at the vast number of ships, and Loren pointed.

"Look."

Half a dozen warships, sleek three-masters, bulwarks heavy with infantry, their rams, beaks, catapults menacing, boiled past under full sail, banners streaming.

Gart stared after them, eyes shining.

"Shows what a damned fool you were, coming to the dragons, when you could be mate of one of them now, coverin' yourself with glory," Vad Feccia said, with more than a bit of a senseless sneer.

Gart looked him up and down, but said nothing.

Hal determined that Feccia would be chosen to supervise some detail, preferably involving dragon shit.

Winds rose, and another storm threatened. Hal saw sailors praying in the small niche behind the *Adventurer*'s mainmast, guessed that seamen aboard the countless smaller ships would be praying even harder.

But the wind blew out before dawn, and once again the fleet sailed on.

Hal took his dragons up daily, staying close to the convoy, under orders not to fly south of the ships, toward land. The last headlands of Deraine fell away to their stern, and Sagene's coastline was, at most, a dim blur they never closed on.

Then the ships turned south, and even the thickest soldier realized they weren't about to campaign in the frozen north.

Morale and mood improved steadily.

They turned a bit closer to land, and twenty Sagene ships,

plus escorts, joined the convoy. They were cheered by the Deraine soldiers and sailors, gave back huzzahs in return.

The fleet was at full strength.

Hal was on the foredeck at night, and one of the watch officers paced back and forth a few yards away.

Something to the landward caught his eye, and he asked to borrow the sailor's glass.

A darker bulk showed – Sagene. He stared at it, then saw a flare of light grow, start blinking.

"What's that?" he asked the officer. The man took the glass, scanned.

"Shit," he muttered.

"What is it?" Hal asked. The officer passed the glass back. The blinking light flashed again, then died.

"Two fingers to starboard," the sailor said, and Hal swung his gaze.

Another light came to life, blinked.

"Navigation beacons?" Hal guessed.

"The charts show none," the sailor said. "More likely signal beacons."

"Signaling what?" Hal asked, then caught it. "Oh."

"You have it," the sailor said grimly, and hurried to the captain's cabin to report they were being tracked.

Storm fairly leapt into the air, and honked in glee. None of the dragons liked being aboard ship. Hal wondered about that – how they could sail like boats, but despise these wooden creations, guessed it might be the stink of men, or perhaps the unnatural swaying as the ship rolled.

He sent Storm high, two other dragons climbing behind him, swooping in pure pleasure.

The wind was from the west-south-west, and almost warm, even here, a thousand feet above the water.

Hal scented a different wind – the wind of battle.

*

Sailors put out long trotlines, and pulled fish in, fish multi-colored and unknown to any of the men and women of Deraine.

The cooks set braziers on deck, and fried the fish, basting them in butter, and drenched them with hoarded lemons from Sagene. Hal thought he had eaten a record number of the crispy small delicacies, then saw Farren Mariah, still inhaling, two bites per fish, no more, not concerning himself with bones, crunching them like he was a beast.

"I'm catchin' up on a d'prived childhood," Mariah explained.

"You mean depraved," Saslic suggested.

"That too."

The dragons also liked the fish – fed to them raw, in bushel baskets.

Signal flags from the flagship went to the *Adventurer*, and Hal took half his flight aloft, flew east obeying the orders from Lord Hamil.

Great headlands rose from the sea, the ocean smashing high against them, empty bluffs that, according to his map, marked the farthest westering bit of Sagene.

Hal looked back, saw the fleet slowly turning west, following the coast toward Roche.

He saw something and, against orders, motioned Saslic to follow him down.

Storm's wings folded, and the dragon dove until Hal pulled the reins back.

The monster flared his wings, came level, and the headland's flat plateau was only a few hundred feet below.

Hal saw half a dozen tents, and something he couldn't quite make out. Then he saw it clear – a large mirror, gimbal mounted. There were half a dozen men around it, some looking out to sea.

Then smoke flared, and a small fire grew below the mirror. It moved, beginning to flash rapidly, in some sort of code, pointed east. Hal squinted through the haze, thought he saw an answering blink.

He hoped this was an unmarked signal post of Sagene, but suspected far differently.

Hal waved to Saslic, and turned, at full speed, back toward the fleet.

A ship's boat took Hal to the fleet's flagship, a huge warship with holystoned decks and brightwork everywhere. Barefoot sailors in spotless uniform scurried here and there, as busy as housemaids, under the shouted orders of boatswains.

Hal saw Thom Lowess on the poop deck, nodded to him, ignored his obvious curiosity.

He was escorted to the enormous cabin of Lord Hamil. Hal thought it almost as large as a dragon pen.

They reported what they'd seen on the headlands to Hamil, Cantabri, two Sagene noblemen and staff officers.

Hamil said calmly, "I like this news but little."

Lord Cantabri nodded grimly, but said nothing.

Hamil got up, paced.

"So we must assume we've been seen ... I'd guess those mirror-men could be Sagene traitors."

One of the Sagene nobles growled in anger, but made no comment.

"Or," Hamil went on, "more likely, long-range penetration agents from Roche.

"In either case, that means we've been seen by the enemy."

He looked worried. Hal couldn't understand – the fleet, and its design, had been known to everyone, including the gods on high, since before they sailed from Paestum.

Why should this latest be an astonishment?

But he held his tongue.

"Ships of the Roche fleet might be readying to sail against us," the other Sagene nobleman said worriedly.

Hamil nodded agreement.

"Very well, Sir Hal," Hamil said. "I'll notify the other three dragon flight commanders, and from now on you'll mount constant patrols to the east and north as we sail on toward Roche.

"You must be totally alert, watching especially for any unknown ships.

"From now on, as Lord Cantabri suggested to me back in Deraine, our fate could well be in your hands."

23

From aboard ship the Deraine fleet was most impressive. But from two thousand feet, the ships weren't nearly as awe-inspiring. Hal finally had a chance to count them, as Storm climbed for height. He made about seventy Deraine ships, thirty from Sagene and, in front and along the flanks, another twenty-five warships.

No one had any idea how many ships Roche might have in their navy, their size or deployment, since most of them were evidently berthed in southern waters.

It had possibly made sense to ignore the Roche navy as long as the war was fought on land, and the only sea-guard that needed keeping was over the Chicor Straits. But how no intelligence could have been gathered once Deraine decided on this amphibious invasion . . .

Hal turned that part of his mind off. He would never understand the thinking of generals and such.

Garadice and Sir Loren flew at Hal's flanks, and he set a compass course due west, eyes searching for any ships. Other than a scatter of fishing smacks, he saw nothing, and turned back after a three-hour flight, half of a dragon's comfortable range.

Hal and his team mates landed on the *Adventurer*'s barge, and another scouting flight took off from another transport.

He reported to Lord Hamil on the flagship by coded pennant, ate, waited for his next turn aloft.

Hal spent the time inventorying the fire bottles he'd had made up, with spells by one of Limingo's assistants, wondering just how he'd use them in the invasion. He dreamed of a new device, something that would really explode, something as big as a man, but had no idea how such a killing machine might be built, either by normal engineering or by magic.

His next shift began at midnight, and so he chose Saslic and Garadice to accompany him as the most capable fliers, and paid close attention to his compass on the way out, and on the way back.

Nothing was seen.

Saslic brought him an interesting sheet of paper.

"Look you," she said. "We're not doing all we could."

"Explain, if you would," Hal said.

"Easily. We fly out for three hours, then back for three. That gives us a known area, like I've drawn here, which is no more than the fleet takes to travel in two days."

"Two days is a long time."

"To plan a battle?" Saslic asked, glanced about. "Particularly with these dunderbrains in charge of us?"

"You have an idea?"

"Surely. If there's such a thing as a good chart . . ."

"Maybe," Hal said, "from the captain."

There was, a merchant seaman's map from before the war. Saslic spread it across the navigator's table, ignored his scowl, and studied it closely.

"Just what are we supposed to be looking for?" Hal asked.

"For this," and her finger stabbed at the map. Hal bent closer, saw three tiny dots, just beyond the Sagene-Roche border.

"Islands. Uh . . . the Landanissas."

"Smart, smaaaart man," Saslic said. "A bit more than – what's the scale on this damned map? – eight hours flight time, assuming the fleet is about here. We wait until we're within six hours' range, then what we do is take, oh, two other fliers, and fly off to those islands. That'll give us a forward base to look for the Roche . . . Assuming they've got any ships out there."

"Supposing those islands, which look pretty damned small, don't happen to have anything like water or something we can feed the dragons with?"

"They will," Saslic said confidently. "Look. This little one's got a littler dot, with the name of the port – Jarraquintah. Damned barbarous names these Roche use. Any place with a name has got people. Any place with people's got pigs and water.

"Admire my strategic abilities, O Sir Hal."

"I'm admiring," Hal said. "Four fliers."

"You, me, Garadice and Sir Loren. The best we've got."

Hal took Saslic's plan to Lord Cantabri, figuring that anything irregular was more likely to be approved by him, or at least go to Lord Hamil with Cantabri's hero stamp on it.

Cantabri studied the map and a brief outline thoroughly.

"You'd need gold," he said. "Both for bribes, and for supplies, assuming Dinapur's right, and the island's inhabited.

"What happens if it's garrisoned?"

"We'll make a sweep first," Hal said. "If there's sign of soldiery, we'll shelter on one of the islands until our dragons are rested, then fly back."

"And if all three islands have soldiers?"

Hal had thought of that.

"The only thing we'll be able to do is fly due north, toward Roche, and land on the water if our beasts are winded. Wait for a time, then go on to the mainland.

"We'll try to find a source of supply there, either by force of arms or with the gold, then fly back to the fleet."

"Assume you can't," Cantabri said.

"Then we'll make our way north, as we can," Hal said. "North and west, toward the Sagene border and our lines."

"And if you're captured?" Cantabri said.

Hal shrugged.

"Try not to talk as long as we can. Then . . ."

"Anyone can be broken," Cantabri said grimly. "I'm glad you're not laboring under illusions of heroism."

"I stopped that the first time I got wiped out," Hal said. "Back with the cavalry."

"A hard lesson to learn," Cantabri sighed, looking about Lord Hamil's cabin and the swarm of brave-looking staff officers. "Sometimes I think . . ."

"What, sir?"

"Nothing," Cantabri said. "I'll have to take this to Lord Hamil, of course. But I see no reason he won't approve.

"Go ahead and make your preparations, and I'll signal the *Adventurer* with the decision.

"And if I don't get a chance to give you my blessings and prayers, for whatever they're worth, when you fly off, you have them now.

"Go, and find the damned Roche, if they're out there. *But come back!*"

The four dragons took off through a lowering rain and cloud cover. Hal orbited the *Adventurer* until all four were together, then pulled Storm's reins back, and prodded its flanks into a steep climb.

He vanished into the clouds, hoping that the other fliers weren't prone to vertigo. Or dragons, either . . . And he realized nobody knew if they could lose their mental balance.

He would've prayed, if there was anyone left to pray to, or cross his fingers, except that bold dragonmasters didn't do things like that.

Then they broke out into warm sunshine, still in the formation they'd gone into the clouds with.

Hal checked his compass, set a course, and then there was nothing to do but wait, occasionally checking the small clock that was the rest of his navigational tools.

Time dragged, for man, woman and dragon. The beasts were laden, carrying emergency rations and weapons.

Hal would have liked to dart through fingers of cloud stretching upward toward him, to relieve his boredom, but didn't dare alter his plot. What wind there was came from the rear, hopefully speeding them on their way, and he hoped there weren't any sidegusts that would drive them off course.

After five hours of monotony, broken only by the occasional fear that he'd gotten all four of them irretrievably lost, to vanish into the wastes of the Southern Sea, Hal blatted on his trumpet, and motioned down.

Again, they went down through the clouds, and a chill drizzle embraced them.

Hal was beginning to worry that the clouds went all the way down to the sea when they broke out, and heaving gray ocean was below them.

There was no sign of land, no sign of the islands.

The other three formed in a tight vee formation behind him. Saslic gave him a worried look, and Hal forced that traditional Leader' s Grin, proving he was in full control, knew exactly where they were, and there was no reason to be concerned.

Half an hour dragged past, and Hal could feel Storm's muscles begin to tremble a little as the dragon tired.

Then Hal saw something gray, grayer than the sea or air, ahead. Land of some sort, and he didn't care all that much what it was.

The gray became an island, then three islands, directly ahead, between Storm's horns.

Hal looked left, right, preened visibly, and his heart slowed to something resembling a normal rate.

Since the chart showed no other islands in the area, let

alone islands grouped in three, these had to be the Landanissas.

He took Storm high, just below the overcast and overflew the islands once, then again. He saw no signs of warships, no other craft except small fishing boats.

Emboldened, he dove down toward the small settlement on one, which he guessed would be Jarraquintah. There were a few men and women below, mending nets, working in small fields or in boats.

They gaped up at the four dragons, but didn't wave.

That might not be a good sign. But to balance that, he saw no one visibly armed, and no sign of uniforms.

Behind the village was a plateau, with a pond in its middle, and he motioned the flight to land.

They floated in, and were down. Hal slid out of the saddle, legs almost collapsing under him, and led Storm to the pond, the others behind him.

"Well, we're here," Saslic said.

"We are that," Garadice agreed.

"Are we ready to go into our song and dance?" Sir Loren said, pointing to a straggle of a dozen men and women coming up from the village.

The original plan was for them to pretend to be a Roche dragon flight that had gotten lost, and to beg the mercy of the fishermen.

However . . .

"They appear to be armed," Sir Loren said. "And their expressions aren't friendly."

"Do we have time enough to run, and get the dragons in the air?" Saslic asked. "Just being cautious, not cowardly, you know."

Hal shook his head, unbuckled and dropped his dagger-belt, and walked toward the fishers, arms out, hand extended.

One of the fishermen drew a fish spear back, ready to cast, and Hal, in turn, got ready to duck to one side.

But a woman in front of the dozen snapped something,

and the man lowered his spear, but looked sullen, not shame-faced.

The woman advanced toward Hal, but didn't put aside the long flensing knife she carried.

"Who you?" she said, in Roche, in a barbaric Roche accent Hal could barely understand. Clearly the islanders spoke their own language, another good sign. "Roche bastards?"

"Not enemy," he said, discarding the original deception plan.

"Who?"

"From another country," Hal said.

"Name?"

"Hal."

"Not Roche name. Name country?"

"Deraine."

"Not hear of," she said, with finality, as if her knowledge should cover the known universe. "You demons?"

"No," Hal said. "Men. Women."

"Maybe."

"What your name?" Hal said.

"No," the man with the spear said. "Demon know name, have power."

"How we know *you* not demon?" Saslic said, walking up beside Hal.

"I real!" the man said indignantly, thumping his chest.

"I real too," Saslic said, doing the same.

Someone laughed.

"My name Zoan," the woman said. "I lead, after Roche take men."

"Why they take men?"

"To serve on ships," Zoan said. "Ships of war."

"Deraine at war with Roche," Hal chanced.

There were grunts, mutters of evident approval.

"You ride monsters?" Zoan said. "I hear men do that now."

"We ride dragons," Hal said. "We fight from dragons."

"How you fight ships?"

"We have ships . . . Back there . . ." Hal waved vaguely. "We look for Roche for them."

"What you want with us?" the spearman said.

"We want to buy pigs. Chickens. Fish. We want to sleep up here. For three, maybe four days. We look for Roche."

"How you pay?"

"We pay," Hal said, not about to show these people any gold until the situation settled down some. "Good money."

There was a buzz.

"What else you want? You want women? Boys?"

"No," Hal said. "We are soldiers, not . . ." He couldn't find the word.

Zoan said a word in Roche Hal didn't catch, explained by running her finger in and out of her fisted hand.

"That," Hal said. "Not that."

"Good," Zoan said. "You buy pigs for you?"

"No. For dragons. For us, chickens. Fish. Or we buy fish and chickens for dragons, too."

"Demons don't eat," the spearman announced positively, as if he were on first name terms with several. "They men, women, I think."

Zoan considered, nodded.

"You welcome in Jarraquintah, that Roche name. We call it Wivel."

And so Deraine came to the Landanissas Islands.

The pigs were scrawny little creatures, but there were many of them, and so Hal bought eight.

The sight of the gold coins made the islanders chatter excitedly.

Zoan took out a talisman from around her neck, touched it to the coins.

"These real," she announced. "Now we have feast for you."

*

The feast was fairly elaborate, several courses of fish, and chicken spiced so hot tears streamed down Hal's cheeks, while Saslic sneered at him for being a baby.

There was drink – home-fermented corn beer. Hal ordered no one to touch it, not sure the islanders wouldn't wait until they were in their cups, then decide to do further testing on whether or not demons bled.

The other three fliers shrugged unconcern, especially after Saslic sniffed one of the great pottery jugs that held the brew. Hal was grateful he hadn't brought Farren Mariah along – the diminutive flier would have found some way into the drink, or else would have had to be chained to a tree.

They'd brought waterproofed canvas sheets, and spread their blankets under them. The night was balmy, a bit misty.

Saslic and Hal had found themselves a place away from the others, and, disregarding their agreement, made love slowly, tenderly, before falling asleep.

The two had the first patrol, at dawn, and flew out for an hour and a half, on a west-north-west heading, then back to the island. They saw nothing except a scatter of boats. Hal, even though she wasn't his best flier, wished he'd taken Gart along, since the seaman might've told him what to look for to navigate: shoals, outcroppings, other clues. He did notice the direction the seabirds flew in, and, watching his compass carefully, discovered they were headed back to the islands.

Garadice and Sir Loren took the next patrol, while Hal and Saslic wandered down to the village, where a woman happily grilled small fish and fresh vegetables, gave them a fiery dipping sauce.

They sought details on the Roche kidnapping, found that it had happened six months or more ago, and so far none of the men pressganged had returned home. Hal hoped this bullying policy was commonplace among the Roche – that, in the long run, might make the war a bit more winnable.

But such thoughts were for another place and time.

Satiated, they went back to their campsite, groomed and fed their dragons, and found their blankets for a nap.

The day was sunny, just warm enough to warrant stripping naked for a bit of sun.

Naturally, that led to lovemaking.

Finished, Saslic yawned, looking up at the sky.

"Now, would this be a life? Get up, go out on your boat, cast your net, come back with fish, and your pigs and fowl and garden would give you the rest.

"Would that be a life?"

Hal considered, was about to answer, when Saslic spoke first.

"Naah. I'm full of shit. I'd go nuts from boredom in a month."

"Not to mention," Hal put in, "if I lived here, I never would have met you."

"Why you romantic demon, you." She kissed him, rolled away. "Now go to sleep. We've got the night shift."

Hal tried to obey, but as he drifted off, a thought came.

Nor would I have ever ridden a dragon.

The sadness that brought convinced him he was following a true course, as Mynta Gart might've said.

Now, remembering what Saslic had said about there being no after the war for a dragon flier, all he had to do was figure a way to live until the killing stopped.

Sir Loren and Garadice flew back. They'd patrolled due north, to the Roche mainland, and had seen nothing.

Hal and Saslic flew out at dusk, keeping a course almost due east. The sky was spotted with clouds, and both moons were clear in the sky.

They were an hour and a half out, Hal trying to keep from yawning, and then, he saw what he thought to be stars, low on the horizon.

He shouted to Saslic, and they changed their dragon's course slightly.

The stars grew larger, were below the horizon, and became ships. Many ships. Hal counted at least twenty masthead lights.

The Roche fleet.

Then Hal saw something else:

Flying in lazy circles above the ships were two, no four, dragons.

24

Hal's orders to his flight had been very clear. He fancied he could see Saslic scowl at him, but she obeyed his instructions, and Nont broke away, back the way they'd come. She was to return to the island, report contact, and get the others ready to move. If Hal didn't return within two hours, they were to assume he was lost, and fly off to alert the fleet.

Hal himself, unobserved as far as he could tell, found a thickish cloud to hide above, ducking out momentarily now and again to correct Storm's direction until he was flying in the same direction as the convoy.

Hal checked that compass heading twice, frowning. The Roche ships weren't sailing west, to make contact as directly as possible wlth their enemies, but in a north-north-westerly direction.

That boded poorly for the invasion fleet, he suspected, but there were other matters to deal with before Hal could duck from his cloud and fly hard for the Landanissas.

He counted the ships below. Sixty, at least, in three waves, sailing close together. All appeared to be galleys, of a fairly uniform size, so Hal assumed they were all warships. Their oars were raised, and they were traveling, at about the same

speed as the Deraine-Sagene fleet, under power of the two
squaresails on each ship's masts.

He thought about going lower, remembered Cantabri's
warning, and climbed, keeping that cloud between him and
the Roche. Once or twice he saw dots that were the patrolling
dragons, but they didn't see him.

Very high, he set his course back the way he'd come.

They'd found the enemy. Now to report his presence, and
also his very obvious intents.

"Very good, Sir Hal," Lord Hamil said. "I have no doubt
that you'll warrant another decoration from the king, since
you've made it possible to obliterate the Roche."

"Uh, sir," Hal said. "There's something else. Something
more important."

"What could be more important," Hamil said, with a bit of
a scowl, "than being able to destroy the enemy?"

The cabin, thick with staff officers, was very quiet, waiting.

"The Roche direction of sail, sir."

"Explain, if you would?"

Hal went to the large map on the bulkhead behind Hamil.

"Sir, we're pretty sure our fleet's been tracked since we left
Deraine."

"There's no certainty of that," Hamil said.

"No, sir," Hal said agreeably. "But consider that these
Roche aren't not sailing toward us. Instead. . . ."

His fingers touched the map where the Roche galleys
should be.

". . . instead, sir, they're on this course."

He traced the heading until it touched the Roche mainland. "They're making for this rivermouth port, sir, Kalabas."

Hamil jolted, and there were gasps from some of the staff
officers.

Cantabri's eyes widened, as he got it.

"What of it?" Hamil tried to brazen it out.

Hal didn't know how to pursue the matter. Of course he

wasn't supposed to know anything about the fleet's point of landing, but he'd remembered Cantabri saying the invasion would be at the mouth of a navigable river, leading north toward the Roche capital of Carcaor, and the great river at Kalabas, labeled the Ichili, met the description perfectly.

Finally Kailas said, rather lamely, "I thought that would be of import to you."

"Mayhap," Hamil said. "An interesting note, and one which I'll take into consideration, after we've destroyed the Roche."

Putting Hal out of his mind, he strode to the map.

"Gentlemen, I propose a simple plan. We'll change our course like so, and sail to catch the Roche on their flank. Our magicians will be casting all of the confusion spells they're capable of.

"We'll take those ships on their weakest point, and smash them. I know a bit about galleys, and how structurally weak they are compared to our ships, which is why we've built none in Deraine for any purpose other than harbor tugs.

"We'll hit them first, hit them hard, and leave them to their fate.

"This blow will ensure our landing will be successful.

"Now, I wish to see all ship division captains aboard here by midday, gentlemen. See to it."

Hal saluted, wasn't noticed in the bustle, and he and Cantabri edged out on to the flagship's main deck.

"Pardon me, sir," Hal said. "But . . . Son of a bitch!"

"Indeed," Cantabri said. "Went right over his head. Lord Hamil didn't live to be as ripe as he is by worrying about anything more than today's sorrows."

"So we're supposed to proceed with the landing," Hal said, "even though it's certain the damned Roche know exactly where we're going ashore, and, noting that river, exactly what our plans must be."

"As you said," Cantabri said grimly, "son of a bitch!"

*

Even if Lord Hamil couldn't see the morrow's dangers, he was good at dealing with today's.

The fleet changed course, curving south-south-east for half a day, then changed its course to north-north-east.

They would be in sight of the Roche in the late afternoon, the fleet navigator said, when the first dogwatch began. All four dragon flights were ordered to be in the air an hour before the meeting. Two were to observe, a third to attack the Roche dragons, and Hal's flight ordered to take its fire bottles against the galleys.

The Roche ships came into sight, and Roche dragons rose to meet the Deraine dragons.

The beginnings of the battle went like an infernal clockwork toy. The transports were ordered to drop sail until signaled to join the fray, and the warships put on full sail.

If Hal could forget about the probable disaster of the invasion, and he tried very hard, it was quite a spectacle, the sails of the Deraine and Sagene ships catching the falling sun, and, ahead of Storm, the vees of the Roche.

The dots of the four Roche dragons were met by the dragon flight, and the monsters swarmed together.

Someone reported the Deraine fleet, and suddenly the Roche sails came to the wind, and the oars dropped raggedly down into the water as men manned their fighting stations. Long waves creamed behind the galleys as they came up to full speed.

Hal had a glass, and saw pennants flap to the mastheads of the Roche ships.

The admiral in charge of the Roche ships evidently decided to split his vees, the left diagonal turning to meet the enemy, while the right formed a broad second line, probably intending to envelop the Deraine and Sagene ships.

But it didn't work that smoothly, or at all.

Ships crashed into ships, lost headway rather than risk collision, and it was a swirling maelstrom two thousand feet below.

Some of the madness may have come from the spells cast by Deraine and Sagene wizards, spells of fear, alarm, panic.

Hal glanced around, saw no sign of dragons, guessed they were fully involved with the Deraine monsters, signaled for his flight to dive on the Roche.

They dove hard and fast. Hal, who'd never done this kind of fighting before, estimated the right moment and hurled a fire bottle out and down. Other bottles cascaded with it.

He pulled Storm up, banked, and cursed, seeing all of the bottles smash harmlessly into the sea, twelve flashes of fire and smoke, hurting no one.

But the Roche must never have heard of such a weapon, because the echelon he attacked went crazy, trying to turn away from the threat. Ships smashed together, and Hal fancied he could hear shouts and screams from his position.

He readied another fire bottle, and sent Storm down, determined he'd hit this time, or by the gods dive straight through that damned Roche galley.

He was low, very low, low enough to see oarsmen screaming, pointing, jumping overside, and he lobbed his fire bottle.

It hit just abaft the foremast, burst into flames, and the sail above it caught.

Fire roared up, took the ship, and Storm was speeding just above the waves, then up, barely clearing another galley's mast, and Hal went for the heights.

He looked back, saw three other ships afire, approved, and went down again with his third and last fire bottle.

This one missed, like his first, but four other fliers had better luck, and fire raged on the waters.

Ships were out of control, some oarsmen pulling pointlessly on one bank, the other side abandoned.

Ships collided with burning galleys, and the fire took them as well.

Hal and his flight, all intact, climbed high, just as the last Roche dragon plummeted past, into the sea.

There was nothing to do but watch now, as the Deraine

fleet crashed into the swirling mass of galleys, their rams smashing, tearing the fairly flimsy hulls of the Roche ships, the galleys trying to send their soldiery across to board.

At first the Deraine ships refused close battle, smashing galleys down, sailing through into the second line, and attacking them. They turned, and awkwardly sailing almost into the wind, struck the rear of the Roche fleet.

Signals went up, and certain Deraine transports sailed into the middle of the battle, closing alongside crippled galleys, and sending infantrymen across to finish the ruination.

Another sweep by the Deraine and Sagene warships, and that was all the Roche sailors could take.

More than twenty of their ships broke away, skittering like waterbugs west, away from the battle.

But ten or so ships had harder men aboard, and fought on, refusing to strike.

They killed . . . but were killed in turn.

By dark, there was nothing left of the Roche fleet but crippled, burning, sinking galleys. The Roche had been shattered, for the loss of half a dozen Deraine or Sagene warships.

The way to the beachhead was now open.

Hal dreaded what might well happen next.

25

Victorious, the armada proudly sailed up to the Kalabas Peninsula. The town of Kalabas appeared abandoned, and there were no Roche warships, save two tiny patrol boats, securing the enormous Ichili River.

The way was open into the heart of Roche.

But the fleet just sat there, for all of a very long day.

Hal took his flight far up the peninsula, saw no sign of soldiery, saw nothing on the river to block Deraine.

But nothing happened. The warships cruised about, the transports sat, boats launched, ready to board the impatient troops crowding the decks.

When Hal brought his dragons at midday, he asked, almost in a stammering rage, what the hells was going on.

The answer, somewhat unbelievably, was that Lord Hamil was holding commanders' conferences aboard the flagship, to make sure everyone understood his orders.

They'd had many weeks aboard ship to rehearse and memorize, but now Hamil appeared to be letting opportunity slip past him.

"Th' bastid's afeared," Farren Mariah said. "He's had nought all his life but little pissyanty soldiering, and now he's got all these frigging ships ready to sail widdershins if he commands, and he's got both thumbs up his arse, walking on his frigging elbows!"

That unfair summation seemed most accurate.

The flight grabbed hasty sandwiches, took off again, without orders. Hal decided to scout the peninsula as far as he could go.

The land was rocky, with high cliffs surrounding the small village. There were only two winding roads climbing to the top of the plateau. They ran north, on either side of the land, through narrow passes broken by open land, with only low brush for cover.

Come on, Hal found himself muttering. Get ashore, before the damned Roche show up, because if you don't take the peninsula now, you'll never be able to hold it.

He passed another dragon flight, and its commander held up his hands in equally helpless anger.

It wasn't until late afternoon that the landing commenced, troops getting into the boats in a leisurely manner, as if they were on a holiday outing.

The cavalry's horses were hoisted on to small lighters, and rowed ashore, to splash about in the low surf.

Hal saw no signs of any of the smaller ships the fleet had brought with them securing the river.

At dusk, on another flight up the peninsula, he saw dustclouds on the roads. He flew lower, saw endless columns of Roche infantry and cavalry pouring toward the peninsula's tip.

Saslic held up her crossbow, pointed down. Hal shook his head. Each bolt could kill one man, and that would hardly slow the horde. And where and when would replacement bolts be available?

Hal flew hard back to the flagship, chanced putting a protesting Storm down in the water almost alongside it. A boat was lowered, and he told the coxswain to keep the reins to the dragon close. He'd be back directly.

Aboard ship, he reported what he'd seen to Lord Hamil, who seemed unworried, telling Hal that the troops were already forming up for an attack from the town to secure a foothold atop the plateau. In fact, Lord Cantabri had just gone ashore, to get the men moving.

There was nothing for Hal to do, except go back to Storm, who was hissing unhappily at the poor sailor. Very grateful for not being eaten, the man shouted for his oarsmen to row hard back to the flagship, away from this damned monster and his demon-bound master.

Hal's next problem was taking off. The sea was calm, and there was almost no wind. Storm tried hard, but couldn't break free of the water.

Hal had to swim his beast to the *Adventurer*, and have Storm hoisted aboard the takeoff barge before he could get in the air. He took a moment to toss his dragon a squawking hen. Storm swallowed it in a gulp, but didn't appear that mollified.

Saslic, leading her flight, swooped low as he took off.

"The bastards have the heights," she shouted.

The Roche infantry, moving at a run, now controlled both roads going up to the plateau.

The Deraine infantry began plodding up the winding tracks. Hal saw a cavalry formation push past them, and try to charge. Arrows, crossbow bolts rained down, and men and horses screamed, died, fell back.

Another dragon flight swooped on the Roche positions. Two riders carried bows, and fired down at the enemy. A shower of arrows came up to meet them. The dragons rolled in midair, clawing at the shafts buried in their sides, stomachs, and smashed into the ground, writhing, dying.

The infantry mounted their attack, and were cut down in rows. None even closed with the Roche.

They tried again, going straight up the rocks, off the road, got within sword-reach before they broke, stumbling, jumping back the way they'd come, leaving men sprawled on bloody rocks.

The Roche seemed to have no interest in counterattacking, content with their commanding positions.

And then the sun dropped into the sea, and the first day's disaster was complete.

Hal and the other dragon flight commanders were summoned to the flagship, where Lord Cantabri awaited them. He was dirty, haggard and worn.

"We're attacking again tomorrow," he said. "I'll lead the assault. Straight up and at them, which is the only way we've got left now." He put emphasis on the last word, which the fliers noticed.

"We must gain a foothold on the plateau . . . or else the whole invasion may be lost.

"I want all of you to put every effort into doing anything to make the attack succeed.

"Sir Hal, I want your flight to scout behind their lines, and give me warning if Roche reinforcements appear."

"Sir," Hal said, "I think I can do better service than that."

Hal told him his plan. Cantabri winced. "That'll burn up – pun not intended – a valuable reserve."

"But you said—"

"I know what I said." Cantabri sighed. "All right. Cabet, you'll do the scouting I assigned Sir Hal to. That's all, gentleman. Pray for Deraine . . . And for all of us.

"You're dismissed."

The attack began at dawn. Men who'd gotten little sleep after the ordeal of the day before took position, and started up toward the plateau.

They moved in line, guides shouting orders to keep the lines even, as they'd been trained. Hal winced, seeing the Roche cut them down like a peasant scythes wheat.

The entire front line went down, and then the second. But the third pressed on, suddenly forgetting their training, darting from rock to rock, archers and crossbowmen firing only when they were sure of a target, closing on the clifftop.

Hal sent Storm into a dive, the rest of his flight behind him, well spread out. Each flier had a fire bottle ready, and looked for a target as the ground rose up at them. Hal threw, didn't know if he hit the knot of crossbowmen he'd aimed at, dragged Storm around, and came in on the level, dropping one, then his last fire bottle.

Flame gouted along the cliff, but Hal wasn't finished. Crossbow ready, he looked for targets – officers, men who looked important. He fired, reloaded, fired, and sent Storm back along the line.

Sometime in this sweep, he lost his first flier – the dragon hit in the throat, screeching, diving down toward the town, smashing through infantrymen moving steadily upward.

But he sent his flight back again, sniping at anything worth shooting.

Then he was out of bolts, and pulled Storm up, looking back and seeing Deraine banners top the cliff, and smash into hand-to-hand fighting with the Roche.

By dark, Sagene and Deraine held a precarious toe-hold on the plateau.

Some infantry units had been completely wiped out, almost all in the attack lost most of their officers and experienced warrants.

Lord Cantabri took an arrow in the side, fortunately a wound that looked far worse than it was. Bandaged and in a stretcher, he swore he could still lead the fight from the village, at the very least.

Hal had expended all the fire bottles he'd brought, as well as 200 irreplaceable bolts.

Instead of being able to sleep, he found every bottle the *Adventurer* had, enough lamp oil to fill them, and had them rowed across to the flagship, for Limingo to cast a spell on them.

The next day, with Lord Hamil himself ashore, accompanied by his staff and a distinctly unhappy Thom Lowess, although sensibly not going as far forward as Cantabri had done, the attack went forward, and Hal's fliers rained fire on the Roche.

By day's end, Deraine held a perimeter half a mile deep, a mile long.

But no more.

The Roche dug trenches, and further attacks were driven back, with heavy losses.

Hal lost another dragon, but the flier managed to save himself.

There were now thirteen left in the flight.

The attack up the peninsula was a failure.

Hal had wondered, rather dully, having other matters on hand, why the damned fleet didn't attack up the Ichili River, since that was the intended invasion route.

Perhaps Lord Hamil had been waiting for the peninsula fight to be over.

But when even he had to recognize there'd be no victory on the plateau, he finally ordered an attack upriver.

Sages cast runes, decided in three days there'd be a favorable wind from the south.

There was, and so the smaller, shallower-draughted ships started up, tacking from bank to bank.

Overhead were the dragons, scouting for an ambush.

There were no surprises for about eight miles, then the river narrowed into a gut, barely a quarter mile wide, the current fast-rushing, more than some of the ships could manage.

Supposedly someone asked Lord Hamil's main wizard for a spell to reduce the water-rush, and was laughed at.

"Gods make those kind of spells," the magician said, "not men. But I'll give you some advice – wait until the tide is on the flow, and that'll make it easier to sail through."

Gart, who'd watched all this from above, sat at dinner in the messdeck of the *Adventurer*, shaking her head.

"It's not so much the stupidity of the godsdamned army that bothers me," she said. "It's that it's somewhat like a disease. There must be seamen, even rivermen somewhere in this expedition of idiots who could've figured that out. But no, they've got to be as thick-headed as Hamil the Dolt."

"Careful," Lord Loren said, grinning. "That's treasonous."

"No, treasonous is the fool who named Hamil as commander of—"

Gart broke off hastily, remembering it was King Asir himself who'd chosen Hamil.

"So what now?" Saslic asked Gart.

"We'll try to force a passage through," Gart suggested. "Unless other things happen first."

Other things happened first.

At dawn the next day, there were Roche soldiers on the heights above the gut, equipped with catapults.

But that gave Hal a target, and so he and his flight went out with fire bottles, and the catapults roared up into flames.

Before the narrow passage could be sailed through, though, patrol boats found the river below the gut blocked, trapping two dozen ships.

The blockage appeared, at first, like a huge net, somehow stretched, in the course of a single night, across a half-mile-wide stretch of the river. The ends of the net were guarded by Roche battalions, who drove off attempts at landing.

Other Roche units reinforced the heights above the gut, until that passage was secured.

Lord Hamil decided to take larger warships upriver, and ram the net. Once the net was holed, the trapped ships could escape.

He also decided to make the attack at night.

It was blowing hard, so none of the dragons could handily fly, which Hal was very grateful for, later.

Three ships drove under full sail at the "net," and it came alive, lifting out of the water like so many conjoined serpents, reaching out for the ships as they closed. Certainly it was magic of a high order as the net took the ships, and tore at them, climbing over their bulwarks and pulling the ships down, until water surged over their rails, pouring down into their holds.

The three rolled, back, forth, then capsized, men spilling into the water, swimming away from the nightmare.

There were creatures in the river, creatures no one could later quite describe, that tore at the men until the river turned muddy brown with blood.

Few of the sailors aboard the three ships made it to the banks, and those that did were killed by Roche soldiers.

The net appearing to be broken, the twenty-four trapped ships tried to push for freedom. But the net, or whatever it was, reformed, ripping at these small ships, tearing out masts, winding like corpse-sheets around the hulls, pulling them under.

Seven of these small boats, carrying as many men as they could pull aboard, until they were down to the gunwales, made it to the river mouth and safety.

Something no one had appeared to plan for, or at any rate hadn't planned well, was resupplying the expedition. The fleet itself had to land all supplies, then sail back toward Sagene for more men, more equipment, more of everything.

Only a few ships were left – picket boats, the flagship, hospital ships and the dragon ships, among others.

With them went Thom Lowess, who'd taken Hal aside the night before sailing.

"I think it's time I moved on."

Hal lifted an eyebrow, Lowess drew closer, making sure there was no one to overhear.

"I came out to write tales that would build morale back in Deraine. This disaster is hardly my cup of tea. And, to tell you my own personal feeling, things aren't likely to improve.

"But don't worry, Hal. I'll make sure your career stays on an even keel. Yours and Lord Cantabri's."

*

Lord Cantabri sourly watched, from shore, as the ships sailed away, leaving the soldiers marooned, and said, "A frigging whale. We're nothing but a damned stranded whale on this strand. Deraine forever. Hurrah, hurrah, hurrah."

26

Ninety days later, the beachhead was even worse. There was more debris along the shore, more broken, abandoned weaponry scattered on the heights and below. The village had been ransacked again and again for materials for shelter, firewood, or simply for the joy of having something to ruin that wouldn't ruin back.

The Roche archers and crossbowmen killed their share, waiting in concealment until someone had a careless moment, and ensured he'd never have another one. More died through Lord Hamil's insistence the Roche would only "respect" Deraine by aggressive patrolling. So every night patrols went out, and were ambushed.

But still more died from disease. The sere Kalabas peninsula hid strange sicknesses, some that killed quickly, others that tore until a man or woman screamed for death's relief.

The expedition had run out of room to bury its dead, and so priests and sorcerers burnt the bodies in tall pyres. Soldiers swore they'd never be able to eat mutton again, the smell being just like that of a burning corpse.

But that was just one of the stinks – decaying bodies of

horses and men, spoiled supplies, burnt wood, decay and shit hung over the peninsula like an invisible fog.

No one had allowed for the winter storms, even in the more placid Southern Ocean, so the supply line was constantly overstrained, in danger of snapping, and the troops mostly lived on iron rations, almost never seeing fresh food. Officers and staff personnel seemed only too ready to "borrow" a cabbage or a ham for their own use, figuring one item would never be missed. Of course, by the time everyone took his little bit on the way up to the plateau, the fighting troops got damn all in the way of foodstuffs.

Reinforcements arrived, were assigned to different formations, plodded up to the top of the plateau, and came back down, wounded, dead or mad.

Hal was down to ten fliers, eleven dragons, and he couldn't tell which was in worse shape, the dragons with their lean sides and nervously flicking tails, or the fliers, with their twitching muscles, and remote stares.

He was, quite illegally, able to make it a little better for his fliers, ordering paired patrols "out to sea, to make sure Roche ships weren't returning."

Of course, the patrols went directly to the Landanissas Islands, one pocket of peace in a world tearing at itself. The fishermen welcomed the gold and strange, new foods, while the fliers were only too glad to trade hard biscuit and pickled beef, standard supplies, for fish or fowl.

Pig-raising had become a major industry on the islands, and so the Eleventh's dragons were a little less lean and weary than other flights'.

But not much.

Hal worried about everything, and had learned the worst of being in command. Sometimes he thought, when a flier died, he would almost have gone down in his place, rather than write the letter to whatever people he had, lying about how the flier had died instantly in an accident, rather than the probable truth that he'd been shot off his mount, and fell a hundred feet, screaming to his death, clawing at the air, trying to make it hold him up or, worse yet, killed by his own mount in its predawn irritation at being wakened for a patrol.

At least, there were no Roche dragons on the peninsula.

Not yet.

Hal worried about that, too, then found a possible explanation – the Roche knew very damned well where the Deraine forces were, and didn't need any scouts.

Hal wondered why the black killer dragons hadn't been dispatched to the Kalabas Peninsula, thought, forlornly, that Queen Norcia and Duke Yasin knew the beached whale was well contained by the forces at hand. But he wondered how soon the Roche would adopt his arming of dragon fliers as policy, rather than a scattered experimentation.

The invasion, to Kailas' eyes, was indeed a beached and dying whale.

But the broadsheets from Deraine swore the invasion was a roaring success.

"Damme," Sir Loren said. "Look at this broadside. You went and did it again."

He passed the sheet across, and Hal read the tale by, of course, Thom Lowess, of how the expedition had been attacked by barbaric Roche warriors, from the far east, barely human, and how they'd broken the lines at the north side of the foothold, and only Sir Hal Kailas and his Eleventh Dragon Flight, heroes of Deraine, envy of the nation, and so on and so forth, had stopped the attack, landing their dragons and fighting as infantry until Sir Hal's friend, Lord Bab Cantabri of Black Island, had arrived in the nick of time with reinforcing infantry, and driven the Roche back.

Of course, no such attack had happened, and Hal certainly wouldn't let his men and women be wasted fighting as simple infantry.

"Wonderful," Hal muttered, handing the broadsheet back. "Aren't the people at home fed up with such crap? Haven't they been able to figure out that if we're such godsdamned heroes, every one of us, why we're still stuck on this sandy-ass desert?"

"Of course not," Saslic said. "You don't think anybody who isn't actually fighting a war *ever* wants to know the truth, do you? Otherwise, there wouldn't be wars at all, let alone fools like us to fight 'em."

"Fine, I calls it *damn* fine," Mariah said, "to be allow't to serve with such friggin' heroes. Almost makes me not wisht I'd stayed at home and learnt more about castin' lovespells. Ain't that right, Feccia?"

The man nodded thinly, forced a smile, and went out on the deck of the *Adventurer*.

Hal wondered how, in such lean times, Feccia managed to keep up his bulk, decided he didn't want to know. The man held up his end, even if he never went beyond what duty required.

These days, that was more than enough.

Hal, scouting up the peninsula, saw more Roche soldiers coming toward the front.

Other flights, over the Ichili River, saw transports heading toward the river's mouth.

But the lines remained fairly quiet, with only the daily probe and nightly raid to make sure no one was likely to die of old age.

Soldiers who'd cheered when they were told they'd be coming south for the winter couldn't find enough obscenities, especially as they realized winter was ending, and they had nothing to look forward to except the increasing heat of spring and the drought of summer.

"I've decided something," Saslic said as they strolled one night, clothes in hand, along one of the empty beaches beyond Jarraquintah. "I think I want to get killed before you do."

"Gods rotating," Hal said in considerable astonishment. "Here we had a nap, a bath, a nice dinner, some marinated raw fish, green vegetables, some chicken that burnt the taste of all that pickled monkey meat out of my mouth, a real salad, another swim, a little hem-heming around, and you go and say something like that!

"Yeesh, woman! You're a true romantic!"

"Nope, just a realist," Saslic said. "Which is one reason I'd better get killed before the war's over, because no gods-damned civilian would ever understand me."

"All right," Hal said. "You're obviously intent on pursuing the subject. Why do you want to get killed first – remembering that I've decided I'm immortal, which means you're safe?"

"Because you're big, strong, brave." She paused. "And dumb. So you'll be able to handle the blow a lot better than I would when you get ripped in half by some dragon."

"What a charming thought," Hal said. "I love you."

"I love you back," Saslic said. "But dumb, like I said."

The Roche hit them at dawn, the day after Hal and Saslic had gotten back from their illicit leave. They struck cleverly, sending the first and second waves across in a suicidal frontal assault, which the Deraine and Sagene defenders cut down.

The Deraine and Sagene forces didn't notice other formations slip through the gullies and ravines of the rutted peninsula, and thought the first two waves were all there were. They relaxed, some coming out of their trenches to exult, to loot the dead, maybe even a few to try to help the writhing wounded.

Two more waves debouched from the Roche positions, and this time there was confusion. Yet another wave smashed into the mêlée of hand-to-hand fighting, and this one broke through to the Deraine trenches for a moment.

They didn't deploy along the trenches as they'd done in the past, trying to kill all the Sagene and Deraine in them, but jumped over the trench's rear parados, going for the edge of the plateau.

The Deraine were about to cut them down from the rear when yet another line of Roche rose up and charged.

Then all was madness, and the Roche had split the position on the plateau in half.

Hal, awaiting orders on the flagship, saw signal flags go up. The flag officer deciphering them turned ashen.

"Lord . . . Lord Cantabri's down."

Hal's stomach shifted, even though he'd realized some time ago that no one could be as impossibly brave as Cantabri and expect to live forever.

"Dead?"

The officer glanced at him, then lifted his glass again to the flags fluttering up from the shore station.

"No. Wounded in the chest . . . Refused to give up command . . . He's being taken to one of the hospital ships now. There's a chiurgeon with him.

"Nobody knows if he'll live or not."

Lord Hamil was on deck, shouting for boats, strapping on his sword, telling all and sundry that he'd lead the counter-attack himself.

Hal went for his own boat, back for the *Adventurer*.

And then black dragons, flying pennons Hal recognized as they swooped close as *Ky* Yasin's, smashed over the plateau top, circled the ships, and went back the way they'd come.

By the time Hal reached the *Adventurer*, they'd torn the patrolling flight from the skies.

Some of the Roche fliers had crossbows, crossbows of a new design depending on a wound-up coil spring, like a clock, for their energy.

But most of them needed no more than the brute ferocity of their mounts, who screeched in joy as they tore riders from their mounts, ripped into the dragons themselves.

Hal waved his flight up, trying to get above the dragons, to gain altitude, then shouts came. Rai Garadice was pointing down at the ruined village.

There was Lord Hamil's banner, atop a pile of rubble, and

wave after wave of Roche infantry attacking. Hal hadn't seen them move down on the village, but now saw Roche cavalry cantering down from the plateau.

Death above, death below, and Hal Kailas knew his duty.

He blasted on the trumpet, and dove toward the embattled Lord Hamil. Out of the corner of his eye, he saw troops, Deraine or Sagene troops, going over the edge of the plateau, retreating back toward the beach.

But there was nothing ahead but the torn banner of his commander, and his dragons, all ten of them, flashed over the pocket battlefield, crossbow bolts raining down.

The surprise sent the Roche reeling back, time enough for the soldiery around Lord Hamil to regroup and begin falling back on their boats.

A shadow came over him, and Hal ducked as a black dragon tore over him, talons reaching, missing.

He fired a bolt straight up, without aiming, but heard the dragon howl as the bolt hit him somewhere.

Then there was another dragon coming at him, jaws gaping.

Saslic's Nont was there, between them, claws flailing, far outsized.

Hal's world stopped as he heard Saslic scream, saw Nont torn by the black monster, a wing coming off, then Nont was spinning, falling, Saslic screaming as she fell out of her saddle, down into death's madness below.

Hal kicked Storm into a turn, trying to get to Saslic, and then the world was night and he smelt death as an unseen dragon, coming up from below, tore at his shoulder, his side, and then there was nothing at all.

27

There was a dull keening in Hal's ears, and he dimly thought he must not be dead – demons of the other world would be rejoicing at having a man for their feast, for surely that was the afterlife he was intended for, not one of gentle lambs and flowers.

He was lying on sand, he realized. Wet sand.

The keening kept on.

Hal tried to force his eyes open, couldn't.

Oh. I'm blind, he thought, ran a hand across his head, felt stickiness. Blood.

The keening changed to a yip. Hal recognized it as a dragon sound. He pushed himself up on an elbow, felt down, found ragged cloth. Hal ducked his head, scrubbed across his face, winced at the stabbing pain, and wiped blood away.

He could see, dimly, through a red mist.

He sat up, used both hands to lift his tunic, ignored the pain and rubbed hard.

Now he could see.

Storm was lying next to him, and now he could smell the dragon's fetid breath. Blinking hard, he reached out, found a scale, and pulled himself to his feet. He staggered, almost fell, but had his balance.

He was on a beach somewhere. Then he heard the smashing sounds of battle to his right, looked up, saw cliffs, vaguely recognized them as being west of the beachhead at Kalabas.

The war was still going on.

He looked down at himself, winced. There was a long tear in his side, up across his ribs, that had missed gutting him by an inch. Another pain came from his shoulder, and there was a gouge there, probably from a dragon claw.

That black dragon had also gotten him across his forehead. Blood ran freely down into his eyes, and he wiped again and again.

He still had his belted dagger, at least.

Then he realized Saslic was down, was dead, and there was no more world for him.

He almost collapsed back on the sand, caught himself.

The hells.

All right. She'd died first, as she'd wanted, his mind said, refusing to allow pain.

But I'm not dead.

That means that I'm to seek revenge.

She wouldn't have wanted me to just collapse here on this damned beach, and give up.

Maybe it was her spirit that made Storm call him back from wherever he was.

All right, he thought again. If that's the way it's to be.

Storm made another noise, and Hal looked at him.

The dragon had a slash down one side, and several head-spikes were torn away, green ichor clotting over the wounds.

There were other cuts down Storm's side. He'd fought hard as he fell.

Hal saw, lying in the low surf, the motionless body of a black dragon. There was no sign of its rider.

"Good on you," he whispered, and his voice sounded as if he was gargling glass.

He wanted to lie down, get his energy back, but knew, if he went back down on the sand, that called to him more loudly than the softest feather bed, he'd never get up again.

Storm made a low cry.

"I hear," Hal said, and pulled himself toward the monster's forelegs. He almost fell, but made it to Storm's neck.

All that he had to do was pull himself up, into the saddle, but that was a million leagues above him.

But somehow he was there, where his saddle should have been, ripped out of its mounting rings, gone. His map case and quiver of bolts still hung to their rings, but his crossbow had vanished.

The reins dangled just out of his reach. He stretched for them, and pain stabbed. Hal almost cried, wouldn't allow himself.

"All right," he said once more. "Up, Storm."

The dragon whined, but came to his feet. Hal tapped reins, and pain came again. Storm thudded forward, slowly, then faster, and each time one of his feet struck, agony rolled through Kailas.

He heard shouts, looked up, and saw, on the clifftop above, a handful of soldiers. His vision was too clouded to tell, but an arrow arced down, then others, and he knew the soldiers had to be Roche.

Storm leaped for the air, wasn't strong enough, came down again, then, just short of the water, was in the air, feet dragging through the waves, then the dragon was up, climbing for the sky.

"Up," Hal whispered. "High."

Storm obeyed, and Hal could look along the coast.

There was Kalabas, not many miles distant, a scattering of ships moving out to sea, ships on fire, men in small boats.

Deraine was beaten, was retreating, the last of its soldiery fighting clear of the peninsula.

If Hal chanced going there, where could he land? Would any of the ships stop for him? Sure as hells, none would take his dragon aboard. He bleared, saw no signs of the *Adventurer* or any of the other dragon flight ships.

"You and me," he said, tapping reins to the right. Storm obediently turned south, out to sea, wings lifting slowly, coming down faster.

Hal found his eyes closing, fought them back open. If he went to sleep, he'd fall, and they were a thousand feet, more, over the water.

His fingers groped to the map case, opened it, took out the compass. No, don't let it go, don't let it fall, and he looped its lanyard around his neck.

He knew the heading well, and turned Storm until he was headed a bit further to the east.

Toward the Landanissas Islands.

Blood clouded his eyes, and he wiped them clear, swayed on Storm's back, refused to allow pain. He considered his revenge, but that could lead to a dream, and in a dream lay death.

All that could keep him awake was his pain, and so he embraced the agony as his dragon flew slowly, limping, across the gray skies.

Below was the water, welcoming water, that would cool the fire raging across his body, and he and Storm would forever roll in the sea's currents, flesh picked by multi-colored fish, white bones being polished as their skeletons turned, turned, turned—

Hal jerked himself awake, started singing, every song he could remember, from the bawdy chants of the soldiers to schoolyard nonsense songs.

And the miles reeled past.

Then there was land, three small dots, ahead, and Storm needed no urging, dropping down.

Hal thought – hoped – the islanders would still be friendly, now that he was begging, not buying.

They were. Zoan summoned the village witch, who used

herbs and spells on Hal's wounds, wanted to give him a sleeping potion.

He refused, fearful that he'd been followed by Roche dragons, or a Roche warship would come on the island while he was unconscious.

But he sagged down into unconsciousness anyway, waking, stiff and in pain a dozen hours later.

Zoan had assigned someone to sit with him, and the boy ran to get the village head.

She came within minutes, ordered the boy to get the witch, and bring broth.

"You must stay until you recover," she said.

"No," Hal said. "I can't."

"You talked in your sleep," Zoan said. "About Saslic. That was woman with you before?"

"Yes." Again, the crashing wave of her death bore him down. Zoan saw his face, patted his hand.

"We all die," she said. "Soldiers die first."

"That's what Saslic said."

"She was wise. Perhaps, when you die, you will meet again."

Hal didn't answer.

"I am sorry to do this," Zoan said. "But men ask questions I cannot answer for what comes next."

"I don't know if I can answer them."

"They are afraid," Zoan went on. "Will Roche come here again?"

"I don't know."

"Did they follow you?"

"I don't think so." Hal struggled up. "Where is dragon?"

"He is well," Zoan said, pushing him back. "We fed him four pigs, and he slept. Witch put herbs, she not know what heals dragons, but work for men, for our beasts.

"Herbs and sew leather . . . pigskin, tanned, on wound, strong bandage. When he woke, he did not tear off. Maybe good for him."

"I sleep," Hal said. "When dragon wakes, wake me."

"What then?"

"I leave."

"For where?"

"For home."

Hal set his course back toward the mainland, but westering. He was in constant pain, but that kept him from falling off Storm.

He'd expected the dragon to be angry, unwilling to fly. But Storm seemed to understand where they were heading, and screeched no complaint.

Below him, high waves swept the seas, a summer storm. From time to time, he saw small boats, tattered and holed, limping their way away from the disaster of Kalabas. Sometimes they waved up, in friendship or thinking Hal was a scout for a rescuing force.

But he had nothing, and could only hope to be able to rescue himself and his dragon.

They made landfall, and Hal flew west, along the Roche coastline, until he found a forested headland where they could land. He and the dragon shared a meal of dried fish, but Storm snorted away from the cornmeal mush Hal offered.

Hal woke, with joints and his wounds screaming, and Storm seemed in no better shape. They watered at a creek, took off, continued their slow odyssey west.

The pain of Saslic's loss tore at him, more painful than his wounds sometimes.

Hal dared not fly Storm longer than a guessed-at three hours, then looked for shelter, a hiding place where no Roche cavalry or dragons could spot him.

If they did, and challenged him . . . No. He would not surrender.

Once, he flew over a bluff, where sheep sheltered against the onshore winds. Storm honked longingly, and Hal obeyed, had the dragon turn back and land.

Storm had a half-grown sheep halfway down his throat before Hal could dismount, swallowed it whole, went for another, killed it, and was beginning to feed when Hal heard shouting.

He saw the shepherd, and his dogs, running toward them, the shepherd waving a club.

Hal admired the man's courage or foolhardiness, killed him with one pass of his dagger. The dogs snarled at him, tried to nip at his heels, and Storm ate one of them, and the other fled, yapping.

He killed a sheep, rough-butchered it, and dragged it on to Storm.

They flew on until they found an abandoned farmstead further west. Hal landed, used the remnants of a shed to build a fire, and ate roast mutton, while Storm slept at his side.

The dragon moaned once or twice, and Hal wondered again if dragons had dreams, and if so, of what?

That far land they appeared to have come from? The northern wastes? Black Island?

He didn't know, vaguely wished to find out some day.

Some day, after he'd revenged Saslic.

At dawn, he went on, west.

Again, he found a herd of cattle, and Storm and he ate. But this time, if there were herders, they were sensible enough to avoid the ragged, bearded, bandaged flier, and his torn dragon.

And west, and west.

Then one day, after he'd flown for a week, a month, a year, he never knew, he flew over a burnt-out village, then wasted farms.

The ruins brought what might have been a smile, and he drove Storm on, harder.

Then, spread out below him, was a soldiers' winter camp.

He swept low over it, saw banners he recognized.

Sagene pennons.

He'd made it, flying all the way across Roche, back to his

own lines, and suddenly, the end a hundred feet below him, pain took him as a terrier shakes a rat.

He brought Storm into a clearing, an improvised drillfield, surrounded by log huts, canvas-roofed, slid out of the saddle.

Men ran toward him, buckling on their weapons, passed by a man in armor.

"You!" the knight barked, sword sliding out of his sheath. "Stand still!"

Hal obeyed. Storm hissed, and the knight's horse jumped sideways.

"Who are you? Are you Roche? And keep your monster under control!" the knight called, fear obvious in his voice.

"Don't worry," Hal said, about to let go. "He won't hurt you. We're on your side. I'm Sir Hal Kailas, Eleventh Dragon Flight. Come from Kalabas."

The knight jolted back.

"You're one of the—"

"I'm one of the," Hal agreed. "Now, if you'll have someone see my dragon's fed, watered, and his wound treated?"

"Why . . . yes . . . but . . ."

Hal smiled gently at him, let go, and slipped quietly to the ground.

He'd made it back. Now it was the turn of the others for awhile.

Then it would be time for red vengeance.

28

There came a blur of dressing stations, creaking ambulances, anxious attendants and, for some unknown reason, the peering curious.

Hal didn't bother with full awareness, except for making sure twice that Storm's wounds had been treated, and that he was safe.

He thought he must be in good hands, and if he wasn't, there wasn't anything he could do about it. So he drowsed, mind floating, trying not to return to that dreadful moment when the dragon tore at Saslic, and she fell away, and there was nothing he could do.

Then one day, he woke to a clear mind. He was in a room by himself, in a bed with clean sheets, warm and cozy. There was a window in front of him, with autumn sleet lashing against it.

He wriggled, realized he was clean. He lifted an experimental hand to his cheeks, realized he'd been shaved while unconscious.

There came a giggle.

He looked to one side, saw Lady Khiri Carstares, as lovely as ever, in a chair beside his bed. She wore what should have been a prim white uniform that buttoned down the front. Khiri had unbuttoned the top three buttons, so the effect wasn't quite what nursey efficiency intended.

"I've never shaved a man before," she said. "Let alone one who's snoring."

Hal blinked, lifted an arm to point out the window, felt his bandages and stiff body.

"Deraine?"

"Of course, silly. You've been here, in hospital, for almost a month. Which gave me time to learn about your where-abouts from Sir Thom – you know he's been knighted for his courage in battle – even though your travels are all over the broadsheets, and arrange things so that I'm your nurse."

Hal blinked again.

"My nurse."

"Until you're well enough to be discharged."

"From the hospital?"

"No, no. From the service."

"What?"

"You've been hurt, remember?"

"I know." Hal started to get angry, realized this was hardly the time, and let sleep wash up on him again. Before he went under, he managed a smile at Carstares.

"Thanks," he mumbled. "For the shave. And . . . for being my nurse, I suppose."

Days drifted by. Hal knew he was feeling better, because the simple broths Khiri spooned into him became boring. She told him he definitely was recovering, since he was being alto-gether too bad tempered.

Hal apologized.

But he *was* bad tempered, and brooding. The news that he was going to be invalided out did not sit easy.

What was he supposed to do then?

Beg in the streets?

Limp back to Caerly to go down the mines?

Logically, he doubted that anyone with a knighthood would end up swinging a pick, but since when have invalids been logical?

What about flying? Starting his own flying show? But that would almost certainly be impossible at the present. He could guess there wouldn't be any dragons on the civilian market, and those that might show up would be thoroughly spavined or rogues.

Lord Cantabri came to call one day. He'd lost a deal of weight, and his face had new lines. He walked with a cane, and talked with a wheeze, but nevertheless said he'd be back in the wars by the time winter ended.

Hal grumped at him, and Cantabri just laughed.

Kailas, feeling ashamed once more, asked for details on the invasion.

"You're sure you're up to it?"

"That bad?"

"Worse," Cantabri said. "Of the hundred and twenty thousand, more actually, when you include Sagene's replacements, we managed to evacuate about thirty thousand."

Hal grimaced.

"And many of those were wounded, too many unable to return to the army," Cantabri went on. "Lord Hamil was killed shortly after I was wounded."

"I assumed that, sir," Hal said. "I was overhead, trying to figure a way to come to his aid. But there were too many Roche down there."

"Too many Roche *everywhere*," Cantabri said, almost to himself.

"I'd ask a favor, sir," Hal said. "Would it be possible for you to look up the Eleventh Flight's casualties?"

"I figured you'd ask," Cantabri said, and took a sheet of paper from his belt pouch.

"You had about seventy-five when the invasion began. Of those, about fifty still live. The *Adventurer*, even though the black dragons tried to attack it, made it to safety. You had ten fliers when that final attack came, and eleven dragons. Six dragons, five fliers are still alive."

Hal asked about his fellow flying school graduates.

"Vad Feccia, unwounded," Cantabri went on, and Hal shook his head, thinking only the good die young.

"Rai Garadice, also unscathed. Sir Loren Damian, wounded. Farren Mariah, wounded. Mynta Gart, wounded. All of them swear they'll be able to return to combat, although I understand this Mariah character voiced his status rather colorfully."

"He would," Hal said.

"Other dragon flights took worse casualties, including one completely wiped out.

"They're training dragons pell-mell upcountry, and realize they've got to build the flights back up, and add more to boot," Cantabri said. "The appearance of those black dragons, and their aggressiveness, has shaken the army badly.

"The formation, by the way, is led by one *Ky* Yasin."

"I knew that," Hal said. "I recognized his pennant."

"As our spies had said, his force is a squadron, more than four flights strong. Word has it, Queen Norcia of Roche has ordered it further augmented. He'll be a force to contend with," Cantabri said.

Hal started to say something, kept his own thoughts for the moment. There would be other matters to clarify first.

Cantabri and Kailas chatted on a bit more about inconsequentials before the lord got up.

"I'll say this, Sir Hal. The army without you will be a far lesser place. Far, far lesser."

"I've the best news," Khiri said.

Hal, who was still brooding about his seemingly unavoidable retirement, grumped something, which Carstares took as interest.

"You'll be permitted to leave the hospital under my care any day now," she said.

"For where?"

"For wherever you want to go. I've got estates in the west, although I don't know if you'll want to go there, they're pooh-gloomy, a dairy farm south of Rozen, sheep holdings on the highlands north of here . . . Or we could even possibly impose on Sir Thom. I'm sure he'd let us stay in that great house in the capital.

"You can decide . . . or I will."

"I might as well let you do that," Hal growled. "Since it appears I'm no better than a lady's handsome man these days."

Lady Khiri froze, her face went hard.

"And just what is *that* supposed to mean?"

Hal should have shut up, but his shoulder was hurting.

"Just what it meant. A nice, scar-faced popsy to flaunt about, eh?"

Khiri came to her feet.

"Has anyone ever suggested, Sir Hal Kailas, that you are more than a bit of a shit?"

Hal opened his mouth.

"No," Khiri went on. "You've said quite enough for the present. It's quite obvious that you have the manners of one of those damned dragons you love so well.

"You think that I've been attracted to you because of your reputation. No, Sir Hal. I despise killers, and you're one of the bloodiest-handed.

"I like – liked – your company because you could make me laugh, which comes hard enough these days.

"I know that you lost your lady in battle. Do you think you're the only one to suffer a loss?

"For your information, my father was killed at the war's beginning, and my only brother, who I loved most dearly, two months later, not to mention someone else I thought I was beginning to . . . to care about.

"That's why I left those damned gloomy stone halls on the ocean, why Sir Thom was kind enough to take me in. I thought I was doing my bit for the war, and it turns out that you thought I was no better than a back-alley whore.

"Sir Hal, you should be very ashamed of yourself. Very damned ashamed, and I hope you treat your new nurse better than you have me."

And she went out, the door crashing behind her.

Hal's anger had risen as she spoke, but vanished moments after Khiri had gone.

He thought hard, staring out at the snow, just beginning to fall, not seeing it.

Very good, you imbecilic moron. If you had brains, you'd take them out and play with them.

At least now, he thought, I've really got something to be glum about.

And try to figure out how to apologize.

If I can.

Hal was still figuring when Sir Thom Lowess bounced through the door.

"And what, my fine young lad, have you done this time? I saw my dear friend, Lady Khiri, crying bitterly in the nursing office, and she said that you'd ruined things.

"Might I inquire?"

Hal reluctantly told his story. Lowess listened, shaking his head.

"Dear me. Dear me. You do, as the soldiers say, know full well how to step on your cock, don't you?"

Hal nodded.

"Just for your information, not only did Lady Khiri tell the truth, but she's given great sums to various hospitals.

"She's also, I suspect, without knowing, still a virgin, or so near to it as to not matter, so your shame should be complete. She originally came to stay with me in the hopes that I could introduce her to suitable men, men who weren't just after tossing her into bed, or looking to marry her estates.

"Have you any ideas on how you're going to recover from this gaffe?"

Hal was about to shake his head, then had an idea.

"Sir Thom – and congratulations on your knighting – how is my credit with you? I haven't been paid since before we left Paestum, and I assume sooner or later the paymasters'll—"

"Don't try to offend your other friend," Lowess said. "Even if you were stony broke, you could still have my last piece of gold."

"Thank you, sir," Hal said, shamefaced. "I apologize if I insulted you, for I need not only some of your gold, but a bit of your help."

Hal explained.

"Well, that might do for a beginning," Lowess judged. "And it's a matter handled just down the street. Sit here and contemplate your sins, Sir Hal, and I'll take care of things."

He was gone for half an hour, came back smiling.

"The lady I dealt with shall be singing your praises until the day she dies, as will all of her friends. And you should be most grateful her shop is – was – very well supplied, particularly for an autumny time of year."

"How long will it take?" Sir Hal asked.

"An hour," Lowess said. "She's bringing in her neighbors to help. And there's a wizard down the street who can provide some spells to keep things fresh.

"Now, while we wait, would you care for any news?"

"What's this about them forcing me out of the army?"

Lowess lifted an eyebrow.

"Of course they're going to retire you, Sir Hal. You're cut all to shreds."

"No more so than Cantabri."

"He's different. He's too mean to let go."

"Some people had best think of me as mean," Hal muttered.

"*Some* people already do," Lowess said.

Hal winced.

"Besides, you're giving everyone a chance to wallow in your heroism, for which I take some measure of credit. You'll be told, in time, that the Eleventh Flight will now be known as the Sir Hal Kailas Flight.

"Great recognition. Plus I imagine there'll be some more medals, most likely a pension. You'll not starve."

"I wasn't quite starving when I got dragooned into the damned army," Hal said.

"So, then, what do you have to complain about? You'll be out, a civilian, not that badly impaired, and with your life, which is a deal more than many can say."

Hal remembered Saslic, kept from snarling at Sir Thom.

"Oh, one other thing, which I'll make much of in one of my tales. It seems there's a man in the flight who's from your own town, and has sworn to get revenge against the Roche in your name."

"From Caerly?"

"Yes, been a flier for some months, saw limited combat with the Fourth Army. You might know him, since he's knighted. A Sir Nanpean Tregony."

Hal, remembering the last time he'd seen Tregony, tormenting a dragon kit, suddenly found everything, from his situation to . . . to the world, hysterically funny.

He burst out laughing, so hard he thought he'd tear a wound open.

Sir Thom smiled with him at first, then looked concerned.

"Would you mind explaining?"

"Sir Thom," Hal said. "In time, I shall. But not right now." And again he started laughing uncontrollably.

Lady Khiri Carstares, eyes still red, opened the door to her room, and gasped.

It was full of flowers, so full she could barely make out her small bed and tiny chest.

There were orchids, many varieties, dancing ladies, hibiscus, roses, protea, night-blooming jasmine, other exotic flowers she had no idea existed in Deraine's winter.

"And I am, truly, a shit," Hal said from behind her.

She recovered from her surprise, forced a hard face, and turned. Hal sat in a padded wheelchair a few feet away. Down the hall was Sir Thom Lowess.

"You are."

"I'm sorry," he said. "I can't say I'll never be a shit again . . . But not in that way."

"Do you expect forgiveness?"

Hal shook his head. Khiri deliberately waited until the silence was very uncomfortable.

"Then you have it."

She came close, leaned over, kissed him on the lips, mouth closed.

"Now, since I somehow forgot to ask to be relieved of your onerous care, shall we start thinking about where your convalescence should be best spent?"

29

Cayre a Carstares sat on a promontory overlooking the western ocean. A high curtain wall enclosed a dozen acres and a small village. The castle itself was octagonal, with a round tower at each corner, and could have comfortably held an army headquarters in its stone magnificence amid the jagged crags.

"My forebears built this to keep off the raiders from the north," Lady Carstares said.

"The people I came from," Hal said, finding a bit of amusement.

"I'll add that it never fell to them."

"Never from without," Kailas murmured, surprised at what he was saying, not displeased that he wasn't entirely soul-dead. "But what of within?"

"What?" Khiri said.

"Nothing."

But it was evident from Carstares' lifted eyebrows and smile she'd heard what he said.

The castle was gray, as Khiri had promised, matching the gray seas beyond, and the wintry land. The dusting of snow made it look even more ominous.

Hal loved it, loved its gloom and dark menace.

It was the perfect place to mourn Saslic.

And to make himself back into a warrior.

The castle was fully staffed, many of the retainers having worked for Khiri's grandfather. They still tottered faithfully about their rounds.

"Don't be in much of a hurry around here," Lady Khiri advised.

Hal wasn't.

He found a round bedroom in the tower of the wing Khiri said was the castle's most inhabited, just below the roof, with shuttered windows that looked out on the wild surf smashing against the rocky cliffs below. Khiri's bedroom, one she'd had as a girl, was one flight down, and she had the local witch cast a similarity spell on two tiny bells. If Hal needed something, all he needed do was tap his, and the one in Khiri's room would tinkle and summon her.

Hal's room was bigger than his parents' house, had its own washroom and dressing room, plus a fireplace, fresh wood brought daily by a man who could've been Hal's great-grandfather, but who refused, utterly shocked, Hal's offer to help.

"Never, Sir Hal," he said. "You're wounded, and to be recoverin', and besides, you're *noble*."

"Only by the grace of the king."

The man's eyes rounded.

"You've *met* our gracious Majesty?"

"Yes," Hal said, realizing the conversation was going in the wrong direction and, from the man's expression, that now he'd *never* be allowed to do anything resembling manual labor.

Khiri found this funny, although she still wondered why Hal had chosen this place.

"Damp, and cold, and full of bad memories," she said.

"Maybe I picked it to exorcise them."

"Yours or mine?"

Hal didn't answer.

He started with slow, creaking walks, hardly better than the pace of the archaic retainers, around the keep. Then, feeling stronger, he went beyond, and walked along the curtain wall, through the orchards, unharvested since Khiri's father's death, and the grazing grounds for the small herd of sheep.

There were horses, and he took them sugar, or an apple he'd picked and thawed in his pocket.

Khiri went with him at first, then realized he wanted no company but his own thoughts, and the howl of the wind.

Hal wore a knee-length sheepskin coat, a matching hat, and thought he looked a perfect fool, a country bumpkin if ever one existed. But a warm perfect fool.

Once, when the storm broke, he went beyond the curtain wall, and found a hollow, out of the wind, warmed a little by the winter sun.

Full of a very good midday meal, he drifted away, then dreamed. All he remembered was Saslic's body falling, falling, and then she was on Nont's back, down below this very castle, the dragon's wings lifted to protect her from the waves.

She smiled up at him sadly, waved, and then Nont's wings closed about her, and the dragon turned out to sea, as Hal came to his feet, awake, pain tearing at him, but the pain hadn't brought the tears on his cheeks.

He began training, lifting small weights, gradually increasing them, forcing his body from a walk into a limping trot. Hal went beyond the curtain wall, found tracks down to the rocky beaches below, went down them. The first time he came back up, he thought he wouldn't make it, that he'd have to fall and wait for someone to rescue him.

But he forced himself on, lungs ripping, and made it, staggering, to the top, before he went to his knees.

Khiri ran up, knelt.

"Are you all right?"

"Just . . . just being stupid," he panted.

"Why do you want to do this to yourself?" Then she realized. "Oh. You want to go back to that damned war."

"It isn't . . . what I *want* . . ." Hal said.

"You're right! You are being stupid!"

She stamped away, back to the castle.

But by dinner that night, her sunny mood was restored.

He dreamed again that night of Saslic, again, on the back of Nont as his wings unfurled, and he beat hard, lifting, leaving a wake of spray.

Again, he saw Saslic waving, but this time, he heard her shouting, words dimly heard against the sea's roar:

"Another time . . . somewhere . . . somewhen . . . maybe . . ."

He strained for more, but couldn't make out what else she said. Then Nont was in the air, flying due west, in the directions dragons seemingly came from.

Hal Kailas woke, and there was melancholy in his heart, but he no longer felt dull, dead.

He was alive, he would live, until he was killed.

Once he might have felt mortal, but now he believed Saslic's words: "There'll be no after the war for a dragon flier."

Strangely, this made him feel better than he had since watching her die.

"I have an idea," Hal said. "I think we should have a party."

"A party?" Khiri said incredulously.

They were in her bedroom. Khiri disliked rising early, so Hal, after his morning run, generally took her a tray with the rusks she preferred unbuttered and some herbal tea.

For some unknown reason, neither one of them had tried romance, beyond an almost-brotherly hug and a brush of the lips at night and in morning's greeting.

"A midwinter party," Hal said.

"You're mad."

"Not at all. Or, at least, not noticeably at the moment."

"Sir Hal, love of my life, you have the brains of a sheep. It's winter. Everybody's huddling around his fire, dreaming of spring.

"And this castle – this whole district – isn't a happy one. The war's cost all of us too much."

"Exactly. That is why we need a party."

"You are not the kind of person who holds parties," Khiri said suspiciously.

"What kind of person does?"

"Sir Thom. Me."

"All right, then. You'll be the one throwing the party. You've got more money than I do, anyway."

"Uh-uh," Khiri said. "If you want to have a stupid party, with everybody glowering around at each other, and thinking about old feuds or . . . Or thinking about people who aren't here, you'd best have some kind of idea on what's going to make it work. Make it sing, as Sir Thom might put it."

Hal grinned.

"That was an evil smile if ever I saw one," she said cautiously.

He reached in his shirt pocket.

"Here's your invitation. You're to come as you were when you received this."

"Like *this*?" Khiri wasn't wearing much under a warm shoulder throw other than a thin nightgown.

"And here are two other invitations for you to give others. Pick the right moment," Hal said, "and we'll all be amazed at how people show up."

A smile ghosted across her lips.

"What about you?"

"When I," Hal said, "received my invitation from a dashing dragon flier, I just happened to be wearing full dress uniform. Hah-ha!"

"Perhaps you're not quite mad. Or maybe you are. I never thought you were the kind of person who would come up with an idea like this."

"I didn't used to be," Hal said, his smile flickering momentarily. Khiri saw it, looked away.

"So who are we to invite to this party? The local nobility, of course."

"Everyone."

"Everyone?"

"Servants, peasants, priests, popinjays, poopheads."

"The whole district?"

"Grandsires, grandmeres, babes, children, even a sheep if you fancy."

"Let's go back to your madness."

"Oh yes," Hal said. "Two other details. For every jewel you somehow decide to wear, you bring a coin, copper, silver, gold, that'll go to the hospital fund."

"That'll keep some people from overdressing," Khiri said.

"And make others pile on the gems," Hal said.

"And the other detail is that everybody is to bring something to eat."

"Why?"

Hal picked his words carefully. "When you've shared another man or woman's meal, you're not quite as likely to be hating them. Anyway, not as hard."

He jumped to his feet, winced.

"Calloo, callay, it'll be a joyous occasion."

There was a broad smile on his lips, but none in his eyes.

Hal's workout grew more intense by the day.

Finally, it consisted, in the morning, of setting-up exercises, then a mile run, regardless of the weather. Sometimes he'd run down one of the half-wild, long-unridden horses, and go bareback with only a rope bridle for a ride out across the bleak landscape.

He made friends – or, if not friends, acceptable

acquaintances, courtesy of sugar lumps – with the completely wild hill ponies, and sometimes he'd chase them over the rolling moors, through the scrub forests, or they'd chase him.

Other days, he'd hunt down the locals, and force an invitation to his party on them. He was quite pleased with the reactions he got, from petrified amazement to grumpiness to laughing joy.

After midday, and a brief nap, he'd begin his real workout.

First came setting-up exercises, then running up one of the ramps to the castle parapets. Another set of exercises, then running down the ramp. He repeated this five times.

Then the hard part, climbing up and down a knotted rope he'd hung from the parapets, forcing his wounded arm to recover.

Then repeating the ramp run and exercises five more times.

Khiri watched him once, shuddered, and went back to one of the great hall's roaring fireplaces.

The afternoon of the party was warmer than usual, an almost tropical wind from the south blowing in from the sea. For a moment, he was reminded of the Southern Sea, and death, but he forced those from his mind.

He wore the dress uniform Khiri had tucked into his trunk, complete with half a chestful of medals. As he'd threatened, he made Khiri wear her nightgown, although Hal had allowed her to cheat, and wear a matching silk bathrobe over it.

The guests trailed in, sometimes singly, sometimes in village-size groups. Some of them were honest, and wore what they had on when invited, others blatantly cheated and wore their best.

From these, one of Lady Khiri's retainers extracted the penalty, dropping the coins into an ornately carved chest that had belonged to her great-grandfather.

Cooks took the viands from the guests, and whatever instructions needed to serve them.

Khiri suddenly gasped.

"But we have no band!"

"Oh yes we do," Hal said, pointed to three women and two men, holding the simple instruments of the peasantry. Their leader wore only a towel, and had been caught in the village sauna.

But they tootled, sawed and strummed mightily, and then there were dancers. Priests danced with beldames, merchants' wives with drovers, young boys with their mothers, young girls with their hopeful lovers.

Khiri had been right – the district had been decimated by the war. There were few young men at the dance, and most of those were clearly unsuitable for soldiering or else they'd served and come home, far worse wounded than Hal.

But they danced, they sang, and they ate.

Hal made a note of some of the dishes, served along two great tables. Perhaps they should have been organized and served in proper courses, but everyone was too hungry, and enjoying themselves too much.

There were small shrimp, boiled in beer and served in a tomato sauce from one of Khiri's hothouse gardens; crisp, fried young smelt, dipped in a seasoned mayonnaise; hearth cakes in butter; oysters, raw or grilled with bacon; grilled lamb sausage; marinated cucumbers; sea trout, poached in wine; potatoes cooked in a dozen different ways; smoked local ham; crab cakes; chicken livers baked with rice; lobster, fresh from the booming seas beyond the castle, served with drawn butter; puddings, from blood to fruit; tarts made from dried fruit; preserved orange cake; pies; filled cookies, and more.

They drank the strong local beer, or mulled cider, or wine from Khiri's, or the district's other minor nobility's, cellars.

There were those who drank or ate too much, and there were wagons outside to carry the casualties home. Or else those incapable of moving were carted off to another hall, where straw had been piled for the eventuality.

It was long after midnight when the last guest stumbled out, or was otherwise disposed of.

"And me for bed," Khiri yawned, waving at the tables. "We can clean up the rest in the morning."

"Good idea," Hal agreed. "I don't think I'm in any shape to be handling the family porcelain."

They went up the curving staircase into their tower. Hal stopped at Khiri's landing, looked out through a tiny-paned window at the sea. The sky was clear, with only one moon out, but that clearly showing the white lines of surf as they marched against the cliffs.

Khiri shivered, came closer.

"I'm glad I'm in here, and not out there."

"So am I."

It seemed appropriate for Hal to kiss her, and for her to kiss him back.

After a very long time, she pulled away.

"Well, I guess you're *not* that wounded."

He started to pull her close.

"Oh no," she said. "If you want to play those games, it won't be with that damned pincushion of a tunic on."

She took his hand, led him into her bedroom, closed the door.

"Now," she murmured, unfastening his uniform's loop and button fasteners, and lifting it off his shoulders. "That's a bit better."

"Sauce for the gander, and all that," Hal said.

"True enough, young sir," Khiri said, and let the bathrobe slip to the floor. "And my bare feet have been freezing all night, so perhaps you wouldn't mind dealing with the problem?"

He picked her up in his arms, carried her to the bed, and pulled back the feather comforter.

She lay looking up at him, half-smiling.

"And I don't want you dirtying my nice flannel sheets with those clompy boots of yours."

Hal sat, obediently pulled off the boots.

He heard a whisper of silk, turned, and saw Khiri, naked.

Hal suddenly felt thick-headed, and it wasn't from the wine. He undressed, fingers feeling like awkward balloons.

"Now, come to me," Khiri said, and her voice was a noble-woman's command.

Hal knelt over her, eased himself down, half across her body, kissed her, felt her nipples hardening against him.

Then it was if the seas outside took them, spinning them high into the night sky.

Near dawn, Khiri said, her face muffled by the pillow, "I guess . . . this means I'm not your nurse . . . anymore."

Hal gasped.

"Probably not."

"That's good," Khiri said, and then lost her words as they moved together.

From that night on, they shared a common bed, and no one in the castle seemed to disapprove.

Hal, in spite of Khiri's best efforts to decoy him into sloth, continued his exercising.

Then, one day, a bright day that hinted of spring, he knew.

He was fully recovered.

And it was time to go back to war.

30

Hal wrote his intentions to Lord Cantabri, but before he had a reply a royal messenger fought his way through the deep new year snows with a summons to King Asir's court.

"Which will be for what?" Hal wondered.

"Why, you dummy, your honors for being a good little hero about to go into retirement," Khiri said. "And then you'll get them all taken away for not being a good little hero who's going into retirement.

"You dummy."

The messenger was very glad to make his return to Rozen in one of Khiri's carriages, his horse tied behind. For an instant Hal had wondered why they were taking two carriages. Khiri had sighed in exasperation.

"Because, dummy, if there's another person in the nice warm carriage, I can't do this to you."

She slipped to her knees, and reached for him.

And so they set out, with three carriages, which included Lady Khiri's entourage and road supplies, slowly making their way east from country inn to country inn, until they reached the outskirts of the capital.

"I suppose we can find somewhere to put up," Hal said. "Still being unpaid, I can borrow money from you."

"You'll not borrow money from anyone," Khiri said. "We'll be staying at Sir Thom's."

"Oh. You wrote him?"

"Shut up, hero dummy. I don't need to."

And so it proved.

They were lavishly welcomed by Lowess, and given a separate suite.

"Now this shall be a tale," he said. "The bravest warrior, in love with Deraine's loveliest lady.

"I can hear the sound of whimperings from those not so fortunate already."

And he licked his lips.

Hal made himself visit the King's Own Menagerie to tell Saslic's father of her death.

"My only daughter," the man said sadly. "Bound and determined to fly, and to fight. My wife's gone, and now Saslic is with her.

"It's a cold, lonely world, Sir Hal. I'm glad to be old, and not long for it, for it holds little warmth for me, beyond my beasts."

The short, fat man was all business. He introduced himself as one of King Asir's equerries.

"Since you've already been presented at court," he said, "I shan't have to inform you as to protocol.

"The king proposes to make you a lord."

Hal blinked.

"In addition to other matters which he'll inform you of personally. One of the reasons I'm here is to ask what title you'd prefer to have.

"Lord Kailas of Caerly, perhaps?"

Hal smiled tightly. He found no need to mention the money he sent his parents every time he was paid.

"No," he said. "I don't think I'll be returning there, ever. Caerly's a good place to be from. A long ways from."

The equerry forced a smile in acknowledgement. "What, then?"

Hal had only to think for a minute.

"Lord Kailas . . . of Kalabas."

"Oh dear," the equerry said, sounding shaken. "The king will not be pleased with that, I know. Kalabas is something I doubt if he wants to be reminded of. Many of his most loyal subjects, including Lord Hamil, died there."

"I had . . . friends who died there, as well," Hal said.

The equerry saw the look in Hal's eyes, nodded tightly, didn't pursue the matter.

"Matters such as your pension, other benefits, can wait until later."

"As long as I'm ruining your master's, the king's, day, let me complete the job," Hal said, and went on.

"Oh dear, oh dear, the king will *definitely* be unhappy," was all the equerry had to say.

King Asir named Hal Lord Kailas of Kalabas with barely a flicker, said, as he had when he ennobled Lord Cantabri, there would be other honors as well, requested Lord Kailas' presence in his private chambers.

Another equerry escorted Kailas down a long corridor, into a surprisingly simply furnished room.

The king was pouring a drink from a decanter.

"You, sir?"

"With all pleasure, Your Majesty."

"I think I said something, back when I knighted you, that Deraine needed new thinkers."

"You did, sire."

"Why are new thinkers generally such pains in the ass?"

Hal sipped at his drink, realized he would probably never have as fine a brandy in his life, didn't respond.

"What I had proposed for you was giving you some estates,

so you wouldn't starve, a proper pension so you could sire sons or bastards, depending on your feelings, who'd become warriors of Deraine as well fitted as you.

"Plus medals, of course. Umm ... Member, King's Household; Defender of the Throne; and Hero of Deraine.

"I also proposed sending you on a grand tour of my kingdom, with recruiting officers in your wake, scooping up all those starry-eyed sorts who'd want to be just like Lord Hal.

"Instead, I get ... What? You don't want a nice, safe life. You want to go back to the damned front, where you'll be lucky to live a month.

"Do you have any idea of how long a dragon flier lives these days?"

Hal shook his head.

"Two, perhaps three months, at best."

Hal jolted, and King Asir nodded.

"It's not just those damned black dragons of theirs, but their tactics have changed. The Roche are now more interested in fighting than scouting, and when our fliers cross the lines, they're immediately attacked, generally outnumbered.

"At the moment, and I do not wish this repeated, we have less than no idea what Queen Norcia and her confidant, Duke Yasin, intend for the spring."

"And that's why I have to go back, sir," Hal said.

"What good will you do, other than becoming another martyr for Deraine?" Asir asked bitterly.

"I have an idea on how things might be changed, sire. *Ky* Yasin – that's the Duke's brother—"

"I know well who the bastard is," the king said.

"Yasin showed up over Kalabas not just with black dragons, but with them in strength. Instead of a flight, he had a full squadron, maybe four flights.

"Four against one, for that's how we were deployed ... Well, those odds are deadly."

"They are," the king agreed.

"Some time ago, my old squadron was attacked on the ground by three flights, and nearly wiped out. I retaliated by striking back against those Roche, again and again, until we'd put the fear of the gods in them."

"I'm aware of the action," Asir said. "I do more than sit on my arse on this damned throne, you know."

"Yessir. I want command of my old flight ... And can we get rid of the new name, and just call it the Eleventh?"

"We can." Asir had a bit of a smile on his lips.

"Build it up, until it's the size of Yasin's. Or bigger. And send us after those damned black dragons. If we hound them from pillar to post, never giving them a moment to strut about ... Sir, I think we can start bending the odds back to where they should be."

Hal didn't speak his other thought – that if it was now fighting in the skies, perhaps one-on-one combat might be a momentary tactic, and other ways of fighting should be explored.

"Well," the king said. "You certainly don't go by halves, do you?

"You realize you're probably guaranteeing you'll get killed."

Hal thought of Saslic's words, shrugged.

"There's one thing I'm good at," Asir went on, "and that's judging men. So I know if I forbid this action of yours, all you'll do is slip away from your estates and somehow end up in Sagene as another dragon flier, probably named Anonymous.

"So I have no other options.

"Very well, Lord Kailas. We'll do as you 'suggest,'" the king said, now with a broader smile. "Now, get out of my sight, you blackmailing bastard."

Hal put his glass down, saluted.

"Oh. One more thing," Asir said. "I've heard a certain term used, and now declare it an official title, you to be the first to hold it.

"Dragonmaster."

"What a tale this will make," Sir Thom Lowess whispered, unable to speak through excitement. "What a tale!"

31

The remnants of the Eleventh Dragon Flight were waiting at their old base. They were a pretty sad relic.

They were tattered and torn, and most of their equipment had been dumped overside from the *Adventurer*, to make room for fleeing soldiers.

Some had been wounded – the black dragons had not only gone after dragons in the air, but had been able to identify the flights' mother ships, and attacked them, as had the Roche catapults as the beachhead was being cleared.

Worse, they knew how badly they'd been beaten. Now, without any real work, with only six dragons and five fliers, they could do little except make-work, and mope about, feeling sorry for themselves.

That would change, he knew, with replacements, new gear and, most importantly, more dragons and their fliers.

Hal noticed Nanpean Tregony, who was busily avoiding him, found Tregony was keeping company with Vad Feccia, which made perfect sense to Hal, the pair in his mind being equal villains.

At least Serjeant Te had survived the withdrawal, and had been doing what he could to take care of the Eleventh.

"But it's damned hard, sir, and I realize there's no excuses to be made but, without an officer in command, your requisitions tend to get ignored, and when you don't have any trading stock, any good souvenirs, it's very damned hard to go a-bartering for what you need."

"No officers?" Hal asked. "What about Sir Nanpean Tregony?"

"Do I have to say anything?"

Hal thought. "You do."

"He isn't worth a bucket of warm owl spit. Oh, he's a good dragon flier, and seems aggressive enough. But he surely doesn't give a damn about anything or anyone else in the flight, excepting maybe his personal dragon handler, and how many dragons he's killed.

"He's got plenty of money – guess his father's mines are really paying off in the war – but won't spend a copper of it on anything but himself."

Hal nodded. It was what he would have expected from a Tregony – except for being able to fly a dragon well.

Kailas set about putting matters in hand – first restoring the flight to its proper strength, then he'd worry about implementing his idea the king had approved.

The first item was calling in Feccia, and asking what had happened to him when the invasion collapsed.

He said that when the black dragons attacked, he'd gone for altitude, but been driven down and inland. Flying just above the brush, he'd managed to elude the two monstrosities on his tail, but his dragon had been exhausted.

He flew west, as Hal had done, found a resting place, with water. Then he'd tried to return to Kalabas, but every time had encountered the black flights, and was always outnumbered.

"I went back to my hiding place, and then, the next morning, my poor dragon was cramped from the attacks of the day previous. I found some wild hogs, and chased them into my dragon's clutches.

"But it was a day and a half later when I was able to fly

back. The fleet was well at sea, only a few stragglers around the landing beaches.

"I followed the ships until I found the fleet, found the *Adventurer*, and was safe home."

That possibly wasn't the bravest story from the debacle Hal had heard, but then Feccia wasn't high on his list of candidates for hero medals. He seemed to scout with a degree of ability, and Hal wasn't sure it wasn't a sign of intelligence for a scout to avoid battle when he was outnumbered.

When the flight changed as Hal intended, Feccia might not fit in, in which case he could be transferred to a more conventional dragon flight, or possibly put in charge of the maintenance section.

Hal had an idea Feccia wouldn't be heartbroken to have an excuse to walk away from flying.

But that would be for another day. Hal was a little reluctant to harshly judge anyone from his flight training, particularly as the numbers dwindled.

Mynta Gart was the first to arrive from hospital. She'd been simply knocked from the sky by a particularly skilled three-dragon combination, not the blacks, Hal was surprised to find.

"Landed – not far from where Saslic crashed – and some bastard put an arrow in my other leg." She smiled wanly. "Now I limp on both sides, like I'm a lubber on her first day at sea."

"Did you see Saslic's body?"

"No," Gart said, looking away. "I saw her poor damned beast – what did she call him, Nont? – trying to get up, with his poor damned wing torn away. And then he fell back and some bastard put a spear in his throat. But I suppose, the way he was, that quick a death was best."

But her eyes gleamed a different story.

Hal didn't need to ask if she wanted revenge. He made a note to put her in charge of one of the new sections he planned.

Sir Loren and Farren Mariah arrived together, with their own stories.

Sir Loren's dragon had been struck by arrows from the ground. He landed, and was attacked by a Roche knight.

"I was fighting my best, which prob'ly isn't all that good, killed the man after he wounded me sore with his blade, then his squire attacked me with a damned great axe. I killed him, too, saw my poor dragon had breathed his last, and, since they hadn't hurt me legs, I took off, running like a stripe-assed ape.

"Passed several dozen arrows, I did."

Farren Mariah had been forced to land by a pair of the black dragons.

"An' I was just standin' there, with me thumbs up, an' this horseshit great rock from one of their bleedin' catapoops slams down next to me, throwin' splinters and shit here, yon and everywhere. Got fragments in my eyes, thought I was blind, and if I lived they'd put me next to the Rozen city gates to beg, which ain't proper for a Mariah.

"But m'beast kept whistlin', and I could see blurry well enough to crawl aboard, and he trampled down some of their friggin' soldiers takin' off, and somehow found the *Adventurer*.

"I may marry the bugger."

Hal found himself missing Lady Khiri, but in a very different way than he'd missed Saslic, when she was still alive. It was a pleasant kind of melancholy, tempered with a selfish gladness that he had something, someone, far distant from these killing fields and, at night, could dream about her great gray castle by the sea.

He smiled wryly at that, remembering that he didn't have to be here in Sagene at all. He could be comfortably lazing about some estate somewhere, and he realized King Asir had been so surprised by his behavior he'd never gotten around to telling Hal just what estates he was being given.

With my luck, he thought, they'll probably be coal mines in some stony waste.

Hal decided he'd made Nanpean Tregony suffer enough, and summoned him into his tent.

Tregony was about two inches taller than Hal, and still good-looking, even if he was starting to get a bit heavy. Hal noted the livid scar along his neck he'd given the man years ago, rescuing the dragon kit, wasn't displeased.

"You may sit," Hal said, keeping his voice flat.

Tregony obeyed.

"So you're the one who was going to avenge me?"

"That was pap the taletellers came up with," Tregony said. "Someone told them we came from the same village, took that, and ran hard with the information."

That could have been. Hal had certainly experienced the taletellers' willingness to brutalize the truth for their own ends.

"Very well," he said after a suitable pause. "Your records don't seem to have caught up with you. Perhaps you'd fill me in. Starting from when you entered the service."

"It was after the siege of Paestum was lifted," Tregony said. "I wanted to do something against the damned Roche, and there was a man – Garadice – who came through the district, looking for dragon fliers.

"I took the king's silver, and they trained me and sent me to Sagene.

"I went to a flight in the Second Army area. We got caught up in one of the Roche offensives, and did what we could – I credit myself with half a dozen or more dragons – then my dragon was taken down by one of their bastardly catapults, and I was captured."

Hal was interested.

"They have a special camp for dragon fliers," Tregony went on. "Far behind the lines, up north, on this island, well up an estuary."

"How many fliers are there?"

"There must have been thirty when I was captured. Probably there were fifty when I made my escape."

"Good for you," Hal approved, against his root feelings for the man. "And how did you make your escape?"

"I'm a bit of an athlete," Tregony said, looking down at his stomach. "Was, anyway. And being a prisoner helps you stay lean. I saw my chance, and kept it secret, since the Roche have spies in the camp.

"It's a terrible place, ruled by threats and cruelty and the lash, I can tell you.

"Anyway, I went out one night, when it was storming. Wore padded clothing. Pole-vaulted the first fence, and the padding kept the spikes from hurting me when I banged into it, landing. I used the pole to help me climb over the second fence, and then I was gone.

"I had some gold, some silver, and kept to the woods. The Roche peasants like their queen and their rulers no better than I do, and were willing to feed me, or sometimes put me up when it was raining. And so I worked my way east, always east.

"I stole a horse and, after that, it got easier. Then I reached the lines, turned the horse loose, and slipped across by night.

"When I got back from my leave, I said I wanted a chance to get back at the bastards for their cruelty, and the way I'd been treated . . . And so they sent me here, to the Eleventh."

Hal thought the story interesting.

"How many dragons have you brought down?" Tregony asked.

Hal shrugged.

"I don't keep track."

"I do," Tregony said. "More than I've killed?"

Hal thought of asking Tregony if he remembered a certain dragon kit, decided there wasn't any point.

"That's all," he said. "Go on about your duties."

Tregony, lips pursed, got up, saluted, went out. Outside the tent, he happened to look back in the tent, and Hal saw a look of utter, cold hatred on his face.

32

King Asir may have ordered the Eleventh Flight's augmentation, but even kings have limits.

There were few replacement fliers arriving in Paestum, and fewer dragons. At least Sagene was finally producing dragons and fliers, but those men and women were going to their own forces.

Hal had Rai Garadice write his father asking what was going on, and got an unhappy reply that the recruiters weren't able to bring in new men as fast as they should, and dragon training, what with many of the best trainers having gone off to the front and gotten killed, was even slower than it had been in peacetime.

"Besides, everyone," he wrote, "wants dragons, for everything from courier duty to parades, and all too many of these are great lords, well away from the fighting, with enough influence to get their way. I'm sorry, my son, but there's little I can do about it, at least for the present."

At least Hal, by pulling every string he could think of, and several Serjeant Te knew of, was able to bring the Eleventh up to a normal authorized strength of fifteen dragons and fliers.

Once or twice, Serjeant Te convinced a replacement depot

officer to call for volunteers from the ranks of the unassigned enlisted men.

Since most of the new blood was headed for the front lines, and the spring offensive wasn't far distant, the idea of being able to stay alive a bit longer sang clearly, and so the Eleventh was actually a bit overstrength in its ground complement.

Te had an idea, which Hal found capital, and so a special, very secret section was set up, manufacturing authentic war relics. Men who could sew made up Roche battle flags, others scoured trash dumps for battered Roche weaponry. The flags were carefully bloodied – "aye, th' man who fell over this standard, defendin' it with his life's blood, as you can see, was a great Roche knight, bravest of the brave" – as were most of the weapons. No one found it necessary to inform the souvenir's new owner the blood came from chickens, bought from local farmers, who were delighting in the flight's presence, since any beast, in any condition, was perfect dragon fodder.

Hal put his experienced fliers to training the new ones, so they might live beyond a single flight when the spring came, and, with the grudging concurrence of the First Army Commander, Lord Egibi, restricted his winter flights to reconnaissance along the lines.

While the storms raged, the soldiers along the front retreated into dugouts or, if they were lucky, huts. The enemy was not so much the Roche as King Winter, and the deathdealers were colds, fevers, the ague.

Magicians cast occasional spells, and fighting patrols went out, on foot or horseback.

But all three armies seemed content to wait for better weather.

On one flight, Hal found what he'd been looking for – a new base for his command. The old farm was not only too far behind the lines to suit him, but a constant reminder of defeat, the scars from the Roche raid still black and ruinous.

The new base was a small village at a crossroads, east of Paestum, a few miles behind the lines. It hadn't been looted too badly, and, best of all, had been a dairy commune, with huge barns ideal for dragon shelter.

The flight moved carefully to its new quarters, trying to ensure the ruined village still looked no better than a ruined village.

Hal's troops welcomed the change, one of the few objectors being Sir Nanpean. Hal puzzled at that – he would've thought any flier as intent on building his kills would have welcomed being closer to the fighting. But he quickly forgot about that, figuring Tregony probably had found a mistress at a farm around their previous station, and now was forced to be as celibate as the others.

Hal, rather gleefully considering his disgust with religion, set up his headquarters in the town church, an imposing high-ceilinged monument whose only flaw was that the tin ceiling leaked badly. But his artisans put that to rights, and Hal took over the gods-shouters' quarters for his own. Priests being priests, there were several excellent stoves, and so the building became an off-duty den for the men. Hal found something interesting – the small cubicle intended for the confession of sins to whatever god or gods this temple had been dedicated to had a small screen in its rear, low to the ground. The screen concealed a listening tube that went directly to the priests' quarters, no doubt for priestly entertainment and possible blackmail. He showed it to no one, except Serjeant Te.

The fliers found their own club/mess, one of the village's three taverns, and more top class relics were manufactured to fill the tavern's shelves as they should be. Hal found one of the replacements had worked in a tavern, and put him in charge of liquid victualing, under Te.

Te had the idea of bringing in whores from Paestum, which Hal quickly rejected. Dragon fliers already had a reputation for rowdiness, and having prostitutes in their quarters might be quite enough for him to be relieved. Hal couldn't quite understand the army's thinking on this, other than people talk to people in bed, and the powers were afraid of spies. But it was a commandment, and so he honored it. Soldiers with exceptionally strong lusts could get permission to visit Paestum and its authorized brothels.

Farren Mariah tried to cast a spell of invisibility around the base, failed completely, muttered about how he should have paid more attention to his grandfather.

Now, all he needed was better weather, and the promised addition of fliers, and he was ready to go after Yasin and his black dragons.

He spent hours in Paestum, at the First Army's intelligence bureau, but nothing came from the spies who crossed the lines as to Yasin's location.

But he knew spring would bring the black dragons out of their dens.

"We have problems, sir," Serjeant Te announced.

"What now?" Hal asked.

"Lord Cantabri's come a-calling."

"Oh shit."

"You can't see the blood on his hands," Te announced. "But you know he's got to have some scheme afoot that'll be killing us."

Hal laughed, asked Te to escort him in, and bring some mulled wine. He didn't need to add that Te should have an ear at the confessional cell.

Hal trusted Te and knew that, if Cantabri's visit had nothing to do with the war or the flight, he'd go on about his business.

"Quite a little establishment you've worked here, Lord Hal," Cantabri said. He looked far better than when Hal had seen him last, ready for the campaign trail.

"So far our friends across the lines haven't spotted it . . . And when the fighting starts, we'll be a bit closer to the action."

"Ah. I thought you might have spied out our intent for the spring."

Hal tried to look sagacious and knowing, failed.

"Oh. You *haven't* spied out the land," Cantabri said, his yellowish eyes gleaming.

"No, sir."

"I think," Cantabri said, "after all this time and bloodshed, we can dispense with the sirs and lords unless we're in formal company."

"Yes, mil . . . I mean, Bab."

"I have two matters of personal business for you. Here's one," and he reached into his belt pouch, took out an elaborately sealed roll of parchment, gave it to Hal.

Hal saw the red seal, knew it was from King Asir. He broke the seal, read, whistled.

"I just happen to have a bit of a guess as to what it is," Cantabri said. "I, in fact, made a request of His Highness, when I heard you were to be lifted further into the nobility, and you'd be granted certain privileges, that if one of them included estates, you be given lands near the ones granted me.

"I do like to have neighbors I can turn my back on. So you're now the proud owner of some dairy land, quite a sufficient acreage, plus some villages, and I suspect fishing rights, along the east coast."

"You called it," Hal said. "Plus some islands off the coast, a rather embarrassing pension and a manor house in Rozen."

He lowered the parchment.

"A question just occurred to me. Where do these lands the king gives out come from? Didn't they have owners?"

"Certainly," Cantabri said. "But the owners perhaps aren't supporters of the king, or the war, or died without heirs."

"A hell of a system," Hal said. "And this business of owning villages. I suppose that means I could evict the villagers if I didn't like the color of their hair or such?"

"You could," Cantabri agreed. "And it *is* a hell of a system.

But if the king heard of your tyranny, there just could be lands awaiting a grant to a newer hero.

"The whole matter comes to whether or not you happen to trust the king. I do."

"As do I," Hal said, glad he was telllng the truth, and remembering Te's ear at the mousehole.

"I can add," Cantabri said, "that the king told me privately he was most sorry for not taking care of this matter at your audience.

"But you, and I am quoting directly, 'shook the shit right out of him.'"

Such language, given Te's near idolatry of King Asir, must've set the serjeant back slightly.

"The second bit of business from His Majesty is that he's most apologetic that your plans for the squadron haven't been implemented as yet, but that hopefully success in the spring and summer will make matters easier.

"He didn't explain, nor did I inquire."

Hal sipped at his mulled wine.

"Now," he said. "Might I inquire as to your business, Bab?"

"Why," Cantabri said, "if you've no better way to spend your afternoon, perhaps you might take me flying."

"Just to get a breath of nice, fresh air?" Hal asked skeptically.

"No more."

"There's enough fresh air about today to freeze your frigging nose right off," Hal said. "And, not meaning to call a greater lord than myself a liar, but you might wish to give me some hints as to which direction the best fresh air might come from."

"Oh, the hells with it," Cantabri said. "I told them you wouldn't be any help unless you knew what we would be going up after. North-east by east." He saw a map on the wall, went to it, and tapped. "Here."

Hal went to the map, studied it.

"I think," he said, now not so sure his clever-clever stationing of Te was that good an idea, "we'd best go on outside, see to the saddling of our mount."

They went out, putting on heavy coats, gloves, against the swirling winds. At least it wasn't snowing, Hal thought.

Cantabri grinned at him.

"You know, back when I commanded my first cavalry troop, I thought I was most clever, and had my most trusted senior warrant with his ear to the back of my tent when I met with superiors, so that if anything of interest to my command was heard, he could be dealing with the matter immediately.

"I won't bother you with details as to how I was caught in my own trap . . . But I was."

Hal didn't think he was capable of flushing any more, but he was, and Cantabri roared laughter.

"Now," he said, after he'd recovered, "let me give you the details of what's planned.

"I'll add that this plan comes directly from the king, after he had some most meaningful dreams his astrologer said must have been sent by the gods. The king, evidently, has felt his fate connected with a great river since a witch told him that, back when he was a boy."

"Oh dear," Hal said in a small voice.

"Perhaps so," Cantabri agreed. "First, you must remember His Majesty is not a man of war, and despises this horror Queen Norcia and, frankly, the prewar weakness of Sagene, forced him into.

"However, he feels he must rise to the occasion."

Cantabri and Hal looked at each other, and their faces were perfectly blank.

"He always felt that the invasion of Kalabas was an inspired idea, together with his plan to invade Roche up the Ichili River.

"It is a pity, in his view, that certain events, and possibly the hand of the gods – King Asir believes very firmly in the gods – intervened.

"Or perhaps he chose the wrong place."

"I see," Hal said, remembering the map. Cantabri had pointed to the fortified city of Aude, on the broad River Comtal. It was about fifty or more miles from the vaguely defined desolation of the lines, and some ten miles from Roche's northern coast. "Just like the last time?"

"Sort of," Cantabri said. "Except that, being closer to Deraine, our supply lines won't be as long.

"We've even now begun building craft for the invasion, but they'll be different, not a mish-mosh of cargo ships and such, but smaller, flat-bottomed river craft, able to cross the Chicor Straits in good weather."

"And of course, there are no Roche spies in Deraine reporting this construction and drawing the obvious conclusions," Hal said.

"The king's aware that there are," Cantabri said, a bit of frost in his voice. Hal reminded himself that Lord Cantabri wasn't near the cynic Kailas thought himself to be.

"Go ahead," Hal prodded.

"There'll be spells of confusion cast along the northern front," Cantabri went on. "Together with other spells I can't talk about right now.

"On a more physical level, we'll interdict all mail leaving Deraine for any foreign shore for the week before the attack."

"None of which will be noticed by Roche magicians or agents," Hal said cynically. "And no one will look to their defenses, remembering that good King Asir has a fondness for rivers."

"This time, there'll be a bit more subtlety," Cantabri said. "I hope. The First and Second Armies will mount an attack on Aude. All plans will suggest that is our only goal, that once we break through the lines, we'll regroup, and then move south and east on Carcaor.

"Instead, holding Aude, we'll have control of the upper hundred or more miles of the River Comtal. The invasion barges will carry the troops upriver, toward Carcaor.

"At the very least, holding Aude, we'll force the Roche lines back on themselves, and break this stalemate."

"If we take Aude," Hal said, but quietly, under his breath.

Hal told Sir Loren and Rai Garadice, his best pilots, although, if Sir Nanpean was telling the truth about his victories, he might well be a better choice.

But Kailas, having the safety of the man he considered Deraine's most important soldier uppermost, wished to take no chances with the unknown.

Storm, recovered from the long flight and his injuries, was sleek, and roared pleasure at the thought of flying.

Hal and his two handlers got Storm ready to fly, with a double saddle. His new crossbow, and five ten-bolt magazines, a trumpet and glass finished Hal's equipage.

The other two fliers were outfitted similarly.

"All right," Hal said. "Now, if you'll just clamber up—"

He looked closely at Lord Cantabri, saw he was as pale as he'd been in the hospital, wondered if the man was concealing wounds worse than anyone knew.

Then he got it.

"Uh, Bab, meaning no offense, how many times have you flown before today?"

Bab said, in a curiously muffled voice, "This will be the first."

"Would you rather wait here? My fliers can scout the area around Aude without being caught."

"No," Cantabri said, iron in his voice. "I must see what we'll be facing."

"Very well, then. Let me give you a hand up."

Hal didn't think it would be wise to add the caution he normally gave first-time fliers, that if they got sick on him, there'd be several hells to pay.

He mounted up, made sure Lord Cantabri had a firm hold, and slapped Storm's neck with the reins.

The dragon plodded out of the huge barn, squishing

through the winter muck, faster, wings swirling up, then thrashing hard down, and Storm was in the air.

Behind him, Sir Loren and Garadice's monsters lifted clear.

Hal glanced over his shoulder, saw Cantabri's eyes were tightly shut, but his hold on the dragon's scales could have bent them.

As briefed, they flew high across the front, keeping a sharp eye out for Roche patrols, then dove down, beyond the archers and crossbowmen.

They flew due east, until the land below was empty of soldiery, turned northerly toward Aude.

Hal flew behind the knoll, then darted up, and landed on the clear crest. Garadice and Sir Loren flew in circles, hidden by the knoll, watching for any Roche dragons.

Beyond, across the Comtal River Valley, lay Aude.

"And here we are," he said, sliding out of his saddle.

Sir Cantabri took his hand, staggered, then went to a patch of brush and threw up in a dignified way.

When he'd finished, Hal handed him his canteen.

"No," Cantabri said. "Get mine. It's got brandy in it."

Hal obeyed. Cantabri rinsed his mouth, then swallowed, sighed.

"I'd be most beholden, Lord Kailas," he said, curiously formal, "if you could find your way not to discuss my body's weaknesses unless you must.

"But I shall admit to you I have a desperate fear of heights."

Hal was surprised, not only that Cantabri was afraid of *anything*, but that he had the courage to admit to it.

He thought he still had a great deal to learn about bravery, took out his glass, and studied Aude. Cantabri did the same.

It was even worse than the map had suggested. The Comtal, deep, wide, unfordable, protected three sides of the city. And it was a city, almost as large as Paestum.

But where Paestum had grown beyond its walls, Aude still

hid behind them. The city had been built on a high bluff. There were double turreted walls, machicolated and strongly held.

Inside the second of these ran the town, zigging, narrow alleys Hal knew would be deadly to fight through, easy to defend, to a final stronghold, with its own walls and round keep.

There was a broad ramp on the third side, but this was well protected with pairs of interlocking gatehouses.

Assaulting this castle would be an utter nightmare. Hal didn't think it could be taken by any human forces, not unless there were enough soldiers willing to have their bodies stacked to the tops of the walls for others to climb on, and then die, in their turn, within the city.

Hal remembered Serjeant Te's words, almost looked at Cantabri's hands, to see if there might really be blood dripping from them.

33

It was a brisk late spring morning when, to the roll of drums and the thunder of horses' hooves, the First and Second Armies went on the attack.

Hal and his flight were reconning for the First Army, and, from high above, it looked splendid – the Roche lines being broken by the heavy cavalry, light cavalry pouring through the gaps, and a steady stream of infantry securing the positions, then moving on.

This, Hal was glad to see, wasn't like the abortive invasion of Kalabas – Lord Egibi had given his commanders explicit instructions that they were to exploit any opportunity offered.

Hal saw two dragons, neither black, and he and his flight attacked, drove them down into the bloody hands of the soldiery below.

Kailas chanced flying south for almost an hour, and found the lead elements of the Second Army, half Deraine, half Sagene.

They, too, had been successful in the breakthrough, and were marching steadily north-north-east, toward Aude and the River Comtal.

They saw three dragons, killed two, and the third fled.

At base that night, most of the fliers were bubbling, sure an attack that began this successfully couldn't fail.

Hal tried to hold back their enthusiasm, but felt a warmth of hope in spite of himself.

The next few days they drove the Roche back again, and now, when Hal swooped low over the soldiers, he could hear singing, and see they were laden with loot the Roche had previously seized from the poor, vanished peasants of the area.

Hal took Garadice and Gart, flew over the Roche lines, such as they were, and on, deeper into the rear. Then an idea struck, and he blew his trumpet, waved for a course change, to east-south-east.

What he saw, or rather what he didn't see, sent him back at top speed, his bewildered wingmates trailing, until he spotted the pennons of the Armies' Combined Command.

He landed, told Garadice to watch Storm, and went looking for Cantabri.

"You're sure?" Lord Bab said.

"I'm positive," Hal said.

"Twice lucky," Cantabri said. "I remember what you didn't see on the day we invaded Kalabas."

"I hope the result is different," Hal said.

"It will if I have anything to do with it. Now for Lords Egibi and Desmoceras."

Bab's eyes were a-gleam.

"This, Hal, could win the war for us, in a week, or at most a month. Come on, man!"

"There appeared to be no Roche formations to the south?" Egibi said, trying to hold back incredulity.

"None, sir," Hal said. "I saw scattered light cavalry, and they were in full flight."

"This is somewhat astonishing," Lord Desmoceras, the Sagene commander of the Second Army said. He was a thin man, a bit shorter than average, but his face and body were seamed with the scars that proved him a fighting man to contend with.

"I have full confidence in Lord Kailas," Egibi said, but there was a slight question in his voice.

"As do I," Cantabri said, without ever a question mark.

"Thank you, sirs," Hal said. "Lord Desmoceras, I'm an experienced flier. I flew very carefully, saw no camouflaged camps or formations.

"The Roche have, from all I could see, been split in half. I'd guess some are fleeing toward Aude, the rest possibly to join up with other elements to our south.

"I'm ready to take out flights to find out just where they are."

Egibi nodded, didn't respond to Hal's volunteering.

"What do you think?" he asked Desmoceras.

The Sagene pulled at his nose.

"I think my Council of Barons would have my head for disobeying their orders, and turning away from Aude. Not to mention we have no spells ready, and it would take at least two days to change the army's orders."

Lord Egibi made a wry face.

"And here we've told our officers to take the initiative, not to be afraid to take chances.

"I myself wonder what King Asir would think if I changed the attack. First, we'll have a supply problem, turning away from the River Comtal, and—"

"Live off what the Roche have abandoned," Hal said, somewhat astonished at his effrontery.

Lord Egibi turned to him, face reddening. Then he controlled himself.

"Yes. Thank you, Lord Kailas," he said, voice cold. "If you'll wait beyond, to see if we have any further orders?"

Hal forced calm, saluted, and left.

An hour later, Cantabri came out, lips pursed, hand on his sword as if he wanted to draw and kill the first person he saw.

Hal didn't need to ask what the decision had been.

"Continue the attack?" he said.

Cantabri nodded, too angry to speak.

Hal stormed back to his dragon, took off for his flight base, barely noticing or caring that his wingmates were flanking him.

A drum kept pounding in his head – we could have won the war, we could have won the war, we could have won the war.

The next day, the advance continued toward Aude.

34

Two days later, Hal still not over his rage, the first scouts reached the River Comtal, facing light opposition from the Roche. Following them were the pioneers, who considered the deep, unfordable river, then began denuding the local forests for bridging material.

Then came the infantry, who looked across the river, and up at Aude's great walls, winced, then settled down to wait.

Logs were snaked to the river's edge, and small lumber-yards put together, to begin planing and cutting the lumber for the bridges.

That night, fires flickered along the riverbank, and the cut lumber, green wood though it was, burst into flames. Aude's magicians were at work.

The next morning, Hal and his flight were told to lift a cadre of magicians to the knoll where Cantabri had first scouted the city.

The magicians conferred, then ordered their acolytes to begin laying out tapes in mystical patterns, and chanting preparatory spells.

Hal noticed Storm was making a low, pained noise, as if

hurt. He examined the dragon carefully, saw no signs of harm, saw other dragons were also showing discomfort.

Magic, he realized, something the monsters liked no better than the layman.

He told the head magician of the dragons' problems, said he'd take them off, circle the knoll from a distance, and return when summoned.

Within minutes, he, too, felt uncomfortable, and knew a great spell was being sent against the sorcerers of Aude.

Then, suddenly, the discomfort vanished, and he saw a tiny, robed dot below, waving to him.

He brought the flight back, and took the magicians and their gear back to the rear area, just behind a ridgeline, where the high command had positioned itself.

The pioneers went back to work, and this time, their piled logs remained intact.

He heard, from a man who had a friend who'd been eavesdropping when a deserter was questioned that something horrible, invisible, had struck at the Roche wizards, killing at least a dozen or more.

He wondered, properly suspicious of the army's rumor machine, how much of that was true.

Replacements trickled in – none of them fliers – and they were a-babble of the new small ships, river barges, tied up in Paestum, or still building in the ports of Deraine, while two bridges inched across the River Comtal, the walls of Aude looming above.

If the Roche didn't know of King Asir's plan, Hal figured they'd gone blind and deaf.

The bridges reached the far side, and ranks of infantrymen trotted across, forming into attack echelons.

From the walls, catapults sent man-long arrows arcing down, and even a few crossbowmen, clearly inexperienced, chanced shots at this impossibly long range.

Hal, soaring above the city, saw a gate yawn open on Aude's landward side, and half a hundred knights debouch.

He scribbled a note, sent Storm diving toward the Deraine infantry, tooting on his trumpet. Someone with rank got the note, and soldiers formed a wedge, ran to meet the cavalry.

Hal pointed at the open gate, dove on it, sent crossbow bolts into the scattering of soldiers atop the wall.

A Deraine light cavalry troop rode around their soldiers, into the Roche horsemen, as the infantry charged.

Then there were Roche dragons coming in, and he had no time to watch the ground. Two dragons dove at him, and he pinned the first's rider to his dragon with a bolt, pulled the charging handle back, forward, and shot the other rider in the stomach. He screamed, fell, and his dragon, unmanned, fled.

Then his flight was around him, and it was a swirl of screeching monsters and shouting men. A wingtip brushed Hal's chest, and he almost fell from Storm's back. He fired a bolt after his attacker, had no idea if he hit or not.

Sir Loren had a dragon on his tail, closing. The Roche rider wasn't watching his own rear, and Hal came down on him, shot him in the back. Sir Loren waved thanks as Hal banked away.

Hal looked around, realized he was very low over Aude. He flashed over the great roofed, turreted keep, big enough to land a dozen dragons on, near the main gate. Bowmen were shooting up at him. He gigged Storm, and the dragon shot away, low over the walls, over the river, and came back across Aude.

The last of the Roche cavalry was being cut to pieces, and the Deraine riders were breaking free, galloping hard for the still-open gate.

Hal thought he might be mumbling a prayer – if the cavalry made it inside, the battle could be a victory before it was even mounted.

Heavy cavalry, moving at a ponderous trot, came up from

the river and around the walls toward the gate, supporting the light riders.

The air above the wall was a swoop of dragons, Hal's flight, and another formation. There were only two Roche dragons aloft, and one of those folded a wing, and spun down to smash across the outer wall's battlements. He looked for the second, but it had vanished.

The Deraine light cavalry was inside the city's outer walls, and there were spearmen running out, forming a wall before the inner gate. The Deraine horses reared, turned away – no horse will charge into a solid mass, romantic paintings aside, and Hal saw the outer gates slowly closing, brave Roche soldiers ignoring the cavalry at their back.

Hal heard the gates slam closed from 200 feet above, saw the last of the cavalry inside the wall shot down by bowman on the walls on either side. The accidental chance at a quick victory was gone.

Now, unless there was a miracle, the battle for Aude would be a long, bloody siege.

The hut was a blurt of excitement as the fliers unwound from the air battle.

"How many'd you get . . . sir?" Sir Nanpean called.

Hal shook his head. As always, he didn't think he was in the business of counting.

"He got four, four, the dirty whore," Farren Mariah chanted.

Tregony's face fell, and he turned away.

"Guess," Mynta Gart grinned, passing Hal a jack of ale, "who's been holding forth on his three victories."

The beer, chilled by sorcery, meant more to Kailas than whether or not Sir Nanpean Tregony was happy.

"I think we've got a problem, sir," Serjeant Te said.

"Of course we've got problems," Hal said. "We're sojers, ain't we?"

Te didn't smile.

"Very well," Hal said. "We do have a problem. A serious one."

"Someone's stealing supplies, sir."

Hal grimaced.

"What sort?"

"All sorts," Te said. "The fliers' club is missing brandy, the supply tent's missing clothing, boots, jackets.

"And I'm missing some maps."

Hal suddenly took things very seriously. The only people who might be interested in maps, outside the army, would be historians, collectors . . . and spies.

Hal doubted there were many collectors hiding in the forests around Aude.

"What sort of maps?"

Te nodded – Hal was beginning to understand.

"Marked ones, sir. Showing last week's deployments, some of the area around Paestum."

"Which naturally, we've been squirreling away, rather than destroying, against orders."

Te held out his hands.

"Tell me somebody who doesn't keep files. More files than he should."

Hal nodded reluctantly, thought.

"The clothing. Any particular size?"

"The first thing I thought of, sir," Te said. "No such luck. All sizes, which means the thief must be selling them."

"I'd haul everybody together," Hal said, "and read them the liturgy about thieving, and how we'll hang anybody we find stealing from the nearest dragon.

"But not with those damned maps gone. That suggests something else. Any ideas on who might be the guilty one?"

"Not a clue, sir," Te said. "So I've got to suspect everyone and no one."

"So it's up to us to play warder and investigate, then."

"Yessir," Te said. "And I'd rather no one be tipped the

wink that we're alert. Maybe I can lay out and catch the bastard first."

"Maybe that's a good idea," Hal said. "And maybe, when
I've got the time, I should do the same.

"It's pure hell when you don't know who you can – and
can't – trust."

"It is that, sir."

Hal was summoned by Lord Egibi, informed the attack on the
Comtal's mouth had been successful, and Deraine and Sagene
were turning the port town into an impregnable fortress.

Now supply barges and small ships could sail or be warped
upriver with supplies and reinforcements.

"However," Egibi said, "our scouts report the riverbanks
are held by partisans – Roche irregulars. Our first convoy
upriver was ambushed and forced back.

"Take your dragons, Lord Kailas, and scout for ambushes,
and drive back those guerrillas. You have royal permission to
land and burn any villages you deem to be supporting the
enemy."

"Nossir," Hal said firmly. "I'll not be doing *that*."

There was an audible gasp from some staff officers, while
Lord Cantabri hid a grin.

"And why are you disobeying orders?" Egibi said, in a
voice that would have passed for summer thunder.

"Because," Hal said, "first, we're in Roche now. Any villages supporting these guerrillas, who I'll wager are no more
than Roche soldiers who've lost their parent units, are no
more than patriots.

"Just as you – or King Asir – would expect our Deraine villagers to stand and be counted should we ever be invaded."

Egibi glowered at him, but Hal refused to look away.

"I suppose," Egibi said, "you're right. Dammit, I know
you are. Very well then. Go wage your damned moral war."

Hal took his entire flight down the River Comtal toward the

sea. Taking off, he could see the pioneers, busy again, building siege engines.

Then he concentrated on ambush sites, flying low, just above the water.

He heard a whoop of glee, glanced back, saw Farren's dragon lifting its head from the water, holding an enormous pike in its jaws.

Hal noted several spots, saw horsemen gallop out of brush a few times, didn't pursue them.

After a two-hour flight, they saw boats in the river. Not trusting their own soldiery to hold fire, Hal draped a Deraine flag from Storm's neck, circled until he was waved in.

He landed on the bank, and one of the barges drew near.

"See any Roche?" the officer in the bows said.

"Probably," Hal said. "We ran them off, but I'm sure they'll scuttle right back. We'll orbit your forward ships, and give the alarm if they're still planning anything."

"Excellent," the man called, and someone on the ship shouted, "Good on the dragons!"

The journey back to Aude took two days. Three times the dragons sprang traps, coming down from above on the ambushers, showering crossbow bolts, and the escorting ships landed soldiers to finish the job.

Then, almost within sight of Aude, their escort duty was taken over by cavalry, and Hal signaled his flight back to their base.

He saw a storm front approaching, was glad it looked as if they'd be stuck on the ground for at least a day. His fliers and, more importantly, his dragons could do with a bit of a rest.

The storm lasted longer than expected, and by the third day, Hal couldn't find any more maintenance for his soldiery.

Serjeant Te reported no luck at all in finding the thief, but Hal told him to keep his watch out.

"I'll do that, sir," Te said, yawning. "But it's damned hard chasing the flight around by day and creeping through the bushes at night. Almost makes me think I'm back being an infantryman."

Hal was jerked awake by the duty officer.

"Sir. It's an emergency."

"It always is," Hal muttered, rolling out of bed and dragging pants and boots on.

"You'd best come armed, sir," the man said.

Hal belted his sword-belt on, went out into the rain.

There was a flare of torches back of the headquarters tent.

Women and men stood around a body in Deraine uniform, sprawled on its face.

"Must've surprised some damned Roche," someone muttered.

Hal knelt over the body, turned it on its back.

It was Serjeant Te, eyes wide, mouth gaping. A long knife was buried in his chest.

Hal knew the knife.

It was the dagger issued only to dragon fliers.

35

Hal ordered the flight to parade, in full uniform, as a gesture of honor to Serjeant Te. Of course, he really wanted to see which flier was missing his dagger.

There were enough shortages and uniform inadequacies for Hal to make quite a storm, and have his adjutant, Gart, make notes of what was missing.

But the dagger gave him nothing.

Some of the fliers swore they'd never been issued a dagger at all, which Hal had no way of knowing. Others, including Gart and Feccia, had lost theirs, somewhere. Sir Nanpean had the best reason – his, of course, had been taken from him when he was captured, and he'd never been able to get a replacement.

Nothing.

Hal, not having the slightest clue as to how to play warder, made what he thought were subtle inquiries, which also gave him nothing.

Worse, from the death of Te on, the thefts came to a halt.

Hal ground his teeth, got on with the war.

*

The pioneers had finished their siege engines, and they began thudding away, hurling huge stones against the landward wall, firing huge arrows at any target that presented itself, lobbing other stones into the center of Aude.

Hal, riding back of the lines for a meeting with Cantabri, saw men going forward. They were lightly armed, and carried the types of picks and shovels Hal recognized from Caerly. He also remembered them from the horror-drenched days in Paestum, waiting for the Roche mine to be fired.

He said nothing to anyone – the mine must be kept a secret.

Deraine controlled the air, although Roche dragons still fiercely contested the issue.

Hal took flights up in the morning and at dusk, and almost every day the Roche rose to meet him.

None were the feared black dragons. Hal began hoping that maybe Yasin had been eaten by the monstrosities, or they'd discovered they couldn't be depended on, or something.

Hal killed his share and more, as did Sir Nanpean, Garadice and Sir Loren. But the Eleventh Flight still took casualties, and the number of pilots gathered in their hut grew fewer and fewer, the revelry louder and louder, sometimes just short of hysteria.

Hal sent inquiry after inquiry back to the First Army Headquarters, some bordering on the insubordinate, raging, begging for replacements.

But none came.

The soldiers on line were put on alert, with no reason being given, and for all dragon flights to be in the air from dawn to dusk, prepared, as the order said "to take advantage of targets of opportunity."

Hal knew what it meant, but still kept silent. Perhaps the still-undiscovered thief/murderer in the flight was no more than that.

But most likely, not.

They were orbiting Aude in formations of three, other dragon flights soaring past them.

It was a summer day that promised heat, but in this morning was crisp and clear.

Hal saw wisps of smoke coming from the base of one wall, watched closely.

The smoke boiled out, and the timbers of the mine below cracked, and crumbled.

The outer wall cracked, tottered, and fell, crashing down, almost into the river below.

But no wave of Deraine soldiers rose to the attack. The space between the outer and inner city walls was too close for it to be anything other than a deathtrap.

Roche reinforcements were hurried to the inner wall, waiting for the assault that never came.

That was the first step.

Somewhere, not far distant, another mine would be dug under the inner wall.

In the meantime, the siege went on, daily patrols by cavalry and infantry to make sure Aude stayed invested.

The Roche developed a new tactic – bringing four or six dragons up just before dawn. These carried the great wicker baskets, but were filled with supplies. They flew out – when they could – with wounded soldiers.

Hal, still fighting his own war, told his fliers to attack the incoming dragons, but let the ones leaving pass.

His fliers, no more interested in slaughtering the sick and wounded than Kailas was, obeyed.

Except for Sir Nanpean, who argued that any dragon and its flier should be a target, and there was no place for mercy in war.

Hal, logically, knew he was right, and didn't ground him for disobedience.

But he liked Tregony no more than before.

*

. . . we lost two dragons today. The first was crippled in
a fight with three other dragons, and we had to put her down.
I frankly feel that the fault is that of the flier, who's less
than experienced, and should have known better than to fly
against such odds.

The other, Sir Nanpean Tregony's, fell sick of some unknown
ailment. We isolated it in a barn, which made the poor beast even
more forlorn. Tregony, of course, refused to spend any time with
his dragon, saying he had no intention of catching whatever
ailment the monster had.

We sent for a wizard, and asked around for an animal doctor.
But no one had any experience with dragons, and the magician could
do little but ease the beast's last hours.

I am starting to wonder if the poor damned dragons shouldn't
have stayed in the west, without matter what enemies
threatened them.

Certainly we haven't brought them anything but grief.
Perhaps, when this war is over, if it ever is, we should free all the
dragons, and let them fly to wherever they wish.

I write this, but I know it's foolish, for many of the dragons are
now thoroughly domesticated, and prefer our company. Also,
those captured young could hardly be released into the wild, for
they'd live but a few days, certainly less if they encountered wild
dragons.

And what of those who've been kept in zoos, thoroughly
accustomed to having their sheep or whatever provided to them
on a barrow?

Once again it seems whatever Man touches he turns first to
his own purposes, then to ruination.

Sorry to end my letter on such a gloomy note, but that's how
I'm feeling at this moment.

I do miss you
Hal

*

Hal hadn't known what would happen between him and Khiri when he returned to the war, and was quite surprised to find he thought of her often.

She wrote him daily, letters about the smallest, most normal things – what was going on with the sowing at Cayre a Carstares, the newest fripperies around the capital, what dinners she'd been invited to, and what she'd worn and eaten.

All of these, things Hal might've thought irritating, took him away from the war.

She was working at one of Rozen's hospitals, still living at Thom Lowess' city home, and missing him desperately.

Hal, in return, missed her, and wrote back as often as he could.

He was learning the loneliness of command, and, without Saslic, had no one to confide in, especially about his feelings about war, and about dragons.

He wondered if he was falling in love with the beasts and also with Lady Khiri.

He snorted. He had no time for such weaknesses, especially not now.

But still, when he thought of her, at the strangest times, a smile came to him, and his mood lightened.

Again, the troops were brought to full alert and, this time, told to be ready for an all-out attack.

Hal, once again, overflew the city, looking for any signs of trouble.

This time, he found them.

He saw, not far from where the first mine had been dug, men suddenly explode out of carefully camouflaged tunnels, running as if there were demons at their heels.

He expected to see smoke, once again, as the pit props were fired.

But nothing came.

Heavy cavalry and infantry moved forward, guarding the tunnels.

Hal wondered what had happened. Something must have gone wrong.

The tale didn't take long to reach the squadron.

The miners had been within a day of undermining the second wall when suddenly – stories varied from nowhere or from a tiny, unnoticed crevice – monsters boiled on them. They were not men, all stories agreed, could not be men, being coal black, with a rigid carapace atop their head like a lizard's. They had sharp pinchers for hands, and tore at the miners as they panicked, tried to escape the trap.

The monsters, whatever they were, feared sunlight or possibly open air, for none of them came out of the tunnel, either by day or night.

Evidently the master spell of two months earlier hadn't gotten rid of *all* the Roche sorcerers.

There matters rested for two days.

Then magicians came up, staying well clear of the tunnel, and began chanting, dancing, weaving in steps as more magic was sent out.

There was no smoke, no fire, but somehow the wizards' thaumaturgy worked upon the tunnel props.

Cracking noises came, Hal was told later. Then, slowly, majestically, the inner wall began toppling, outward, just as the miners had intended.

It leaned out at an impossible angle, but its stones never shattered. And then it stopped leaning, and held at that impossible angle.

Hal shook his head. Wizardry confounded wizardry.

Then he heard a squeal from one of the dragons, looked away from Aude.

Hurtling toward the city, above Hal and the other dragon flight, came *Ky* Yasin's black dragons.

36

Hal had time for one warning trumpet blast, then had to concentrate on Storm, on trying to overcome Yasin's height advantage.

The other, experienced fliers of the Eleventh were doing the same, but the other flight over Aude, and some of Hal's less-seasoned fliers did little more than gawp at the black death coming down on them.

Yasin's fliers were experienced – they tried to avoid combat with their equals on the climb, and struck at the newer fliers.

They'd stolen a lesson from Hal and their own experimenters, and all their fliers were armed with short recurve bows, harder to fire accurately than Kailas' crossbows, but with a much heavier weight. The Roche fliers had become adept in clinging to their dragons' backs with their knees, reins looped around the flier's neck while he was shooting.

A Roche dragon veered away from Hal, but he launched a bolt, and hit the beast in its wing. It shrieked, and its rider fought the reins.

Hal slid another bolt into his crossbow trough, and was just under the Roche's wing. He fired, this time at the flier, hit him in the leg. The man reflexively grabbed at the wound, and Hal fired again, this bolt taking the man in his chest.

The black dragon, feeling no control at the reins, shrieked again, and flapped away to the west.

Hal banked Storm sharply, looked down at disaster.

Deraine dragons were falling, fleeing. He saw no more than half a dozen of his fliers still looking for a fight, dove down to support them.

He put a bolt in a black dragon's neck, another in a second beast's tail, enough to make it coil in surprise, hurling its rider down toward Aude.

A black dragon was flying at him from dead ahead, and Hal, dropping another bolt tray on to his crossbow, forced himself to hold his course.

At the last minute, the black dragon turned aside, and Hal swore the flier was Yasin himself. He fired at the man, and missed.

Then the blacks were gone, and it was time to limp home and count the losses.

They were severe. Hal didn't know how many fliers the other flight had lost, but he'd lost four himself.

One of them was Rai Garadice, who'd been seen trying to fight his crippled dragon across the river, into his lines.

Hal and Sir Loren went back into the air, flying low along the river front, hoping and looking.

It was just before dark when they saw the broken remains of a dragon, landed, and found Garadice's body a dozen yards away. It appeared as if he'd tried to jump for the leafy branches of a tree, hoping to cushion his fall. But he'd missed by feet.

Another of the old guard was gone.

It took Hal almost until midnight to find the right words for the letter to Garadice's father.

They buried Rai, full ceremony, the next day.

Then Hal found a horse, rode to command headquarters, and found Cantabri.

He was less than properly military, angry and demanding,

that he had less than half his fliers left, and no more than one spare dragon.

As of this moment, he was standing down his flight, unable to accept any further assignments until his unit was properly rebuilt.

Cantabri listened, didn't show signs of anger at the insubordination, said the matter would be taken care of.

"When?" Hal half-snarled.

"Before the week is out," Cantabri said.

Hal stared at him, turned, remembered his courtesy, turned back, saluted the lord and stomped out.

"Isn't it a bitch," Hal said, staring at the half-empty bottle of wine, "that not only are you the only one I can feel sorry for myself around, including Khiri, but I can't even let myself get drunk."

Storm made what a serious dragon fanatic might have defined as a sympathetic noise, especially if no one considered his breath, palatable only to someone who likes the aroma of very dead sheep.

"Troubles," Hal went on, leaning back against the dragon, and considering the empty, dark barn. "Not enough fliers, and the ones I've got are fodder for that frigging Yasin. We're low on supplies, and nobody's answering Gart's requisitions for anything and everything from socks to crossbows.

"Plus I can't find that . . . that person I'm looking for," he said, cautious even when alone.

"I don't think we're fighting the Roche in the right way, but I'm just too damned tired keeping up with this minute's emergency to rethink matters.

"If I could have a month or so to myself . . ." His voice trailed off, and he wished he could uncork and finish the bottle.

"First, I'd go to Cayre a Carstares," he decided. "And I'd sleep for a week. Then I'd spend the next week in bed with Khiri. Then I'd eat for a week. Eat and drink.

"After I got over my hangover, I'd sit down, in that tower, and get the mud out of my brain on some of those ideas I had that looked so promising."

Storm made a noise.

"All right," Hal allowed. "You can come too. And we'd go out flying every day, or, anyway, every other day. Flying west, and looking at some of your relatives as they sail toward us."

Hal heard a flapping noise, looked out the open door of the barn, saw, not far distant, flying low, one of Yasin's black dragons.

Storm made a keening sound.

"You'd rather not go? You'd rather stay here and kill black dragons?"

Hal pulled himself to his feet.

"And me talking to dragons. There was more wine in that wine than I allowed for.

"I'm for bed."

At the far end of the barn, a canvas blocking a doorway moved, very slightly.

Hal Kailas didn't notice.

Cantabri's word was good. Three days after Hal had stormed his battlements, seven new dragon fliers appeared. They weren't nearly as trained as Hal's flight had been what seemed like a century ago. But they were present, didn't seem to have any significant flaws, and could be trained.

Or else they'd die.

"Now, yer see," Farren Mariah said to the seven replacements, "there's a gatillion an' three ways to fight a dragon.

"And all of 'em's right, as long as it's you that comes home all heroic and shit, and not the Roche."

"We don't need generalities," a dragon flier named Chincha said.

"Hold on, woman," Mariah said. "You'll get statistics and such, if you want."

Hal had happened by the open back door of the fliers' hut, heard Farren holding forth, listened, grinning.

"We'll start-a-tart by comparin' our two grayt hee-roes, Lord Kailas, who I can call Hal but you can't until you've gotten your paws thorough blooded. The other is Sir Nanpean Tregony, who'll, thank you, prefer you use his title. Or you can simply call him a god.

"He won't object t' that."

"Clearly a friend of yours," Chincha said.

Mariah turned serious.

"I'll tell you someat that'll stand you in great standings as you wobble through thisyere life.

"You don't got friends. Friends take yer heart with 'em when they die. Your friends are the people who can pull one of them friggin' black dragons off your arse, and who'll carry her, or his, end of a horrible dawn patrol wi'out snivelin' overmuch.

"Anyways, to turn serious. You takes Lord Kailas for starters. Now, he ain't the best shot in th' world. Good enow, but he'll win no country rumpkin-bumpkin fairs for shootin'. Which is why he gets as close to his target as he can.

"Ne'er shoot 'til you smells the reek of its breath, might be his motto in his grotto if he had a motto or a grotto.

"So he's friends – if friends you can ever be – wi' his horrid beastie. And he uses th' dragon's flyin' to get right up a Roche's butt. You'll note he steers wi' his foots an knees as much as the reins, which gives him a better chance t' take aim. Not to mention hangin' on, since it's not considered respectickle to fall off yer mount while chasin' some other sod.

"Also, he uses his wingmen, generally likes to have one t'either side, to keep th' Roche from tippytoein' up behint and arsassinatin' him, and in front to steer th' bad sorts into an intractabobble situation.

"A nice thing, if you're one of those wot counts bodies, he'll share or even give up a win to you.

"Now, *Sir* Nanpean, he's different. A dead shot. I mean

that in earnest. He gets in 'til he's got a shot, and that's as he sees it, near or far, and then plonks 'em.

"He don't care what he hits . . . Which brings up another matter about our Hal. He rather goes for the rider, not the dragon.

"Got a soft spot for the beasties, he does.

"Back to *Sir* Nanpean."

Hal noted Farren's emphasis on the sir.

"He don't have much use for a dragon. If he weren't scared of Lord Kailas finding him out, he'd prob'ly pack a whip.

"I remember a flier, back in trainin', thought he was some kinda drover or shit, did that. Dragon went and killed him, it did.

"Another thing about Sir Nanpean. He don't have use for wingmen, neither. He figures it's your place to help him make kills. Never'll be the day come when he shares credit."

"What about you?" another replacement asked. "What's your secret, since you've been out for such a long time?"

Hal could imagine Farren's sweet smile.

"Why I gots none, other'n bein' a helladacious wizard on my mother's side, wit' charms and all *kinds* of shit. I just flies along, lookin' cute, and when somethin' moves, I shoot."

"How many dragons have you killed?" Chincha asked skeptically.

"Ours or theirs?"

Hal buried laughter.

"Dozens," Farren went on. "Hunnerds and hunnerds. Back of the Roche lines looks like a secret dragon graveyard."

"Then why aren't you the darling of the taletellers?" Chincha asked.

"That's a bit complicated," Farren went on. "Yer gots to start with me bein' the illygitymate daughter of King Asir, and—"

Hal, not having time for the rest of the tale, went on about his business, his dark mood of the night before gone.

*

Now the war became static once again. But more men, horses, dragons died, on both sides, than ever before.

There were more attacks against the walls of Aude, each time driven back. But each time, more of its defenders died.

The city walls were pockmarked from the huge stones hurled by trebuchets, and unshriven and unburied bodies lay scattered across the barren landscape, the bloated bodies of horses and oxen among them.

The soldiers were either entrenched or sheltered behind rocks, in gullies, folds in the ground. On the battlements of Aude were arrow-firing catapults, whose crews grew more and more deadly in their aim.

There were demons brought forth and sent into battle by both sides. Sometimes they fought men, and the carnage was terrible, and sometimes each other. And sometimes the other side's magicians were quick enough, and the demons vanished harmlessly into the air. But not often.

Neither Sagene's Council of Barons nor King Asir would give up their foothold in Roche terrain, and Queen Norcia was only too aware if Aude fell and the River Comtal became an open waterway, her country was very much at risk.

Hal took his dragons up over the city, against Yasin's black monsters day after day, trying to always choose the terms for combat: never less than three against one; never without the advantage of altitude; always with at least one other dragon flier in constant support.

There were other Roche dragons in the air – evidently training the blacks was as hard as Garadice's father had said it would be.

These other dragons Kailas wasn't as choosy about the fighting conditions for.

But still, he lost fliers.

Of the seven replacements, he lost four within two weeks. But the other three learned, and became as canny as the rest of the flight.

Hal was amused to see the tall, blonde Chincha become

more than friendly with the short, dark, stocky Farren Mariah. He said nothing, however, after the night Sir Nanpean made some crack, unheard by Kailas, about the woman, and Farren beat him so badly he couldn't fly for three days.

Hal punished Mariah by making him fly Sir Nanpean's patrols in addition to his own.

Even though Hal refused to admit it, even to himself, a killing war began between him and Tregony. One day one would be up, the next the other.

Since Kailas frequently forgot to put in a claim, or gave the kill to one of his fellow fliers to make, there was no question within the flight as to who was the real dragonmaster.

It didn't matter to Hal. All he wanted to do was have more dead Roche dragon fliers than could be replaced.

Very secretly he hoped one day to meet, in the air, the bastard who'd killed Saslic.

That would be a victory he'd loudly claim.

In the meantime, he concentrated on the hard targets – Yasin's black dragons. But they flew in close support of each other, and took a deal of killing.

Then one day, Yasin's blacks vanished from the skies over Aude.

They reappeared, two days following, along the River Comtal. Flying very low, in pairs, they attacked the small supply ships bringing replacements and materiel to the besiegers, tearing rigging, raining arrows down on helmsmen and boat commanders and, when they got a chance, ripping apart any unwary soldier or sailor.

They also scouted for prepared ambushes, and forced Deraine to escort the boats with cavalry on the banks, which slowed progress.

"We have new orders," Hal told his assembled fliers. "You won't be surprised.

"We're to go after the black dragons, and at least make them stop harrying our ships."

"Shows what happens," Sir Loren said, "when your flight is the best. You get sent to do the impossible and, by the way, don't get killed until you've done it."

"Hell of a morale builder you are," Vad Feccia said.

"If you can't stand the heat," Sir Nanpean put in, silkily.

Feccia turned, glowered at Tregony. Hal lifted an eyebrow – he'd thought the two were the closest of – well, perhaps not friends, because he couldn't imagine either of them actually having a friend – but compatriots.

"We'll do it in flights of four," he said. "Two pairs, the second pair back of the first by, say, a hundred yards or so.

"If you spot a dragon, try to get height on him, and force him down into the water or riverbank. If you're seen by them first, and they've got height, get away from the river, and stay low. Maybe you can veer enough so the bastard that's diving on you'll eat rocks instead.

"Don't be too quick to fly around any of our barges," he said cynically. "Sailors have a great reputation for shooting at anything in the air, no matter whose pennons they're flying. Each dragon'll fly a banner with Deraine's colors on it, but don't depend on that being much of a shield.

"This time, everybody draws trumpets, and if you see anything – an ambush, a dragon – blast your little brains out.

"Gart, since you're the seaman among us, I want you to tell everybody how these river barges sail, so we can maybe anticipate what they'll do when they get hit.

"I'll lead the first flight out tomorrow. We'll fly north, where we'll link up with a river convoy. Chincha, on my wing. Mariah, you'll fly number two. Pick your own wingman."

The dragons lumbered into the still, summer sky at dawn. Hal led the four to the river, turned north. They flew slowly, Hal peering ahead to look for signs of the enemy.

Storm began snaking his head back and forth, sensing something.

Hal decided to trust him, waved for the other three to climb.

They rounded a bend, and saw two black dragons, sitting on a sandbank.

They waddled into the air, necks stretched like geese, but it was too late. The Deraine fliers were on them, bolts slamming into the fliers. One dragon squawked like a wounded goose, slammed into the water, a gout of spray around it.

The other ducked through river-edge brush, and flew hard east, deeper into Roche territory.

Hal let it go, signaling the others back toward the river, expecting the pair had been waiting for the Deraine boats to appear, which meant there should be an ambush laid nearby.

There was – twenty cavalrymen, some in uniform, some in ragged civilian attire.

They had only a moment before the four dragons were on them, talons ripping, tails lashing down, smashing horses and men.

The riders broke, and were harried by the flight away from the river.

Only a handful escaped.

Hal returned to base, sent an exuberant message to Lord Cantabri:

"Dragons love fishing. Took about eighteen bottom feeders this morn."

Another flight went out in the afternoon, and jumped soldiers setting up a block where the river narrowed, and attacked.

Hal heard, a day later, the Roche troops assigned to ambuscades along the river had started calling the dragons "Whispering Death," from the slight rush of air across their wings as they attacked.

"I would like," Limingo the wizard said precisely, "a flight around Aude."

"I have read the orders here from Lord Cantabri saying you're to get anything you want," Hal said, tapping the scroll the magician's extraordinarily handsome assistant handed him. "And I obey my orders."

"I know," Limingo said. "But it's always nicer to have some enthusiasm, rather than simple rote obedience."

"You can have that, and more," Hal said. "Provided you do me two small favors."

"Magical, I assume."

"Of course."

"No love philters until the war's over," Limingo cautioned and started laughing at Hal's annoyance until he caught on.

"I'd especially like," Limingo said, "you to fly me—"

Hal stopped him with an upraised hand.

"Tell me when we're in the air."

Limingo lifted eyebrows, but obeyed.

Unlike his master, Limingo was eager to clamber up behind Hal, and positively glowed as the dragon lumbered into the air, and changed from a waddling monster to a graceful creature of the heavens.

He leaned forward. "Are we a little suspicious of our fellows?"

"I'll explain later – when we're alone," Hal said. "Now, what do you want to look at?"

"The far side of Aude, particularly the main gate," Limingo said.

Hal did, swooping low, and getting a few arrows in his general direction for his bravado.

"They're getting better," he said over his shoulder.

"Let's hope," the wizard said, "this marks the limits of their expertise. If you could do what you just did, two or three more times?"

Hal obeyed. The magician seemed to have no idea of bodily harm.

"Very well," Limingo said. "I think I have enough."

Hal flew back to the base, landed Storm a ways from the barn, and explained his caution.

"My," Limingo said, "a possible spy. What happened to that dagger that was used to kill your serjeant?"

"I still have it. The matter hasn't been reported, by the way."

"Aren't you playing your cards a little close?"

"Maybe," Hal said. "If I let the provosts know, they'll be kicking through my whole flight, looking here and there and everywhere.

"We've got a war to fight, and it won't get any easier if my fliers are looking over their shoulders for spies or, for that matter, warders who'll suspect everyone."

"Why don't you give me that dagger," Limingo suggested. "A spell here and there might give some fascinating answers."

"That was one of the favors I was going to ask," Hal said. "I assume, the reason you wanted to fly where we did is there is a plan afoot?"

"I hope so," Limingo said. "This crap of sending men against solid stone is doing nothing but guaranteeing Deraine and Sagene are going to have some very empty counties for a couple of generations.

"But everyone, even our noble lords in command, know the Roche have paid close attention to their gates, so it's not a matter of just wandering up and knocking politely.

"I thought I might be able to devise something. And I think I was right, assuming the Roche thaumaturges don't pay attention to every detail.

"You mentioned you could use two favors. One we've discussed. What about the other?"

"I could do with some help looking for a dragon base," Hal said. "I took one of their flights out of the war once by attacking their base.

"Now we've got those black dragons, who're giving everyone a rough way to go. Maybe a good wizard could be of assistance?"

"I might," Limingo said. "Especially if you happen to have any scales, banners, whatever that belonged to the Roche or their dragons."

"I think we have a couple of souvenir keepers," Hal said.

He put Gart to rooting through the flight, and produced a pennon and an arrow that'd wounded one flier.

"Excellent," Limingo said. "My assistant and I'll set up this very night."

That night, at the far end of the field, there were strangely colored lights, flickering, and chants that seemed to come from more than two throats.

The soldiers of the flight shivered, and held close to their quarters.

In the morning, Limingo said, a bit angrily, that there were some heavy counterspells on what he'd been given.

"Perhaps," he suggested, "the leader of this black dragon unit is aware of the flight you obliterated, and is taking thorough precautions?"

"Perhaps," Hal said. "Yasin is no idiot."

"I'm sorry, Lord Kailas," Limingo said. "Perhaps, with my other incantation, I'll be more successful.

"In the meantime, stand by to be given special duties in the not distant future."

Three days later, Hal returned from a river sweep to find he had visitors.

Thom Lowess had arrived.

With him was Lady Khiri Carstares.

37

Hal followed his first instinct, and kissed Lady Khiri thoroughly. After awhile, she pulled back and whispered, "I'm certainly glad you're not one of those who believe in propriety."

Only then was Hal vaguely aware, through the roaring in his ears and his mind yammering for him to lug her into the nearest tent and work his lack of will on her, the cheering from the men on the dragon line.

He blushed a little, let her go.

"You know," she said, still in that wonderful whisper, "what they say about fliers is true. You all do smell like dragons."

"Uh," Hal managed. "I guess so. I suppose it's because—"

Khiri interrupted him. "I don't mind it at all. It makes you smell like sex."

A few feet away, Thom Lowess coughed discreetly.

"I'm also glad to see you, Lord Kailas."

Hal came back to himself, half-saluted Lowess.

"And I you, sir. What brings you here?"

"I, and my aide," Lowess said, indicating Khiri, "are in

search of good tales. Tales to embolden the hearer, tales of victory and hope."

He made a face.

"And, right now, the dragon fliers are about the only good thing of notice around Aude. Although . . ." He let his voice trail off.

Hal looked at the taleteller questioningly, but got only a bland smile.

"Well," Khiri managed. "You certainly don't have to make any protestations of your virtue after that."

"Sorry," Hal said. "I didn't mean to lose control . . . at least not so quickly."

"So shut up," she said, lifting her legs around him, "and don't stop."

She moaned, then bit his ear.

"What would you say if I said I thought I was falling in love with you?"

Hal covered her mouth with his, didn't answer.

Hal vaguely expected some comments from his fliers about Lady Khiri, or at least some raised eyebrows. If there were any, they were very much behind his back, and it seemed that most soldiers in his flight thought it was perfectly all right for the "old man," as he'd come to be known, not yet twenty-five, to have a little joy in his life.

Both Khiri and Lowess busied themselves during the day interviewing everyone in the flight, including the dragons, or so it seemed.

"*Good* tales, m'boy," Lowess said. "Especially this duel you're having with Sir Nanpean Tregony for being the ultimate Dragonmaster. Especially especially with you both having come from the same town, and now being friendly rivals.

"It's the buzz of all Deraine, you know."

Hal thought of explaining, decided what he and Tregony

felt about each other was no one's business, so long as it
didn't get in the way of the war.

He did have one question of Lowess – how had this matter
of their purported competition spread so widely?

"You certainly don't think you're the only young hero
who's got a taleteller hanging to his coat tails, do you?"
Lowess answered briskly. "You just happen to have gotten
lucky and drawn the best."

Hal and his flight element, now down to ten fliers, nine dragons, went about their mission, escorting the convoys up and
down the River Comtal. Sometimes they met the black dragons, and fought them if they had the advantage, but mostly
were forced to flee, swearing at Hal's absolute orders, and
sworn at by the sailors below, who had no reason to understand their abandonment.

Hal realized, after a day or two, that Lowess was just passing
time, waiting for something.

Since he didn't get in the way much, and his presence kept
Khiri around, that was well and good with Kailas.

He wanted her not to leave until he finished puzzling this
matter of love over in his mind.

Now the rumor was everywhere – Deraine and Sagene were
getting ready for a great offensive that would end the siege
once and for all.

Hal cursed the inability of anyone in the army to keep his
mouth shut and his nose in his own business, but it didn't
change matters.

Alarms were shouted, trumpets blared, and there was chaos in
the village. Hal made it out of his sanctuary, no more than a
towel wrapped around him, in time to see a huge black
dragon climbing away from the village.

"What is it?" Khiri asked sleepily, coming out to the head

of the steps. It was just dawn, and they'd been up later than they should, still delighting in each other's body.

Hal shook his head, saw a soldier running toward him, waving a tube.

"Sir!" the woman shouted. "It's for you."

Hal blinked, took the tube. Tied to it was a pennon Hal recognized – *Ky* Yasin's!

And his name was neatly written on the tube.

He twisted it open, forgetful of sorcery, and took out a note.

It read:

Lord Kailas:

   There appears to be a matter of honor between us, that you might find amusing to settle at your convenience.

   I have heard that you are the ranking dragon killer of Deraine and Sagene, and have even had the temerity to dub yourself Dragonmaster.

   I will meet you, just the two of us, over any place you name, at a time and date of your choosing, where we may discuss this matter at greater length.

   If you have interest, and consider yourself an honorable man, return this container with your conditions across the walls of Aude. It will reach me.

                                                    Ky Bayle Yasin
                                                    Commander
                                                    First Guards
                                                    Dragon Squadron

Hal read it once, again. A smile came. He had an idea that might possibly solve two problems at the same time.

The dragon fliers listened closely as Hal outlined the challenge from Yasin. Lowess hovered in the background, beaming at yet another superb tale falling into his lap, pen scribbling frantically.

"First question I've got," Hal said, "is the bastard being honorable. Opinions?"

He pointed around. They ran from Mariah's "friggin' impossible. He's a Roche," to Gart's "maybe. Just maybe," to Sir Nanpean's "who gives a hang. What a chance to go down in history, win or lose."

Indeed, Hal thought. Especially if I lose, Tregony'll be the one going down in history. I'll just be going down.

"My own opinion," he said carefully, "is it's worth a shot. I personally don't believe Yasin'll be the only one to show up.

"But that doesn't mean we should play the utter fool."

He went to a large-scale map of the Aude region.

"Now, here's what I propose. I'll drop the message over Aude, agreeing to the meet. I'll set it for . . . oh, five days from now. At dawn. We'll meet here," and his finger stabbed at the map about ten miles downstream from Aude.

"Away from the front lines, and this is a huge damned meadow," he went on.

"I'll agree to fight him at, say, 500 feet."

"That'll give you some advantage," Sir Loren said judiciously. "The air's thicker down there, and his black will be a little harder to handle in tight turns."

"More than one advantage," Hal said. "Just in case he brings friends, I'll want the rest of you on the ground here," and he indicated an area about a mile from the meadow.

"Light trees, which'll give the dragons cover. If he fights fair, you can stay where you are. But if he shows up with his squadron, then you can get in the air fast, save my young ass, and maybe wipe out some of those blacks.

"Rumor has it we'll be needing all the help we can get in the not too distant future."

"You're a damned romantic fool," Khiri said.

"So it appears," Hal agreed. "But I happen to believe I

can tear Yasin's nose off, and feed it to his damned black dragon."

"As if he'll be the only one there!"

"If that's the case, then I'll have the whole flight behind me. I don't think he'll bring his whole squadron to wipe out one dumb Deraine."

"You think!" Khiri said. "Men!"

"Shut up, and come here."

She came across the room, sank into his arms.

Hal nibbled on her ear, then whispered, "Even a romantic can be a sneaky bastard."

She lifted her head back, considered his smile.

"You have a plot."

"Maybe."

"Which you won't tell me about."

"Not now. Now, give me back that ear, if you will."

Hal rode to Command Headquarters, looked up Limingo.

"I'm sorry, Lord Kailas," he apologized. "But I've been running myself ragged, like every other magician with the army, with . . . with this plan we're developing. But I promise you, within the week, I'll let you know what clues that dagger gives."

Hal wasn't happy – he'd hoped sorcery could keep him from having to play out the game with Yasin.

But since it wouldn't, he found Lord Cantabri, asked him for a small favor, and explained.

"One company, only?" Cantabri looked at the map again. "I'll have two there, I promise. That might improve the quality of slaughter.

"You know, your duel with Yasin has shot around the army like an arrow-chase."

"What are the odds?"

Cantabri hesitated.

"Six to five," he admitted. "No one feels that the Roche will live up to their end of the bargain."

"Six to five," Hal mused. "That's the best life gives you, isn't it? Either way?"

Cantabri grinned.

"Perhaps, knowing what you told me, I might be convinced to have a bit of a go myself."

The days crawled past. Hal watched his fliers closely, but none of them behaved differently than before, and he wasn't able to narrow his search for the spy, if spy there was.

A courier came down to summon Sir Thom Lowess to the Armies' Command, the day before the duel. Hal knew that meant the offensive was drawing near.

Lowess sent the courier back, saying he'd be honored to join them, in a day's time, but he had another matter to take care of first.

"I don't know," Khiri said, "if I should be here, or not. If something happens . . ."

"If something happens," Hal said, "wouldn't you rather hear it directly?"

"I suppose so. Oh, dammit, I'm going to cry."

Hal slept badly that night. He was glad to be roused by the orderly warrant two hours before dawn.

He dressed quickly, went to the fliers' room. He'd ordered guards around the building, and the only people to be admitted were Sir Loren, Farren Mariah, Mynta Gart.

"I'm changing the orders," Hal said briskly. "I want each of you to take two other fliers out under your absolute orders.

"But don't, I repeat, do not, land where I ordered you to.

"Instead . . ." And Hal outlined his orders.

"A question, if I might?" Sir Loren asked. "Why the change?"

"You can ask, but you'll not get an answer. At least, not right now.

"You're dismissed. The other fliers and the dragons should be getting rousted out and fed by now."

Half an hour before dawn, the rest of the dragons in the flight took off. Hal had told each of them to obey any commands signaled by the three team leaders, no matter what they were.

He waited until they disappeared into the darkness, then went to Storm.

The dragon bubbled a greeting.

Khiri Carstares was waiting.

"I just wanted to say I love you."

Hal, mind already in the air, thinking about the meeting over a certain clearing, had to force himself to smile, give her a hug.

"I love you back," he said. He still wasn't sure if he did, but if he didn't come back . . .

He forgot that possibility, clambered into Storm's saddle, tapped the dragon's neck with his reins.

It snorted, ran forward, and leapt into the air, somehow sensing this day was different.

Hal let Storm climb until he was about 700 feet above the trees, the dark mass just beginning to lighten. He needed no compass or map to navigate to the Comtal, and up the river toward the clearing.

Just above him, about a thousand feet above the ground, was the usual scattered predawn cloud cover.

Very good.

Darkness became gray, and Hal knew, above the clouds, the sun could be clearly seen.

It was light enough to make out the clearing. Flying in lazy circles, about a hundred feet below him, a mile distant, was a single black dragon.

Hal checked his crossbow, eased a bolt into the trough.

"Let's go kill him," Hal said, snapping his reins.

Storm had already seen the dragon and, shrilling a challenge of his own, was flying toward it.

The dragon climbed to meet Hal, trying with its talons for Storm's head.

Hal jinked his dragon to one side, couldn't find a clear shot at its rider. But he saw Yasin's banner clearly.

He pulled Storm up as the black dipped a wing, turned hard, came back at him.

An arrow whispered past him, a foot or two distant.

Hal held his fire, still not happy with his shot. The two dragons sped past each other, talons reaching for a grip, finding none. Yasin's black flailed at Hal, missed him, and Hal fired a bolt into the monster's tail.

It thrashed, almost caught him, then the two were clear, climbing toward the clouds for an advantage.

The black shrieked three times, and, as Yasin turned back toward the attack, five black dragons dove down at their brother's signal.

Yasin *hadn't* played fair. Hal grinned tightly, did the unexpected, and instead of diving for the ground, came in again on Yasin. He fired at the man, cursed as his bolt missed.

Then he turned for the ground, diving toward the edges of the clearing, looking back as if he were panicked as the six blacks came after him.

None of the Roche saw the nine Deraine dragons plummet down toward them, from behind, from where they'd been flying, at Hal's orders, just above the clouds.

Hal had set a double trap, one for Yasin, one for the spy.

If there was a spy, Hal assumed Yasin had been told, somehow, about Hal's plans, which is why he'd changed them at the last minute, ordering his dragon flight to fly high above the meadow, and attack anything they saw below them.

Hal pulled Storm up, into a wingover, was rushing headlong at the Roche dragons. An arrow went above him, and he aimed carefully, shot one of the Roche fliers in the chest at point blank range. The Roche slumped, and the dragon banked, into Storm's talons. The beast howled, tried to dive away, but Storm's tail caught him, smashed his neck.

Then the Roche saw their pursuers, just as the Deraine monsters were on them. There was a swirl of fighting, and Hal heard shouts from men, screeches from dragons, and two black dragons went plummeting toward the meadow.

A trumpet blared, and the three surviving dragons dove toward the ground, intending to escape by flying at treetop level.

Well-trained, as Hal had assumed, they went low, very low.

Lord Cantabri's two companies of archers came out of their hiding along the fringes of the meadow, and arrows sheeted up toward the Roche.

They pincushioned the rear beast, and he squealed, lay over, and smashed into the ground, bouncing to stillness.

Two, Hal thought, and then, past him, came Sir Nanpean Tregony, having a bit of height, enough to close on the forward black. He was almost atop the beast, and Hal wondered if Tregony's dragon would tear the flier from his mount.

But Tregony was leaning out, aiming, and his crossbow bolt took the Roche in the back of the neck. He contorted, and fell away.

Hal was closing on the last dragon, Yasin's, but the black had speed on him, and slowly pulled away from him.

Hal broke off the fight, banking up and around, trumpet blasting the signal to return to base.

"An' you're a cagey, cagey bastard," Farren Mariah said admiringly. "Remind me to never wager with you, least not unless we're usin' my cards."

"And how did you know they'd be waiting for us in the clouds?" Gart asked.

"I pray regularly," Hal said piously, and Sir Loren snorted in laughter.

Hal, surrounded by congratulating members of his flight, leaning against Storm, who was almost purring in content, pulled Lady Khiri to him.

"I love you," he whispered, leaning back against Storm, and this time he meant it.

He smiled, as if well content with the day.

In some ways, he was. He'd lived.

More importantly, he'd confirmed the presence of a spy in the formation.

But he still didn't know who he was.

And *Ky* Bayle Yasin still lived.

38

Reinforcements started coming in thick and fast, as did supplies. Hal's flight came to full strength, and, wondrously, was given two extra dragons.

Kailas knew the attack was very near.

As did the enemy.

Ky Yasin's black dragons, also reinforced, were withdrawn from raiding along the River Comtal, and now flew close cover over the city of Aude.

Three other dragon flights, including Sir Lu Miletus', Hal's first combat unit, were stripped away from the Third and Fourth Armies. Hal was delighted to see that his former tentmate, Sir Aimard Quesney, was still alive, and, he discovered in the few minutes they had to chat, as wryly cynical as ever.

But there was little time for reminiscing. Hal spent almost as much time in conference at Command Headquarters as he did with the Eleventh.

He was pleased to see Lady Khiri, who he'd convinced to stay with Sir Thom, was the absolute darling of the staff officers. It kept her from worrying about him, he hoped, and, not being the jealous sort, he didn't worry about any of these popinjays being invited to share her bed.

He was not as pleased to see just how luxurious a life these back of the line slackers had carved for themselves, from the best rations, which should, by rights, have gone to the front lines, to uniforms and living equipment.

Cantabri told him to forget his anger. If these staff sorts spent their time trying to connive themselves a fine case of Sagene wine or whatever, instead of their job, perhaps the line units might not be as subject to their killing whims.

But Hal still wanted to put all of them in a long line, armed with their favorite pens and foolscap, and send them against the walls of Aude.

The Eleventh was chosen for special duties – to escort the army's magicians wherever they wanted to go to cast their spells on the day of battle.

Hal would rather have flown against Yasin, but Cantabri told him this was far more important.

"We'll not hit the Roche with one or two great spells," he said. "But little ones, here and there. If they pry open a crack, you'll be responsible for bringing in more wizards to reinforce the first spells.

"Also, since magicians don't seem to have much awareness of their own mortality, you'll be responsible for keeping them alive.

"Not that you can't take advantage of any targets of opportunity, once your two primary duties are in hand."

"Wonderful," Hal muttered.

His mood wasn't improved when Limingo told him he still hadn't had the time to pluck whatever secrets the dagger that murdered Serjeant Te held, but he would do it immediately. Or within the day . . . or perhaps tomorrow.

Hal took no chances that the spy within his flight might be able to give away their duties, and how much of the attack would be dependent on magic.

He grounded the flight, and had their base surrounded by

troops, who were ordered to let no one except Kailas in or out.

His fliers seethed, not knowing why they were being held hostage, and, for most of them, that they were going to be nothing but a ferry service during the great battle.

Hal decided a little anger would be good for them when they were finally permitted to fly against the Roche.

Then, one day, the siege engines went into constant action day and night, smashing stone ball after stone ball into Aude's outer and inner walls, targets carefully chosen for structural weakness.

Troops moved out of their encampments, into attack positions.

The Roche were at full alert, but they didn't seem to know, any more than Hal or anyone outside the high command, just where the attack was going to be mounted.

For once, the flapping jaws of the army didn't have anything to chew on.

For the moment.

Limingo arrived at the base with four acolytes, a cheery face, and interesting news for Hal.

"I was going to put you off yet again," he said. "Then I realized if this was that important for you to consult me, it might have a great effect on the performance of your flight, which might mean on this battle.

"Which, incidentally, will begin tomorrow afternoon. Everyone fights at dawn, to give them the benefit of the day.

"Which is one reason Lord Egibi chose the time he did.

"Also, this fight is expected to last over several days, and probably won't accomplish much on the first day, beyond, hopefully, putting our spells in place and clearing the walls of Roche archers.

"There'll be a courier arrive sometime today with your orders, but I thought you might like a bit of an advance warning.

"I can give you specifics on what I'll need. I want you, and four of your fliers, to take myself and my staff to that knoll we visited once before.

"At that time, I'll cast my own spell. You might have guessed it would have something to do with those gates on the main entrance.

"They're protected by Roche magic, but I'm betting they haven't thought of everything. Gates require hinges, and hinges, even huge ones such as we saw, corrode.

"Magic isn't all that great in building from nothing, but one of its great strengths is to destroy. To corrode.

"We shall see what my magic can do against them. If those hinges can be smashed, the gates can be toppled.

"And if the gates are toppled . . ."

Limingo smiled tightly.

"I do wish that there was a way we could get closer. The power of sorcery isn't improved by distance.

"But I'm hardly fool enough to try to thaumaturge from either the back of your dragon or, worse, from the front ranks amid an arrowstorm."

Hal let the man run on, realizing the magician was brave, but no one, except probably Lord Cantabri, could face the morrow's slaughter equably.

Limingo caught himself.

"Very well," he said. "Now for your business. Are we in a place where no one can overhear us?"

"We are," Hal said. He'd had the spy-ear in his quarters blocked after Te's murder.

Limingo nodded to his acolyte, who handed him a pouch. Inside was the flier's dagger that had killed Te.

"I can't give you everything," he said. "Magic doesn't generally work that way.

"However, I can suggest that the proper owner of this knife would be large and thick, a man, yes definitely a man, who'd look like a drover or a blacksmith. I don't think, though, that he was the one who committed the murder.

"There's a layer of blood and fog between him and that

death. That's a very imprecise way of putting what my spells showed, but I can't find better words.

"This other person, and I cannot give you anything about him, would have been the killer.

"I'm sorry, but that's all I can divine. Possibly, with more time, and thought, coming up with greater spells, I might be able to divine a bit more for you.

"But not much."

"Thank you," Hal said. "I'll think on what you've said. It might be enough. Meantime, we'd best be preparing ourselves for battle."

All that day, and night, as the Eleventh readied itself for battle, making sure every bit of leather harness was oiled and soft, that the crossbow trays were fully loaded, that armorers had spare bowstrings and prods, Hal pondered the dagger, and Limingo's words.

He sat, staring at it, late, the sounds of dragons wailing in their sleep, aware of change and not happy with it, and the sounds of the smiths' wheels, sharpening already needle-like bolts, swords and knives.

He finally pulled himself away, checked his own gear and harness.

There were still lights about the former village, handlers making sure there was nothing amiss with the sleeping dragons, cooks preparing cold rations for the morrow, and, in the hut he'd assigned to Limingo, the muttering of voices and the occasional sharp reek of herbs being burnt.

His last visit was to Storm, who snored contentedly, head occasionally curling out, fangs yawning, as he destroyed another enemy in his sleep.

"When this is over," Hal said, "I promise you I'll find you the highest crag for your own, a herd of sheep and a cow worthy of your attentions."

Storm snorted, sighed.

*

Just after dawn, Hal was roused by Limingo, who wanted a flight close to Aude. "To get a feel for my castings," he explained.

The roads around Aude were alive with troops, making last minute moves. Heavy cavalry moved ponderously forward, pioneers bustled around the huge siege engines, which were never still, light cavalry trotted across the bridges toward the city, and infantrymen crept closer, keeping well under cover.

"Very good," Limingo shouted to Hal. "Now, all we have to do is wait."

Hal was making sure all was in order, yet without chivvying his fliers into despair, after the noon meal, on the dragon line as the monsters were being led out, saddled and ready, when it came to him.

He felt like a dunce for not being able to figure things out without magic.

He thought of letting matters wait until after the battle, decided he couldn't. He might have been able to keep the spy sequestered for a time, but once the fighting started, that would be impossible.

"I want to see Vad Feccia," he told Gart. "And Sir Nanpean Tregony.

"Have four men standing by, armed, for my orders."

Vad Feccia's eyes darted about the room as he entered. He visibly twitched when he saw the dagger, the only thing on Kailas' table.

Sir Nanpean Tregony looked appropriately bored and upper class.

"I hope this won't take too long, sir," he said, the usual subtle emphasis on his last word. "We're to be aloft in minutes."

"No," Hal said. "Not long at all. Vad Feccia, I formally accuse you, with Sir Nanpean Tregony as my witness, of the following crimes: Theft of war supplies; murder; spying for the enemy in time of war; and high treason.

"The last three are hanging offenses.

"You will be taken into custody by men I have waiting, and closely confined until you are brought before a court martial.

"I have used certain means to determine this dagger was originally issued to you, and falsely claimed to have been lost, after you murdered Serjeant Te for apprehending you in your crimes. There can be no doubt what the penalty—"

"No!" Feccia shouted. "Not me!"

"Be silent, you," Sir Nanpean said. "Stand up like a man for once in your monstrous life."

Feccia whirled.

"Stand up? And be hanged? No! Not ever! Mayhap I'm a thief . . . I'll admit to that, wanting my little delights, and never minding having a bit of cash about.

"But murder . . . Never. Nor treason.

"You're the spy, Tregony.

"And the damned traitor.

"You were the one who had me find out where Te kept his files, his maps. And you were the one who borrowed my dagger when you said there was a lock that needed prying.

"No, you son of a bitch! I'll not hang for your crimes!"

"Enough, Feccia," Hal said coldly. "Those words can wait for the trial.

"However, you, Sir Nanpean Tregony, now stand accused of most serious crimes."

"Lies by this thieving bastard," Tregony said loftily. But his eyes didn't meet Hal's.

"What was it?" Hal asked. "What did they buy you with? Was it gold? Or favors? Or just a chance to get out of that wretched prison camp? If you ever were in one at all, and rather turned traitor the instant you fell into their hands? Or maybe you were a Roche agent, right from the beginning. Certainly that'd hardly surprise me, knowing you for what you are, what you were as a boy.

"And how did you report, after we moved forward, and
you weren't able to visit your contact?"

"I said lies, and lies they are!"

"Feccia surely can lie," Hal agreed. "But magic, especially
magic of the highest order, cannot.

"And magic is what made me summon you and Feccia, in
the hopes he'd behave as he did."

Tregony shook his head sadly, as if he felt sorry for Hal's
foolishness, and then he moved.

His hand swept up the dagger on the table, buried it in
Feccia's stomach. Feccia screamed, clutched himself, as
Tregony dove into Hal, knocked him, breathless, to the floor.

Tregony rolled to his feet, and ran out the door.

Hal staggered up, gasping for breath. He took no notice of
the dying Feccia, but went after Tregony.

The man was down the sanctuary steps, running for his
dragon.

"Stop him! Shoot him down!" Hal gasped.

The four soldiers he'd ordered to stand by did no more
than gape, utterly lost.

Hal swore, stumbled down the steps, his wind coming
back, as Tregony reached his dragon, leapt up into its saddle,
and shouted for it to move, move, dammit.

Hal thought of shouting for archers, but hadn't the breath,
and ran toward Storm, pulling himself up, as his hands found
the reins, and slapped the dragon into motion.

Tregony's dragon was at full gallop, and then in the air, as
Storm, startled, began moving.

Then they were both airborne, climbing.

Tregony headed for Aude, kicking his dragon to full speed.

Hal called to Storm, words of encouragement, orders, and
his dragon closed on Tregony.

Kailas was vaguely aware of the sound of the siege engines
getting louder, more frequent, and, dimly, the shouting of soldiers from below.

The attack had begun, but he had no time for that.

The walls of Aude loomed up, and Tregony went over them, skimming the battlements.

Hal was just behind him, reaching for his crossbow.

Tregony glanced back, realized he was out of time, and steered his dragon toward the flat roof of the main keep.

He brought his beast in roughly, and jumped from the saddle, running toward one of the two closed doors that led down into the keep proper.

Hal reined Storm in hard, and the dragon's wings flailed.

Kailas fired, and the bolt took Tregony in the leg. He screamed, fell, came back up.

Hal, red rage dimming his vision, rolled out of his saddle, dropped ten feet to the roof of the keep, his dagger coming out.

Tregony turned, pulling his sword.

"Good," he said, "good. Come on, you damned peasant, with your hogsticker, and see what a *real* nobleman can do."

He lunged at Hal, and Hal barely parried with his long knife.

Again he struck, and this time his blade scored Kailas' ribs.

Hal spun, and whipped his dagger across Tregony's face, slicing it to the bone.

"Remember the last time, Tregony," he hissed. "Remember that piece of wood I scarred you with, back in Caerly."

Tregony screamed incoherent rage, dove at Hal in a long lunge. The man was very fast, but now time slowed for Kailas.

He brushed the lunge aside with his knife, smashed a fist into Tregony's face.

The man staggered back, sword clattering away, hands coming up in protest.

His mouth was opening to say something, but there was no time, as Hal's dagger drove up, under his ribs, thudding home in his heart.

Tregony mewed like that dragon kit he'd tortured long ago, fell.

Some measure of sanity came back to Kailas, and he realized where he was. There'd be Roche soldiers on the roof within moments, not likely seeking a prisoner, nor would Hal allow himself to be taken.

He had Tregony's sword in hand, and then Storm slid in, not a dozen feet away, and there was safety.

He was in the saddle, Storm needing no command to get away, and they were just clear of the roof when a shadow flashed overhead.

Hal had a moment to look up, saw *Ky* Yasin's pennon, his dragon, and the man glaring down at him.

The dragon's talons took Storm in the wing, tore it, and gashed his back, almost grabbing Kailas.

Storm howled in pain, turned, wing going out from under him, and they slammed down on the keep roof once more.

Hal rolled off, grabbing his crossbow, recharging it as one of the keep's doors came open, and two spear-carrying soldiers ran out.

Hal fired, worked the forehand, reloading, fired again, and both men were down, motionless.

There was a dragon flying toward him, and he took aim, saw Farren Mariah in its saddle.

He brought his mount down.

"Let's be gone! There're those about tryin' to kill us!"

Hal started toward him, heard Storm, keening in pain.

He stopped, stood still.

"Come on, man!" Mariah called.

Hal remembered Storm saving his life on that desolate beach, helping him time and again, and once more that red rage came.

"No!" he shouted back. "Both of us go, or none of us!"

"You're godsdamned daft!" Mariah called, and then there were three more soldiers at the stairs.

Hal spun, shot one, then the other was on him, and he dropped the crossbow, parried the man's pike, spitted him, looked for the third man.

He was stumbling toward Hal, a bolt sticking out of his guts, and then he toppled.

"You stupid bastard," Mariah growled, coming up beside him, reloading his crossbow. "Sir."

"Get your ass out of here," Hal said. "There's only room for one damned fool."

"Shut the hells up. Sir," Farren said. "Get another rack, and get over by that door, and don't make 'em come to us like we was ballroom dancers.

"I'll take the other one."

"Stupid!" Hal called, obeying.

He had a moment to pat Storm, say something meaningless, comforting, he hoped, then ran toward the open door.

Stairs led down, and there were men coming up. Hal shot three times, quickly, and the stair was blocked for a moment by bodies.

He saw Farren, at the other door, pressed by two swordsmen, and shot one out of the way, and Farren killed the other.

Hal heard screaming from above, looked up, saw two black dragons being swarmed by Deraine monsters, like owls in daylight being savaged by crows.

They dove, flapped away to the east, and the sky, at least for the moment, was Deraine's.

"Block the door," Kailas shouted, running back for his flier's dagger, pushing the door closed and ramming the blade into the jamb and kicking it home as a block.

Mariah was doing the same, using a Roche sword.

Then, for a moment, there was peace, except for the slam of the siege engines, the shouts of men attacking the walls, and the screaming of men hurt and dying.

Hal's panting slowed, and the world speeded up to reality.

Storm was looking at him, mouth opening, closing, like a stranded fish. But Hal could see his wounds, and knew, though ghastly, they wouldn't be fatal.

If he could get the dragon off this roof, and out of the enemy redoubt.

Which none of them would be able to do.

"Thanks," he shouted to Mariah.

"Fer what?" the small man asked. "Provin' there's more'n the one damned eejiot in the flight?"

Hammering sounds came from behind one door, then the other.

"Where's your dragon?"

"I slapped the silly git's butt," Mariah answered. "No need for everybody to die.

"And I damned well hope, when this is over, and they start handin' out the medals, there'll be a nice posthumerous one for Mrs Mariah's favorite boy."

"I'll be sure and write the citation myself," Hal said. "But it won't be posthumous."

Mariah stared at him.

"Yer actually thinks yer gonna live this one out?"

"Surely."

Mariah shook his head, and the hammering got louder.

Hal heard the sweep of wings, looked up, and saw Mynta Gart's dragon coming in. Behind Gart was Limingo and an assistant. Both of them carried bundles of gear.

Gart landed, and the two wizards slid out.

"Had I known you planned this," Limingo said, "I would've designed my spell differently."

He went to the edge of the keep, ducked back as arrows shot up.

The Roche soldiers had been cleared from the walls, and there were Deraine and Sagene soldiers between the outer and inner walls.

But they were still barred from entrance to the city, and there was a host of Roche milling around the keep's base, filing into it, toward the stairs.

"Unfriendly sorts," Limingo said. "I think we'll not need corrosion, this close. A nice melting will do fine."

His assistant nodded, began digging through their clutter.

"We'll need," Limingo went on, "a double triangle. Use the blue and the orange markers. Some flax—"

"No flax, sir."

"Hmmph. Well, then, fireweed of course, moonrot, and let me think now . . ."

Hal saw two more dragons coming in, Sir Loren and Chincha flying them, their backs loaded with an impossible number of soldiers. Both dragons sagged in for grateful landings.

"Grabbed all the spear-tossers we could," Sir Loren called. "Thought you might need them."

Hal felt for a moment as if he might actually live.

Then one door was smashed open, and Roche soldiers were on them.

There was a swirl of fighting, and a man stumbled toward Hal. Kailas was about to spit him, when the man's mouth opened, blood poured out, and he fell.

For a moment, the surge up the stairs stopped, and Hal heard the steady chant from Limingo:

> "Burn and build
> Grow, take strength
> Feed on what you have
> On what you are
> On the memory of the casting
> When all flowed, poured together."

A wave of nausea struck, and soldiers went to their knees. The Roche magicians were moving against them.

Overhead, three black dragons dove down at the roof. Hal saw Yasin's pennant in the fore.

He knelt, having all the time in the world, seeing nothing but that huge black dragon coming at him, then the pennant, then Yasin, grinning in anticipation.

He touched the trigger, and the bolt shot home, burying

itself in Yasin's shoulder. The man jerked, almost coming off his mount, slumped forward.

Hal had a moment of triumph, hoping he'd killed Yasin, then the man sat up, shouting at his dragon, and it banked away from the roof, away from Aude, his two fellows guarding him.

Hal swore. It would have been perfect if he'd been able to kill the man responsible for the black dragons, and end the threat to Deraine . . . But the last bit of luck hadn't been given him.

Once more, there was a swirl of dragons overhead, and again the Roche attacked up the stairs.

This time, it was a steady stream, and Hal was attacked by two men. He wounded one in the arm, and felt pain tear down his leg.

He swore, lunged, and took the second soldier in the throat.

Hal looked across, saw Mariah down, clutching his arm, a Roche soldier about to spear him. One of the Deraine soldiers hurled a shield, taking the man in the head, and he jerked like a broken-necked chicken, fell on top of Farren.

"And there we have it," Limingo said in a calm, satisfied voice.

There was a great booming sound and Kailas, heedless of danger from the archers below, had to look over the keep's edge. One of the huge main gates was falling inward. Hal saw molten metal dripping down the stone wall.

It crashed down, and Kailas thought the sound filled the universe.

Then the other gate tottered, and creaked across to lie at an angle.

But the way was clear, and lines of soldiers came out of their hiding places in rubble, turns of the earth, and ran through the hole in the city wall.

Roche soldiers came to meet them, but they were no match, and Kailas heard cheering start.

The Roche on the keep roof realized what had happened, that they were now outnumbered, pelted back down the stairs.

Hal, ears sharpened, heard another sound, the sound of Whispering Death, and dragons plummeted down, sweeping the roofs clear of the enemy.

A dark wave beyond the wall grew, rolling toward the breach, and Deraine and Sagene cavalry crashed through their own troops, into the city streets, lances down, shouting their battle cries.

The last Roche lines broke and ran, into the heart of Aude, and the battle was won.

Hal Kailas, suddenly feeling the pain of his wounds, limped to Storm, stroked him, and the dragon's keening grew quiet.

39

It was dusk, a day later.

Hal Kailas uncomfortably sat a horse in the middle of a victory parade, through the shattered streets of Aude.

Now there would be an absurd ceremony, the keys to the destroyed city gates handed to the Sagene and Deraine Lord Commanders of the Armies.

Kailas had heard it took most of the night to bring the looters to bay, for few soldiers took kindly to a siege like this one had been, and had wreaked bloody revenge on the women and shops of Aude.

Windows were smashed, emptied wine casks were scattered here and there, and there were bodies, still unburied, sprawled and beginning to stink.

But that was the way of war, though Kailas despised it.

At least he'd gotten Storm off the keep's roof, and under an animal chiurgeon's care. He would heal, and fly again.

As would Hal Kailas.

Trumpets blared, drums thundered, and soldiers cheered.

But this was but one battle.

The might of Roche lay unbroken.

Kailas heard a faint noise, looked up, and saw, far above the city, a circling black dragon.

Perhaps it was *Ky* Bayle Yasin.

His, and Roche's, debt to Hal Kailas was still unpaid.

The Dragonmaster knew the war, and the killing, had only begun.